Advanced Praise for *The Odyssey of Fletcher*

"At its heart, *The Odyssey of Fletcher* has a very earnest message, and one that deserves to be heard. A solid story of identity, morality, and personal growth for the last man on Earth."
- *IndieReader* (An "IR Approved" & "Best Reviewed Books of the Month" selection)

"The author's comedic prose flows easily. A comic interrogation of manhood ... more timely than it may seem."
- *Kirkus Reviews*

"A clever dystopian novel with a big splash of humor. A work of speculative satire that is at once far-fetched and believable."
- *SPR*

"This is one of my favorite reads from this year. Funny, witty and satirical. 10/10 character development. And even though it's satirical, you find yourself moved by the end of the book. I think everyone should read it at some point, because wow. What an excellent debut!"
- Celina Tran, *Erato Magazine*

"Erik Dargitz delivers a beautifully observed walk through his book's post-apocalyptic world, and the journey does not disappoint. *The Odyssey of Fletcher* is a unique, compelling, and tender exploration of not only what it means to be a man, but of what it means to be human."
- Katrina Mathewson, Screenwriter (*Jury Duty, Hawkeye*)

"I can't remember many novels that have been able to achieve what *Odyssey of Fletcher* has. I liked Fletcher. And then I didn't. And then I *really* liked Fletcher again. It's already an uphill battle ... to get readers to relate to characters. Dargitz did that twice. I highly recommend this title to fans of speculative fiction. A dystopian that comes across as smart, challenging, but never heavy-handed."
- Lisbeth Ivies, *Reedsy Discovery*

THE ODYSSEY OF FLETCHER

ERIK DARGITZ

EDDERKOPPEN
PRESS

Edderkoppen Press

Printed in the United States of America

ISBN: 979-8-9882728-1-6 (paperback)
ISBN: 979-8-9882728-3-0 (kdp print)
ISBN: 979-8-9882728-0-9 (ebook)

Library of Congress Control Number: 2023916661

Cover Design by Brendan Rice

First edition 2023

www.erikdargitz.com

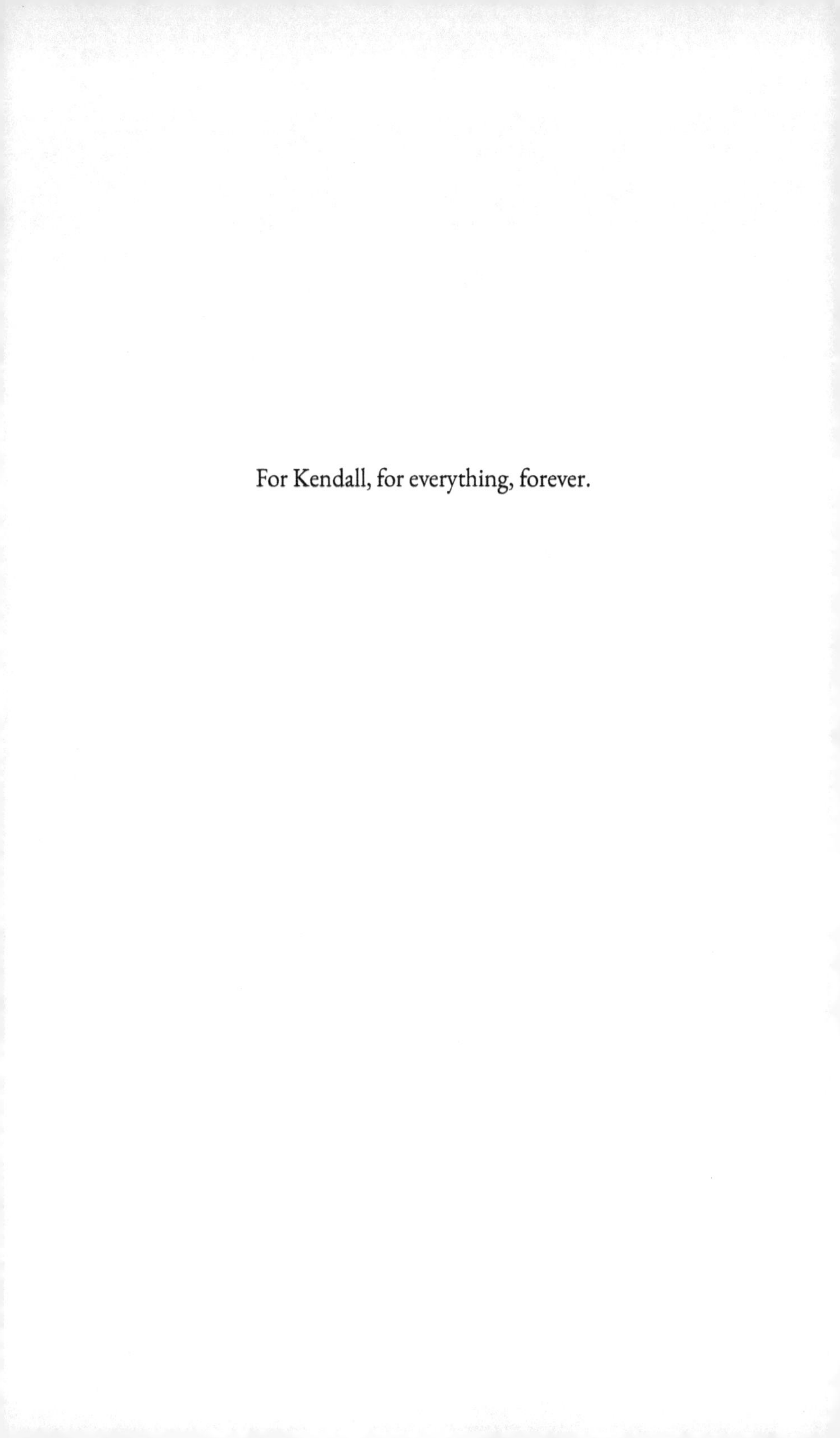

For Kendall, for everything, forever.

PART I

THE LAST MAN ON EARTH

Chapter 1

Fletcher Sinclair prepared to step out into the Southern California sun for the first time in months, knowing there was a pretty good chance it would kill him.

There was a pretty good chance he'd lose his mind, then control of his bowels and then his life. That's how all the others had gone.

Fletcher didn't exactly know how Delilah worked her way into her victims, but he was going to protect himself as best he could. He sat on the cool tiles of the kitchen floor, unspooling a Costco-sized roll of aluminum foil and meticulously covering every inch of himself—mummifying his skinny body in silver. He labored in dim light, the sun barely bleeding through the lining of beach towels and bedsheets he'd hung over the windows so long ago. The bulbs overhead were merely decoration since the power had gone out. Working it with his hands, Fletcher formed the aluminum to the bony contours of his joints, eliminating all menacing gaps, until finally he was confident in his coverage.

He stood and pulled a stretchy gaiter mask down over the bottom half of his face. Then he strapped his brother's old ski goggles over his thick glasses. The rest of his head was already covered in a hood of foil, massaged to form-fit over his mop of hair. He looked like a deranged, low-budget robot, but to Fletcher he was his own knight in shining armor—the bravest knight in Rancho Bernardo.

While Delilah and death were likely waiting for him on his doorstep, Fletcher knew starvation was all that remained in his basement sanctuary.

He needed supplies. He needed food. He needed to leave.

So, he opened the door and stepped outside.

His aluminum suit crinkled and scratched, the only sounds in the dead summer morning. Fletcher closed his eyes, clenched his teeth and waited. A bubble formed in his stomach, followed by a foreboding gurgle. He was certain it was the harbinger of his doom.

But the bubble dissipated. He swallowed. He was still alive.

Fletcher opened his eyes to a tangerine world, tinted through his ski goggles. He hobbled down the front steps in his makeshift hazmat suit, lumbering like Frankenstein's monster to the old Ford Explorer in the driveway. The gas tank was open—not a great sign. He climbed up, leaned across the driver's seat and tried the ignition. Nothing. Fletcher didn't know how one siphoned gas, but he was pretty sure someone had done it to the family car.

So, he would have to walk. The store was two miles away.

Fletcher hadn't been a big fan of long walks in pre-Delilah times, so he wasn't thrilled about it now that he was starving and steaming like a baked potato under fifty feet of Kirkland Signature foil and a 73-degree sun. He was sweating before he left the driveway.

As he shuffled his metallic legs in the direction of salvation, he saw no movement. The world had been abandoned. The air carried a silence that could break glass.

He knew it would be bad, but this—

Fletcher had grown up in this quaint San Diego suburb, but as he walked down the middle of the street, everything looked surreal, almost unrecognizable, an upside-down and inside-out version of itself. There was trash everywhere, piles and piles of it: in the streets, on the sidewalks, heaping in front yards like raked leaves. A strange amount of ash dusted everything gray. The windows of many houses were boarded up. Many others were shattered. Forgotten cars sat in driveways under layers of sooty filth. At the end of the street stood a tan stucco sign, once simply bearing the name of the community. Someone had spray-painted the words "here lies" above it.

Here lies Rancho Bernardo.

He turned onto another street. One house had burned down, leaving behind only a dark skeleton. The houses on both sides were licked black from the long tongues of the flames. While they had survived the threat, their doors now hung open and they were surely empty.

The first movement Fletcher saw was a pack of dogs: a pug, an English bulldog and a few lab-like mutts. The dogs looked as if they were strolling through an abandoned movie set. They wandered aimlessly, whipping their heads at random, like they were looking for their humans. When they saw Fletcher, they scurried off between two houses. Fletcher felt a pang of sadness for the animals.

Then he felt one for their humans, who were most certainly dead.

Fletcher turned left onto San Salvador Road. There was a home with black spray-painted writing on the side facing the street, five feet tall and taking up the width of the house. It read: "SAFETY HERE. FOOD & SHELTER." The windows were smashed, and the front door was in splinters. Fletcher was pretty sure those words weren't true anymore.

He walked on, and suddenly—

A person.

His heart clenched. There, in front of a house on the left, standing in the middle of a garden, was a real, live human being. Fletcher was paralyzed with simultaneous swells of relief and terror, and for the same reason: others were alive.

This human was the first Fletcher had seen in exactly thirty-three days, and the first non-Sinclair he had seen in months longer than that.

This human was, of course, a woman. The Delilah Virus only killed men. While the ensuing wars, riots and overall shittiness of the world killed without such prejudice, Delilah only ever had an appetite for Fletcher's kind.

The woman was old and gray and wore old and gray clothes. She stood looking at Fletcher like a wax figure at Madame Tussauds. All that moved was her long, charcoal hair, waving in the gentle breeze like dying grass. Even her expression was still. It was the look of seeing a ghost and, to be fair, she wasn't far off. The men of the world were dead, yet here one stood.

Or, what appeared to be a man. Covered in foil.

There was no wave, no nod, no acknowledgment between them.

Fletcher just kept walking, faster now, too terrified to do anything else. Fletcher had never cared much care for the unexpected—and the old lady had been horribly so.

•••••••••••

When Fletcher arrived at the grocery store, he was relieved to find that the scary old lady had not followed him. And that the store was empty.

Although ... it had clearly been visited. The windows that faced the vacant parking lot were shattered, leaving jagged mouths of glass. Fletcher stepped through an opening, shards crunching under his sneakers.

The inside of the store was a war zone. Shelves lay on their sides, knocked over, their remaining contents spilled and scattered. The polished concrete was stained with strawberry ice cream, soda and wine, looking like the psycho butcher's killing room floor in one of Fletcher's old horror games. Cash registers were smashed open—not that money could be of much use to anyone now.

Fletcher grabbed a cart and stepped deeper into the store.

The produce section at the front offered him nothing. Anything left was gray, furry and deflated. Whatever. Fletcher hated vegetables anyway. More concerning was that the freezers and refrigerated shelves were worthless. The few chicken nuggets and mini burritos that remained were now floating in pools of water, inedible since the power had gone out.

The trip was far from fruitless, though. Fletcher rolled his cart around the toppled shelves, digging out packaged goods that had been unpicked by previous scavengers. He excavated bags of chips, Fig Newtons and beef jerky. He uncovered cans of peaches and soup. He found jars of pickles and applesauce. He threw in cans of green beans, too, figuring he could suffer through a vegetable if his life depended on it. Then, water: at first glance, the section seemed bare—the shelves just a pile of metal bones—but Fletcher dug desperately. In a stroke of luck, under a layer of smashed Styrofoam coolers, he found a collection of single-gallon jugs of water. The last thing Fletcher stacked onto his cart was a couple cases of Agent Orange, his beloved energy drink. It looked, to his wonder and good fortune, as if nobody else had taken even a single can. He cracked one right there in the back of the store, pairing it with a bag of crushed salt and vinegar chips.

The walk home was far worse than the one to the store. He had never noticed that the road was a hill. It was too subtle to feel in a car, but it was very, very clear while sweating under a second skin of aluminum foil and pushing an overflowing shopping cart.

Plus, he had to go a longer route to avoid the old woman.

"This will all be over soon, honey." His mom's words echoed in his head, as they so often did. She used to say that to Fletcher growing up, any time he got sick or upset, and it always made him feel better, like a warm blanket or homemade lasagna. It's what she had said when the virus started taking people out, too.

This will all be over soon.

She had been right, in a way. Not long after she said those words, all the men Fletcher knew were gone and so was she, after the riots at the hospital where she worked.

Fletcher heard a door to one of the houses on the street slam shut. He quickened his pace. Then he thought he saw someone looking at him from a window of another home. Then a movement, or maybe not, but—

He suddenly felt very much on display, like a lizard in a terrarium. He felt very unprotected, too, like the terrarium was missing its lid and the cat had just noticed.

He was also exhausted, and his stomach was growling, and he was pretty sure his insides were beginning to boil. He tried to hurry his heavy legs, desperately wanting the shelter of his home, to get away from the prying eyes he now imagined in every window. Each of those imagined eyes fired brilliant beams of white-hot Delilah Virus straight at Fletcher, intent on bringing his foil-covered ass down for good.

By the time Fletcher got home, his armor wasn't very armor-like. It had slid around from all the sweat and all the movement, revealing many open places that were perfect for viruses to creep into. He ignored this reality, too afraid to think about what it could mean.

Back in his fortress, Fletcher shed the foil like a molting snake and looked at his bounty of processed goods with pride. Fletcher Sinclair had successfully acquired food for survival.

He felt pretty accomplished. Pretty resourceful. Pretty damn heroic, even. He felt that way all night while he dined on the spoils of his bravery and sipped Agent Orange as if it were champagne.

Of course, when he woke up, he was still just a young man with no plan and death all around.

But he was still breathing.

So, he stayed the course, stayed inside, stayed alive. Sure, he made exactly zero progress toward any long-term solution, but that kind of problem-solving was above his paygrade anyway.

He remained in lockdown for three more weeks, until his food and water ran out again, at which point he got out the Kirkland Signature foil and stepped back out into the world that surely wanted to kill him.

He did this once a month, whenever his thirst and hunger grew louder than his fear of the outside. He visited all the stores in walking distance, some nearly five miles away. He briefly considered hijacking a neighbor's car, but he now knew what the world looked like out there. He imagined all the horrible things people were capable of in a world like that, and he decided the last thing he should do was draw attention to himself. So, each mission was conducted by foot.

When he ran out of stores to go to, he started breaking into houses and ransacking kitchens and garages.

He got used to seeing dead bodies in those houses, each in their various stages of decomposition—sunken, empty sockets watching him from lonely faces on the couch, in bed, at the dinner table, in a pile of their own laundry, on a yoga mat surrounded by small rubber dumbbells. He saw occasional glimpses of what could have been living people, too—watching him from behind cars two blocks away, peering out from windows in houses down the street—and he wondered what evil they had done to survive this long. His own survival, he knew, was merely luck, but that couldn't be the case for everyone.

This is how Fletcher lived for six months.

No people to talk to. No idea what was going on in the rest of the world. No real hope.

Just surviving. Just cold canned foods. Just reading his mom's *Reader's Digests*. Just periodic mental breakdowns.

This is how Fletcher lived for 191 days.

On Day 191, just two days after another valiant return with supplies from the houses of a cul-de-sac down the street, there was a knock on the door.

There wasn't a valiant cell in his body as he tossed himself over the living room couch—hiding, frozen, cowering, vision blinded by a pulsing panic, awaiting the horrors these visitors brought.

Chapter 2

FLETCHER'S TRESPASSERS WERE THE first people to step foot in his house since his family had died. When they busted the door open, here is what they saw: to the right was a living room, as musty and dingy as an opium den, littered with empty cookie boxes, crumpled bags of chips and dented Agent Orange cans. The windows had been poorly covered with towels and bedsheets. Unlit candles lay scattered around on the counters as if in preparation for a half-assed séance. To the left was a kitchen, dishes piling out of the sink like a piece of modern art. A few happy flies buzzed in endless circles. In the middle of the kitchen was a shopping cart, overflowing with cans and bags of food. Directly in front of them, kicked to the side of the foyer, was a pile of glimmering foil that still held the shape of body parts in a few places.

Here's one thing they didn't see: down the hallway, through the second door on the right, was a bedroom that once belonged to Fletcher's older brother, Adam. His body, or what was left of it now, was still in there, lying on the bed. Fletcher wasn't proud of the lack of a proper burial, but it was what it was. He'd told himself he was going to bury him in the backyard (the body pickup service had died before Adam did), but he kept making up reasons to postpone the ceremony. Eventually he just sealed Adam's tomb with a dozen layers of Saran wrap and duct tape and tried to forget that the room existed.

As Fletcher's trespassers crept through his house, he lay as still as possible behind the couch. They had rapped on the front door and called out before eventually busting the lock, but Fletcher hadn't fallen for their false politeness.

The big, bad intruders were three women, none of them over five foot seven. They wore blue hospital scrubs. One was as skinny as Fletcher and just as white—although twenty or so years older. She had bright orange-red hair pulled back in a ponytail. Her lips formed a severe line that didn't move. The second was a Latina woman in her fifties. She was a large woman with a friendly face, deep laugh lines sprouting from the corners of her eyes and a gentle smile that looked permanent. The third was a younger Black girl with a head of tight curls and dimples like upholstered buttons. She was Fletcher's age, maybe a year or two older, and was the smallest of the three. The intruders were not scary-looking whatsoever, but Fletcher couldn't know this from his hiding place behind the living room couch.

"Hello?" they called out with the soft voices used when consoling a child or coaxing a puppy. "Anybody home?"

Fletcher shivered with fear.

He knew that a real man would face them with his chest out and his chin high.

But this—this was something Fletcher could not do.

"Hello? Hello?" Their voices were sweet, tender as a grandmother's. "If anyone's home, we're here to help."

Fletcher clenched his teeth.

He would hide forever.

Or not. They found him in minutes, his hiding spot being as terrible as it was. As soon as the older Latina woman discovered him—in a fetal position behind the couch—it should have been obvious they were not a threat.

It should have been, but it wasn't.

"Don't hurt me," he whimpered. "I didn't do anything. You can have all the food. Don't hurt me."

They nodded and cooed—encouragingly, patiently.

Eventually they got Fletcher to move from the floor to the couch. They brought him one of his Agent Oranges and some cookies. They sat across the living room from him, not making any sudden movements, not wanting to startle the poor thing.

Fletcher realized soon enough what he should have earlier: these women were not there to harm him. His fear unclenched, but there would be no relief. That fear simply shapeshifted into a pulsing, red-hot embarrassment.

· · · · • • • · · · ·

The three women introduced themselves to Fletcher. The pale one with the stern expression and the fire-colored hair was Lynne Reid. She was a pathologist. The Latina woman was a doctor named Lucia Gomez. The young Black girl was a nurse named Jordan Johnson.

Dr. Gomez explained to Fletcher—softly, slowly—what they were doing. And what they were doing was trying to save the world.

As soon as the mighty wheels of civilization had stopped turning, the three women had grouped together, with a couple others, in a nearby hospital. They had been there for a few months, while the last of the men died, and communication with the rest of the world died, and then finally all went quiet and still—as if the world itself had died. They'd spent their time examining the virus, running tests on stored blood, running tests on stored semen, running tests on stored ovaries. They even ran tests on each other. The one thing they couldn't run tests on was a living man.

They believed that a living man—someone who had survived the virus—would be the key to finding a solution. Of course, the trick was finding one.

They learned of a real live man sighting from a woman they met on a supply run. The woman said she had seen a foil-covered thing that looked like a boy walking down the street, and followed him home out of curiosity. This news had given Dr. Gomez and her team new hope.

"I know you must be scared," said Dr. Gomez, "but you should also feel extremely lucky. It appears you're rather special."

Fletcher had never been rather special.

"How do I know I won't just die as soon as I leave here?" he asked. "How do you know I'm immune?"

"To be honest, honey," said Dr. Gomez, "we don't. We don't know anything. But you've survived until now. And you can't stay here forever."

"Listen," said Dr. Lynne Reid. "People tried everything to hide from this virus, and it's clear that *hiding* doesn't work. Even with this kind of protection."

She gestured to an orange beach towel, its corner peeling sadly from the window.

"If you weren't immune, you'd be dead," she said.

"Now, honey." Dr. Gomez softly touched his shoulder. "We believe you might be able to help us find a cure to the virus. To put it not-so lightly: the human race might very well depend on you, dear. What do you say? Will you help us?"

Few had ever depended on Fletcher before, let alone the human race. What choice did he have?

··········

Dr. Lucia Gomez, Dr. Lynne Reid, Jordan Johnson and Fletcher Sinclair drove through the empty streets of Rancho Bernardo. Fletcher had felt only a mild panic when he stepped outside for the first time without his aluminum foil suit, but there were no signs of Delilah. That is: no gibberish, no irritable bowels and no dying. He soon found himself in the backseat of a small electric car, a baby blue Nissan Leaf, with three strangers.

Dr. Gomez drove. She was quite heavy, and the driver's seat seemed a size too small underneath her. She kept smiling at Fletcher warmly in the rearview mirror. Dr. Reid sat in the passenger seat and stared straight ahead like a redheaded mannequin. Jordan sat next to Fletcher in the back. She kept looking at him curiously. Her light eyes sparkled with life—something Fletcher hadn't seen in a long, long time.

Dr. Reid opened the glove compartment and placed a handgun inside. Fletcher's eyes grew, and Jordan caught his gaze.

"You never know out here," she whispered, shrugging.

Fletcher nodded, pretending to understand, and looked out the window. Abandoned cars lay scattered along the freeway like turtles sleeping in strangely colored shells. Some of them were burned to blackened lumps. Shopping carts and other refuse sat forgotten here and there. Dr. Gomez quietly weaved around the obstacles, taking them south. In the distance, Fletcher could see plumes of black smoke signaling fires where fires weren't meant to be.

"So..." Jordan looked at Fletcher, a crooked grin spreading. "How does it feel to be the last man on Earth?"

"Oh, come on," said Dr. Reid.

Jordan just laughed.

Fletcher's eyes narrowed. "You don't actually think—"

"Oh, I'm sure there are others like you out there," said Dr. Gomez.

"When was the last time you saw one?" asked Fletcher, his voice cracking. "Or even heard of one?"

"Well, we did meet two trans men in Chula Vista last month." Jordan turned her head to Fletcher. "But from a chromosomal, species-reproduction standpoint, you're the first living man we've heard of in a very long time."

Fletcher stared at her.

"Months," said Jordan. "A lot of them."

"To be fair," said Dr. Reid, "we have no communication with anyone outside of driving distance."

"Yeah, who knows what's going on in other parts of the world," agreed Jordan. "But you're the only dude in the neighborhood. Far as we know."

"Whoa," said Fletcher, blinking rapidly. "Whoa."

"Until proven otherwise, let's call you the last man on Earth," said Jordan, smiling at Fletcher. "Sounds cool."

Fletcher considered the idea with his man brain, which appeared to be quite the novelty now. If he actually was mankind's last man standing, he couldn't help thinking that was a pretty big bummer for mankind. The last-man-on-Earth responsibility should be bestowed upon a male of unquestionable qualification, a man worthy of such a title. Good God, there had been so many better specimens to choose from.

Not so long ago, about four billion men had shared the planet with Fletcher, all clambering over each other in their efforts to be a somebody. Fletcher had never been a very good clamberer, and had solidified his status as a certified nobody. A speck of dust, as they say. A speck of dust with glasses that were too thick and hair that was too greasy and a nose that was too big and round. Any one of the more skilled clamberers, one of the *somebodies*, might have actually made a fine last man on Earth.

But alas.

Fletcher looked back out his window. There was no movement outside except the distant and faint smoke: no people, no moving cars. Jordan told Fletcher that gasoline had become nearly impossible to come by. There were electric cars, sure, but those required power, and few people had access to such a luxury. And there weren't many people to drive them anyway.

Including most of the male *Homo sapiens*.

Maybe all.

Except Fletcher.

The last man on Earth (for all intents and purposes) adjusted his glasses. They were fogging up.

Chapter 3

WHEN THE APOCALYPSE ARRIVED, it went to work fast. That's how Fletcher came to be in this peculiar situation—a real, honest-to-God apocalypse.

Here's how Delilah did her damage: a guy would appear healthy as an ox one minute, then he'd suddenly stop making sense, start talking all crazy. Phase two: the guy would defecate. After that, he'd die. Just like that. Three quick steps and it was all over. It was not a very dignified end, but at least these poor folks weren't alone. Everyone was doing it.

It could have been worse—suffering-wise, that is. Take the bubonic plague, for example, where you had to deal with all the pus-and-blood-filled boils *on top of* the certain death. Or a zombie outbreak, where you might have your undead mother chasing you down the street, trying to eat your flesh. Delilah's victims just had a short spell of insanity and unreliable bowels. Well, and the dying part.

It started with just a few random people here and there. The first time Fletcher saw it for himself was in his Computer Science class at North Park Community College. Josh Ackerly stood up and announced, rather triumphantly, that he was the kangaroo prince and that he was also rather hungry. The class fell silent. Then poor Josh crapped himself. Then he collapsed. The rest of the class laughed and laughed and laughed—until they realized that their classmate was dead.

There were a few more instances like Josh, whispered about in coffee shops like dirty rumors, until, seemingly overnight, it exploded. Just like that, it had overtaken Fletcher's social feed and his parents' nightly news. Suddenly it was all anyone could talk about. It didn't take long before the men around Fletcher—and only the men, not the women—started dying by the hundreds. Then the thousands. Two weeks after Josh died, it was utter chaos. Men were dying everywhere. All over the world. By the millions.

And so humanity hit the big, red Panic Button.

•••••••••••

While the whole global shitstorm was raging, Fletcher Sinclair hunkered down at home with his family. His dad had worked at a marketing firm in downtown San Diego, which closed its doors as soon as things started getting hairy. Fletcher's brother, Adam, had been a senior at San Diego State, which was also shuttered. His mom, however, went to work at the hospital every day. Nurse practitioners were needed now more than ever. Aside from Fletcher's mom going to work and Fletcher's dad making occasional supply runs, the family stayed in lockdown for four months. A cabin-fever-fueled anxiety crawled up and down Fletcher's spine.

As Fletcher waited out the days with his family, he'd hear strange sounds in the distance; all he could do was guess at the grisly stories behind them. He'd hear military jets ripping through the skies from the nearby Miramar naval base. Sirens he didn't recognize. Explosions far away, and sometimes not-so-far away. He would hear commotion in the street right outside their house, too—the cries of a newly discovered death, families piling into their cars to head to some place of believed safety, the shouts of angry and scared suburbanites. He even heard what he was pretty sure were gunshots on more than one occasion.

Other than listening, though, it was just a lot of waiting.

Over the next two months, Fletcher's known world came crumbling down. First, there were the hospital riots, which took his mom. The news came in the form of a letter slipped under the door by a coworker. It said that the hospital fell to a mob of people demanding care, demanding medicine, demanding equipment, demanding a cure. Fletcher's mom and many others died in the madness, but the coworker had escaped and was fleeing town. The next Sinclair to die was Fletcher's dad. The strong and pragmatic patriarch of the family, his final words, spoken to his two sons, had been this: "I will run naked through the poppies and the world will tremble before me." Then he had soiled himself, slumped over and was dead. This was when the body pickup service was still running, so Fletcher and Adam carried their dad to the porch, where he was collected and taken to one of the mass burial sites that had been set up out in the county.

The next casualty, not long after, was the communication industry. Cable, cell service and the almighty Internet disappeared in a flash. By killing the Internet, Delilah ripped the guts out of more companies than not, crippled financial institutions and severed the heads off of news outlets and all communication tools. Fletcher and Adam were now cut off from the world.

And then Adam died.

Adam had been the golden boy. He'd been studying to be an architect. He'd played football. He'd had biceps. He'd had girlfriends. And yet he'd died like all the others. Fletcher had none of those things, but here he was, alive and well enough.

And now very alone.

This will all be over soon.

By the time the last bomb had boomed and most of the fires had gone out, Fletcher was hiding in his parents' basement, all by himself, with no intention of leaving any time soon. He felt like a kid in a high school slasher flick, whose friends had all been cut down by some maniac, leaving him looking over his shoulder, waiting for Death to come for him.

Fletcher waited alone in his family-home-turned-private-bunker, with duct tape sealing the spaces around the doors where air could get in, and the windows covered with whatever he could find.

All he had was a chest freezer full of Hot Pockets and taquitos, a cabinet full of canned chili and SpaghettiOs, a few flats of Agent Orange Energy Elixir and the entire DVD collections of *Dr. Who* and *Star Trek: The Next Generation*, as well as a show his mom had watched called *Little House on the Prairie*. He was settled in for the long haul, just hoping some manlier man would save the world before he had to resort to the prairie show.

But no manlier man did any such saving. In fact, by default, Fletcher was the manliest man around: a scared twenty-year-old kid locked away in his dead parents' Rancho Bernardo house, slowly watching his stock of frozen, deep-fried Costco goods shrink and shrink and shrink.

On Day 4, Fletcher turned the faucet on in the kitchen and watched it choke and sputter out some brown water, then stop. The city's water system had gone kaput. He checked the garage and found four flats of Kirkland Signature water bottles, the 16.9-fluid-ounce size. On Day 8 the power went out. He was mid-episode on a *Little House* binge when the TV flickered, popped and died. (Yes, he had resorted to *Little House on the Prairie*, but, for the record, not before watching every single other DVD he had, and some a few times over.) After a brief panic about the death of digital entertainment, he realized his problem was bigger than passing the time: everything that was in the fridge and freezer chest was not long for this world, and the electric stove in the kitchen was now just taking up space.

That night, on Night 8, he feasted on an obscene number of cold taquitos.

From then on, he ate only dry goods and canned food. Cold canned food. Cold chili, cold SpaghettiOs, cold corn and cold peas.

For light, all he had was his mother's obsessive collection of scented candles.

··········

As Fletcher faced his shitty predicament, he was well aware of how unqualified he was for surviving in this kind of environment. He often wondered what a good old-fashioned apocalypse-fighting dude would do in his situation. What a real man would do.

But God, he had no idea.

That was the weirdest part about all this: that Fletcher was still kicking, and all those better men weren't. Suave actors, beefed-up linebackers, larger-than-life rock stars, popular kids at school—all of them, no matter their superior maleness, seemed to have met the same fate.

But there was Fletcher, surviving the wrath of Delilah. A 150-pound socially awkward beta male with an ill-advised addiction to Agent Orange energy drinks. He was just a college kid, with the milk-white skin of a cave-dweller and the body of a sixth-grade girl. He couldn't grow a beard, had all of four rogue chest hairs and exuded the natural charisma and swagger of a guy who'd spent the majority of his life playing video games in his parents' basement, which he had.

Fletcher didn't know why he hadn't died yet, but that was the thing about life, he figured. It didn't have to make sense. In *The Odyssey of*

Zordallus, there were rules and reason, and they couldn't be broken. You couldn't cast a spell in a temple. Broots were strong as hell but couldn't swim. You'd never find a Flamegoblin outside the Firelands. A Dazzler would always heal you back to 100 percent as long as you had a dandelion seed for her. And, when your hit-points reached zero, you died. These were absolutes, and they made logical sense to Fletcher. Life wasn't logical at all.

The Odyssey of Zordallus, of course, was a fantasy game; a massively multiplayer online role-playing game, to be specific, or an MMORPG to those in the know. This had been Fletcher's life. It was another world—another universe—where thousands of real people from all over built kingdoms, hunted treasure and waged honorable war against each other. It was full of wizards and trolls and sages and potions and all that kind of stuff. And Fletcher had been good at it. You should have seen his kingdom. He had turrets the size of some people's castles. That universe was the one in which Fletcher had thrived the most.

But those were the good ol' days. Before the Delilah Virus had killed Zordallus, too.

So, what would a real man do? A real man like Pa would have parked his covered wagon and made a life and a home for his family. Pa was resourceful. Pa—Charles Ingalls, that is, of *Little House on the Prairie* fame—would have made the best of the situation. He'd have built a house out of logs and hunted for food and found a way to survive and thrive without bitching and wishing for better fortune.

But he wasn't Charles Ingalls. He was Fletcher Sinclair and he was running out of SpaghettiOs.

Still ... he survived. Night 8 became Night 9, and then Night 10, and then Night 191. And he remained hidden. He found food when he needed it. For six months, Fletcher Sinclair stayed alive.

And then, just like that, he found himself in the back of a Nissan Leaf with three strangers, off to save the world.

PART II
THE ONLY PATIENT

Chapter 4

EVERY FOURTH GRADER AT Deer Canyon Elementary School took a field trip to the locally famous Rattlesnake Gold Mine. It was in Julian, an old mining town about an hour away, that was full of bed-and-break-fasts, pie shops and other such quaintness. The trip to Rattlesnake Gold Mine was part of the school's curriculum on California history and, specifically, the Gold Rush.

It had been an especially hot day for November when Fletcher's class had their turn to walk in the footsteps of nineteenth-century prospec-tors. By the time the bus had wound through the dry mountain roads and arrived at the mine, Fletcher was sweaty and uncomfortable.

At first glance, Rattlesnake Gold Mine looked as if it had been un-changed since its boomtown days. But first glances are usually wrong. A second look revealed that the buildings' wood was fresh and the walls were thin and fastened together with shiny bolts and screws. Everything had been built recently—and cheaply—to recreate the look and feel of an 1850s mining camp. There was a saloon, a jail, a mercantile and feed store, as well as a boarding house.

There was one clearly modern building: the public restroom. Visitors loved the old charm of this mining camp, but they couldn't be expected to pee in such shabby obsolescence.

The guide on Fletcher's field trip was an old guy, a really old guy, called Pops. Pops looked like Rip Van Winkle, with a white beard that practically reached his belt and a floppy felt hat sitting on his ancient head. He wore a flannel shirt in spite of the heat and had a red bandana tied around his neck. He carried a pickaxe all day, using it as an extension of his arm, gesturing with it, picking things up with it, leaning on it. Pops was friendly, energetic and fun—like a skinny, prospecting Santa

Claus—and looked like he belonged right where he was. Fletcher imagined that Pops had been living there since the Gold Rush.

Pops led the kids to the creek and showed them how to pan for gold. The creek had been stocked with pyrite—fool's gold—and the kids got to shake their pans until a sparkle appeared and they could pretend they were rich beyond measure.

There was a quick lunch, the classic miner specialty of peanut-butter-jelly sandwiches with apples and crackers from a brown paper bag. During lunch, Pops regaled them with stories of long-ago life in the hills of Julian.

Finally, Pops held an auction, where the young prospectors could bid on souvenirs from the Rattlesnake Gold Mine with the treasure they'd found that day. Up for sale were items such as a fake beard, a jar of local jam and some chocolate gold coins. Fletcher didn't bid on anything, already old enough to know that public attention was to be avoided at all costs.

When it was time to leave, the kids said goodbye to their new old friend and headed toward the yellow bus. Fletcher had to pee, and he remembered how long the bus ride was, so he walked into the one modern building in town. He thought about telling his teacher, but she was talking to a group of students, and talking to her meant interrupting them just to announce his bathroom needs, and that felt worse than holding it.

So, he went to the bathroom on his own.

When he came back out, the bus was gone.

He looked around: there was not a soul at the mining camp. It was an 1850s diorama.

He made his way to the picnic tables at the center of the site and sat down, waiting for the bus to return. His skin flushed with the thought of facing his class. They'd all have to come back to the mining site just because of him. Just because he'd had to pee. He'd never live it down.

He waited and waited. Now it would be even worse. Now they had been gone a while, meaning they'd have farther to drive back.

How come nobody had noticed yet?

He waited and waited some more.

Maybe they had to find a good spot to turn the bus around on that narrow mountain road.

The sun dipped a little lower in the sky.

Maybe they'd notice when they got back to school.

The sun sank lower still.

"What in Sam Hill?" a voice burst behind Fletcher. Fletcher turned, and it took him a second to recognize the strange man. Pops was walking out of the boarding house, but he didn't look like Pops. He wore jeans and a T-shirt and had a Padres cap on his head. The only thing that gave him away was his epic beard.

That's when young Fletcher cried.

The truth finally sunk in: nobody had noticed that he was missing. They'd been gone more than an hour. They might already be sitting down to dinner with their parents, showing off their souvenirs.

Pops did his best to console Fletcher. He gave Fletcher some chocolate coins, which helped a bit.

"Well," he said, "come on. I'll take you home."

Pops led Fletcher to a green Subaru Outback, which was noticeably not a covered wagon. Fletcher didn't like seeing behind the curtain. He wanted to imagine Pops as the Gold Rush relic he'd been sold.

More than anything, though, he wanted to be home. In his room. If he was going to be the nobody that everybody forgot about, it might as well be there. If he was going to be a nobody, let him be a nobody by himself.

··•·•·•··

Now, as he sat in the backseat of a small electric car with three women he didn't know, he wondered what the better fate would be: to remain unknown and alone in the relative safety of his parents' house, or to be found by these strangers and taken to whatever strange place they called home. He was used to being forgotten. Being searched for—being the center of attention—was all new.

At least his new friends had food and water.

They arrived at what used to be a hospital in La Jolla, which used to be an affluent coastal town north of what used to be San Diego. The grounds looked like a college campus, with multiple large buildings and artsy sculptures growing out of concrete. Gardens—once lush, now withered from neglect—lined the walkways.

"Welcome to our humble abode," said Jordan. They worked and lived in the hospital. It turned out abandoned in-patient rooms made pretty good studio apartment units. They even came furnished with beds.

The women led Fletcher into the largest building. There were signs of damage—black fire markings, chunks missing from the stone wall, a couple windows that were boarded up where the glass had been shattered, a few broken tiles—but overall, the place was in pretty good shape. All things considered. Dr. Gomez explained that the inhabitants had managed to put together the pieces after the riots. She said they didn't get many visitors anymore.

Other than its scars, the inside of the hospital was like the inside of every hospital: fluorescent white lights radiated off of eggshell-white walls and ricocheted off of ice-rink-white floors. The place even smelled white.

"Wait," said Fletcher, looking around in awe. "Lights?"

"Thank the good Lord for solar power," said Dr. Gomez cheerfully. "And for Beth, who knows how to keep them running. You'll meet her shortly. She's a genius."

Fletcher nodded absently, taking it all in.

"The fourth floor is the living quarters," she continued. "Let's show you your room."

They walked through the lobby and into the elevator. It rumbled and lifted.

Thank the good Lord for solar power indeed.

They spilled into the hallway of the fourth floor, which was lined with rooms that once held sick people. Now it was home sweet home for a few lucky survivors. A woman poked her head out of her room to stare at the strange organism carrying a Y chromosome. Fletcher's skin tingled.

"What, never seen a man before?" Dr. Gomez called to the woman, leading Fletcher down the hall in the opposite direction. She smiled at him. "I told you you're special. Don't worry, introductions will come soon enough."

Dr. Gomez and Jordan rounded the corner and stopped at Room 4031. At some point, Dr. Reid had left without Fletcher noticing.

"Welcome home," said Dr. Gomez, opening the door. The room looked very much like a hospital room. "Well, just for a bit."

This will all be over soon.

Dr. Gomez had explained to Fletcher back at the house that they were hoping he'd agree to stay at the hospital so they could examine him and try to solve Delilah's riddle. In exchange, he'd get everything he needed: food, water, supplies—even DVDs.

"Also," Jordan had said, "you get to hang out with human beings. Which is a lot better than hiding behind couches by yourself." She'd smiled a playful, lopsided grin, and Fletcher had found himself smiling back.

"We'll let you get situated, honey," said Dr. Gomez, standing in the entry to Room 4031. "You have a shower in your room, and there should be some essentials in there, too—towels, a toothbrush, all that good stuff. One of us will come get you in an hour for dinner. Then you get to meet the team!"

Fletcher pictured being shown off at the top of a marble staircase like a debutant at a ball, and his stomach clenched.

"Don't worry, dear," said Dr. Gomez, sensing Fletcher's anxiety. "We're a nice bunch, I swear."

"See ya soon," said Jordan as she closed the door. "Don't die."

········

Fletcher flung his duffel bag onto the bed. It was filled with his clothes, enough for a week-long vacation. The bed was connected to a machine that could fold the mattress like a taco, forcing whoever was lying in it to sit up. The machine was unplugged.

Fletcher's general discomfort became more optimistic as he settled in. Here he was, Fletcher Sinclair, facing a real opportunity to be a real hero. Hell, he could save the human race. If things went well, history classes would teach about Fletcher Sinclair.

He could picture the cover of a magazine, maybe *Time*: "Fletcher Defeats Delilah!"

Fletcher decided that this was going to be a good thing. A great thing. He'd stay there for a bit, help them find the cure, and then become an international star, living the rest of his days gabbing on talk shows and touring a book he would write about his courageous adventures saving humanity. Oh, and just wait for the movie version.

Yeah, he'd be the man.

The soon-to-be man unzipped his duffel bag and pulled out a bright orange T-shirt. It featured a big Agent Orange Energy Elixir logo on the front. He folded it sloppily and put it on the bed. Next was his "Property of Kiltania Athletics" shirt, a good joke about the warrior realm in *Zordallus.* He unpacked the rest of his clothes and stacked them in the dresser. It looked a lot like moving in, but it didn't feel like it. He was sure he wouldn't be there long.

The room was large for a hospital room, meant for long-term patients. Apart from the dresser and the motorized bed, the room also had a small coffee table and a stiff couch with a strange brown pattern. The couch sat underneath the window, which looked west. In the distance, a smattering of buildings made up what used to be University of California San Diego. Not far beyond that, although not visible from Fletcher's room, lay what was still the Pacific Ocean.

Fletcher wondered when he'd return home, and he realized that his home would never really be his home again. No matter what happened here.

An uninvited lump grew in his throat. Fletcher made an ugly groaning noise to push it back down. There was no time for that. There was a world to save.

Fletcher took a shower and got dressed. Afterward, he stood and looked at himself in the mirror. His baggy shirt flapped around like an empty potato sack, as if he wasn't even in there. Now that he was suddenly surrounded by women, he wished he wasn't so damn skinny. He frowned as he examined a big old zit right next to his big old nose, looking like a smaller nose was growing beside his real one.

Fletcher sat on the bed and turned on the TV. There was only static. He wasn't sure what he had expected, knowing all too well that Delilah and her minions had killed cable and Internet streaming months ago. Old habits.

Just then there was a knock on the door.

"Room service," the voice said.

Fletcher hurried to the door and opened it. Jordan stood there, smiling at him with that amused, crooked grin.

"Look at you, all cleaned up and ready for your big debut," she said.

Worms swam around in his guts. He did not want a big debut.

Jordan led Fletcher down the hallway toward the elevator.

"Okay," she said. "What's your favorite post-apocalyptic movie?"

She was clearly trying to make him feel comfortable, and it was a much-appreciated gesture.

"*Mad Max*," said Fletcher, maybe too quickly. "Specifically *Fury Road*, but the old ones are great, too."

Jordan raised her eyebrows. "That was easy for you."

"Um, do you have—what's your favorite?" he asked.

"*Planet of the Apes*," she said. "The original one."

"I like that, too," choked Fletcher.

"Maybe someday they'll make a movie about us," she said.

Fletcher blushed.

"And it will be the first historical post-apocalyptic story ever told."

•••••••••••

Fletcher's big debut took place in a conference room. There was an impressive wooden table in the middle; a giant oval where doctors once met and discussed important doctory things. A window stretched the length of the room, revealing the pale sorbet of an early sunset.

Five women sat around the table. Dr. Lucia Gomez rose from her chair, walked over to Fletcher, and wrapped him in a big, chubby hug, pinning his arms to his side. Next to Dr. Gomez's chair was Dr. Lynne Reid, still looking all business. To her right was an attractive brunette in her thirties, with eyes that sparkled with amusement. She smiled at Fletcher the way you smile at a towering cheeseburger being delivered to your table, and Fletcher squirmed. Next to her was a small, serious middle-aged woman with short black hair. The woman did not smile at Fletcher. Then, finally, there was a frizzy-haired girl with glasses as thick as Fletcher's. She pursed her lips politely, flatly, in a way that didn't really feel like a smile at all.

"Ladies," said Dr. Gomez. "Meet Fletcher Sinclair. Fletcher, meet our team."

Fletcher was back at summer camp, being forced to speak his own name in front of his cabin mates and tell an interesting fact about himself. He was back in elementary school, having to share what he did over Christmas break. He was back in English class, reading someone else's words aloud. Fletcher wanted to retreat to his new hospital room.

Skin burning and eyes darting around like the *Pong* ball, he followed Dr. Gomez's directions and took a seat. Jordan sat next to him. She gave him a look that slowed his racing heart and cooled his burning skin. It told him that everything would be alright.

This will all be over soon.

Dr. Gomez sat down herself and introduced the team.

"You already know Dr. Reid," she said, gesturing toward the redhead. Dr. Reid smiled curtly. "Then, this is Natalie. She was, or *is*, a lab technician."

Natalie was the brunette with the dancing gaze. Fletcher realized she was the one he'd seen in the hallway. He couldn't maintain eye contact with her. "Hey, boy," she said, grinning. "You've become quite the hot commodity, haven't you?"

"And this," Dr. Gomez continued, ignoring Natalie, "is Beth." Beth was the woman with the short dark hair. A dried-out-piece-of-driftwood of a woman. She looked at Fletcher with a stern face carved with stern lines. She appeared annoyed, but Fletcher was nearly certain he hadn't done anything to annoy anyone. Not yet. "She's sort of our Jaclyn of All Trades," said Dr. Gomez. "She worked as an electrician before. You can thank her for the solar power we got."

"And this," she continued, pointing to the frizzy-haired girl, "is Megan."

"Nice to meet you," said Megan.

"She was in nursing school, too, and helps out with all sorts of things. And of course, you've met Jordan."

"Yo," said Jordan.

"Hi, everyone," said Fletcher. He imagined what a confident man's first impression would look like and promptly leaned back, casually, coolly. "Nice to meet you all."

He was proud of the successfully feigned sureness in his voice. Fake it 'til you make it, right? His chair, however, the one in which he was leaning, had other plans. It suddenly slid back on the hard tile floor, and Fletcher threw his hands forward to grab the edge of the table and stop himself from falling backward—a violent, loud and uncoordinated flurry. Natalie and Jordan laughed, while Beth, Megan and Dr. Reid all looked at him as if they couldn't comprehend that *this* was their shining symbol of hope. Fletcher's face turned the tomato red of pure embarrassment as the universe balanced things back out.

"And we'd like to keep you in one piece," said Dr. Gomez. She waited for the room to settle down. "Thanks to Fletcher's cooperation, we're closer than ever to a solution. Tomorrow, we start working toward that solution. Tomorrow we start saving the human race."

"It'll be a grand old time," said Jordan.

"I look forward to playing with your blood and semen," said Natalie.

••••••••••

Sometimes you don't know how lonely you are until you're finally around people. As Fletcher closed the door to his room, his loneliness closed in around him like a tomb. He felt lonelier than he ever had in those six months he spent by himself in his parents' basement. Lonelier than in his days as an outcast in the cruel halls of high school. In his post-Delilah isolation, the whole thing had felt like a nightmare, and all nightmares eventually end. In his high school days, he'd at least had his family and his friends.

As he sat on a hospital bed, facing a strange new future, Fletcher found his mind drifting to the people of his former life. He had developed a nice little defense mechanism during his isolation that acted as a firewall to most forms of sentimentality. When an apocalypse is at your door, wallowing is an indulgence you simply can't afford. Because wallowing is just one little hop away from giving up, and giving up means curtains.

But now, he was safe. Relatively speaking. He was safe enough to let himself finally remove the firewall for a moment. And he did. He let his mind float away, back to the pre-Delilah days. Back to his family—his mom, dad, brother. And then his friends.

What would his old pals think of him now? God, that band of oddball outsiders. Simon, Jake, Stephen, Anton, Ash. (Ash, short for Ashley, had actually been a girl, but her womanhood was a detail forgotten most of the time.) His friends were the only company in which Fletcher had ever felt he was really, truly himself. Really, truly comfortable. They had been six strangely shaped puzzle pieces that somehow fit together. They had a lot in common, sure—a shared love of the same games, movies and comic books—but their bond had been forged in something far stronger than nerdy hobbies. In fact, those hobbies were more of a byproduct than a cause. No, these were friendships born out of pariahdom, an inability to emulsify with the Great Majority.

But they were all gone now. Even Ash. Her family had died in an early air raid. He'd heard it from Simon, before Simon likely met Delilah.

Simon had been Fletcher's best friend since video games came in plastic cartridges you had to blow into when they froze. Poor Simon always thought Fletcher was going to do something big. For some reason. Well: how about this, Simon?

His mind slipped further and deeper into a state of nostalgia, to a tapestry of everyday nothingness that now didn't feel like nothingness at all. He allowed himself to get nostalgic about regular old daily life, so long ago, now a memory of a memory of a time: the smell of pasta sauce from the kitchen; the soft buzz of his PlayStation; the way his hands would leave a faint orange trail of Cheeto dust on the corduroy couch; pining for girls he was too afraid to talk to; telling himself those girls were probably dumb anyway; his dad asking him to go outside for once, it was a big world out there; summer blockbuster season; the way his mom would set his folded laundry on the foot of his bed; his online video game friends he'd never met; playing cards at lunch with the few real friends he had; his dad trying to learn one of his video games so he could play with him; Christmas mornings; his mom's giggle fits; his brother's bad advice; his brother's good intentions; people-watching in the cafeteria; helping a girl with a problem in Trig; that girl laughing at one of his stupid jokes; imagining them together, an unlikely duo in love, even though he'd seen one of the basketball players put his arm around her in the hall; mandatory family dinners.

It felt good to wax nostalgic. In a bad sort of way.

He let the bittersweet comforts of a dead time carry him off to sleep.

Chapter 5

T HE NEXT DAY THE sun rose as it had done for more than four billion years. It meant a new day, but this new day was unlike any in a long, long time. This morning, a little sprout of hope grew from the earth—hope that the human species might walk said earth a while longer.

By the time the sun's rays reached La Jolla, California, there were people already milling about in an abandoned hospital, excitedly preparing for the great things they were going to accomplish.

Fletcher was not one of them.

He was fast asleep in his hospital sheets when a knock on the door woke him up. He got out of bed, put on his glasses and, upon seeing his white, hairless chicken legs sticking out of his boxers, snatched his jeans from the day before and pulled them on.

When he opened the door, Jordan was on the other side.

"Good morning, sunshine," she said. "Ready to save the world?"

She gave him fifteen minutes to shower and change, but he did none of those things. He sat on the bed as the hospital-standard clock on the wall ticked. He wondered what the day would bring. What his new life would look like. When Jordan returned, he swapped T-shirts and opened the door again, this time following her down the hallway toward the elevators.

Jordan led him to the cafeteria on the first floor. It was empty except for Beth (the small, short-haired, grumpy-looking lady with skin that seemed to be made of bread crust) and Megan (the quiet, curly-haired girl with thick glasses like Fletcher's, whose lips were permanently pursed). Megan was clearing the tables and stacking plates on a pale blue plastic tray. It appeared the others had already eaten. Beth was sitting at a table staring at the wall across from her.

Jordan and Fletcher sat down at another table, and Megan soon reappeared with a tray. On it was a stack of beautiful French toast, yellow and brown and fluffy. A bottle of maple syrup, too.

"Enjoy," mumbled Megan as she set it down at Fletcher's table.

"You too," said Fletcher, immediately wanting to die. "I mean, thank you. But I do hope you enjoy your breakfast, too. If you haven't had it yet."

Beth broke from her trance and looked at Fletcher as if he had just sprouted a second head. She stood up and walked through the swinging doors into the kitchen. Megan followed. Neither of them said anything.

Jordan just laughed.

The French toast was delicious, despite Fletcher's curdling self-consciousness. He had gotten far too used to cold meals from a can.

Jordan explained their food situation. They had a working industrial refrigeration system, but finding refrigerated supplies to fill it wasn't as easy as going to the grocery store. They did have a shit-ton of frozen ground turkey from a Jennie-O distribution center in Vista, and a good amount of other frozen randomness they'd found in a local college dining hall. They had also procured a bunch of doomsday prepper survival kits from a Freedom Fighter Fuel storage facility in Vista. This was early on, when the place was still unraided, so the nurses had stocked up. The kits were heavy-duty buckets with freeze-dried meals that could last for twenty-five years—things like Flag Waver Fettuccini, Patriot Rice Pilaf and Uncle Sam's Mashed Potatoes. So, Fletcher had that to look forward to. Of course, they also had tons of canned food. There was no escaping canned chili in this new world.

The bread, though, like that used in the French toast, was baked fresh by Beth, right there in the hospital.

"That was really good, thanks," he told Beth when she came to grab his plate.

"You too," she said, somehow smirking without moving a muscle in her face.

"See," said Jordan. "All you have to do is save humanity and you get to eat like a king."

············

Jordan led Fletcher away from the cafeteria and back toward the elevator.

"So, it's just you six here, right?" Fletcher asked. "The six I met last night?"

"Were you expecting the Johns Hopkins staff?" she asked.

"I guess not."

"Well, we don't exactly have many patients," she said. "But our little group can actually handle most medical needs. Our main focus is figuring out Delilah, but we've had the occasional lady wandering in here looking for help."

"Gotcha."

"However," said Jordan, "I hear there's a good surgeon in Phoenix that's still alive if you're ever looking for a transplant or something."

Fletcher laughed. "What about LA? There's gotta be doctors up there, too."

Jordan looked at him. "You've been cooped up too long. LA is a shitshow. At least that's the word on the street. That you want to avoid LA."

This was nothing new for Fletcher. LA had always been something he tried to avoid. The way he saw it, there was no place in Los Angeles for a nerd who wasn't nerdy in an ironic way, who wasn't also a social media influencer and in a band and maybe did a little modeling on the side.

They arrived at an office on the second floor. Fletcher was relieved to find Dr. Gomez inside. It was still too early to face Dr. Reid or Natalie.

"Okie dokie," said Dr. Gomez. She sat on a rolling stool, while Jordan took a seat in a chair in the corner, clipboard in hand. "We're gonna do a basic little check-up before we get to the fun stuff. We need some baseline readings on you, just some general health stuff, so we know what kind of superhero we're dealing with."

She winked at Fletcher, and he forced a laugh.

First, they took some measurements. Fletcher was five feet and ten inches tall. Next, he stepped on a scale. Dr. Gomez pushed around some sliding metal weights. He was one hundred and forty-three pounds.

"Okay, let's check your breathing," she said, pulling out a stethoscope. "Lift up your shirt, por favor."

Fletcher quickly turned pink and shot a glance at Jordan. She didn't look up from her clipboard.

Fletcher lifted his shirt, revealing his skin-covered rib cage.

"Might be a liiiitle cold," Dr. Gomez warned. She put the metal disc on his chest. "Big breath in."

Fletcher took the big breath and turned his head again. This time Jordan was looking right at him. She smiled reassuringly and Fletcher found himself grinning back. It felt natural, oddly enough. Historically, all girl interactions were far from natural.

"Big breath in," said Dr. Gomez again, now holding the disc against his back. "And out. Good. Well, your lungs sound great. You pass the test."

They checked his heart rate, too. Dr. Gomez said some numbers to Jordan, who scribbled them down on her clipboard. Dr. Gomez said his heart rate was a little high for a twenty-year-old, but no worries. Then she took his blood pressure, which was also a little on the high side.

Next, Fletcher followed the good doctor to another room down the hallway. It seemed to be a sort of hybrid between a doctor's office and a gym. On one side there were the typical medical paraphernalia: a sterile countertop, white cabinets, jars filled with Q-Tips and cotton balls, boxes of rubber gloves and antiseptic wipes and a poster that showed the insides of a human being. On the other side of the room were some weights, a treadmill, some colorful elastic bands and an inflated yoga ball. Fletcher wasn't sure which side was more intimidating.

"Okay, let's see how that ticker does with a little exercise," said Dr. Gomez. "First, why don't you throw these on for us? Megan picked them up last night. A little welcome present."

She handed him some bright blue running shorts, a plain white T-shirt and some gray athletic shoes with electric yellow stripes. She took him across the hall to a room where he could change. He did so and returned to the office-gym, feeling ten shades of ridiculous.

"Look at you," said Jordan. "A regular jock."

"Yeah, right," laughed Fletcher.

"This is called a Stress EKG Test," said Dr. Gomez, untangling some wires. "It lets us learn more about your heart and blood flow, to see how it responds to a little push."

She asked him how much he exercised. He lied and said occasionally.

"That's fine, dear. Whatever you've done has kept you alive," she said.

Dr. Gomez asked Fletcher to remove his shirt—completely this time. He shot another glance at Jordan.

"I know it's uncomfortable," said Dr. Gomez, "but I need to attach all these fun little wires to you."

It was indeed uncomfortable, but he obliged. Jordan didn't even seem to notice, and Fletcher found that this bothered him as much as the idea of her seeing him shirtless. Dr. Gomez proceeded to attach the sticky little pads at the ends of the wires to Fletcher's hairless chest.

"These are called electrodes," she said. "You'll look like that Russian guy in the *Rocky* movie."

Fletcher had never seen the movie she was talking about—sports movies had never really been his thing—but he laughed politely anyway.

"Okay, let's move," she announced. Fletcher stepped onto the treadmill. It whirred. It moaned. The belt started to turn. He began walking.

Dr. Gomez occasionally said some numbers to Jordan, who jotted them down on her clipboard. "Let me know if you feel dizzy, short of breath, anything weird," said Dr. Gomez.

A push of a button and the treadmill groaned a little louder and the belt moved a little faster. He was now jogging. It felt horrible.

Another button push. Soon Fletcher was running. Then there was sweat in his eyes. There was sweat dripping off his face and splashing onto the belt below him. He was no longer aware of time—just his body and how much it hated him.

For those who *were* aware of time, six minutes had passed when Fletcher slammed his feet on the unmoving platforms on the sides of the belt. He bent over, sucking in air. There were tiny black spots floating in his vision. The belt whined, high-pitched and sad, and so did he.

"Step on down, dear," Dr. Gomez said, pressing a couple buttons as Fletcher climbed off the sadistic torture machine. She walked over and said something to Jordan, who wrote down whatever failing grade they had given him.

Fletcher finally looked up to see Jordan's lopsided grin. "Only nine more rounds," she said. Fletcher glared at her. "Just kidding."

··········

Fletcher was given a little break after his display of athletic prowess, but it felt more like a timeout. Back in his room, he showered and changed. Then he laid face-down on the bed, with his arms at his sides.

A knock on the door pulled him away from the safety of his mattress. Once again, Jordan was waiting on the other side. She was holding a plastic lunch tray with two tuna sandwiches and two apples.

"Figured you might want to have lunch up here," she said. "I know this is all a bit overwhelming."

"That'd be great." Neither of them moved.

"And," she said, "I thought I'd join you, if you didn't mind."

"Oh, yeah," said Fletcher quickly. "That'd be great, too."

She followed him into the room, her tight curls bouncing, her whole self bouncing. Fletcher scooped up his sweaty clothes from the floor and stuffed them into the provided laundry hamper, kicking it into the corner.

They sat on the stiff brown couch with the lunch tray between them.

"What do you think about our little gang?" she asked. "Quite the ramshackle crew, right?"

"Quite the crew, indeed," said Fletcher.

"They're good people, once you get to know them. Crazy, but good people."

"Yeah, I feel like they're pretty easy to figure out," said Fletcher.

"Oh yeah?" Jordan took a big bite of her sandwich.

"Sure," said Fletcher. "Dr. Gomez is the nice one, the mom of the group. Am I right?" He felt a high of unwarranted confidence.

"Go on," said Jordan.

"Well," said Fletcher, "Dr. Reid is the serious one. Seems pretty no-nonsense. Megan is the shy, quiet one. Beth is the grumpy one. Natalie is ... I don't know. The psycho one. Is she psycho?"

Jordan looked at him, eyebrows raised. "That easy, huh?"

Fletcher shrugged.

"So," she said, "which one am I?"

Fletcher had not thought this through.

Jordan saved him by bursting into song, off-key and through an enormous mouthful of tuna sandwich: "I'm a bitch, I'm a lover, I'm a child, I'm a mother, I'm a sinner, I'm a saint..."

"Oh, that's beautiful," said Fletcher. He knew the song. It had floated around for as long as Fletcher had been alive, popping up on his mom's pop rock radio station, all the way up until Delilah had killed music, too.

"But seriously," said Jordan with that wry little crooked smile, "you actually think a person can be boiled down to one thing like that? Just, boom—nice one, psycho one, etcetera, etcetera?"

"Oh, I dunno," said Fletcher, not wanting to dig any more of his grave.

"Well," she said, matter-of-factly, "personally, I feel like I can be nice one day but grumpy or psycho the next, you know?"

"Yeah, I guess so," Fletcher conceded.

Fletcher and Jordan finished their lunches, but continued talking for more than an hour. Fletcher learned that Jordan had grown up in Sacramento, moved south to go to UC San Diego and had never left. He learned that she, like Fletcher, had been classified as the nerdy type. Only Jordan fell into a different genus in the nerd taxonomy. Fletcher's world had been filled with escapes to other ones: video games, sci-fi movies, comic books and anime. Jordan's world had existed deeper within the real one. She was one of those people who liked to read (Fletcher, meanwhile, had never understood what was so exciting about frozen words). She was one of those people who liked history (Fletcher, meanwhile, had never seen the allure of things that had already happened). She was one of those people who liked philosophy (Fletcher, meanwhile, had never seen the point).

They talked about their passions and what was left of them, and about life in pre-Delilah times. Jordan told stories of past adventures with past friends, and with her two brothers, whom she missed greatly. Fletcher told some stories, too, although he may have taken some creative liberties to spice his up a bit.

As they talked, Fletcher felt alive. He had never once had a conversation this great with a girl this pretty. It felt easy. It felt effortless. He tried his best not to question it too much, afraid it would burn his eyes if he stared directly at it. Against all odds, Jordan seemed genuinely interested in what he had to say.

Just two kids trying to save the world.

Fletcher wondered what had changed. Painless conversation was a trait reserved for other guys, not for him. Then again, maybe it was him who was changing.

Maybe all the death, disease and global disaster were having a positive effect on the young man.

············

A knock on the door put a pause on the conversation. Jordan had just been telling Fletcher about the time when her debate team had discovered that a rival had been stealing and photocopying their arguments, and what a big scandal it had been. The knock belonged to Dr. Gomez, and Natalie was with her.

"Good afternoon!" said Dr. Gomez. "How was lunch, dear?"

"Great," said Fletcher, a little too excitedly.

Natalie grinned. "We're not interrupting, are we?"

"Don't be dumb," said Jordan. "I should get going."

Fletcher blushed for the millionth time since arriving at the hospital.

"Jordan, you want to get started on tomorrow's schedule?" asked Dr. Gomez.

"You got it," she said. "Have fun, guys."

Jordan closed the door behind her. It felt to Fletcher like she had sealed the remaining three in a cell. He tried to recall that feeling of effortless communication, to grasp at the smoky wisps of self-assurance he had owned only minutes before. It seemed like a faulty memory. He was now unsure he had ever felt that feeling in his life.

"So," said Dr. Gomez, "how we doing?"

Fletcher stumbled over an answer.

Dr. Gomez then went over the plan for the rest of the day. Just some testing in the lab, then a little questionnaire, then dinner, and that was it.

"And off to the lab we go," sang Dr. Gomez. The three of them walked toward the elevator, but Dr. Gomez passed it. "Let's take the stairs, shall we?" she said, allowing herself a quick glance at Fletcher.

He knew what that meant. It meant: "I saw you almost die on the treadmill." It meant: "Let's make healthy choices." It meant: "We need you to not be a dumpster with arms and legs."

They walked down only one flight of stairs to the third floor. Down the hallway was a sign that said "Laboratory."

"Welcome to my playground," said Natalie.

Fletcher sat in a padded plastic chair. The two physicians moved around the room, opening cabinets, grabbing supplies, snapping on rubber gloves. His eyes darted around, following them, as his palms moistened. He felt like the test subject for some experiment in some twisted horror movie. He wasn't far off, he supposed.

"Five liters, give or take," Natalie said out of nowhere.

"What?" squeaked Fletcher.

"That's how much beautiful blood you've got in you." Natalie poked him in the chest with her finger.

Fletcher saw the needles that would be poking him next.

"Five thousand milliliters," Natalie continued. "And all I'm taking is ten. Ten milliliters, leaving you with around four thousand nine hundred and ninety." She stopped and leaned closer. "Now, that's not asking too much, is it?"

Fletcher saw the vials where his beautiful blood would be going.

"Don't be nervous, dear," said Dr. Gomez. "Easy, peasy."

"Easy, peasy," Natalie repeated. It sounded different when she said it.

Natalie jabbed the needle into Fletcher's arm. Despite wanting to wince, he willed an unfazed scowl onto his face.

This will all be over soon.

Dr. Gomez talked to keep him occupied. "Now, I know nobody likes fasting. Lord knows I don't!" she said, putting two hands on her large belly. "But the next time we do one of these we'll have you fast for about eight hours beforehand. Fasting blood glucose, your lipid profile, your iron tests, B12 ... all of those will require some fasting to—Fletcher? Fletcher, are you okay, dear?"

Fletcher was not okay.

And besides, someone was dimming the lights.

And suddenly he felt extraordinarily heavy. *How strange*, he thought.

And then he passed out.

···········

Fletcher awoke with Dr. Gomez and Natalie standing over him.

His first thought was that a real man would not have passed out from an itty-bitty blood test.

Dr. Gomez reassured him it was fine, that people fainted all the time during blood work, and that he'd totally get used to getting his blood drawn.

"Wait 'til we check your prostate," said Natalie.

"She's kidding," said Dr. Gomez.

They gave him a can of apple juice and put a cold washcloth on his forehead. He felt like a child.

Fletcher lay there for fifteen minutes until he was good to walk.

"Grab the kit for the second part," Dr. Gomez said to Natalie.

The second part?

They led him back to the elevator, where Dr. Gomez went her separate way.

"We can take the elevator," said Natalie, pressing the up button. "You've had a tough day, haven't you?"

"It's been something," said Fletcher.

As they got to Fletcher's room, Natalie reached into the bag she was carrying and pulled out a plastic cup with a white screw-on lid.

"Alright, now for the fun part." She extended the cup to him, pulling it back when he reached for it. "We need your semen."

Fletcher wanted to disappear.

Natalie stepped closer to Fletcher. She bit her lip softly. "Do you want me to help?" she whispered.

Fletcher wanted to pass out again.

"I'm just kidding, sicko," she said with a far-too-satisfied laugh.

Fletcher wanted to die.

"But, yeah, we do need your baby batter," she said. "Maybe you're hiding the secret to defeating Delilah in your testes. Who knows? So, uh, yeah. You just come in this here cup, at your convenience, and leave it outside your door. I'll grab it in an hour."

"Okay," Fletcher choked.

She handed him the cup. "Have fun!" she said with a wink. She cackled again and bounced away.

Fletcher stood there, looking at the cup in his hand, and wondered if anyone had ever died from embarrassment.

Chapter 6

Day Two's breakfast wasn't as exciting as the previous day's French toast. It was a big bowl of watery oatmeal and raisins.

After that, he was given a questionnaire. It had been on the schedule for Day One, but Fletcher had replaced it with fainting.

Fletcher answered the questions in the conference room. They asked about his family's history with diseases, any allergies he had and his medical history. They asked about his diet, too.

"We're going to get you eating healthier, that's for sure," said Dr. Gomez, frowning at the filled-out questionnaire in her hands. "But that's not for you to worry about."

Jordan sat next to her at the conference table. She was looking at the questionnaire, too. "Fletcher Sinclair!" she said, mocking the voice of a stern mother. "Do you really drink one of those nasty energy drinks every day?"

Fletcher grimaced.

Fletcher had been riding the orange wave of chemically induced stimulation ever since he discovered the beautiful beverage during his freshman year of high school.

"That shit is literal poison," Jordan said.

That shit is literal bliss, thought Fletcher.

At around noon, Jordan, Dr. Gomez and Fletcher were back in the half-office-half-gym. Jordan was showing Fletcher some exercises he could do on his own to get his baseline health up. It was going rather humiliatingly, as expected, when Natalie walked into the room. Fletcher looked down at his silly blue shorts and the five-pound weights in his hands. He braced himself for Natalie's commentary.

Instead, she walked straight to Dr. Gomez and whispered something. Dr. Gomez nodded.

"Fletcher, dear," said Dr. Gomez, "we're going to leave you alone for a little while. Maybe try some of the exercises Jordan just showed you? Jordan, you're with us." She looked at Fletcher. "See you soon, dear."

Fletcher sat on the yoga mat and considered stretching. Fifteen minutes passed and his new coaches still hadn't returned. He stood and studied the anatomy poster on the wall. He looked at the spleen and the pancreas all squished in with the rest of the guts in the skinless man looking back at him. He realized he had no idea what those organs did.

When the door finally opened forty minutes later, Fletcher was kneeling on the inflated yoga ball, trying to balance for as long as he could without touching the ground. His record was seven seconds. The opening of the door startled him and he fell forward, catching himself with his hands. He quickly flipped around and sat on the ball.

Smooth as a buzzsaw.

Jordan smiled slightly and shook her head. She was the only one at the door, and Fletcher followed her back to the conference room, where Dr. Gomez and Natalie were waiting. They took a seat at the table.

Dr. Gomez smiled sweetly at Fletcher. "Well, honey, we have some unfortunate news."

"Okay," said Fletcher, shifting in his seat.

"It appears that you, well..." She winced slightly. "That you are incapable of reproduction."

"What?" asked Fletcher.

"Ran your boys through some tests," said Natalie. "You're shooting blanks."

"You sure?" Fletcher continued shifting and could feel the weight of the eyeballs on him.

"Which sucks," continued Natalie, "because we really thought your semen might hold the answer. But it doesn't hold anything, unfortunately."

"Now, now," said Dr. Gomez. "There is still plenty to learn from your semen, and from your blood, and from your hair ... from all of you, dear."

Like a cadaver.

"So, I'm infertile?" he asked.

"That's what it looks like, yes," said Dr. Gomez.

Fletcher had a feeling he knew why his swimmers weren't swimming right. The truth was Fletcher drank more than the one Agent Orange

Energy Elixir every day. He drank an average of four, and had for years: one right when he got up, one after breakfast, one at lunch and one in the afternoon. (God, he'd been itching for one ever since arriving at the hospital.) Every time he had grabbed a can, there was a big, fat label looking up at him that read: "WARNING: This product contains Xploserine, a chemical compound that has been linked to infertility and some cancers."

He'd never paid it any mind. He figured everything could be linked to something bad. He once noticed that the tag on his parents' couch pillows said they contained a chemical known to the state of California to cause birth defects.

But ... well, shit.

On the bright side, at least he didn't have cancer. Hopefully.

Fletcher was silent for a moment. A real man would own up to this, he thought.

"This one might be on me," he muttered.

"What?"

He repeated himself, a little more clearly. Then he told them his honest energy drink habits. Jordan's jaw slacked open.

Dr. Gomez did her best not to act disappointed, reassuring Fletcher that the past was the past and that they would help build a healthier future and that, who knows, maybe they could reverse some of the damage.

"Your treadmill performance makes a little more sense," said Jordan, smirking.

"Just our luck," said Natalie. "Our greatest hope for humanity voluntarily drinks toxic waste."

Fletcher walked back to his room, feeling like a puppy that had just shit on the carpet.

· · • · • · • · • · ·

Later that day, Fletcher was sent to Natalie's lab to give a urine sample. She handed him a jar and sat down in her chair, as if waiting for a show to begin.

"Let's get on with it," she said.

Fletcher looked around. "Can't I..."

"Well, I need to make sure that the urine you're giving me is really yours."

"Are you serious?" asked Fletcher, feverishly adjusting his glasses.

"No," smiled Natalie.

Fletcher sighed. He couldn't maintain eye contact with her, but he also—desperately—didn't want to look at that place where her blue scrubs stretched across her chest. So he looked at her shoes. They were perfectly boring tennis shoes.

"Use the restroom over there," she said, laughing to herself.

Fletcher shuffled into the lab's restroom and closed the door. It was very quiet. He could hear Natalie's chair squeak as she shifted her position. He could hear her humming. He knew Natalie would be able to hear him pee, and that made it impossible to do so.

"How you doin' in there?" she said in a singsong voice.

"Fine," croaked Fletcher.

He was not fine. Stage fright had taken over.

This will all be over soon.

The anxiety became all-encompassing, squeezing his body like a giant hand, as he started to sweat. He tried picturing a waterfall. He tried pushing on his bladder. He tried positive self-talk. He tried negative self-talk. It was all hopeless: his urethra had shut its gates.

He opened the door. "Can I come back? I don't have to go right now."

"No worries, just hang out here," she said. His stomach tightened. "We can get to know each other."

He sat down in the chair across from her. She lifted her right leg and put her foot on her left knee, leaning back.

"So, Fletcher," she said. "Tell me: what do you miss most about the good ol' days?"

Fletcher thought about it. "I guess my family," he said. "And my friends."

Natalie nodded, but seemed a little disappointed with such a vanilla answer.

"You?" asked Fletcher.

Natalie thought. "It's the little things I miss," she said. "I miss good food. Like, really good food. Like, somebody-takes-you-out-to-a-way-too-nice-dinner-because-they-think-you'll-sleep-with-them food. Like foie gras and lamb chops and shit."

"Yeah," said Fletcher. "I miss home-cooked meals."

"Home-cooked meals! My God, yes," she said. "I heard you were like, buried in Pop-Tarts and Pringles when they found you."

"Pretty much." Fletcher smiled.

"I miss the sound of a busy store," Natalie continued. "You know? Like, you're shopping, there are people everywhere, sort of a buzz all around."

Fletcher nodded, but he couldn't really relate.

"And I had this constant hum from the freeway outside my apartment window," she said. "I miss that, too."

"I miss video games," offered Fletcher.

"I bet you do." Natalie smiled.

"You have no idea."

They sat for a moment, lost in their individual daydreams.

"Let's see," said Natalie. "I miss my sister calling me on her way home from work and bitching about her coworkers."

"I miss movie theaters," said Fletcher.

"I miss having a reason to wear heels," said Natalie. "Or anything that's not this." She pointed at her tennis shoes. "But also, I miss those days where you never change out of your sweatpants 'cause goddammit, you deserve it. You know what I mean?"

Fletcher nodded.

"Let's see..." she continued. "Uh ... I miss the Internet."

"Amen," said Fletcher.

"Like, mindless dumb Internet. Scrolling Instagram and shit. I miss reality shows and the bad movies that were on late at night." She was on a roll now. "And I miss fresh fruit. Happy hour with the girls. And I miss men. They can be so dumb, but Lord, I miss men." She paused, looked at Fletcher, and grinned. "Not that you're not enough man for all of us, of course."

Fletcher's skin turned hot, but he smiled back.

"I dunno," she said, a little absent-mindedly, finishing her stream of consciousness. "I dunno. I guess there's a lot I miss that I never really thought about."

Despite his awkwardness, Fletcher felt that electric current of person-to-person connection—a feeling he'd also had with Jordan, a feeling he'd missed for so long. It was a glimpse of Natalie's own real, raw, limited-edition humanness.

It felt like she had given him something personal.

Just then, he had to pee. He got up, walked into the bathroom with the plastic cup, and peed without pause.

············

Jordan came by Fletcher's room later that day.

"How ya doin?" she asked.

"Fine," he said.

"The infertility thing," she said, "and the energy drink talk … I don't want you to feel like you did anything wrong."

"I mean," said Fletcher, "I kinda did. I could have *not* slugged four cans of Agent Orange a day."

"Well, don't worry," said Jordan. "We'll be limiting your energy drink intake from now on. To … about zero. Give or take nothing."

"I figured."

"You'll learn to like coffee," she said.

"We'll see about that," said Fletcher. There was a pause. "Hey, I have a question. What about sperm banks? Can't women use those to get pregnant?"

"They can," said Jordan. "Well, with the sperm banks that are left. A lot of them are useless thanks to power outages."

"But some are okay? So…?"

"It doesn't matter. Yeah, women can get pregnant from the frozen sperm that's in there, in the solar-powered centers and whatever, but it doesn't change anything." Jordan spoke with a solemnity Fletcher hadn't seen yet. "Any pregnancy of a baby boy ends in miscarriage. No boy has made it to childbirth since Delilah."

"Oh."

"But the good news is that if we find a cure," she said, "we do have frozen sperm, ready to launch. Maybe we can apply what we learn to those sperm cells, you know? We just thought that maybe whatever made you immune would be passed on to your offspring. But it's all good.

There's still something in you that made you survive. We'll find out what it is."

Fletcher had no idea how this immunity had been bestowed upon him, but it seemed like one big, random accident. Or one big, mean joke.

·····•·•····

Fletcher tucked himself into bed that night and stared at the black square of the dead TV looking back at him through the darkness. He felt incredibly low. He pulled the comforter up to his chin like a child listening to the ghostly creaks of an old house.

He imagined turning on the TV and flipping through the channels, the lullaby of his youth. He wondered what the news would show, if such a thing still existed. Fletcher had never been much of a news guy, much of a current-events guy at all, but in his months of lockdown he'd adopted the habit. He figured every living soul had. By the end, Fletcher was watching it every night. First with his whole family. Then his dad and Adam. Then just Adam.

God, those nightly updates. That steady escalation of terror.

Early on, there were the scientific explanations. The attempted rationalization of it all, with fancy terms like "viral dysphasia" for the symptom of talking nonsense, and "sudden fecal incontinence" for shitting oneself.

There were the gas-mouthed politicians, first claiming that it wasn't a big deal, then, okay, maybe it was kind of a big deal. Then, fine, it was a very big deal.

There were the shelter-in-place and quarantine orders. The facemask mandates. The shutdowns: schools, restaurants, any businesses that weren't essential. The boarded-up windows, painted with messages of we'll-get-through-this optimism.

Then, if anyone still doubted the bigness of the deal, those first politicians had to be replaced with more alive ones.

Then, there was the dark realization that the damage had already been done. The scientists and their talks of incubation periods, of this virus's horribly long one, and how it meant that it had likely spread to every sad sap on the planet before anyone showed a single symptom.

Then—

Then, the hysteria.

The riots, the looting, the global terror.

The TV preachers proclaiming the End Times. The worldwide gas shortage. The grocery raids. The haunting shots of all those abandoned cars on the sides of roads. The people starving to death in their living rooms, either too scared to go outside or there being nothing for them if they did. The cruise ships stuck out in the harbors, not permitted (or maybe not willing) to port. The twenty-two city blocks burned to the ground in Brooklyn. The mass suicide outside of Atlanta.

From an apocalyptic standpoint, the rest just took care of itself.

Fletcher remembered watching the political blame game play out. If people couldn't find a solution, a scapegoat would have to do. From what Fletcher gathered from those locked-in evenings on the couch, trying to make sense of the varying stories from each news network and online article, some folks thought the virus had come from a rat in Vietnam. Other theories pointed to a bat in Thailand or a monkey in Indonesia. Then, some speculated that it could have come from a laboratory. Specifically, maybe, a lab in Russia. Well, Russia didn't like that, and they said it had to be a chemical attack from North Korea. North Korea was sure it was Iraq, who said it was definitely the US.

And so on and so forth.

And round and round they went.

And that's how the wars sprouted up. Lots of them. All over.

It turned out to be a very ineffective way to cure a pandemic.

The Sinclairs watched as the news continued, the worst horror story to ever play on a screen.

One day, Fletcher noticed, there were only women newscasters. He never saw another man on TV again.

The reports came in about countries running out of medical supplies. Trade stopped, and some countries began to run out of food. All in all: fantastic methods to turn up international tension even more.

And just like that, you've got yourself a full-scale world war.

All of this just helped Delilah send Earth down the shitter even quicker. By the time it was only Adam and Fletcher watching the news, much of the world's infrastructure—trains, hospitals, roads, government buildings, power plants, cell towers—had become casualties of war. Industries collapsed and died, accelerated by the fact that half the workforce was collapsing and dying, too. The stories showed the remaining women doing their best to pick up the slack left behind by the falling men, but there just weren't enough hands to repair all the buildings and bodies that kept getting blown up, let alone run a functional society. And plenty of women were dying, too. They may have been immune to the virus, but nobody was immune to a bomb or a bullet.

And plenty of bombs and bullets were flying.

Then, sanitation rounds were halted, and trash piled up in alleys like big, stinking snowbanks. Police forces were weakened, crippled and finally nonexistent. The United States Postal Service even disappeared. If that's not the sign of a dead civilization—the day the bills stop coming—then what is?

Now, interspersed among the news stories depicting the world going up in flames were ones of people trying to save humanity, too. Doctors and scientists and other smart people had tried to understand how the Delilah Virus worked and how it could be stopped—people like Fletcher's new friends. But nobody could figure it out. It all seemed to be in vain, anyway. The main stories now were just the violence and chaos, which became only more violent and chaotic. Right at the end, Adam had called the people still working toward a cure "ghost heroes"—invisible do-gooders all but forgotten in their abandoned hospitals and labs. He said they were trying to build a house of cards in a windstorm.

Maybe he was right, but Fletcher hoped—then and now—that he wasn't.

And then all forms of mass communication finally ended. There were no more updates. Fletcher and Adam got no more information on either the global destruction or the hope for a cure.

And then Adam died.

Fletcher pulled the sheets tighter in his strange hospital bed. He was glad there was no news to watch. He knew it would be the bleakest of stories.

Chapter 7

OVER THE FOLLOWING DAYS, a slight feeling of normalcy settled into Fletcher's new life at the hospital. There was routine. There were solid schedules. There were very few surprises. Those days eventually turned into weeks, as days tend to do.

For Fletcher, those days usually looked something like this: at 7:00am his alarm would ring. He would mutter obscenities to it and turn it off. At 7:30am Jordan would knock on his door and then he'd have no choice but to get out of bed. She'd be in her blue scrubs, ready for another day of work. The scrubs, Jordan told him, helped make them feel like they were still physicians. Plus, they were super comfortable. Plus, they had an endless supply.

After his wake-up call, Fletcher would go down to the first-floor cafeteria for breakfast. Beth cooked most meals while Megan acted as sous-chef-slash-dishwasher. Beth never smiled and Megan rarely spoke. Fletcher couldn't tell if Beth liked him or not, but she didn't exactly glow with joy for anyone or anything else, either. Megan, amazingly, seemed more socially unequipped than he was. Or maybe just socially uninterested. Fletcher usually ate breakfast alone, with a significant amount of coffee, which tasted like battery acid. He missed Agent Orange with all his just-slightly-unhealthy heart.

Fletcher would then go to the doctor's-office-gym hybrid room to improve said heart health, along with that of the rest of his body. He despised that room, although in the few short weeks of daily exercise he noticed it was getting a little easier. Jordan and Dr. Gomez would be in the hybrid room with him every day, giving him his workouts. They were training their longshot racehorse, their only desperate chance to win the big one.

"We need you to keep living, and healthy people seem to be better at that," Dr. Gomez would remind Fletcher.

Along with his workouts, they'd also monitor, test and track anything that could be monitored, tested or tracked. After four weeks, his cardio-vascular and respiratory health had improved significantly. He still hated breathing hard and sweating, but he no longer felt as if he'd pass out after a few minutes on the treadmill.

"Baby steps, baby," Jordan would say.

After his daily sweat session, Fletcher would shower, change and head back to the cafeteria. Since lunch was followed by a break, Fletcher would often take the food back to his room. Fletcher would sit on the stiff brown couch and eat, and then sit there and let his mind overanalyze various awkward encounters, or what the others at the hospital thought of him, or his anxieties of the future.

Sometimes he was saved from all that thinking. Sometimes Jordan would join him for lunch, and she would do most of the thinking for the two of them. She read a lot of books from people Fletcher had never heard of, and would tell Fletcher all about them, including the ways she agreed and disagreed with the men and women who wrote them.

After the lunch break it was time for more testing. Every afternoon Fletcher would meet with some combination of Dr. Gomez, Dr. Reid, Natalie and Jordan for a slew of tests. He was Fletcher, the human lab rat.

The tests were a mixed bag of poking and prodding and spitting and stretching. Some days were horrible, others were fine. The anticipation was the worst part; at least with the morning workouts he knew he'd hate them.

Some days consisted of simple X-rays or CT scans. Others included allergy tests. Natalie would often ask for a sample of some kind. He gave more blood tests, and only fainted one other time. He gave more urine and more semen, and also saliva. He gave hair—from his head, his armpit and also his pubes. He even gave a stool sample, which was almost enough to make him walk out into the world and never come back. He wondered if Natalie was ever messing with him. Fletcher also took mental tests, which were the least comfortable of them all. Dr. Gomez or Dr. Reid would sit him in a room and drill him with psychoanalysis, memory assessments, intelligence exams, personality quizzes, tests for mental health, anxiety, depression and on and on and on. These peep shows into Fletcher's brain were the worst … and if Dr. Reid was running the show, they were the *worst* worst. She wasn't mean, but her concrete personality—her utter lack of bedside manner—made it feel as though he had failed before he even started. At least Dr. Gomez would reassure him that he wasn't a lost cause damning human civilization with his stupid brain.

Fletcher would return to the cafeteria for dinner. Usually, he was joined by more of the team. Dr. Gomez would tell stories or ask fun questions to the group. She'd also deftly steer conversations away from any doom and gloom. Everyone knew what she was doing, but followed her anyway. You always follow Mom.

After dinner Fletcher would retire to his room. They'd finally given him a DVD player, so he'd usually put on an old movie and fall asleep halfway through.

Nobody tells you: trying to save the world every day is a tiring business.

·····•··•·····

One day Jordan came to see Fletcher, and she was unable to keep her big, sideways grin at bay. "Want to see something cool?"

Of course Fletcher wanted to see something cool. He followed Jordan down the hallway.

"So, Beth has been working on this for a while," said Jordan. "But I helped! A little. Barely. Not very much. But I did hold some shit while Beth welded it," she laughed.

"Beth welds?" asked Fletcher.

"She does everything," said Jordan.

"Who *is* this lady?" he asked.

"Beth?" Jordan laughed. "She's one of a kind, my friend."

Jordan led Fletcher to the underground parking garage. There was a series of giant floodlights connected by long extension cords to outlets in the concrete walls. The floodlights stood in a circle, staging the scene and washing the object of interest in a blinding studio light.

"Meet Big Nurse," said Jordan.

Fletcher's mouth hung open like a cartoon character, like an idiot.

Big Nurse was an ambulance. Or, it had once been an ambulance. It was now a beefed-up, tricked-out, get-out-of-our-way apocalypse-mobile. Welded on both sides as well as the back doors were great sheets of shiny steel, looking like the armored ribs of a giant armadillo. Attached to the front was a massive snowplow.

"Badass, right?" asked Jordan.

"This," said Fletcher, "is awesome."

Behind the floodlights sat a big, gray, cube, which Fletcher learned was a 275-gallon gas container. In this post-Delilah reality, fuel was more valuable than gold, and harder to find.

Jordan gestured to the snowplow. "Some of the roads are totally undrivable now. Trash and shit all over them. Pieces of old cars, I don't even know what. Anyway, this baby solves that problem."

"And the armor?" asked Fletcher. "Is it … like, for bullets? Is it that bad out there?"

"It can be," said Jordan. "Not everyone left is as lovely as we are. Here, stay there. Check this out."

Jordan heaved open the back doors, which swung heavily under the weight of their new metal reinforcements. Fletcher watched from the left side of the ambulance, unsure of what he was looking for. Suddenly a panel not much bigger than a mail slot slid open. Jordan stuck out her hand, making the shape of a gun. "Pew, pew!" she shouted.

Fletcher pretended to be shot, putting his hands to his stomach and keeling over dramatically. Jordan laughed.

"One more thing," she said. At the back of the ambulance, under the rear bumper, was a metal box. "We pull a lever on the inside and *ka-chunk!* This thing opens up and dumps a bunch of nails and old pots and pans and stuff on the road for anyone driving behind us."

"Oh, hell yes," said Fletcher. "It's like James Bond meets *Dawn of the Dead*."

They hopped in the back. "Smoke grenades?" asked Fletcher, as Jordan reached into a box and held one up.

"Why not?" she said. "Found 'em at the police station."

Fletcher looked in geeked-out awe at the gutted back cabin.

"So yeah," said Jordan. "Our thought is that the look of this thing is probably enough to keep away trouble. Nobody would want to mess with this beast."

"Totally," said Fletcher.

"But if they do," said Jordan, opening up another box. "Beth also found this at the police station." It was an assault rifle the size of a fire hydrant.

"Awesome," said Fletcher. "Hey, how come you didn't show me this earlier? This is the coolest thing here." He knew the women did all sorts of things without his knowledge, always coming and going, meeting without him. He wondered what else he didn't know.

"Baby steps, baby," Jordan smiled.

"If you say so," he said.

"Plus, we just finished it."

"If you say so."

"Hey," said Jordan, "wanna get in the driver's seat?"

"Um, duh."

They got out and hopped in the front, Fletcher behind the wheel and Jordan in the passenger seat. "This is so cool," he said, for what might have been the twentieth time. He pretended he was driving it, like a kid behind the wheel of his parents' car—making all the noises, turning the steering wheel and clicking random switches on the dash.

"Fletcher, this is dispatch," said Jordan in a nasally radio voice. "There is a horde of zombies we need you to plow down over on 20th Street. Please take care of it at your nearest convenience. I repeat, please take care of it. Do you copy?"

"Roger that," said Fletcher.

Fletcher finally stopped being a six-year-old and turned to look at Jordan, smiling. He found she was looking at him, too. Her eyes seemed to shine with an extra brilliance, sparkling in the strange lighting of the parking garage. They sat and looked at each other for what felt like a decade, the silence making Fletcher's head swim. He could hear his heartbeat in his ears, and he felt at once both invincible and hopelessly fragile.

He thought, what if, right now he—

Suddenly, Jordan reached for a switch above her head and the sirens exploded to life, piercing the quiet air, red and blue lights bouncing around the garage, breaking Fletcher free from his frozen trance.

They laughed awkwardly.

"Johnson!" barked Beth, bursting into the garage and standing in front of Big Nurse. "Sinclair!"

Jordan shut off the sirens, and the two hopped out of the vehicle.

"She's not a toy," grumbled Beth.

Jordan and Fletcher grinned. "Just wanted to show off your hard work," said Jordan.

"It's so cool," Fletcher told Beth—his attempt to assuage her ire—as he and Jordan scurried off. "So cool."

··········

Fletcher began looking forward to the moments he got alone with Jordan, of which there were plenty. She would often spend the afternoon break in his room, or they'd go get fresh air in the grass field behind the hospital or in one of its open-air courtyards.

Before Delilah, Fletcher had never had a girl in his room, yet, somehow, in some end-of-the-world miracle, Jordan's company felt natural.

Back in the old days, there had been only a few girls Fletcher could talk to without sweating or feeling his tongue swell up. There was Ash, of course, the lone girl in Fletcher's friend group. She played *Zordallus*, too, and they'd all hang out at LAN parties, watch tournaments or play the fantasy card game *Orcs & Oracles*. She almost didn't count, though. She was one of the guys. There was also the chubby girl at GamerNation, the video-game-and-trading-card store he frequented. He eventually saw her as something close to a friend. Besides his mom and cousin Libby (who he almost counted as a friend and who even liked some anime) that was about it.

With almost any other girl in the world, Fletcher would feel his words get caught in his throat like big chunks of poorly chewed bread. His skin would burn and tingle. His breath would hitch. And cute girls, of course, were the worst. He'd felt awkward checking out from cute grocery clerks. He'd felt awkward ordering from cute waitresses. He'd felt awkward trapped in forced conversations with cute barbers.

Fletcher was pretty much a virgin, depending on your qualifications. He had one fumbling encounter with girl at a Coder Camp in the summer before his junior year of high school. He hadn't even known her—just the right place at the right time, so to speak. The girl had pulled him into a janitor closet on his way back from the bathroom, and then there was some sloppy kissing and a little hand stuff, but that was it. She sent him on his way as suddenly as she had pulled him in. It hadn't been all that enjoyable, but he still looked back on that day with pride. Not so much for the act itself, but for the experience of telling Simon, Jake, Anton, Stephen and Ash about it during the hackathon that evening. He may as well have told them he'd discovered alien life. Even Ash was amazed.

Fletcher had always wanted to be confident and cool with women, and nothing made him want that more than Simon. Simon had been even more shy than Fletcher, and thought Fletcher was hilarious, witty, whatever—which made it all the more agonizing when Fletcher found himself lock-jawed and red-cheeked in social situations. Like: he had let Simon down. Like: if Fletcher couldn't manage, then Simon was helpless.

All this to say, Fletcher had never been good with the fairer sex. But he could talk to Jordan. No sweating, no stuttering, no temporary loss of brain function.

As a bonus for Fletcher, Jordan often had the start of a conversation flying out of her mouth as soon as she walked through the door. This made Fletcher's life much easier.

Even the way she spoke intrigued Fletcher. She talked about deep things with casual ease, with a simple and excited natural curiosity about the world. When she was about to drop something really good, some sort of knowledge bomb or a razor slice of wit, she had a tell that would warn Fletcher: it was that slow, wry, Han Solo smile, and it would appear even when she tried to poker-face it.

No matter what they talked about, it was always a two-sided conversation, as if she actually believed Fletcher had a valuable opinion on anything other than video games, energy drinks and sci-fi.

Some days Jordan would start conversations about trivial things—top movies of all time, favorite music, the three things you'd bring to a desert island, which celebrity you wish you could marry, and so on. She'd often talk about whatever book she was reading, too. She read a lot of history, a lot of philosophy, a little fantasy and a fair amount of capital-L Literature. Fletcher pretty much only read comic books, but he enjoyed hearing her verbal book reports. She was like his human SparkNotes.

On other days, Jordan would dive into a more nitty-gritty topic of conversation, attempting to dissect some subject she'd been reading about. One day it was a psychological dive into nature versus nurture. Another day it was the afterlife. She talked about different forms of hypothetical government, she talked about different forms of God and she talked about different ways that various Ancient Greek philosophers said to live. Your typical lunch chat topics. One day she talked about how it was classic male arrogance that led to the pickle humanity was currently in. No offense, she told Fletcher.

"I mean, think about it," she said. "And I'm not shit-talking men in general. Just that dick-headed macho mindset that so many of the men in power had."

"Shit-talk away." Fletcher looked to his left and right. "Who are you going to offend?"

Jordan laughed. "Well, that's kind of my point. Not you. You're not like that. But there were plenty who were, and I think this whole thing is their fault. Ask me why."

"Why?"

"I'm glad you asked," said Jordan. "Well, the disease started. We don't know how that happened. But, instead of trying to find a logical solution to what was wrong with men—medically speaking, with men dying left and right—the whole focus was on *who did this to us?* That's your stereotypical machismo way of thinking. An inability to realize something is wrong with them, refusal to get help, always pointing fingers, etcetera, etcetera. Instead of working together with all the top minds around the world, the men in charge, our *world leaders*, just blew each other up. They went out doing what they loved, I guess."

"Never mind; I am deeply offended," said Fletcher.

Jordan smiled. "No, you're not."

"No, I'm not."

"And another thing!" said Jordan, somewhat playfully. "Look at the name they gave the virus."

"Delilah."

"You know where that comes from?" Jordan continued. "The story of Sampson and Delilah? You know, from the Bible?"

"Yeah," said Fletcher. "Sure."

"Sampson was the super strong warrior guy, right?" said Jordan. "The ultimate man, right? But if he cut his hair he'd lose his powers. And Delilah fucks him over and cuts his hair while he's sleeping. And so he gets captured, gets his eyes gouged out, dies. And it was a woman's fault."

"I see."

"So naturally," said Jordan, "when all the big, strong men started dying, we gave their killer the name of a woman. A woman who slays big, strong men."

She let it sink in. Dramatic effect.

"So you're like, a pretty big feminist then, huh?" He sounded like an idiot.

"Are you not?" Jordan smiled.

"I don't know," laughed Fletcher. "I mean—I'm a..."

"It's just wanting women to be equal to men," she said. "It's not so scary."

Fletcher nodded. "Never really thought about it like that."

"So are you?"

"Am I what?"

"A feminist."

"Oh," said Fletcher. "Sure, why not."

"You gotta say it," she said.

Fletcher sighed. "I'm a feminist."

"Good," said Jordan, satisfied. "Now that we've enlightened you on gender power dynamics, shall we move on to systemic racial inequality? Or would you like to save that for tomorrow?"

Fletcher laughed. "Hit me."

·········

Fletcher, the newly born feminist, and Jordan talked about anything and everything, but he didn't have this rapport with everyone. With Beth and Megan, his dialogue rarely ventured beyond "good morning," "thanks for the food" and "no, it was good, I'm just not that hungry." He talked with Dr. Reid only when necessary, and it was always spiritless. Their conversations were technical and sterile dialogue—a doctor and her patient, or maybe a mechanic and her engine. He spoke plenty with Dr. Gomez, who went out of her way to make sure Fletcher was comfortable, or as comfortable as he could be. She reminded him of his mom, in a way. They had similar, soothing ways of speaking. Like, if you were to burst into flames, they'd calmly lead you to the garden hose and douse the fire and tell you what an impressive little trick that was. Both medical professionals, both caretakers to the core. Fletcher's conversations with Dr. Gomez usually didn't last long, though. Dr. Gomez was a busy woman, always with something else to rush off to. Besides Jordan, the voice Fletcher heard the most belonged to Natalie.

Natalie ran the lab, and Fletcher had plenty of tests to take. Fletcher would often be trapped—with a needle in his arm or whatnot—and would have no option but to hear Natalie out. So, they'd play their favorite unnamed game: Natalie would try to make Fletcher uncomfortable, while Fletcher would try and pretend he wasn't.

It was sort of their thing.

"Before all this went down," Natalie asked Fletcher once. "How'd you do?"

"What do you mean?" asked Fletcher.

"I mean," she said. "Was Mr. Sinclair getting any or what?"

This will all be over soon.

Fletcher could feel hot needlepoints spreading over his skin. He was losing already. "Oh, come on," he said with a chortle that was meant to be a laugh but sounded more like being waterboarded.

"No, seriously," she said. "So—what, you were in college? That's primetime sexy time. Did you have a girlfriend or anything?"

"I did not," he said.

"Just playing the field, huh?" She rolled her chair back across the tile. "You dog."

"Oh, my God," he groaned.

"What about high school?" she asked.

"What about it?"

"You run through the chess team or what?" She basked in his discomfort. She radiated. "Things get steamy in the after-school science club?"

"That's not really any of your—"

"Shit, I mean, when I was in high school," she said. "The things I used to do in the backseats of boys' cars..."

Fletcher had never had a car, and at that moment it was his biggest regret. His skin burned and his big, round nose shined a deep red as he tried not to picture Natalie in the backseat of his car he never had. Her mouth curled into a satisfied smile. He had lost the game.

This is how a lot of their conversations went. She'd ask him when he had popped his cherry, watch him squirm, and then share a story about losing her virginity at fourteen. She'd ask him if he'd ever been with a man, or had thoughts about a friend. Then she'd tell him about her same-sex encounters. On and on it went, but over time a weird thing happened: Fletcher didn't dread their forced conversations as much as he used to. Sure, he usually writhed with awkwardness, and sure, he always lost and would blush a glistening crimson, but he realized that her bark was far worse than her bite. He wondered if her stories were even real, or just fabricated for her own entertainment. *Their* entertainment, really. Either way, she was lonely just like him, and this strange ritual connected them in their own strange way.

Chapter 8

"Hey, so, I was wondering," Fletcher asked Dr. Gomez one day in the hybrid room. Dr. Gomez wore a headband with cat ears sticking up and had drawn whiskers on her face with eyeliner. It was Halloween, and she said she refused to let an apocalypse ruin all their fun. Fletcher was stretching on a squishy yoga mat in his little gym shorts, which felt like enough of a costume to him.

"Yes, dear?" Dr. Gomez thumbed through the papers in her hand.

"Would it be cool if I took a little field trip to GamerNation?" Fletcher wiggled his fingers as he tried to reach his toes.

"Pardon?" She looked up from her papers.

Fletcher explained that the TV in his room had the right ports to connect a video game console. While he had no Internet—meaning games like *Zordallus* were off the table—he could still play the built-in story modes of countless titles. He longed for that sweet, satisfying sting his thumbs would get after a good button-mashing.

Cabin fever had begun to settle in. He had watched the six DVDs they had given him a few times over already, and really, how many times can a guy watch *Sleepless in Seattle*?

"Fletcher, dear, I completely understand," said Dr. Gomez. "Here's what we'll do: You write a list of the games you'd like, and we'll send someone to go to Gamerland."

"GamerNation," Fletcher corrected.

"GamerNation. One of the girls will go and try to get you all the video games you need."

"I don't *need* them," said Fletcher.

"Of course not," said Dr. Gomez. "*Want*, dear. All the games you want. Does that work?"

"That's fine," said Fletcher. Then he paused. "Dr. Gomez? Am I not allowed to leave?"

For the first time he considered whether he was truly a patient and not a prisoner.

"Fletcher," said Dr. Gomez, her voice warm and gentle. She sat down next to him on the floor as she carefully chose her words. "You are *allowed* to do whatever you want. Of course you are, honey."

Fletcher sighed, reassured.

"But let me be very clear," she said. "It's dangerous out there. More than you know. We don't want *anyone* to get hurt, of course, but you … you *can't* get hurt. You know that. And I am aware of the enormity of that responsibility, dear. But, this being our reality, we'd like to avoid any unnecessary risks. So, if you'd like to leave, nobody will stop you. You're free to do what you will. But you'd be jeopardizing everything we're working toward with every step out that door."

Fletcher had been looking at his feet in front of him, avoiding eye contact. He finally looked up at her. She looked ridiculous, speaking with such sincerity in her eyeliner whiskers. And it made Fletcher's little heart swell up, just a little.

"We're all making sacrifices," she said sadly. "Just different kinds."

Fletcher knew he had no choice. When he returned to his room he wrote down the console he wanted and a list of games. He looked out the window and thought about how big and beautiful the world was. How much there was to do. How much there was to see. He had never really considered it before, and now he wasn't supposed to go do or see any of it.

This will all be over soon.

As he lay in bed that night, bored, he thought of the gerbils in those big, elaborate gerbil cages with all the brightly colored tubes twisting and turning in every direction. He knew Dr. Gomez wanted the best. And he understood his role. It was what it was. Still, he couldn't help feeling that this hospital was his own personal gerbil cage. Except he didn't even get the fun colors.

·········

On the subject of boredom, Fletcher never would have dreamed that he'd miss meeting new people. There in the hospital, however, with the same six people, all day, every day, Fletcher would have appreciated a new face every now and then.

Occasionally, visitors would come to the hospital seeking help of one kind or another. It was a hospital, after all. The policy was that, if a stranger showed up, Fletcher was to remain out of sight. Whoever was closest to him would take him into a room and see to it that his existence remained a secret.

Someone would get Beth, and Beth would speak to the visitor. In the simplest terms, she was triage. Her job was to assess the level of risk for the hospital. Did the stranger truly need stitches or medicine or whatever? Or did they just want a meal and a cot? Most importantly: were they dangerous? Beth did the assessing with a pistol on her side. Part of the policy was no handouts, no free lunches and no new residents. This wasn't a soup kitchen and this wasn't a boarding house. This was survival.

Fletcher would hear about the visitors from Jordan, of course. There had only been a handful in the nearly two months since Fletcher had joined the team, but they provided at least a small source of entertainment. There had been the woman who had lopped off her finger chopping firewood. The woman with the horrible headaches. The woman with a bullet in her shoulder. They'd all been helped to the best of the skeleton crew's abilities and sent on their way.

There had also been two women who had begged to be taken in as an act of charity, who said they would cook and clean and whatever else was needed if they let them stay. They'd been turned away, which gave Fletcher a strange, icy feeling in his stomach.

Apparently, one of the women had offered endless sexual favors for any and all women living there in exchange for shelter and protection. This, of course, was the most interesting story to Fletcher, and gave him a whole other kind of strange feeling in his stomach. Unfortunately, Jordan didn't give Fletcher any juicy details. And now she was back wandering the hellscape from which she'd come.

The new world was a cruel, cold one.
Cruel, cold and monotonous.

··········

Dr. Gomez stopped by Fletcher's room one evening to check in. She seemed to have that motherly instinct that he was a little disheartened after the conversation about GamerNation and his voluntary confinement.

She sat gently on the foot of his bed. Fletcher was slouched, like a big bag of flour, on the stiff brown couch. He wasn't really in the mood for another pep talk on the importance of his safety.

"I was married," she said. "Did you know that?"

"No," said Fletcher, fighting a yawn. "I guess I didn't. What was his name?"

"*Her*," she corrected, smiling.

"Oh," said Fletcher, blushing slightly. "Sorry. So ... is she ... did she..."

"Yes, she died," said Dr. Gomez. "And her name was Emma."

"I'm sorry," said Fletcher.

"She was a teacher," Dr. Gomez continued. "First grade."

Fletcher nodded.

"And I swear she thought each and every one of those kids was her own."

"Sounds like a good teacher," said Fletcher.

"Too good, if you ask me," she said. "I had to fight every day with those dang kids for my Emma time. And date night? Ha. I should be so lucky."

She chuckled, and Fletcher smiled politely.

"You know how some people have fancy art walls in their homes?" she continued. "With stylish prints in frames, all arranged just so?"

"Sure," said Fletcher.

"Well, we had a wall that was kind of like that," she said. "But full of fingerpaint turkeys and macaroni art on paper plates and all these insane crayon drawings. Stuff her kids had made her. It was really something, Fletcher. Not exactly Monet, but you get used to it.

"Oh, and I did my own share of arts and crafts, too. More than any full-grown woman should do, let me tell you. All for her little class. Once there were these paper mâché planets ... oh, those planets!"

She shook her head, smiling. She was somewhere else now.

"We were up half the night painting the rings of Saturn and Lord knows what," she said. "At one point, around one in the morning, she looks at me, completely serious..." Dr. Gomez giggled. "She looks at me and goes: 'Lucia, once I'm done painting Uranus we can go to bed.' Oh, I've never laughed so hard in my life."

Fletcher grinned, watching Dr. Gomez.

"I loved every second of it," she said. "Those nights, working our butts off for her kids, with all the Elmer's glue and cheap wine and random conversations ... those are the nights that stay with you. That make it all worth it."

There was a pause.

"She carried nine kids out," she said suddenly. "One by one, she carried nine kids out of the school where she worked. It had been hit in one of the air raids. But she got nine kids out who would have died in there, Fletcher. Nine. And I believe, deep down, that some of them, maybe some of the girls—that they're alive today. Somewhere. Of course, she could have saved herself, too, but that—that wasn't her. She wouldn't have gotten nine."

Fletcher looked at the floor, feeling impossibly tiny. There was a thick, muggy silence in the air.

"The reason I'm telling you this," said Dr. Gomez, "is to remind you that we're all in this together. We've all lost so much. Each of us. Jordan, Natalie, Dr. Reid, Beth, Megan, you, me. We lost our men to the virus, our women to the violence. We've had almost everything taken from us ... but not *quite* everything. That—the little bit of what's left—that's what we're fighting for. We need to grab onto it. We need to hold onto it, and nurture it, and eventually grow it and bring it back to life. Because it's up to us, Fletcher, it's up to the few who are left to keep alive the things we love."

Fletcher looked at her.

"Just remember you're not alone, is all," she said. "And remember why we're doing what we're doing." She stood, patted him on the knee, and turned to leave. "Goodnight, dear."

·········

Dr. Gomez was skilled at delivering delicate doses of perspective when Fletcher needed them most. She found ways to remind him of their greater purpose, as well as ease his anxious mind.

She tried to assure him that his whole staycation situation likely wouldn't last long. After all, Fletcher held the answer, and they had the people and equipment to find it. Science, she said, eventually solved everything.

Well, that may have been the case, but science was taking its time. Weeks went by with no progress, nothing to celebrate.

Then those weeks turned into months, as weeks tend to do.

Fletcher tried to hold onto Dr. Gomez's words and the power they had carried. The righteous cause and all that. He wanted to stay passionate about their mission, but boredom can dilute even the most noble of intentions.

And those months turned into a sinking, mucky boredom indeed.

This will all be over soon.

Everything was the same, all the time. He was a ghost walking through his own memories, reliving all the slow minutes that weren't worth reliving. The food all tasted the same. So much freeze-dried doomsday prepper mush, all of it looking like clam chowder. Cup after cup of coffee all had the same burnt bitterness. Each test felt like one he had already done a hundred times. Every step down the white, sterile hallway was an echo of a previous step, each leading to another fruitless medical examination. Everything stitched together to create a big, fat, gray quilt of monotony.

Everything, that is, except Jordan.

Jordan—and not the importance of their cause—was the electricity that kept Fletcher running, kept him excited about the next day. She was full of an addictive fire, a kaleidoscopic unpredictability. And with it all, a seemingly unconditional acceptance.

Fletcher knew that the feeling he was feeling was the feeling of falling for someone. He'd never felt it before, but he knew it without a doubt. Of course, he had no idea how to pursue a female specimen, but at the moment that didn't matter. The idea that one day—and maybe one day soon—he could ... that was intoxicating enough.

He just knew that his restlessness wasn't so bad when she was around.

They began spending all their free time together. They played board games. They watched movies. They talked for hours. Conversation as an activity was still a strange concept to Fletcher, but he only wanted more.

Jordan taught Fletcher how to fold origami (a hobby she'd picked up out of pure boredom in the post-Delilah era). Fletcher taught Jordan how to play video games on the PS5 Megan had found at GamerNation. Sometimes Jordan would just hang out in Fletcher's room and read. Fletcher would flip through a comic book while Jordan would read some old dead guy's philosophical ramblings on God knows what.

"Okay, so really," said Fletcher one day. "What's like ... the actual point of philosophy?" Jordan had her nose in a small book called *On the Shortness of Life* by some old dead guy named Seneca. The title alone made him want to take a nap. He had his nose in a comic book from a little series called *The Incredible Hulk*. Here, even the cover was cool. The Hulk was halfway in the mouth of a giant shark, punching the shit out of the great white's face, while more sharks circled in to join the fight.

"I mean, if people haven't been able to figure it out," Fletcher continued, "in the thousands and thousands of years that we've been philosophizing, doesn't it seem like kind of a waste of time?"

"A waste of time?" She lifted her head up from the book, her dimples giving away her amusement.

"Just sayin'," he said. "If we haven't been able to figure out how to reach enlightenment, or the secret to happiness, or the meaning of life, or whatever, then it sure looks like we won't. So ... yeah. What's the point?"

Jordan considered this for a moment. Then she smiled, already proud of her answer. "Philosophy, my friend, is more of a back rub than a blowjob."

The word *blowjob* hit Fletcher in the stomach like a cannonball. "Excuse me?"

"Well," she said, "it's not about achieving something, or reaching some big ... climax." She paused again, still pleased with herself. "I mean, it's not a means to an end, you know? I think the journey is the point. It's the process that is enjoyable, that makes you better, that gives you tools to, like, live life differently."

"If you say so," said Fletcher.

"It's like exercise, you know?" said Jordan. "Small improvements every day. Baby steps, baby."

"You know," said Fletcher, "I think maybe you've been reading too much of that stuff. You should try *The Hulk*."

There was a pause.

"Oh my God," said Jordan suddenly, her eyes wide. "This is it."

"What?"

"Just now! I just reached enlightenment." She put her hands behind her head, lifting her feet and leaning back. "Man, sucks to be you."

············

Natalie kept things interesting, too. He looked forward to their encounters, no matter how helpless he was at their game—the one where she always got him to squirm or blush. Because it wasn't as much of a cornered-animal relationship as it seemed at first. The truth was, she treated him like a real person. Not a test subject, not a hero and not a disappointment. And while his insides sometimes bubbled and boiled with awkwardness, at least it was a source of entertainment. That was hard to come by in these times.

"So, how are things at home?" she asked one day.

"Oh, good," he said. "The kids keep us busy with soccer and band practice, but you know how it is."

"Nice," she said, smiling. "Hey, so you banging the nurse or what?"

"What?!" said Fletcher. His face blew up with a deep strawberry burn. He had already lost their game.

"Jordan," she continued. "You guys doing it or what? Give me some *gossip*, please!"

"Come on," Fletcher wheezed.

"You *are*! Fletcher Sinclair..." she said, feigning disapproval. "She is a *medical professional*."

"I'm not—"

"I slept with a doctor once," she said. "He was *my* doctor, actually. My doctor, but someone else's husband. *Oopsies*."

Natalie went on to tell the story, which included using various medical paraphernalia for purposes for which they were not designed. Fletcher was happy the attention was off of him. And Jordan.

And hey, it sure beat boredom.

··········

A short time later, Jordan shared the meaning of life with Fletcher.

They were drinking coffee and folding origami in Fletcher's room. Jordan was showing him how to make a swan. Fletcher's looked more like a dinosaur, and Jordan pointed this out to him.

"You could call it a *Fletcher's-fingers-are-sore-aus*," she said, giggling at her own joke.

But Fletcher didn't really see the humor in it. He wasn't really seeing the humor in anything at the moment. His usual excitement around Jordan felt numbed, too. He was, as they say, in a funk.

Fletcher felt homesick. He missed his old life. He missed his family. Simon and the gang. He missed his creature comforts.

He felt surrounded by hopelessness, like he'd be there in that stupid hospital forever, failing forever. Slowly letting down the human race one day at a time.

Plus, it was a weird week. Dr. Gomez and Dr. Reid had gone on some secret errand, leaving the rest of the crew to float around aimlessly for a few days. They'd just returned that morning, and Dr. Gomez was being all cagey about it. Jordan reassured him, said they had no reason to worry, but Fletcher couldn't help but feel—

Again: in a funk.

"Hey," Jordan said, studying his face. "What's wrong?"

"Nothing," Fletcher lied. A real man wouldn't mope and bitch and moan and go all woe-is-me. He faked a smile. "I'm fine."

"Bullshit," she said. "I've known you for a while now, Mr. Sinclair, and I can tell you're very much not fine. You didn't even laugh at my dinosaur joke. And that was a good one."

"I'm just feeling whatever," he said. "About nothing. About everything. I dunno, I'm just being a baby."

"Hey," she said. "It's okay to be bummed out—for no reason or for any reason. Everyone feels down from time to time."

"I don't know," he grumbled. "The *last man on Earth* should probably be a little more... I dunno."

"More what?" Jordan prodded. "Manly?"

Fletcher wished he could rewind a few seconds. Now he sounded both gloomy and stupid.

Jordan looked at him, her expression unreadable. "Oh, my sweet, silly little friend," she said. "To live is to feel. And to feel all of it."

"Is that Descartes or Plato?" Fletcher said flatly, not in the mood.

"That," she said, "is the personal philosophy of Jordan Johnson."

Fletcher looked up at her. "Oh yeah?" he said. "That's actually not bad."

"But for real," she said. "Let yourself feel shit. Don't be a robot."

"I suppose."

"Embrace the feels," she said. "The wonderful paint splatter that is *human emotion*." She waved her hands in a purposefully over-dramatic fashion. "The good, the bad, the ugly. The more you feel, the more you live. Those little *feelings* are you getting your money's worth out of this thing."

"I guess that makes sense," Fletcher said.

"So go ahead and be bummed," she said. "It's all part of the game."

"Thanks," said Fletcher.

"Hey," said Jordan. "You want to know the meaning of life?"

"Yes," Fletcher laughed. "Hit me."

"The meaning of life," she said, "is to allow yourself to feel *alive*. Simple as that. And that means the whole gamut of human emotion." She shrugged. "And I think the manliest man in the world would be as full of life as anyone."

Fletcher looked at her. She amazed him—just the way she saw things. There was no one more full of life in the whole world than Jordan Johnson.

"You're welcome, by the way," she said. "For the meaning of life."

Chapter 9

"Alrighty, dear," said Dr. Gomez. "Hide-and-seek time!"

Fletcher was in Natalie's lab. She was plucking hairs from his head and putting them into little vials, telling him how hair analysis could reveal certain genetic diseases or heavy metal poisoning or maybe his secret heroin addiction. And hey, anything could lead to a cure.

"A visitor?" asked Natalie.

Dr. Gomez nodded. "I'll get you when it's safe to come out," she said, closing the door.

"And now you're stuck with me," said Natalie, adding her best evil villain laugh.

"All part of your diabolical plan," said Fletcher. "Hey, do you ever get to talk to the outsiders that show up?"

"Sure," said Natalie. "I talked to one a few weeks ago. Some chick named Jessica."

"What was her deal?" asked Fletcher. "Was she hurt?"

"No. Just wanted us to take her in." Natalie clicked her tongue. "Sounds like things have gotten worse out there, dude."

"Worse?"

"Worse," she said. "When people run out of food, things can only get worse. According to Miss Jessica, most people have grouped together into either little camps or little gangs of like … scavengers or marauders. I don't know what you'd call them. But these little gangs—I guess they just go around raiding the nice communities and demanding you hand over your food, and let them siphon gas from your car, and anything else you might have that they want. And if you refuse, well … it ain't good."

"Damn," said Fletcher.

"Yeah," said Natalie. "Brutal shit. And here we are, with goddamn electricity."

Fletcher spun on his little wheeled stool. "I never thought I'd say this," he said, putting his foot down when he was facing Natalie again, "but I'd kind of like to meet one of these visitors. My amazing people skills are getting rusty."

Natalie laughed. "Tough luck, kiddo."

"Why *is* it so important for me to stay hidden?" asked Fletcher. "I mean, from the nice ones. Like, say we determine that someone is friendly. Why couldn't I meet—"

"Don't be stupid," said Natalie. "You know word getting out would be bad."

"I guess."

"Think about it." Natalie took the jar of cotton balls on her counter and gave Fletcher a handful. She began tossing them toward an empty garbage bin on the floor. "If word got out, people would come looking for you. That's bad enough. Remember: we have a lot of food and supplies, and there are a lot of people who would like to get their hands on them. So, the more people that come knocking, the less safe all of that is. The less safe all of *us* are."

"Sure," said Fletcher.

"And raiders aside, think about *who* would come looking for you. And *why*." Natalie sunk a cotton ball into the bin and fist-pumped the air. "The nice ones would want to hitch their wagon to your scrawny ass. Probably screw your itty-bitty brains out and tell you how amazing you are and blah blah blah in hopes that you'd fall for them and their little seductress tricks. That you'd want to *keep them around*. I mean, they'd know that the only man for miles around would be taken care of. Fed and protected. Which he is, if you haven't noticed our luxury accommodations."

Fletcher was only half listening now, though. He was picturing Imaginary Jessica, coming all the way to the hospital, across the starving wastelands to seek him out. To screw—

"God, you little perve," said Natalie. "I see those wheels turning. You're focusing on the screw-your-brains-out part. Not the taking-advantage-of-you-and-all-of-us part. And you're forgetting there's a second option. Introducing: the women who'd want to kidnap you. Either make you some prisoner they run tests on and God-knows-what, or ransom you off. You'd go for a pretty penny, after all."

Fletcher nodded. He decided not to bring up all the tests Natalie herself ran on him.

"Long story long, it's all bad," said Natalie.

All bad, yes.

But that night, Fletcher couldn't stop thinking about Imaginary Jessica. He pictured her walking into his room, all dolled up. Slipping her dress off her shoulders like in the movies. That dress falling to the floor in a pile around her. There before Fletcher: things he had never seen in the flesh. There before Fletcher: Imaginary Jessica, prepared to offer him something he'd never had before. Years of adolescent inferiority flashing before him, the top of the unclimbable mountain suddenly in reach. And then—

But he wouldn't. He couldn't. Not in real life. Because of Jordan. Duh. He was just torturing himself. So be gone, cruel visions. Be banished.

But then again ... would it really be so wrong? He wasn't even dating Jordan. Who knew if she even had any feelings for him? It was impossible to betray a romantic relationship that didn't yet exist, right?

He wondered if, given the chance, he'd actually do Imaginary Jessica. Let her do him. However it worked.

No way.

If he really wanted to have a shot with Jordan, he'd need all the help he could get, and one-night stands with strangers wasn't a recommended courtship technique.

Not that Imaginary Jessica was anything but imaginary.

But still.

There was a new feeling—actually just a hint of a feeling, a little seedling, but it was there. It was the faintest wisp of a feeling of power, or at least the potential of it. Natalie was right. He was worth a pretty penny. Imaginary Jessicas and Imaginary Raiders all fought over him, all because he was special. Because of who he was and the position he held. The more he thought about it, the easier it was to feel it.

And it felt pretty good.

·········

A feeling of importance was nice, but in the week that followed a much more tangible thought began demanding attention. This idea, which had crept into Fletcher's head, grew into a little monster—setting up camp in there, making all sorts of noise and refusing to move out. The little monster of an idea was this: for the first time in his life, Fletcher thought he might actually have a shot with a girl he had become quite fond of.

Hell, he had just mentally denied a naked Imaginary Jessica for this girl. If that didn't say something...

The thought became inescapable, almost overpowering. It followed him around everywhere he went—when he went to get blood drawn, when he ate breakfast, when he took a leak.

There had been times during their afternoon hangouts where a simple look from Jordan could have been interpreted as something more, times where brief pauses in conversation seemed to fill the room with a new noise, a noise that surely both of them could hear. God, it was deafening to Fletcher. The occasional touch of the hand here, a little smile there—all these small moments had added up into one, big possibility. On more than one instance, Fletcher felt as if somebody with more game might have even gotten away with kissing her, right there and right then.

Fletcher wanted to do something nice for Jordan—a small sign to show he cared. Fletcher didn't know much about women, but he knew they liked it when guys gave them flowers, so he decided he would do that.

Problem: he had no access to flowers. He'd surveyed the gardens in the hospital grounds, but everything had either withered away or been overtaken by bullish weeds.

Solution: he would make a flower instead.

Jordan had taught Fletcher the basics of origami. Every few days those thin sheets of soft, colorful paper would come out, and the two of them would fold away. Jordan was pretty good, making all sorts of things—boats, butterflies, cats, frogs. Fletcher was not very good, but he was getting better. There was a book that had instructions for 202 origami creations, and Jordan kept it in Fletcher's room, along with the paper. Toward the back of that book was a beautiful flower—one with detailed petals and complex layers, not some stupid tulip like in Lesson Two. It looked impressive. And very difficult to make. Fletcher decided that this was the only flower worthy of her.

The flower had five outer petals and a collection of little paper stamens. On the first night Fletcher attempted the flower, he couldn't even make one petal. When his fingers grew too stiff and tired he went to bed, discouraged.

He tried again the next night, and the night after. On the fourth night he completed a petal. It was a rather sad petal, but a full petal nonetheless. After a week, he could make a petal no problem, but he still couldn't connect more than one. The whole thing would come apart like a cardboard box in the rain. He got close once, but he spilled his cup of water on the origami, leaving a defeated pile of brightly colored oatmeal.

There were times he thought he'd never figure it out, that his fingers just didn't have the dexterity to complete such a task. But those fingers kept folding every night and finally, two weeks after he started his floral adventure, he held, in the very hands that created it, a flower with five petals, stamens and all. He did it a few more times until the folds were crisp and the structural integrity was uncompromised.

He finally had a flower for Jordan.

On the bottom of one of the petals, he carefully wrote: "To: Jordan" and "From: Fletcher." Romantic letters and heartfelt poetry would have to come later.

With the origami flower hidden safely in his underwear drawer, he thought about how he'd give it to Jordan. He didn't want to come on too strong, but he wanted to be confident. And the thing was, he *felt* confident. Look how far he'd come! It had been three months since he had been found hiding behind a couch, but it might as well have been three years.

He decided he would wait until the time was right and casually give her the flower, with suave nonchalance. He ran the simulations in his head, and in each one he was smooth and sure.

Now he just had to find the right time to give it to her.

Unfortunately, an unexpected staffing update got in the way of Fletcher's courtship.

....

Fletcher was feeling uncharacteristically debonair, ready to bestow his homemade flower upon a deserving young maiden, when there was a knock on the door. It was evening, so he figured it had to be Jordan.

Was it time? Was this the night? Was he prepared? Was he overthinking it?

He was definitely overthinking it.

However, it wasn't Jordan at the door. It was Dr. Gomez and her big, warm smile.

"Good evening, dear," she said. "All-staff meeting. 7:30. Main conference room. Be there or be square."

Twenty minutes later, the whole hospital family sat around the conference table. The short winter day had ended hours ago, and the world out the window was pitch black. Fletcher and Natalie were teaming up on Jordan, making fun of her for bringing a book to a team meeting, when Dr. Gomez stood up.

"Well, hello!" she said. "Feels like we haven't had an official meeting in ages. Should we take roll?"

The peanut gallery chuckled.

"Well, I'll get right to it," she said. "Big changes are coming, folks!" She rubbed her palms together excitedly. "Yeah, yeah, change is scary and all that. But it's also important. And what we're doing here is important. It might be the most important thing happening in the world, right? Trying to give us a future. So, I believe it's our responsibility to take every measure to ensure our success. To give us the best shot."

Where was she going with this?

"That's why I'm bringing in some help."

Jordan, Natalie and Fletcher exchanged glances.

"There's a hospital in Palm Springs," continued Dr. Gomez. "It had a reputation for having some of the brightest minds around. The good news is that fifteen of them are still alive, still together. Like us, they're trying to find a cure. The bad news is that most of their equipment was destroyed or stolen. And all leadership is dead or gone. The fifteen that stuck together are the young guns, the fresh nurses. The Jordan Johnsons of the group." Dr. Gomez smiled at Jordan. "I visited them a few weeks ago, and they're lovely girls."

Her secret errand.

"They will make great—"

"Wait." Natalie cocked her head to the side. "You're not saying..."

"I am!" said Dr. Gomez. "Think about it. We're spread thin. Too much to do and not enough hands. Not enough perspectives and new ideas. They can help us. With the medical side of things—they have recent infectious disease training, some even with focuses in virology and immunology—but also with the operations side. They can help Beth and Megan keep this place running."

Beth grunted.

"I know, it will be a big change. But they'll help us. And we can help them. They are smart and full of hope, and we can give them access to equipment and, well ... our secret weapon." She winked at Fletcher. "Fletcher is invaluable, and it's silly for us to keep him to ourselves."

Fletcher considered the word *invaluable.* It had a nice ring to it.

"And safety. They'll be safer here. We'll all be safer with a bigger group." She paused. "It's a good fit. And this isn't on a whim, I want you to know. Dr. Reid and I have been discussing it for weeks, and I truly believe this is the right move." Her smile grew. "And besides, we could use some new friends, don't you think?"

Fletcher had recently told Natalie how he'd like to meet one of their visitors, but now that meeting outsiders was really going to happen, he wasn't so sure he liked the idea. He actually had enough new friends after all, thank you very much.

With that, Dr. Gomez opened up the floor for questions. There were a few, like: When were they coming? (Answer: Next week.) What could they do that the current staff couldn't? (Answer: They'd have to wait and see, wouldn't they?) How would they feed this newly expanded team? (Answer: Some of the new girls would be responsible for procurement missions.) Why did Dr. Gomez keep it a secret? (Answer: Because she was a cruel dictator.) Everyone laughed at the last answer. The tension in the room softened. Dr. Gomez explained that she needed to be sure, one hundred percent, and now she was sure.

Fletcher watched Dr. Gomez speak. He wondered if leadership was something that came naturally to people, or if it was a skill that could be developed.

After the meeting ended, Fletcher, Jordan and Natalie stayed behind, chatting into the night. Natalie had already decided that she hated the new girls. She didn't want "some new bitches coming in and messing with their shit." But Jordan was passionate that it was a good idea. That it increased their chances. She thought the whole experiment could be fun, too. Fletcher was just anxious about it all. Eventually, though, both Fletcher and Natalie agreed that, at the very least, even if they weren't thrilled about it, it made sense.

It was an interesting night, to say the least. But not interesting in the way that Fletcher had hoped.

Fletcher's flower would have to wait.

··•••·•••··

Dr. Gomez, Megan and Beth were gone for a couple days. They took Big Nurse, the Nissan Leaf that Fletcher had arrived in, and another car—the caravan needed to chauffeur fifteen new hospitalmates. They left behind an uneasy atmosphere. One collectively held breath. Jordan, Natalie, Dr. Reid and Fletcher kept glancing out the windows the way a first grader does when waiting for their friend to come over. Finally, the caravan returned.

Fletcher was down on the first floor with the other three, finishing up breakfast in the cafeteria. The four of them had picked up the culinary slack in Beth and Megan's absence, and had a newfound appreciation for their ability to make palatable food with their dystopian ingredient list. Natalie had made a powdered egg scramble that resembled cottage cheese. Fletcher was poking at the mush with his fork and sipping on his second cup of coffee—which no longer tasted like motor oil to him—when he heard a commotion. All four heads rose, watching in anticipation. First came Beth and Megan, their expressions no different than if they were returning from the bathroom. Dr. Gomez followed, her face a sunbeam of excitement. She greeted her team, then nodded back at the cafeteria door. Fletcher watched the opening, waiting for something else to come through.

And then the something else came through.

The something else was a young woman in a mint green nurse's tunic. She was followed by another. Then another. The girls kept appearing at the mouth of the door, and it looked like they might never stop—a procession of bouncing ponytails and bright eyes, all seeming to be in their early twenties. It was like some sort of beauty pageant walk and Fletcher felt like their petrified judge. Fletcher looked at them, his mouth slacked like a caveman's. To his horror, they were all very pretty.

Chapter 10

Dr. Gomez introduced the new cast to the old guard. There were two Michelles, a Lori, a Serena, a Heather, an Amanda and a whole bunch of other names Fletcher feared he'd never be able to remember. Then the La Jolla crew introduced themselves. When it was his turn, Fletcher's voice shook like he was jackhammering concrete.

The girls—the Palm Springs 15, as they were dubbed by Natalie—were given a tour and a meal, then shown to their rooms. They were assigned departments and positions, based on their areas of expertise as well as needs around the hospital. The girls with virology backgrounds would work with Dr. Reid directly. Natalie was given a lab assistant, too, to her dismay. They would all take rotating shifts in the kitchen or as janitors. Overnight, the office had turned into a sorority, and Fletcher had never felt more out of place.

Girls ran this way and that, popping out from behind doors and appearing out of thin air to offer bubbly hellos. These females were eager to speak with Fletcher, and that, of course, terrified him.

Well, hold on. It terrified him *at first*. But he couldn't ignore that some of the girls seemed to be amazed by him—by his very existence—and that made things a little easier.

Fletcher Sinclair: the man who survived Delilah.

There was also that word Dr. Gomez had used: *invaluable*. Plus, he still had Imaginary Jessicas seeking him out, and the Imaginary Raiders fighting over him, and that faint notion of unrealized power. Thoughts like those definitely helped soften the intimidation of so many new faces.

Not long after the new hospitalmates arrived, two separate strangers stumbled in. Both times, Fletcher was taken into the nearest room to hide. Visitors had always sent a wave of fear through the hospital. What if they weren't just seeking medical help? What if they had more nefarious intentions? But things were different now. There was safety in numbers. It was reassuring to know there were twenty-one other people nearby. Of course, both of these strangers were harmless: one had an infected knife wound and the other was simply looking for food. The first received treatment and antibiotics. The second received nothing. Then both women were sent on their way. And both, Jordan told Fletcher, likely wouldn't be alive much longer.

Soon after, Christmas came. A few of the Palm Springs nurses strung up lights on a tree in the lobby. One set up a menorah in a window. Dr. Gomez brimmed over with enthusiasm, helping the girls organize supply runs to get decorations. Fletcher had to admit: the new girls brought some new energy. Dr. Gomez organized a big Christmas feast, telling everyone to find their most festive attire.

"You know what I love about Dr. Gomez?" Jordan asked Fletcher as they were making their way to Christmas dinner. They were both wearing ironic ugly sweaters that Jordan had found on a supply run in the back of a Target. Hers had a hideous tree design and the words: "Festive AF." Fletcher's had Darth Vader in a Santa hat. "Dr. Gomez keeps morale up by sheer will power," said Jordan. "Like, she won't let an apocalypse ruin Christmas."

Fletcher laughed. She was right, too. But what Jordan didn't realize was that she was exactly the same way.

Beth had cooked up a big ham she'd been saving for a special occasion, but because their population had skyrocketed, everyone only got a small slice. But there were meatballs and mashed potatoes and jars of cranberry sauce. They even had some Oreos for dessert. It wasn't exactly a Norman Rockwell painting, but it was a small piece of niceness in a not-very-nice world. And that was something. The Palm Springs 15 were all effervescent holiday cheer, singing carols and laughing and drinking wine that Beth had found. Dr. Gomez gave a speech—a hope, love and this-is-what-the-holidays-are-about kind of thing—and Fletcher noticed Heather and Serena wiping their eyes as she spoke. Fletcher had a thought, and he couldn't tell if it was incredibly stupid or incredibly profound. It was this: a little niceness can make a big difference.

The year came to a close a week later. All twenty-two of them stayed up until midnight. They drank champagne and played charades and at one point some of the Palm Springs girls started dancing to a Spice Girls

CD they'd found. There was another speech from Dr. Gomez, and as she spoke Fletcher felt a warmness for this team, even some of the new girls. Because this was a nice night. And a little niceness can make a big difference. They counted down the seconds to midnight, and as they all cheered and whooped, Jordan grabbed Fletcher's head and kissed him on the cheek. Of course, she kissed Natalie on the cheek, too. And Dr. Gomez. And Beth, who tried her best to avoid it. There was no private moment for any real kiss to happen between Fletcher and Jordan. But besides, he thought, a New Year's kiss was a little cliché, wasn't it? He'd find a better time.

·········

And then another week went by. And then another.

Things settled down as the new girls began to find their natural fits within the hospital, and Fletcher got used to having them around. Routines became routine once again, even with the new recruits. Tests were tested, trials were tried, charts were charted and plans were planned. There were many days where Fletcher wasn't needed at all, and those crawled along with a torturous sluggishness. He still had his daily workouts, and—while he wasn't exactly ready for his calendar shoot yet—he did look (and feel) healthier than ever. But, God, it was still exercise.

A hard truth suddenly became apparent to Fletcher: boredom wasn't a rat in the attic that could be driven out by a few plucky exterminators. It was a hulking, scaly beast in the basement, and it needed to be fed, continuously, or it would climb those stairs and devour you whole.

He was chewing this hard truth when Dr. Gomez came in to check on him one night. See how he was adjusting to things—one of her occasional mental health check-ups. It was a kind gesture, but Fletcher wasn't in an especially receptive mood.

And so he began whining. About the boredom and the blahs. "Sometimes I get so stir-crazy I just want to leave," he said. He was sitting on the stiff brown couch. Dr. Gomez sat across from him in a plastic chair. "Don't you? Just want to go live your life?"

"This is my life," said Dr. Gomez. "This place. These people. Including the most handsome man I've seen in months." She reached across pinched his leg.

"Yeah, yeah."

"My Emma always said: 'if you don't like something, change something,'" said Dr. Gomez. "So, what could we do to spice things up a little?"

"I don't know," said Fletcher.

"Come on," she goaded. "A solution for every problem. What do you like to do? Or, what did you like to do before Delilah? Maybe there's something we can bring back to life?"

"Can't bring back the Internet," muttered Fletcher.

"No, I think that's a little advanced for us," she agreed. "Let's see. Did you play basketball? We could—"

Fletcher laughed.

"Fair enough," said Dr. Gomez.

It was all video games and movies, wasn't it? The occasional card game, sure, but really, his life happened on screens. And he already had a PS5 and some DVDs. He did miss going to the movies, he thought. The biggest screen of all.

Wait.

"What if we made a movie theater?" asked Fletcher, eyes suddenly electrified, alive.

Dr. Gomez grinned. "Now you're talking."

"We could do it in one of the small conference rooms," said Fletcher. "Just need a projector and a screen. Oh, shit—and a popcorn machine!" He was on a roll now. "We should set up a little makeshift snack bar, too, you know? Like, with Junior Mints and Now and Laters."

"See?" laughed Dr. Gomez. "A solution. Make it happen, good sir. You talk to Megan, tell her what's needed. Let's give this place a movie theater."

On a Friday evening, just over a week later, the theater had its opening show. Fletcher urged everyone to come for the premiere. He decided, proudly remembering Jordan's favorite post-apocalyptic movie, they'd play the original *Planet of the Apes*. He thought it a hilariously ironic choice, too, given the state of the world.

Fletcher was only slightly disappointed in the turnout: Jordan and Natalie showed up, as well as about half of the Palm Springs 15. Lack of a sellout aside, he was still in awe: he had said the words "movie theater" and—without even a snap of a finger—here was a movie theater.

"Speech!" shouted Jordan when Fletcher got up to insert the DVD.

Fletcher laughed loudly and suddenly, with the sound you make when you get punched in the stomach.

"No speech," he said, starting his speech, "but I will say, well, thank you for coming and I, you know, I thought everyone—all of us here, we're all together, you know—and that we'd all like—I mean, who doesn't like movies? I thought we would all enjoy this. Something new and exciting. I dunno. Okay, well, please silence your cell phones ... just kidding ... but, uh, yeah ... enjoy the show!"

A satisfactory inauguration, he thought.

As the movie started, Fletcher looked around at the lights dancing across the faces of those in the audience chairs. Even though a few girls slept and a few left early, and even though Natalie kept throwing popcorn at girls and pretending it wasn't her, he felt proud. This was his doing.

He said the words, and the thing appeared.

Welcome to Sinclair Cinema.

···•·•····

A week later, Fletcher was bored again.

It wasn't that he didn't like Sinclair Cinema, as he now called it in his mind. He did. It was just that, well ... it wasn't as much of a cure as he thought it might be. First of all, while he watched plenty of movies in the new theater, he was often alone. He had imagined the twenty-one women joining him, packing in for his movie nights like it was the hot ticket in town.

Whenever a big group *did* use the theater, it wasn't how Fletcher had envisioned it. He had only imagined the theater to show exciting blockbusters, the way the good Lord intended. But that wasn't the case. Occasionally, some of the Palm Springs 15 would gather to watch reruns of *The Bachelor* on DVD, or silly rom-coms from the 90s. Fletcher didn't approve of such blasphemy within his sacred cinematic temple, but it wasn't like he could say anything. He desperately wanted them to like him, and playing theater manager wouldn't help his campaign.

On that matter, it was hard to tell how the new girls felt about him. It seemed that some had a bit of well-placed respect for him as the only known man who had survived the virus. But not all of them. In fact, a few didn't seem impressed by him at all. (Specifically, for the record, a girl named Arlene, who tended to roll her eyes and do this weird little laugh whenever Fletcher spoke.)

Did he mention that he was the last man on Earth? Or, at least, the only one around?

Now, even though the theater didn't quite live up to his imagination, there was still something about it that sent a current of dark electricity through his veins whenever he walked by it. It was there because of him. Just because he was who he was. And God, that felt good.

But back to his boredom.

He thought about Dr. Gomez's question—about what he used to do for fun, before Delilah went and stole it all away. He didn't want to admit it out loud to anyone, but oh, how he missed *The Odyssey of Zordallus*. What he would give to lead a team on a raid into the Giant's Forest, slay a few oversized enemies and lug back as much gold as his satchel could carry.

What else did he do? He went to GamerNation a bit. He used to play laser tag occasionally, but that place had gone out of business a year or two earlier. Sometimes he would go to the arcade to play some of the classics, but he hadn't been in quite a while.

Fletcher stopped in his mental tracks. That was doable. An arcade. Why not? All it would take would be the machines and electricity. Plug 'em in and you've got yourself an arcade.

So Fletcher told this to Dr. Gomez, as the word *invaluable* swelled in his mind.

Dr. Gomez gave him her patient smile. It was identical to one that his own mother used to give him. "Is an arcade something that everyone will enjoy, you think?"

"They could," said Fletcher. The word *invaluable* ballooned up even bigger, and he could feel it pressing against the inside of his skull.

"Maybe we try to think of something that's a little more—"

There was no room in his head for good, honest thinking anymore. So the words came: "I don't mean to be—I don't know," he said, "but I kind of feel like it's not too much to ask. Being that I'm the only one of me."

The polite smile on Dr. Gomez's face hardened, just a little.

Then, with a weird smile like maybe he was joking, but maybe not, he said, "I could always leave."

Fletcher winced inside. *Where did that come from?* He was pretty sure he didn't mean it.

Dr. Gomez sat for a long time, the seconds clawing forward. Fletcher wished he could pull the words back into his stupid mouth, tell her he was sorry, hug her, be hugged by her, have her forgive him for being an ungrateful prick.

Finally, she spoke. "Fletcher, dear." Her voice was soft and warm and deliberate. "I won't pretend like we won't do whatever it takes to keep you here. I guess my silly little dream is you stick around because you want to. Because you believe in what we believe. Because we're all in this together. Not because you're … compensated highly enough for the unique position you're in."

Fletcher didn't know what to say, so he didn't say anything. He just looked at his dirty shoes. But the silence seemed to say something to Dr. Gomez. Seemed to be interpreted as an animal far fiercer than the cat that had his tongue.

She sighed. "We'll make your arcade, honey."

Fletcher looked up.

"We'll do this for you," she said. "Think of it as a token of our commitment to you. But then, from here on out, let's focus on doing things for the good of the whole team, okay?" Fletcher nodded. "We're family now."

As Dr. Gomez walked out of his room, Fletcher flopped backward on the stiff brown couch. He looked up at the ceiling in amazement.

Jordan had once asked him if he felt special that he was somehow spared, that he—and only he—had survived. Fletcher had been in one of his bad moods when she had asked.

"I think it's silly for anyone to feel special," he had said. "There are—er, there *were*—like eight billion people on Earth. Did you know there have been more than 100 billion people over the span of humanity? I read that once. So, think about it: the odds of being *special* is well … pretty bad, I'd say."

Jordan had just laughed.

"Feeling special," Fletcher had continued, "is probably some built-in evolutionary thing that keeps us moving forward. Otherwise, why would we care?"

"Well," Jordan had said, "you wanna know what I think?"

"I assume you'll tell me either way?"

"Of course. *I* think everyone has their own brand of special, and that's what makes people so cool. The number of human beings that have *not* been like you is what's really impressive. In my humble opinion. 100 billion or whatever you said. 100 billion people and none were like you."

Fletcher had grunted a response.

"So, maybe," she'd said, "we each just need to figure out what makes us special."

"You're certainly special," Fletcher had joked.

As he now stared at the ceiling tiles of his hospital room home, an arcade in the works just for him, he realized that maybe he was a little special. He had been a nobody before, but he was an honest-to-goodness somebody now. Somebody important. People went out of their way to make arcades for him. Movie theaters for him. Imaginary Jessicas threw themselves at him. Simply because he was him.

At that moment, Fletcher decided that if he was going to be in this position, if he was going to help save the world as only he was qualified to do, it was not only *okay* for him to benefit from it. It was *right*.

The world needed him.

He was invaluable.

PART III
ODIN, KING OF THE WORLD

Chapter 11

Fletcher was a freshman in high school when his brother, Adam, won the Glenn R. Bachman Leadership Award. The honor was given to the member of the football team who best exemplified the leadership qualities that Bronco Football valued so very much. This award was bigger than Team MVP. It was a tool for college applications. It was a sign of future success. It was a message to Fletcher's parents that they had raised a hell of a young man.

At least one.

That night, the whole Sinclair family had been in attendance in the high school gymnasium for the awards banquet. Fletcher's parents swelled with triumphant pride, nearly bursting, when their eldest son was announced as the winner of the night's most prestigious prize. Tears streamed from his mom's eyes. His dad kept grinning like a lunatic. To Fletcher, the whole night was boring as shit, but he clapped earnestly when his brother walked up to accept the honor. He loved his brother, and if this made him happy, then Fletcher was happy for him. Bored, but happy.

The four Sinclairs went to get ice cream after to celebrate. The parents kept looking at Adam as if he'd just cured cancer, patting his shoulders over and over again and smiling at him without saying anything. Smiling and patting, patting and smiling.

Later that night, Fletcher was in the basement per usual, playing *Zordallus.* He walked up the stairs to get a glass of water, but a sound stopped him at the top. His parents were whispering, and he gave in to his curiosity. Parents can be so smart, he thought, but also so naïve. They often talked like this, as if their words existed in a glass bubble that was impenetrable to underage listeners.

"Let's not worry about Fletcher now, honey," his mom was saying.

"I'm not *worrying*," his dad said.

"He'll be fine," said his mom. "Plus, Adam's accomplishments are independent of Fletcher, and..."

"Of course. I know. I'm just saying it's ... frustrating. No, that's not the right word." His dad paused, thinking. "It's just hard to understand how Fletch didn't get any of the ... ambition that Adam did. The go-getter-ness."

"Honey, they're just different."

"I know," Fletcher's dad said. "And I love that they're different. I just sometimes wish Fletcher wanted more, you know?"

"Some kids are late bloomers."

"I just wish he wanted to *do* more." His dad's voice was wistful. Perhaps trapped in memories of his own youth. "To *be* more."

"I know, honey," his mom said. "But everyone wants different things."

"Man, if I could go back to high school," said his dad, "I swear I would never turn on a TV. I wouldn't even sleep. There's too much life to live at that age."

"But it's his life," said his mom. "And who knows who he'll become?"

Fifteen-year-old Fletcher no longer wanted water. He went back downstairs, feeling even smaller than usual.

··········

Years later, Fletcher decided that it was finally time for him to be more. Maybe even make his old man proud.

A week after Fletcher surprised himself with the boldness of his request, his wish was granted. A large break room on the fifth floor was gutted and converted into a beautiful, buzzing, bona fide arcade. Fletcher's heart jumped with nostalgic joy when he laid eyes on the finished product. The walls were adorned with lit-up neon signs that must have been found in whatever abandoned coin-op they'd taken the games from. They read "Fire Away," "Level Up," "Turbo Mode" and "Tilt." Painted on the far wall was makeshift lettering: "Fletcher's Arcade." His throat tightened unexpectedly and he coughed it away.

Fit snugly alongside each other, against all four walls, were no less than a dozen full-sized arcade games. There were some classics (*Dig-Dug*, *X-Men* and *Super Off Road*) and a few fighting games (*Mortal Kombat*

2 and *Soulcalibur*). There was a good selection of shooter games (*Area 51, Big Buck Hunter, House of the Dead 2* and the one good *Jurassic Park* game). There was the *Cruis'n World* racing game. There was a pinball machine, too. They'd even included *Dance Dance Revolution*.

It was glorious. It was electric, glowing, humming, beeping and glorious.

Fletcher got right to work. Each of the machines had been turned on "free play" mode, so he was mashing buttons and setting high scores in no time. He was no longer a lone patient in a hospital. He was a kid again. Then he was a professional racer, and then he was a feared, sword-wielding fighter and then an alien hunter. He played and played and played—until Beth popped the bubble around him and brought reality back into full, three-dimensional color.

"You're late for your blood work," she said humorlessly. Fletcher had lost track of time, but he obliged. He followed Beth away from the arcade, his fingers tingling and sore from his feverish abuse of the buttons and joysticks.

"It's awesome, Beth," said Fletcher as they rode the elevator to the third floor. "Awesome."

"It cost Big Nurse a new bullet hole," she said.

"Oh, shit," said Fletcher. "I didn't want any..."

"Not for you to worry about," she monotoned. "Nothing Big Nurse can't handle."

They walked past Sinclair Cinema and then to the laboratory in silence.

"Hey, Tinkerbell," Natalie said as Fletcher entered. She was talking to a tiny blonde girl in the room with her. "Why don't you go get Fletcher some juice?"

"Can you not call me that?" the girl said. Her real name was Amanda. "And ... does Fletcher even *want* juice?"

"Yes, please," said Natalie. "Lord Fletcher gets a little fainty sometimes. We need some sugar on hand just in case."

"Fine," said Tinkerbell-slash-Amanda. She smiled a little too sweetly at Fletcher and walked out.

The girl closed the door behind her, and Fletcher and Natalie were alone. Just like old times.

"So," said Natalie, "you wanna give her a poke or what?"

Fletcher wheezed a response: "What?"

"Yeah, why not?" Her eyes danced gleefully, gobbling up Fletcher's squirminess. She played it up, all no-big-deal, casually sweeping a strand of cola-colored hair behind her ear. "Tinkerbell. Want me to have her give you a little something-something?"

"Come on," said Fletcher, suddenly bright red, meaning he'd already lost.

"She has to do what I say, you know," continued Natalie. "I'm her boss."

"No, she doesn't," said Fletcher.

"No, she doesn't," Natalie conceded, laughing. "But I *am* her boss. And she better damn well act like it. That girl is annoying as *shit*."

She cackled her sing-song cackle, and Fletcher laughed, too. The game was over, and now he could relax.

"It's been a while, dude," she said. It was true. With the incendiary bomb known as the Palm Springs 15, one-on-one conversations had become a rarity. "How you holding up?"

"Not too shabby," said Fletcher.

"So," said Natalie, flashing a wry grin, "somebody thinks he's the big dick in the locker room, huh?"

"Excuse me?"

"What's the king's next request?" she asked.

"Oh, the arcade thing?" Fletcher scratched his head and swallowed.

"And the movie theater…"

"Well," said Fletcher, as matter-of-factly as possible, "I think they're really going to be enjoyed by everyone. It's not…" It was a sentence he had no plans of finishing.

"Oh, don't get your panties in a bunch, Your Highness," she said. "If I were you, I'd do the same thing. Might as well make the most of your position. Just don't forget us little people."

"Hey, I just want to bring some fun to this place," he muttered.

"He says, right before ordering a harem of women."

Fletcher looked at her tensely.

"Dude, I'm fucking with you," she laughed. "You are so uptight. You might *need* a harem of women just to loosen you up."

Fletcher let himself laugh back. She was right, after all. About being too uptight.

"You ever think about how this all would be different if it were the other way around?" asked Natalie.

"Huh?"

"I mean, if it were one woman left in a world full of men. Instead of you and all the ladies."

"Oh," said Fletcher. "Not really."

"Call it the Samson Virus."

Fletcher smiled.

"God, that poor girl," laughed Natalie. "It'd be some sort of *Handmaid's Tale* nightmare."

"Yeah," said Fletcher. "Guess so."

"She'd just be kept in a cell and ... well ... yikes. And all the men would probably kill each other fighting over her. And then one day she'd just be like: 'Um, hello? Anyone out there?'"

"Totally," said Fletcher.

"Or she wouldn't even make it one day. Just be ripped apart in every which direction, like a piece of meat being fought over by dogs."

"Lovely," said Fletcher.

"Guess it's better this way," smiled Natalie.

The door opened, and in walked Amanda with her juice box.

It was good to chat with Natalie again, to be lovingly harassed by her again.

And he knew damn well he hadn't asked for the theater and the arcade strictly for the good of the masses, like he said. It was mostly because he desperately needed entertainment. And, he supposed, it was possible of course, that maybe—just maybe—he had also wanted to show that he knew where he was on the totem pole. Was that so bad? Natalie said she'd do the same thing herself. In a perfect world, he thought, his new arcade would address all three issues. In a perfect world it would be enjoyed by everyone, it would cure his boredom and it would maybe earn him the respect that a few of the girls around were still withholding.

This world was far from perfect, though. So very far from perfect.

·········

Jordan also had something to say about Fletcher's recently granted wishes. She was sitting in his room one evening, a Risk board between the two of them. They were in their usual loungewear: her in yoga pants and a "Sally Ride is my Homegirl" T-shirt, Fletcher in sweats and a plain white tee. The board between them was looking more red than blue. Fletcher's armies were blue.

"So what's next, big shot?" she said.

"Well," he said, "it looks like you're going to take South America from me, so there's that."

"This is true," said Jordan. "I am going to do that. But I meant with your recent … *requests*." She smiled that crooked grin.

"Oh," said Fletcher.

"Wanna get me something nice?" she asked.

"What do you want?"

"I'm kidding," said Jordan.

"You sure?" Now it was Fletcher's turn to smile. "I mean, life is short."

"It's also the longest thing you'll ever do," said Jordan.

"What?"

She laughed. "I dunno."

"Okay, but seriously," said Fletcher. He wanted to nip this in the bud right here and right now. "What are you worried about?"

"I'm not," she said. "Nothing."

He looked at her and raised his eyebrows.

"I *guess* I just want to make sure you don't get too far out over your skis or whatever," she said.

"Oh, yeah, no," said Fletcher. "I'm just … I'm not like, trying to do anything crazy here. It was just a couple fun *suggestions*."

"Oh, I know," she said. "I just… No, that's all." She laughed. "I'm done. Lecture over. I shouldn't have said anything."

"Do you think I'm being…?"

"No, no," she said. "I'm blabbering. Don't listen to me."

"Okay."

"And hey," said Jordan, "the movie theater is sweet. That was a good idea."

"Jordan," said Fletcher, "I'm not an asshole."

"I know you aren't," she said, looking at him with a look. One of *those* looks. A look that made Fletcher wish he could just man up and kiss her.

There was a long pause.

"You are what you repeatedly do," she said suddenly.

"What?"

"Aristotle," she said. "One of my favorite quotes. *You are what you repeatedly do.*"

Fletcher nodded as if he understood. He didn't really.

"It's kinda powerful, right?" Jordan continued. Fletcher nodded some more. "Like, we have control, I guess. Like, if you want to be a good person, you just need to repeatedly make good-person choices. And you only become an asshole if you do asshole things over and over."

"Yeah." Fletcher adjusted his glasses.

Jordan laughed, loud and sweet. "It just came to mind. I'm still rambling. I'm sorry."

"No, no, it's cool," said Fletcher. And he meant it. "I like when you ramble."

"Okay, good," she said. "Ramble, continued. To me, the quote means that anyone can change, and I like that."

Fletcher considered this, scratching the scalp under his mop of hair.

"Like, I might be a person with a messy room," said Jordan. "But if I clean my room today, and tomorrow, and the next day, and the next hundred days, then eventually I'm just a person with a clean room."

"And I'm a person with less armies than you," Fletcher said, looking at the board.

"Exactly," Jordan said. "Because you repeatedly lose them to me."

Another one of those sweet, heavy pauses.

"Well, your move, Ms. Johnson," said Fletcher.

Jordan collected a few territory cards in her hands and stacked them on the side of the board, collecting a scoop of army figurines from the box in return.

"You know," she said, "I don't really like my last name."

"Johnson?" said Fletcher. "What's wrong with Johnson?"

"That name was a gift from my dad." She shrugged. "And, as you know, he kind of sucked."

"I see."

"I have more opinions on the matter, if you want 'em." She grinned.

"Oh, I can't wait."

"Okay," she said. "Well, I mean, look at the etymology of names like that, with the 'son' at the end. Johnson. Ericson. Jackson. It's just another example of male self-importance."

Fletcher looked at her, one eyebrow raised.

"No offense," said Jordan, smiling.

"Well," said Fletcher. "Lucky for you, we're in a whole new post-Delilah wonderland. Who says you can't be whoever you want?"

Jordan laughed.

"Let's do it," said Fletcher.

"Let's do what?" asked Jordan.

"Let's be whoever we want." Fletcher shifted his position excitedly. "New world, new names. If you could be called anything in the world, what would it be?"

"Oh, I have no idea!" said Jordan. "That's hard. You go first."

"K, let's think," said Fletcher. "Finish your turn. And stop taking my armies."

They played for another couple minutes, Jordan taking over South America and finally moving the turn to Fletcher.

"Okay, I got it," said Fletcher. "From this point hence, I shall be known from land to land by the great name of Odin."

Jordan burst. "Odin?!"

"Yeah," Fletcher said. "You know, the old Norse god."

"I love it."

"He was also a really cool character in the game I used to play," he admitted.

"*Zordallus*," said Jordan. "Oh, I've heard." She paused. "Well, okay, Mr. Odin. Let me think for another minute."

Fletcher, who was now also Odin, took his turn. He conquered Madagascar, but that was it.

"Ooh…" said Jordan. "I have a good one."

"Hit me."

"My new name shall be … Hypatia."

"Hi-what?"

"Hypatia," she said.

"Hypatia," repeated Fletcher.

"She was one of the earliest female philosophers," said Jordan.

"Of course she was."

"Pretty badass chick," said Jordan.

"Of course she was."

"Well, okay," she said. "I like it. Odin and Hypatia, taking on the new world."

"Odin and Hypatia," said Fletcher. He imagined this becoming a cute thing between them. Little pet names. Every couple had inside jokes. He knew that much.

Chapter 12

Sinclair Cinema. A new arcade, just for him. And now this cute little nickname-inside-joke thing with Jordan? Things were finally grooving for Fletcher.

He made no more requests—or demands—from management. If he were to be honest, he'd felt a little conflicted after sort of threatening Dr. Gomez with leaving. Plus, Jordan and Natalie's remarks were still freshly burned into his brain. He desperately needed their approval—Jordan's, especially.

But he wanted so much more than Jordan's approval. He wanted her affection. He wanted her to feel the same way he did—like it could be the two of them, forever, and they'd be all right. Everything would be alright.

Fletcher spent most of his free time during the day in his arcade, which was indeed a happy place for him. He felt at home there, and he always had the place to himself. It felt good to see his initials at the top of every high score list, despite there being zero competition. As he mashed buttons, his eyes tractor-beam sucked into a screen, the little monster that had set up camp in Fletcher's head would come to life. The monster—that persistent idea that ended with Jordan and him falling madly in love—paced around in his cranium, scratching his claws at the place where Fletcher's skull met his spinal column. Fletcher knew there was only one way to get rid of the monster and its scratching.

One night Jordan came to his room to hang out for the evening, like normal. But Fletcher had decided this would not be a normal night at all. This, Fletcher knew, was The Night. It had to be. He had pumped himself up all day, rehearsing what he'd say, playing potential scenarios in his head.

Strong. Charming. Unafraid. Confident. The man he needed to be would be all of these things. The man he needed to be would welcome this new challenge with a smile—a square, suave, handsome smile. Fletcher grinned in the mirror. His smile was an oval with a lot of pink gums showing, and his big red nose seemed to compete with it.

Whatever.

The plan for his courtship was simple. He knew Jordan. She wouldn't want a whole lot of pomp and circumstance. She would want honesty and openness. Fletcher's plan was to say: "Hey, Jordan, listen—there's something I need to tell you."

Then, he would proceed to tell her how he felt. He had it all memorized, pretty much. He was going to tell her that seeing her was his favorite part of the day, and that she made him feel like he really *was* special—not because he might be the last man in the world, but because he was Fletcher. And how he wanted her to feel special, too. His plan was to then reach below the couch, where he had placed the origami flower, and hand it to her. Then he'd finish with a closer, something about how he couldn't live his life without knowing he took his shot, and that he was falling for her, and he just wanted her to know how he felt.

The next part was a little sketchy. His plan was to read her body language if a clear answer wasn't given. If she looked at all receptive to his confession of love, he'd go in for it. He'd lean in and kiss her—not a sloppy makeout, and not a little peck either, but a good, real kiss. Then, from there, he didn't even care what happened. They had the rest of their lives to figure that out.

When Jordan came into his room that evening, she looked perfect. She wore a slim-fit baby blue T-shirt and some black sweatpants, strolling in without a care in the world—so unaware of the claws scratching the base of Fletcher's skull, so unaware of his sudden nausea.

"What ... is ... up!" she said.

"Oh, you know," said Fletcher. They small-talked for a few minutes, until Fletcher knew he had to pull the trigger.

This will all be over soon.

"Hey, so ... Hypatia," he said, chuckling.

Was his voice shaking? How do you make your voice stop shaking?

"Yes, my dearest Odin, King of Asgard."

"Listen, there's something I need to tell you." He was keeping to the script.

"Yes?" she said. Her eyes looked huge, and inside them was more beauty and complexity than he felt he had in his whole body.

"Well," he said.

Wait, shit—

God, what made him think he was worthy of a girl like her?

"Well," he said again. Suddenly a scenario played out in his head that he hadn't really entertained before. He saw her laugh, desperately trying not to but unable to help herself. He saw her stand up, tell him she was sorry, but no, but that she still wanted to be friends. Then she left. Then she never came back again, evening after evening, and they only ever talked when in groups, and usually only about medical bullshit. Every night he sat alone, and the loneliness felt like gravity had doubled.

Fletcher could feel the extra gravity even now, as Jordan looked at him with those big, beautiful, unattainable eyes, waiting for him to speak.

"I wanted to tell you," he said, "that I'm ready for another round of Risk. I know you smashed me last time, but that was a total fluke."

The scratching in Fletcher's skull went quiet, as if the monster, too, was broken and ashamed.

"Why do you torture yourself like this?" she asked.

He was asking himself the same question, and he had no idea.

"Fine," she continued. "If you want me to wipe you off the map again, I'm game. Let's do it."

They set the board game up on the floor. Five feet away, under the couch, an origami flower sat like a discarded empty bag of chips.

• • • • • • • • • •

It was a Wednesday morning, not that Wednesdays meant anything. Spring was just around the corner, and long golden shafts of light pierced the hospital lobby, giving it the feeling of some important Greek temple.

Fletcher had just finished his breakfast—oatmeal again, for the love of God—and was walking from the cafeteria with Jordan and Natalie, through the lobby, toward the elevators. Sarah, Carly and Shannon, who were sweeping and cleaning the lobby tables, waved good morning.

Fletcher had started to kinda-sorta be friends with some of the Palm Springs 15. They really weren't so scary, once you got to know them.

Hey, maybe that was true for most women.

As Fletcher, Jordan and Natalie walked through the lobby, a crash erupted from the front door. The door was kept locked 24 hours a day, for obvious reasons. The crash was the thick tempered glass shattering to the ground. Fletcher froze. So did everyone else.

Three women stepped through. They wore filthy jeans and filthy T-shirts. Their gaunt faces were filthy and one wore a filthy Padres hat. Their eyes were wild and hungry. A short stocky tan woman held the shotgun that had just blasted the hole through which they'd appeared. One of the others, an athletic Japanese woman, the one in the Padres hat, held a three-foot-long fire axe. The last one was exceptionally tall and exceptionally pale with a skeletal face, her eyes in dark sockets. She held a machete.

"On the ground," said Shotgun, waving the barrel at Sarah, Carly and Shannon. They dropped to the floor, whimpering. "Okay. Food. We know you have it."

"What the hell?" said Axe. She had seen Fletcher, Jordan and Natalie, who were statues in the back of the lobby. "Is that a man? You have a man?"

"No," said Sarah from the floor, turning her head toward Fletcher, who was indeed a man.

The three intruders looked at Fletcher. Machete's head tilted to one side. A small grin pulled at Axe's lips. Fletcher stood there, motionless, like maybe these three were actually from the Church of Jesus Christ of Latter-Day Saints and were there to ask if Fletcher and his hospitalmates had a moment to talk about their Lord and Savior.

Jordan acted first. She yanked Fletcher's arm, pulling him away from the scene. "Move!" she barked.

Shotgun turned to her partners. "Go get them. Bring the boy back alive."

As Fletcher, Jordan and Natalie ran toward the door, Fletcher stole a quick glance over his shoulder. Axe was already running after them. Machete walked, but her long legs crossed half the lobby in a single step.

Jordan led the way, taking a right down a hallway. As they took another right into the cafeteria, Fletcher saw their pursuers turning the corner into the hallway. He could feel his blood pumping maxed-out through his veins. He thought he might just explode.

The three burst into the cafeteria and looked around. There was a door on the other side. There was also a door to the kitchen.

"Kitchen," whispered Jordan. "We'll hide. Plus there are knives."

They snuck through the double swinging doors—the ones without locks—into the kitchen. They looked around wildly for anything that could help them; hide them; protect them.

"Here," said Natalie, grabbing two chef's knives by the blades and offering the handles to Fletcher and Jordan. Fletcher held the blade in his hand and swallowed hard, hoping he had what it took to—

"Down," said Jordan. She yanked Fletcher's arm again, leading him to the back of the kitchen, crouching behind the giant stainless-steel worktable. Industrial-sized bags of rice sat on the bottom shelf, providing a little cover. Jordan put a finger to her lips, then pointed to her ear, then out to the cafeteria. Translation: she could hear them. Fletcher gripped the knife with one hand, the other on the floor, steadying himself. There was a layer of flour on the concrete, and his fingers absent-mindedly wiped it back and forth.

Murmured voices from the cafeteria.

The door leading out of the cafeteria, away from them, opening and closing.

A sigh of relief from Natalie.

And then—

The kitchen door inched open.

Between the bags of rice and the pots and pans, Fletcher had a postage-stamp window to look through. He saw Machete's torn jeans step into the kitchen and stop. The long blade swung into view as she slapped the flat end against her palm.

She then tapped the point of it against the concrete floor with a metallic clack, then took a slow step. Then another. As she did, she dragged the blade along the floor, like drawing a line. Like toying with her prey. Like a thousand nails on chalkboard. Fletcher's spine melted into useless goo. He realized he hadn't breathed in forever, and found he couldn't take a breath if he wanted to.

The blade screeched across the concrete toward the back of the kitchen. Toward them.

Jordan looked over at him and gave a strange expression. Kind of like a smile, but kind of heartbreaking, too. Maybe like she'd loved every second she'd spent with him, and regretted that they would never get to see what they could become. Or maybe that was just Fletcher projecting.

Now Machete was nearly to them. Fletcher could see her legs through the worktable, her jeans all ripped and stained and coming ever closer. He could smell her, too. She smelled like something burning; something decaying; something dead. Natalie nodded at them, and Fletcher could see her knuckles go white around the handle of her knife, ready to fight to the goddamn death, because that's who she was. Her body tightened, like a sprinter on the blocks waiting for the starter gun, and—

There it was.

The crack of the gun.

It nearly split the kitchen in two, exploding in Fletcher's ears, vibrating his eyes in their sockets.

And then a thud. Machete fell to the ground, slumping next to a stack of Freedom Fighter Fuel survival kit buckets. Fletcher, Jordan and Natalie rose from behind the worktable to see Beth, holding a handgun. "Stay here," she said, nodding once and then running off.

Fletcher, Jordan and Natalie held each other in a team-huddle hug. Finally, one of them spoke.

"Holy fucking shit," said Natalie.

"Yep," said Jordan.

"Yep," said Fletcher.

They shared the quickest and smallest of smiles at their new shared near-death experience. And then the crack of a gunshot again, this time farther away. Another one. And another. Their smiles died.

"Let's go," said Jordan, ignoring Beth's order. "You stay here, Fletch."

Jordan began moving, Natalie following her. Now it was Fletcher's turn to ignore an order. Jordan looked at him, definitely not staying put, but he just shook his head, like he was coming, like he couldn't let Jordan go into whatever was out there without him. She nodded, understanding.

They stepped around the body of Machete. Natalie reached down and grabbed the long blade, swapping it in for her chef's knife. They crept through the kitchen and down the hallway toward the lobby. Fletcher looked at the knife in his hand, very aware of how little help it would be against a woman with a shotgun or a fire axe.

They peered around the corner and saw Sarah, Carly and Shannon now standing, no longer prisoners on the ground. They stepped out into the lobby and saw Shotgun lying on the ground. Blood leaked from a bullet hole in the center of her forehead.

Beth rushed toward the three newcomers. "Are you hurt?" she asked.

"There was another!" cried Jordan. "The girl with the axe!"

"She ran off," grunted Beth, gesturing toward the shattered window at the front of the lobby. "She's gone."

"Holy shit," said Fletcher. "That was—that was—"

"Intense," said Jordan.

"Beth, you've got one hell of a shot," said Natalie. "Where did—"

That's when all three of them noticed it. Sarah, Carly and Shannon were standing, yes, but they were standing around something. Along with Madison and Annie. And Beth's assistant, Megan. They were all standing around something.

Or someone.

More of the Palm Springs 15 crept into the lobby, too, to see what the commotion was all about. They floated toward the growing crowd. Fletcher did, too.

But he knew what he'd find, didn't he?

He did.

Two women lay on the ground. One was Heather, her arms splayed, blood pooling around her from a shotgun wound to the stomach.

The other was Dr. Gomez.

Her shotgun wound had ripped through her chest. Her arms lay at her side. Her eyes were open, staring at the ceiling. Fletcher waited for her to blink, for her to move a finger. But she didn't. She wouldn't. She was already dead.

There would be no inspiring last line like in the movies. No chance to say the magic words that would point Fletcher in the direction to walk from here.

All the death he'd seen. All the bodies. And how different this was. How different these two victims looked and felt from those Delilah had claimed. But Fletcher already knew one thing was the same: virus or violence, death was always ugly. And the ones it destroyed most were the ones it left behind.

Fletcher looked at his hands. They were shaking.

Death always destroyed the ones it left behind.

Chapter 13

The next day was one of mourning.

Fletcher had hardly exchanged any words with Heather, but her Palm Springs sisters were devastated. Fletcher knew the feeling.

Dr. Gomez, of course—everyone had been close to her. She was the mama bear.

There was a funeral, or something close to it, in the afternoon. It was awkward. The remaining twenty of them stood in a circle. First, those close to Heather each said a farewell to their lost friend. Then everybody took turns saying something about Dr. Gomez. Fletcher stumbled over his words, trying to say how she had always been nice, even when he did stupid stuff, and how she always made sure he was okay. His speech wouldn't win any awards, but he meant it with all his heart.

The day after that, the crew tried to go back to business as usual. They had all dealt with their share of death since Delilah came to town, but—while they could perhaps expedite the stages of grief on account of experience—things would never go back to how they were.

Fletcher spent the next few days moping around. He often locked himself in his room, and when he did come out, a dark cloud floated above him and he didn't talk much. Meanwhile, the rest of the hospital staff hustled about, working long hours at a rapid pace, trying to figure out what they were going to do without their leader. Fletcher had moments where he felt guilty that they were all working so hard while he was wallowing, but it wasn't the same for them. None of them knew what it felt like for a boy to lose his actual mother, and then this post-Delilah stand-in. No, he decided, his pain was surely worse.

This will all be over soon.

While he brooded, he couldn't help but replay the last big one-on-one he'd had with Dr. Gomez. The one where he asked for the arcade. Where he sort of demanded it. Where he sort of threatened to leave. God, how dickish he had been. For what?

Meanwhile, Dr. Reid stepped in as the new head honcho. She was the natural next in line, and it wasn't like anyone else could really do the job, let alone wanted it.

However, Fletcher soon realized that Dr. Reid was not a born leader. She didn't radiate hope, like Dr. Gomez had. She didn't radiate confidence, like Dr. Gomez had. She didn't radiate a feeling that everything was going to be okay, like Dr. Gomez had.

Dr. Reid had always displayed a concrete shell—unshakeable, unemotional, unamused. But now Fletcher could see the cracks. They showed up with the slightest pressure, like the spiderweb fissures in ice beneath your feet on a barely frozen lake. She was insecure and unsure, often asking Natalie and Jordan what to do, what tests to run, what possible solutions they wanted to study. In her new role, she seemed unorganized and uncomfortable—a stark contrast to the stern, steady demeanor she'd displayed as Dr. Gomez's right-hand woman. No, Dr. Reid was born to be second in command.

· · · · · · · · · · ·

Plywood was nailed up over the shattered windows. A handgun was placed in a big ceramic planter in the lobby, in case there were other intruders. A rotating security schedule was set up to have someone on watch at all times, with a big siren-equipped bullhorn for them to sound the alarm if ever there was a break-in. Beth gave firearm lessons to anyone who wanted them. Many of the Palm Springs 15 (now 14) accepted the offer. Fletcher did not. If he were to be honest, he was nervous the girls would be better than him at something that years of *Halo, Call of Duty* and *Doom* should have made him an expert at. Annie started teaching morning kickboxing classes, too. She said she'd never hit anyone before, but it was a good workout and it couldn't hurt. Fletcher declined this, as well.

People always talked about the feeling of vulnerability after a home invasion—that your safe place didn't feel safe anymore. That may have been the case for some of the women, but Fletcher didn't think much of it. His mind was poisoned with other thoughts. Such as: self-pity and grief and hopelessness and trying to get back on track with Operation Make-a-Move-on-Jordan.

Despite some of the more positivity-and-sunshine girls' best intentions, the noxious gloom that clung to the walls of the hospital was hard to clear. For starters, there was the devastating hole left by Dr. Gomez and Heather—an untended wound they all shared. Then there was the unorganized and uninspiring new leadership. And then ... then the hospital had its first departees.

Chelsea and Lori decided it was time for them to leave. They were sent on their way with backpacks full of peanut butter sandwiches and water bottles, plus a twenty-minute cryfest in the lobby with their Palm Springs girls. Jordan said, in the days prior, Chelsea and Lori had started talking about the amount of time they'd all spent trying to find a cure, to no avail—even with a living man at their disposal. Eventually they said they wished their hospitalmates the best of luck, but they were going to go live what was left of their lives.

And then the Palm Springs 15 was the Palm Springs 12.

Dr. Reid gave a speech at dinner that night, about how they had to stay focused even though times were hard, but it was about as stimulating as a wilting head of cabbage. Fletcher could practically see team morale evaporating up and into the ceiling vents, gone forever.

Everything seemed to be falling apart. Everything, that is, but one thing.

There was still Jordan. There was still hope for that mission. That's where he'd put all his energy.

It was time for the hero to get the girl.

·········

Fletcher tried to be easy on himself for chickening out in his last opportunity with Jordan. The night he was going to give her the origami flower. Before the scavengers broke in and put a pause on all romantic endeavors.

Hey, the important thing was that he hadn't ruined anything. He'd get another shot. He just had to build up his confidence.

But all that was going to be a lot harder given the new plan.

"What's going on with you?" Fletcher asked her one night while they folded origami boats in his room. Jordan was being uncharacteristically silent and serious. "Is everything alright?"

Jordan looked up at him, her eyes big, wet and full of an emotion that Fletcher couldn't quite identify, but certainly didn't like.

"Fletcher," she said, her voice lower than usual, "I have some news."

"What's going on?"

"I'm leaving for a bit," she said.

"You're what?" Fletcher did not hide his shock.

"I need to go away," she said. "But I'm coming back."

"What do you mean?" Fletcher asked. His stomach felt like hot soup.

"I'm going to Phoenix with Natalie and one of the Michelles," said Jordan. "We're leaving tomorrow first thing."

"*Tomorrow*?" Fletcher squeaked. "Why? What for?"

"Well, we need medical supplies," said Jordan, "but that's just part of it. Fletcher, the thing is, we're the only ones who have *you*. And we've like ... tried everything we can think of. We need to let others—other experts, other minds—give it a go. There are—or, there used to be—some really good doctors in Phoenix. If any of them are still around, it'd be stupid not to give them a chance to solve this, not to give them access to you. You're the best chance we have. And, Fletch, well ... Dr. Reid—I mean, she's not meant to be the leader, you know? She doesn't *want* to be the leader. To be honest, I think she's hoping we can find a new leader. A new Dr. Gomez."

There was a pause.

"How long will you be gone?" Fletcher asked quietly.

Jordan looked down. "Hard to tell."

"Try," said Fletcher.

"Depending on what we find in Phoenix, we might bounce around, maybe Tucson, maybe Albuquerque. There are great minds still out there—there have to be—and they deserve to know as much as we do."

"So," said Fletcher, "a long time."

"Maybe," said Jordan. "Maybe a few months? But you've seen what's happened here. This place is falling apart. With Dr. Gomez gone ... and we're running out of ideas. And eventually more raiders will come and—we just need to crack this. And we need the leadership."

"Couldn't you or Natalie run this place?"

"No," said Jordan. "We need a new Dr. Gomez."

"I assume there's no use trying to persuade you to stay," said Fletcher, his eyes on the floor. He was studying the tiles. They were off-white, with long gray lines, like claw marks.

"You are correct," said Jordan, offering a sad sort of smile.

"I hate it," he said.

"I know," she said.

"But it's so dangerous out there," said Fletcher.

"We'll be extra cautious," said Jordan. "We're staying far away from LA, I promise."

"Phoenix could be just as bad," said Fletcher. "Or worse."

"We'll be smart," she said.

"You're taking Big Nurse, right?"

"No," she said. "We're leaving that beast here for short supply runs."

"What?"

"We're taking the Leaf," she said. "The little electric guy."

"No."

"We don't want to risk running out of gas and not being able to find any," she said. "Plus, the less attention we can attract the better."

"But why you?" Fletcher stood up. "Why do *you* have to go?"

"Natalie and I are going because we can best explain what's been going on here," she said. "The Palm Springs girls don't know the history, the full story, like we do. We can explain it best to whomever we find. Plus, you think any of them could handle this?" She smiled, trying to lighten the mood. It didn't work.

"You're too important!" said Fletcher. "Just give someone else a letter to show someone they find, or—"

"Fletcher, you know I need to do this."

"Yeah," he said. "Because you love the human race and all that shit."

"Yeah, something like that." Jordan thought for a moment. "I think it would be a bummer if we didn't try our damnedest to give us lowly humans a shot at staying on this planet. And Fletcher: Natalie, Michelle and I are the right people for the job."

She said it with such conviction that Fletcher knew it had to be true.

Before she left the room, Fletcher decided he had to give her that stupid origami flower. If not now, when?

Before she left the room, Fletcher decided he had to tell her how he felt. He decided he had to kiss her. If he had been waiting for the right time, this was undoubtedly it.

Soon after he decided those things, Jordan left the room.

He hadn't told her how he felt. He hadn't kissed her. And that stupid origami flower sat next to a granola bar wrapper under the couch, now frosted with a light coating of dust.

The last thing he said to her was this: "Be safe and hurry back, Miss Hypatia. This place is going to suck without you."

·········

That night, Natalie came to say her goodbyes, too. She rarely came to his room, but had no problem making herself comfortable. "You better miss me," she said as she flopped down on his bed, putting her hands behind her head as if she was going to take a quick nap. Fletcher sat on the couch.

"I guess I can do that," said Fletcher.

"You're the man of the house now," she said in mock seriousness, glancing over at him. "I need to know you're going to take care of this place."

"I'll do my best," he said.

They talked about the trip for a few minutes, then she got up to go. "Well," she said. "I guess it's time to say goodbye. Don't you go crying or anything."

She walked up to Fletcher and hugged him. Not in a joking way, either. It surprised Fletcher, but at that moment he realized how much he really was going to miss her, too. She was a weirdo, but she was on his side. She was his friend. With both her and Jordan leaving, who was he left with?

"Don't have too much fun without us," said Natalie.

"Deal," said Fletcher. "And be safe. And look after each other. And come back soon."

"I'll bring her back," said Natalie, winking. "See ya when I see ya, Fletch."

And with that, she was gone.

Chapter 14

When Fletcher woke the next morning, it was to a new hospital. No Jordan. No Natalie. (And only one Michelle, not that Fletcher really knew either of them.)

This will all be over soon.

He suddenly felt very alone. He rarely spoke to Beth or Megan, and he was still unsure if they were on Team Fletcher or not. Dr. Reid was hardly ever seen, and when she was, she wasn't much good for entertainment. Then there were the Palm Springs 15—well, 11 now. Sure, some of the Palm Springs girls were fine, but they were such a big, intimidating group that it seemed impossible to infiltrate their ranks on his own. He'd always had Jordan as a buffer.

Fletcher had once quite enjoyed being by himself, and he was amazed at how quickly he could now feel lonely.

On the first night that the girls were gone, Fletcher lay on his bed and thought about Jordan. That mischievous little grin, their weird conversations, his feelings toward her and how he had failed to make a move. He thought about her trip and realized his emotions were a little complicated. First, unexpectedly, he found he sort of envied her. He was jealous that she was doing something truly heroic. When would he get his chance to be the cowboy instead of the prized cow? Of course, he was proud of her, too, for her selflessness and courage. But there was a third feeling. It turned out he also felt a little, tiny, itsy-bitsy bit betrayed. She did *choose* to leave. They *could* have found another way. He was preparing to finally ask her out (and he would have—soon, too, he knew it), and then she left. He knew he shouldn't feel this way, that she was doing everything for the good of humanity, but hey—the heart feels what it feels, right?

Stupid heart.

....

Boredom quickly rushed in again, rising like the water in a flooding basement—an annoyance at first and then, suddenly, a five-alarm emergency. It hadn't even been two weeks since Jordan, Natalie and the one Michelle had left, and Fletcher was already going stir-crazy.

Jordan was the sparkplug that had been yanked from the engine, and now Fletcher was stranded on the side of the road in the middle of nowhere. On top of that, even if the remaining crew got the car up and running, Fletcher was pretty sure nobody knew where they were going. Least of all Dr. Reid.

So there he was.

Even when Fletcher was feeling social enough to give it a shot with the new girls, he often found himself twiddling his thumbs alone anyway. His hospitalmates spent much of the days poring over cartoonishly dense-looking medical tomes in hopes of finding a past case or a wild hypothesis that could spark an idea. And this neo-analog research didn't involve the patient at all. On top of that, they developed their own hobbies. Krishna, Madison and the remaining Michelle started painting—like, art painting. Serena and Annie began crocheting, for God's sake. Carly and Sarah took up gardening, transforming one of the courtyards with planter boxes, each filled with hopeful herbs and vegetables. Fletcher wasn't sure when they had all turned 80 years old.

It was weird to think how not-boring the world was outside those hospital walls. Perilous and horrifying, sure, but not boring. But there on the inside...

So, it was usually up to Fletcher to entertain himself. He spent the majority of his hours drinking coffee in Fletcher's Arcade, mashing buttons and staring unblinking at the screens.

But even video games—yes, even the soothing hum of the machines, the satisfying beeps and boops and bells and rings and the warm glow of the various 32-bit worlds—even video games eventually lost their luster.

His mind wandered and wondered what could improve life at the hospital. He remembered how quickly his theater and arcade requests had been granted. He remembered Dr. Gomez saying that they'd do whatever it took to keep him there. Then he remembered how bad he'd felt for being rude to Dr. Gomez. Then he remembered Jordan and Natalie's skeptical comments.

Then he remembered that all of them were gone.

Everyone is on their best behavior when they're being watched. It's easy for a kid to leave a plate of cookies alone when Mom is in the same room, but as soon as she steps outside ... oh, what's one cookie?

Someone once said that character is what you do when no one is watching, but that someone wasn't Fletcher. And Fletcher was bored and lonely.

Oh, what's one cookie?

It was an especially warm spring day outside, and Fletcher thought back to days like that growing up. He thought of backyard barbecues. He thought about how repetitive and bland their meals had become at the hospital.

By God, they needed a backyard barbecue.

Fletcher found Dr. Reid and told her his request. Or, his *recommendation.*

"It's not just for me, though," he assured her. He remembered Dr. Gomez asking that he think about the whole group. Well, here he was. He thought she'd be proud. "Wouldn't everyone love a barbecue? Don't you think everyone deserves it? After all the hard work?"

"I don't know," said Dr. Reid. "I don't think now is the time for this kind of thing. We have a lot on our plates."

Fletcher knew they had next to nothing on their plates. They were clueless. He also knew that Dr. Reid wouldn't risk losing Fletcher. Like Dr. Gomez had said.

"Listen," said Fletcher. Bravado is easier when the other person doesn't have a choice. "I could walk out the door, you know. Leave for good. But a summer barbecue ... that would sure help convince me to stay."

Dr. Reid's mouth opened, just slightly. "You wouldn't—"

"I sure might."

Dr. Reid stared at him a moment. "Okay."

"Great!" said Fletcher. "Hey, see if you can get cornhole, too. And a speaker for music."

"Cornhole?"

"You know," said Fletcher, "that beanbag toss game."

Dr. Reid grunted. It was not a yes or a no.

"I'll have Megan get the full list of demands from you," she said.

"They're not *demands*, they're…"

Dr. Reid looked at him as if another word might send her to her grave, so Fletcher didn't give her one.

And besides. They kind of *were* demands, weren't they?

Megan met with Fletcher later that afternoon to get the supply list. Fletcher tried to get her excited about the barbecue idea, but she was unenthusiastic. Oh, well, he thought. The Palm Springs girls would love it. This could be his way into the group.

The barbecue commenced the following Saturday in a grassy area next to the parking lot. Big Nurse sat parked with her back facing the lawn, doors open from unloading.

Bags of chips and big bottles of soda sat on two picnic tables, both covered with plastic red-and-white-checkered tablecloths. Beth and Megan cooked frozen hotdogs on portable charcoal grills. Tom Petty played through a small battery-powered CD player, and Fletcher could feel the warm sun on his skin. He realized how rarely he ever stepped outside anymore.

He poured some Sprite into a red plastic cup, looking around. The chefs weren't smiling, but he figured they were just lost in concentration. He looked at the eleven Palm Springs girls in their tiny tank tops and colorful rompers. Surely *they* were having fun. To Fletcher's delight, he saw smiles. He heard laughter mixed in with the music. The smell of the grill, the spread on the table, the Palm Springs girls giggling: Fletcher had done it. He had brought life back to the doldrums of the hospital.

There are many different types of heroes, he decided.

He took a sip, satisfied. Then, riding the high of a job well done, he walked up to the fourteen girls.

"What we really need is beer," one girl said.

"Totally," said Fletcher. All eleven girls turned to look at the source of the nasally male voice that had snuck into their circle.

"This is fun, right?" he asked.

"Yeah, it's nice to get outside," said one.

"It can get so boring in there," said another.

"I'm excited for a goddamn hotdog," said a third.

"I'm vegetarian," said a fourth.

"Well, anyone wanna play cornhole?" asked Fletcher, nodding toward the wooden boards and beanbags.

"Hell yeah!" said Annie, a cute Asian girl in a yellow tank top.

"We need two more..."

Madison and Shannon also volunteered. Madison was taller than Fletcher, with long blonde hair. She was as lanky as one of those inflatable tube characters outside car dealerships, and moved just as sporadically. Shannon was an olive-skinned brunette who wore a flattering yellow floral romper and smiled with her eyes at everything.

The four began playing. Fletcher felt like he was ten again—except for the whole being-surrounded-by-beautiful-women thing.

The rest of the girls stood by and watched, talking to each other. He couldn't help but hear one of them (Arlene) ask how long they had to be there. Another (Amanda) asked if this was supposed to boost morale, and if so, they were going to need more than frozen meat tubes.

It hurt Fletcher to hear that. He just wanted all of them to have fun and, if they ended up liking him more because it was his idea, well, then that was nice, too.

But then Fletcher saw that a few of the girls were tossing a disc back and forth. He looked at the girls he was playing with and saw that they were grinning ear to ear, giggling at bad throws, high-fiving good ones.

Fletcher's heart swelled with pride. So what if a few sour apples refused to have a good time? They weren't going to spoil his, or the rest of the group's. Except for those couple girls with the bad attitudes, people were having *fun*. That's what he needed to focus on. He couldn't please everyone.

Fletcher and Annie, who were teammates, got destroyed. Fletcher only got four bags on the board the entire game. He didn't even care, though. This was a full success.

"Hey, thanks for planning this," said Madison, bending down a little to get to Fletcher's level. His smile almost broke his face in two.

After the game, Annie hugged Fletcher, catching him off guard. "We tried, Fletch," she said. "Damn it, we tried."

"Fletcher—think fast!" the girl named Serena yelled. Fletcher turned to see a Frisbee rocketing toward him. He ducked as if it were a ninja throwing star, the disc landing gently on the grass beside him. He flushed, and looked up to see Serena and a couple of the other girls laughing. They weren't laughing cruelly, though. These were the laughs of people who were hanging out with their friends.

These girls don't just like the barbecue, he thought. *They like me.*

Fletcher felt on top of the world—a world that had been on top of him his whole life. He could get used to this.

The hotdogs were a little freezer-burned, and there was no watermelon or Agent Orange, but it didn't matter. This was a backyard barbecue for the history books.

Chapter 15

When you have a glass of wine and you feel all warm and fuzzy, there's some warped logic that jumps in and says: well, gee, one glass sure feels good—imagine what two would do! What about three? What about twelve?

Well, Fletcher was feeling good and ready for that next glass.

He called for another meeting with Dr. Reid. This time, unlike before, he didn't even have a plan. Just a problem. He said that he was bored of the movies they had. He was bored of movies in general. There was no good entertainment in this joint.

"What do you want, Fletcher?" she asked. "You have a theater. You have an arcade. We can go get new movies."

"I know," said Fletcher. "I don't know."

"You want to be entertained," she said, "but not by more movies."

"Well," said Fletcher, "yeah, I guess."

"I'm sorry, but if you don't know what you want, then I don't know how to help you. You want the girls to all dress up and perform *Macbeth*?" She said it condescendingly, but that was lost on Fletcher.

"A play?" He raised his eyebrows.

Dr. Reid just looked at him.

"That's a great idea!" said Fletcher. "Let's do it. Let's do a play. As long as the girls want to, of course. As like, a fun thing for them. For everyone."

"You're serious."

"Why not?" said Fletcher. "I bet they'd love it."

"A play," Dr. Reid said. "Yes, I'm sure they'd love it."

She left without saying anything more.

The next day, Fletcher ran into Arlene in the hall. She was the one who rolled her eyes a little too much. She had a stocky, athletic build and a caramel-colored ponytail.

"I hear you guys are making a play," said Fletcher, enthusiastically.

"What gives you that idea?" said Arlene, less enthusiastically.

"Oh, Dr. Reid mentioned it," said Fletcher.

"Wasn't it your idea?"

"Oh, no." Fletcher scratched his head. "Dr. Reid came up with it."

Arlene smiled a smile that said: *sure she did*. "Sorry to break your heart," she said, "but I won't be playing theater."

Later Fletcher talked to a few of the other girls—Serena, Annie, Madison, Michelle, Carly, Shannon—and they showed much more excitement.

To hell with Arlene and whoever else had a stick up their ass, he thought. If you didn't want to have fun while you're here, that was your choice.

Sarah took charge, playing director. She told Fletcher one evening how thrilled she was, and how great the play was coming along. They practiced every night.

Five short days later, it was showtime.

The performance was to be held in Sinclair Cinema, and Fletcher sat in the middle of the front row. The best seat in the house. Dr. Reid, Beth and Megan sat scattered behind him, as well as a handful of the girls who weren't in the production. Arlene, of course, was one of them.

In front of the movie screen was a makeshift curtain—a sheet hung on a line connected from one side of the room to the other. The lights dimmed, and someone stepped out from behind the curtain. Fletcher narrowed his eyes, trying to make out who the shadowy figure was.

The lights on the far side of the room, the ones pointing down at what was clearly going to be the stage, switched on, revealing Sarah. She was wearing a little black dress and makeup, her hair curled and bouncing on her shoulders.

"Ladies and gentlemen!" she said. "Well, gentle*man*. Welcome to a special performance of *Taking Down Delilah*. I hope you enjoy the show."

The lights dimmed again, and when they came back on, there was Serena and Annie.

"We must hide!" cried Serena, in a weird faintly British-sounding accent.

"Nay!" shouted Annie awkwardly. "We must go find help!"

"It's too dangerous!" cried Serena.

"It's too late!" said Annie. From the other side of the stage, a large green mess appeared. It was a girl in an ambitious monsteresque costume made from green sheets and clothes hangers, with a paper bag over her head. The bag had been painted green, with big, angry red eyes. Even with the mask Fletcher knew it was Madison, as she stood a good six inches above Serena and Annie.

"Oh, no!" yelled Serena, cowering. "It's Delilah, the horrible, mean dragon bitch!"

"RUN!" screamed Annie as the two girls scurried off stage, Madison's dragon lumbering behind them. She let out a roar.

Fletcher was enthralled, gums flaring with an enormous smile. He looked around to see if the other audience members were enjoying it as much as he was. It was too dark to tell, but they had to be. The show was off to a better start than he could have possibly imagined. And it only got better.

Next, Shannon was introduced as the hero. The fearless knight. To Fletcher's delight, the knight's name was also Fletcher. Shannon wore a suit of armor made from cardboard and aluminum foil, and Fletcher briefly and embarrassingly remembered the foil armor he had worn to brave the outside world on his supply runs back home—six long months ago.

The play featured a very intense scene where a village was slaughtered by the dragon. Later, there was a group of damsels in distress, seeking refuge after Delilah had destroyed their homes. Then, there was a moving speech by Shannon's Fletcher, in which the character swore to defeat the evil dragon bitch, Delilah. It was now a story of vengeance. Finally, Sir Fletcher faced the monster with his cardboard-and-foil sword. The dragon vomited crumpled-up balls of orange tissue paper toward the knight, and it was no easy fight, but in the end Fletcher slayed the mighty beast. The townspeople surrounded their savior, praising such a lionhearted hero.

As the lights dimmed, Fletcher shot to his feet, applauding loudly. He was proud, overjoyed and flattered—almost to the point of tears. This was for him. He was the guest of honor. He was the hero.

It was the greatest play he had ever seen.

Sarah announced the actresses, and they took a bow as a cast. Fletcher rushed the stage. He told them how wonderful he thought it was. The actresses beamed with the satisfaction of a performance nailed. As for Fletcher, he felt like he could defeat a dragon himself, and he swore some of the girls looked at him as if his *Zordallus* shirt was a suit of armor indeed.

A knight was charming, handsome and brave. While Fletcher had never described himself by those adjectives, he was certain of one thing: he was certainly the most charming, handsome and brave man around.

··•••·•••·

The next morning, before Fletcher left his room for breakfast, there was a knock. He hopped to the door, still floating from the previous night's show.

"Dr. Reid!" he said. "Beth! To what do I owe the pleasure?"

"May we come in?" asked Dr. Reid.

"Sure," said Fletcher. "Hey, thanks again for organizing that play."

"I didn't organize it," Dr. Reid said. "I just told them they had to do it."

"Well," said Fletcher, "it was fantastic."

"Let's take a seat," said Dr. Reid.

Fletcher suddenly wondered if he was in trouble, nervous for a second before reminding himself that he was the irreplaceable one. Supply and demand. Supply and demand. Supply and demand.

Fletcher sat on the edge of his bed. His two guests took the couch.

"I get it," Dr. Reid started. "You understand your position. You're a rare commodity, and that gives you weight."

Fletcher paused and considered. He nodded slowly. Supply and demand.

"And," she said, "you want to be paid as such. Paid what you're worth. We're still capitalists, I suppose."

Fletcher swallowed hard and shifted his position.

"And," she continued, "since money is no good anymore, theaters and arcades and plays are what you value. You want to use your position, and I don't blame you. I won't pretend that we don't need you; that we won't do what it takes to keep you here. You know it. Everyone knows it."

Fletcher nodded.

"So, let's make this easy on ourselves," she said. "I'm too tired for games. Whenever you need anything, you go to Beth. She will be your right-hand woman. I can't tend to your every wish. I'm running a hospital that is trying to find a cure for an apocalyptic virus. But Beth will work with you to get you whatever you want. I will tell the rest of the staff that Beth's orders are my orders. Whatever she says, goes. She is your person."

Beth looked at Fletcher, and Fletcher at Beth. The hard lines in her catcher's mitt face revealed nothing. Fletcher tried to smile, but it came off as something like a grimace.

"All we ask," Dr. Reid continued, "are two things: One, that you don't ask the impossible. Be reasonable. Two, that you continue to participate in the medical side of this. That's the trade. Remember: the reason you're here—the reason all of us are here—is because, somehow, Delilah doesn't affect you. We have to believe that we can still uncover what that is. So we need your cooperation."

She paused.

Fletcher took a deep breath.

"How does all that sound?" she asked.

Fletcher looked from Dr. Reid to Beth and back to Dr. Reid. "That sounds great."

"Good," said Dr. Reid. She shook his hand to seal the deal. Beth shrugged and the two women walked out.

·········

Beth's new responsibility was to be at Fletcher's beck and call, and she was good at her job. Beth was austere, stern and seemingly void of any humor—save the occasional smirk that Fletcher never understood, and that made him only a tiny bit self-conscious. Above all, though, she was loyal. She asked no questions and, if the request was possible, executed it fully. Big Nurse began working overtime, her spacious cabin repeatedly stuffed with the paraphernalia to cater to Fletcher's whims.

How about a bowling alley in the hallway? No problem. Plywood was hunted down, brought in and laid along a stretch of carpeted hallway on the eighth floor. A mattress was set up as a backdrop to catch the bowling balls. Fletcher was told he'd have to accept the reality that automatic ball returns and pin replacers were pre-Delilah luxuries, but he didn't mind. He and a few of the Palm Springs girls spent a week bowling every night and, even though the girls usually beat him, he loved the new addition to their home. Any distraction was a blessing.

So Fletcher kept the blessings coming.

His next request was a giant laser tag arena. Welcome to the new ninth floor. A maze-like course was erected with more sheets of plywood and salvaged billboards. All the necessary laser tag gear was lifted from a nearby abandoned family fun center—vests, guns, scoreboard and all. They'd even found some neon lights.

"You really outdid yourself this time," Fletcher told Beth. And he meant it.

"I did it out of the goodness of my heart," said Beth. She didn't mean it, but her almost-smile was enough for Fletcher. He grinned a big, toothy grin.

"Paid for it all myself, too," she added.

Fletcher was pleased to discover that not only were some of the girls excited to play laser tag, a couple were even halfway decent shots. Maybe Beth's firearm lessons were paying off.

···•·•····

More and more over the past few months, an evolved Fletcher—Fletcher 2.0—had been gaining strength, swelling under the lame, dusty old husk of the original Fletcher, making itself more and more known, slowly taking control over the host. And Fletcher 2.0 had big plans.

Those plans weren't going to stop at some plywood sheets, a few bowling balls and a couple laser tag guns. Why would they?

Fletcher asked for a pizza party, which was honestly enjoyed by every-one.

Fletcher asked for a video game tournament, which was honestly enjoyed by very few.

Oh, Fletcher was living the good life, alright. In this living, breathing fantasy, anything he dreamed up appeared before him. Besides, women respected him now. They laughed at his jokes, played his games. Even—he was pretty sure, maybe, sometimes—flirted with him. Hell, they'd put on a theatrical performance strictly *for his entertainment.* Fletcher was special, and specialness felt fucking great.

Sure, the eradication of all other known males helped, but it seemed like more than that. It seemed like maybe he'd always been special, deep down, only it hadn't been visible before. Like a caterpillar waiting to become a butterfly. Or a dormant volcano waiting to explode and change the shape of the world. Hadn't there been signs before Delilah? He was sure there had been. Either way, Fletcher was just happy to recognize his specialness now. Because he deserved this. All of this. He was going to be the hero of the goddamn human race, after all.

If that's not special, what is?

Chapter 16

One day, Fletcher was sitting with a group of Palm Springs girls in a conference room that had recently been turned into a rec room. The early May sun poured in through the floor-to-ceiling windows, and tiny dust motes danced around in the air. The group was gathered around a sterile corporate table playing Uno.

It had become clear which of the girls were on his side, and which were the party poopers. The No Fun Committee's proudest members were Arlene and Amanda (Natalie's assistant, or "Tinkerbell"). Fletcher no longer cared what they said or what they did, as long as they didn't burst his bubble. If they wanted their post-apocalyptic world to feel like one, that was their problem.

The girls playing Uno with him? They were some of the good ones.

Shannon put a red Eight on the deck. Madison laid down a red Skip.

"Ah, fuck you, Raff," said Annie as the turn jumped her and went to Serena.

"Oopsies," said Madison.

"Reds again?" said Sarah. "Lame."

"Hey everybody, something tells me Sarah has all blues," said Michelle, smiling. She was always smiling, and for good reason, too. She was one of those people who was friends with everyone.

"Are you looking at my cards?" accused Sarah.

"Maybe."

"Wait, hold on," said Fletcher, looking at Annie. "Just a second ago. What'd you call Madison? Raft?"

"Raff," said Annie matter-of-factly. Madison cackled.

"What's *Raff*?" asked Fletcher. "Where did..."

"Short for *giraffe*," said Shannon.

The girls giggled. Fletcher tilted his head, smiling dumbly.

"Have you seen Madison run?" asked Michelle.

"Can't say I have."

"She runs like a newborn giraffe," said Michelle. "It's like she's never done it before."

"I have other talents," smiled Madison.

"The name just kind of stuck," said Carly.

"So now you're Raff," confirmed Fletcher.

"Now I'm Raff," said Madison.

"That's amazing," he said, laughing. She did have some rather giraffe-like qualities, her towering height not the least of them. He remembered the day he and Jordan had chosen new names for this new world: Odin and Hypatia. He thought about Jordan—Hypatia—and wondered what she was doing at that moment, and when she'd come back to him. *If* she'd come back to him.

And then the cartoon light bulb appeared above Fletcher's head.

"Guys, guys, guys!" he said, his voice crackling with excitement. "I have an idea."

The girls all looked at him, curious. Attention didn't make him nervous anymore. In fact, he was giddy.

"Okay, hear me out," he said. "This is a new time, right? A new era, you could say. Like, we're living in the post-Delilah era. Right?"

"Sure."

"Well," he continued, "our names are from the *pre-Delilah* era. In the *post-Delilah* era, we can be whoever we want to be. There are no rules."

"What are you—" said Shannon.

"I'm saying..." Fletcher set his cards down and put his palms flat on the table, emphasizing his point. "Wouldn't it be awesome if we all picked new names? Madison, you can be Raff, if you want. Or you can pick another one! This new world is your oyster."

"You mean, like, we can all have post-Delilah nicknames?" said Annie.

"Yeah, but—they could really be our new names!" said Fletcher. "We can do whatever we want. Who says you can't be Princess Peach?"

He wasn't sure if the *Super Mario* reference landed. "Or Rainbow. Or California. Or whatever!"

"Actually," said Madison, "I kinda love it. And I'm good with Raff." She lifted her head in dramatic fashion. "I am *proud* to be Raff."

"Raff!" cheered Fletcher.

"Okay, then," said Serena, "who are you going to be?"

"Me?" said Fletcher. "I'm going to be Odin."

"Odin?" asked Michelle. "Like the Greek god?"

"Norse," corrected Fletcher. "And also a super badass character in *Zordallus.*"

"That was quick," said Annie.

"Odin it is," said Michelle.

"Odin!" cheered the girls.

"Who's next?" asked Raff (who used to be Madison).

The girls talked and thought and one by one came up with their new names.

Shannon was now Sunshine, because of her bright and cheery demeanor.

"Sunshine!" the table cheered.

Michelle was now Lobster, after her favorite food, which she hadn't eaten in a year.

"Lobster!" the table cheered.

Annie was now Morning, as this was her favorite time of day.

"Morning!" the table cheered.

Serena was now Bobina, which is what her dad, whom she missed very much, had called her.

"Bobina!" the table cheered.

Sarah was now Ripley, after Sigourney Weaver's iconic character in *Alien*, her favorite movie. She earned silent bonus points for the sci-fi nod.

"Ripley!" the table cheered.

Carly, the shyest of them all, was struggling. "I don't know!" she said. "I need to think about it."

"I have an idea," said Sunshine (who used to be Shannon).

"Yeah?" said Carly.

"Crash," said Sunshine (who used to be Shannon). The table erupted with laughter, except from Fletcher. He didn't get it.

"Well," said Ripley (who used to be Sarah). "You know the laser tag arena?"

"Yeah," said Fletcher.

"Carly here helped Beth out. Picking up the stuff. A few of us did. Beth parked Big Nurse at the main door, but then decided we should move it to the alley. Easier to load. Anyway, she told Carly to do it. Long story short, there's a Volvo in that parking lot that is basically folded in half now."

"No…" said Fletcher.

"Yep," said Raff (who used to be Madison). "It was amazing."

Carly laughed. "Big Nurse is faster than I thought! And I forgot about the big shovel thing in front."

"It's called a snowplow," said Bobina (who used to be Serena).

"And so…" said Lobster (who used to be Michelle). "Crash crashed."

When the laughter died down, Fletcher looked at Carly. "The name is yours to choose," he said solemnly. "It's up to you."

"I like Crash," she said. "It's cute."

"Crash!" the table cheered. So there they were: Odin, Raff, Sunshine, Lobster, Morning, Bobina, Ripley and Crash.

Later, during a full-team meeting, Fletcher explained to the rest of the hospital inhabitants this new opportunity: everyone could pick whatever name they wanted. He listed off the newly created names, handing out nametags as he spoke.

"I'm game," said Krishna. She decided that she was now Xena, like the Warrior Princess from the 90s.

"Xena!" the girls with new names shouted.

Eva, a girl who sort of kept to herself, said she'd change her name to Stardust. She said there used to be people who called her that, anyway. Fletcher found this very odd. But either way—

"Stardust!" the girls with new names shouted.

Fletcher did a quick tally. That left Arlene and Amanda—plus Dr. Lynne Reid, Megan and Beth.

Arlene and Amanda both scoffed at the idea of changing names. Fletcher had a feeling that would happen.

Dr. Lynne Reid, Megan and Beth all abstained as well, albeit more respectfully. Dr. Reid said she had quite gotten used to her name over the years. Megan grunted that she was fine with Megan. Beth said that she had already chosen a new name: Elizabeth was her birth name and Beth was her name now.

Even with the holdouts, Fletcher was thrilled with the participation. It was a new era, alright. It was the era of Fletcher—or rather, of Odin—and he was making changes.

··········

The next week, Fletcher took it upon himself to be the New Name Police. The girls with post-Delilah names seemed to love it. "Feels like summer camp," Raff (who used to be Madison) had said, but the party poopers had a hard time remembering Ripley, Crash, Lobster and all the other new monikers. So, Fletcher made sure to remind them any time they used a pre-Delilah name.

One day there was a knock on his door.

"Come in!" he called from the stiff brown couch.

Beth walked through the door, as warm and joyful as a garden shovel. "Sinclair."

"You mean Odin?" Fletcher lifted his mug of coffee, his fourth of the day.

"There's a girl here to see you. Says she knows you."

Fletcher froze before the mug could reach his lips. He looked up at Beth.

"A girl?" he whispered, like he'd never heard of the concept before. Beth nodded. "Says she knows me?"

"She's probably full of shit," said Beth, "in which case I'll send her on her way. But just in case she's not: Does the name Dani Calloway mean anything to you?"

Fletcher felt his eyes grow into baseballs. Of course the name *Dani Calloway* meant something to him. It meant something to anyone who had set foot in his high school during the couple years she had graced those grounds. That name had practically been an utterance of lore, the name you used as hyperbole for any hot girl. You might say "Yeah, sure, and I'm taking Dani Calloway to prom" when someone said something you didn't believe, or "That girl was Dani-level" if you saw some knock-out. In high school, if Fletcher had been given three wishes, he'd have asked for a billion dollars and Dani Calloway, and would have donated the third to charity.

Dani had been a year older than Fletcher, which, by the rule of high school hotness, had made her even more of a mystical siren—and all the more unapproachable. She had spoken to him twice in his life. The first was Fletcher's sophomore year, when they were in the same math class and Dani had asked Fletcher if there had been homework. (There had been.) The second was his junior year, when Dani asked if Fletcher could move seats on the bus so she could sit next to her football player boyfriend. (He could.) Both were glorious days.

But what was she doing here? And how did she know about him?

Fletcher asked Beth to bring her in.

A few minutes later, something Fletcher had never dreamed of actualized. Dani Calloway—*the* Dani Calloway—walked through his door.

Another post-Delilah miracle.

She looked just how Fletcher remembered her: piercing blue eyes above high cheekbones, the model kind; long hair that was dark and shiny like gasoline; a lean body that tugged at her T-shirt in all the right places; a smile that dazzled and made you believe that she was as genuine as she was beautiful. Dani Calloway was still perfect.

She walked in, looked at him, smiled that smile, and ran across the room, wrapping her arms around him. Her embrace was how he imagined a defibrillator would feel.

"Fletcher," she said, "I can't believe it's you—that you're alive. It's so good to see you."

Hearing her say his name was a weird phenomenon, too. It was proof that she really, honestly, knew who he was.

They started talking. Dani told him of the horrors she had seen, all the people she had lost, all the violence she'd encountered, all the fear she'd faced. In the eight months or so that Fletcher had been at the hospital, life on the outside appeared to have continually devolved. Dani told of a world in total ruin, where gangs and scavengers were the new law of the land. He wondered if all of Southern California had caught up to the dangers of LA. As she regaled him, Fletcher saw flashes of all the movies that had tried to predict what this would look like. *The Road. The Book of Eli. Children of Men.* All the *Mad Max* movies. He wondered, if you lined them all up on one big shittiness scale, where reality would fit in.

Fletcher shared a little about his own journey, and the losses he had endured. They swapped some funny stories about how they'd survived, too—like Fletcher's aluminum-foil-armor missions—Dani even giggling and putting her hand on his arm.

Eventually, Fletcher was unable to deny the truth he had been avoiding out of terror: Dani Calloway was flirting with him.

"Oh, hey, Beth," said Fletcher, remembering that his personal bodyguard was standing sentry just outside the open door in the hallway. "You can go. It's okay; I don't think she'll kill me."

Dani laughed with perfect pitch, a bright and resonant bell. "Yes, I promise I won't kill the last man on Earth."

Fletcher stopped and looked at her, eyes suddenly narrowing behind his glasses. "Hey," he said, "how did you know I was here?"

Beth was now in the doorway, leathery face watching silently.

"Oh," said Dani, looking from Fletcher to Beth. "Well, sure. There were these girls, see? They came into the camp I was staying at near San Onofre. There was a group of us living there, but people came and went all the time. Anyway, these two girls stayed with us for a few weeks. One of them got pretty drunk one night and told me what she'd been doing. Said she'd been at a hospital working with the last man on Earth. But—you're not actually the last one, are you? If there's one, there has to be..."

"We don't know anything," said Fletcher, a little curtly. "We can't exactly chat with people around the world, you know."

"Of course," she said.

"Who was the girl?" asked Fletcher.

"Her name was Chelsea," said Dani.

"And her friend was Lori?" asked Fletcher. The two deserters, the ex-Palm Springs 15 girls.

"Yep," said Dani, beaming. "And eventually she said your name." Dani over-enunciated it, drawing it out: "Fletcher Sinclair."

Fletcher shook his head. It was still a small world, wasn't it?

"And I thought," said Dani, "Fletcher—*the guy from my math class*—is alive!"

Dani Calloway had remembered him. What was he so concerned about again?

"Beth," he said, "it's all good. You can take off."

Beth lingered for a moment, shrugged, and walked away.

"Pretty tight security you got here," said Dani. "You know I was literally strip-searched by that old lesbian?"

Fletcher wasn't sure if Beth was actually a lesbian or not, but either way: he didn't exactly love the way Dani said it. But whatever.

"Oh," he said, about the security, "well, we had a thing." *A thing that had included Fletcher hiding from a machete-wielding psycho and ended with four bodies—two intruders and two friends. Including Dr. Gomez.*

"Anyway," said Dani, "I just thought that a familiar face would be wonderful. And that somebody in your shoes might need a familiar face, too. I mean, it's gotta be a lot to handle. A lot of pressure. I thought you could probably use a friend."

Fletcher didn't say anything. He had forgotten how to make sounds with his mouth.

"It must be tough," she said. "I bet you feel like a lab rat in here!"

He did, at times.

"I bet it's hard to know who to trust," she continued earnestly. "Like, who really cares about *you*."

It was, at times.

"It's gotta be lonely, too," she said. "Even surrounded by people. Do you get lonely, Fletch?"

He swallowed what felt like a dry, rolled-up sock. "Sometimes," he squeaked.

They stood in the middle of his room. She put both of his hands in hers.

"In this new world," she continued, "this messed-up, scary, new world, I feel it's more important than ever to know who to trust."

Fletcher tried to say something, but it just came out as a series of awkward little grunts.

"I think we could trust each other, don't you?" Somehow, she continued to move closer without seeming to move at all. "Think about it. We could be a great team. The two of us, trusting each other, helping each other. Side by side."

"Yeah?"

"Yeah." Then, without warning, she kissed him. Fletcher's head spun as the world vaporized around him and gravity lifted. She kissed him long and wet. And then with her tongue.

It was real: Dani Calloway was making out with Fletcher Sinclair.

Post-Delilah Earth was a crazy place, and it kept getting crazier.

Dani grabbed Fletcher's shirt and lifted it over his head, revealing his brittle rib cage and collarbones. Then she lifted her own much more gracefully, flashing a smile that could literally kill someone with a heart any weaker than Fletcher's.

"Is that what you want?" she whispered.

There was nothing in the world he wanted more.

But wait! There was Jordan. Jordan, Jordan, Jordan, Jordan. Who was Jordan? He focused. She was the one with the dimples, the crooked smile, the one who talked with him for hours, the one who taught him about old dead philosophers and the one he played stupid games with. She was the one who saw him for who he was.

Yes, that was Jordan. He tried to focus on her.

But the thought wasn't alone. There was also a series of thoughts about high school, back when Dani Calloway was queen. He thought about what little he had done. What little he had been. He didn't want to be little anymore. The new Fletcher—Odin, perhaps—could be as big as he wanted. And he wanted to be unignorably big. He wanted to be the kind of man who shaped the world; who made the world his own.

In the midst of his teetering thinking, Dani had closed the door and removed Fletcher's pants. And with it, the last of his armor.

And then: a surge of confidence. And then: a draining of the brain.

And then: Fletcher Sinclair did the deed with Dani Calloway.

The Dani Calloway.

It was quick and sloppy, but, as he lay there in bed afterward, staring at the ceiling, Fletcher felt primal in a way he had never come close to before.

She put a hand on his chest and giggled, pushing her face into his bony shoulder and kissing it.

But Fletcher's world was already being ripped in two.

Instead of post-coital bliss, Fletcher's spongy brain was immediately being used as the rope in a game of Tug of War.

On one side was a sense of pride. Even though he hadn't really *done* much, he felt like he had just accomplished something. He looked over and there, naked, next to him, was Dani Effing Calloway. If only he could tell his friends. What would Simon say if he knew about this? He wanted to laugh aloud at the very thought.

On the other side, though, was a small feeling of shame. He didn't like that side, but as time pulled him farther from That Thing That Just Happened, he could feel it growing stronger. Maybe it stemmed from the fact that, deep down, he knew Dani was only there because he was all that was left, and tethering herself to Fletcher meant ensuring her own safety. That this was just a calculated move of self-preservation. Of course it was. Natalie had warned about this happening. Or maybe it was because of Jordan, because she deserved him so much more than Dani did. He tried to push those ideas out of his brain. There was no time for that. No room for that. Not here—not in the godless, lawless land Delilah had created.

Pride and shame kept pulling, but through it all one thing was clear: this was one of those moments that divided life up into a Before and an After, and he was now living in the After.

Fletcher and Dani got dressed. Just as they were finishing up, there was a knock on the door. Fletcher zipped up his pants and opened the door to find Beth. Fletcher stepped into the hallway to talk to her.

"Just wanted to check in on you," she said lowly, so only he could hear. "Looks like she hasn't killed you."

"Thanks." Fletcher realized his skin was burning.

Beth looked over Fletcher's shoulder and he turned to follow her gaze. Dani was looking in the mirror, brushing her hair.

"Would you like her to stay?" asked Beth. "I can talk to Dr. Reid."

Fletcher gulped. He hadn't thought through the logistics. Shit—he hadn't thought at all.

"Or," Beth continued, eyes narrowing slightly, "would you like me to escort her out?"

Fletcher was startled. "Like, take her away?"

"Whatever you want."

A burst of color exploded in Fletcher's mind. Suddenly everything was clear, clouded no more by Dani and hormones. There was Jordan—sweet, incredible, one-of-a-kind Jordan. The Tug of War was over and Shame stood victorious.

Jordan could never know of Dani. Ever. Dani had to go. She had to leave and nobody could ever know she had been here.

God, what had he done?

"I think you should take her away," he said quietly. The words almost surprised him as they spilled from his weak lips, even if he knew they were the right ones.

And so Beth did.

Fletcher just stood and watched, his insides turning into a nest of snakes, his tongue to concrete. Beth told Dani it was time for her to go, that they couldn't have any outsiders stay, that, come on now, let's make this easy. Dani's face twisted with pain, terror, sadness and shock. It was a face Fletcher knew would haunt him forever. And there he stood, unmoving, unhelping, uncomforting. Dani looked out at Fletcher in the hallway and begged him to explain. She cried. She yelled. And then—worse—she went quiet. Beth finally walked her out of the room and down the hallway. Dani looked back at Fletcher the entire way—a steady glare of fiery disbelief. He couldn't make eye contact with her.

Beth returned minutes later. She told him that Dani was gone and doubted she would come back.

"Hey, um," said Fletcher, "can you keep her visit discreet?"

"I will," she said.

"Especially to…" he was going to say Jordan, but decided against it. "To everyone."

"I will," she said.

They looked at each other knowingly. "It's always been inevitable, I guess," said Beth. "That word would get out about your being here. Reckon it'll keep spreading, too."

Fletcher's skin burned and itched and he wanted to be alone.

"There's Chelsea and Lori," said Beth. "Also, that looter that got away. Now this young woman." She clicked her tongue. "People talk. Always do."

Beth studied Fletcher, the hard lines of her face as unreadable as always.

"Okay," said Fletcher.

Beth didn't blink. Maybe she never blinked. "If another woman does come looking for you," she said, "do you want me to bring her up? After I vet her, of course."

Fletcher looked down at his bare feet. He needed to clip his toenails. He needed to shower, too. For a year. "Not … not like this." He didn't know how else to say it. "No."

"Say no more." Beth nodded and walked away. Unlike Dani, she didn't look back.

Chapter 17

ONE THING'S FOR CERTAIN: you can't unvirginize yourself.

Despite his mixed feelings about his romp with Miss Rancho Bernardo High (pride, shame, thrill, regret, etcetera, etcetera), Fletcher couldn't get it out of his head. He thought of his recent copulatory expedition like the discovery of aliens. There was no undiscovering it. There was no unlearning it. And, while it might scare the living shit out of you, God, was it fascinating.

It was now a song in his brain that begged for him to start humming along throughout his daily tasks. Images would jump up in front of his eyes without warning: flashbang bursts of Dani's long tan legs; her delicate collarbones; the smooth way she peeled her shirt over her head; her hands searching him, searching him; her—

Fletcher had to rip himself from these hypnoses, coming to like a man being pulled from the sweetest, cruelest dream.

Soon after, Beth's prediction proved true. Another visitor came. It seemed that word spread quickly in the nearby camps and communities. Gossip was in short supply in the post-apocalyptic world.

Beth told Fletcher that a woman had arrived asking for him. Her name was Chesa, and she was a student at the University of California San Diego. Well, that's who she had been. But who was she now?

He made his way to a small office on the second floor with a window that overlooked the lobby. From there, he could creep on the scene. Waiting for him was a young Filipino woman. She smiled as Beth approached, but Fletcher recognized the desperation in her eyes. The same he'd seen in Dani's, now that he thought about it.

As Fletcher watched, he imagined Chesa pulling her shirt over her head like Dani had done. He imagined a lot of other things, too. A lot of other things indeed.

He saw Beth shake her head. He saw Chesa's eyes plead.

Fletcher wasn't dumb. He reminded himself that Chesa (and Dani ... and good old Imaginary Jessica) simply saw Fletcher as a golden ticket. A golden goose. If they could get Fletcher to like them, they would be taken care of.

But what if they just wanted male company in a world that had none?

What was so wrong with that? The question buzzed like a mosquito in his ear, and for a second he almost couldn't remember. Well, it was Jordan, right? But it wasn't like they were even dating, so he really wouldn't be doing anything wrong. You can't cheat on someone you're not with. Maybe he would go down and talk to her. Maybe he'd—

But she was gone. Beth was escorting her out, telling her that they were in the business of saving the world, and that they couldn't take in any more people, and that, sorry, but she couldn't come back here.

Sometimes there are no good outcomes.

Over the next week or so, life at the hospital home was business as usual. He kept up with his mental exams, bloodwork and physical regimen. Of the latter, he was continuing to get in better shape. He was still skin-and-bones thin, but he could run for a half hour without needing to stop, and apparently his blood pressure and heart rate were no longer reasons for the nurses to exchange judging looks.

But those flashbang bursts continued, and now it wasn't just Dani, either. Images of Chesa, of what could have been, slipped before his vision like old-school projector slides. Before long, his hospitalmates entered the theater of his imagination, too: Sunshine (who used to be Shannon), Crash (who used to be Carly), Lobster (who used to be Michelle) and so on. It was like a new part of Fletcher had been awakened.

One afternoon he sat on his stiff brown couch, uncomfortable in every possible way. His back ached, maybe from his workouts, maybe from that damn couch. His mind ached, too. Guilt could do that. He thought about Dani—what they'd done just feet from where he was. He thought about Jordan, and how she could never know. He shifted and cracked his neck and tried to relax, but his skin crawled with something that felt like claustrophobia. He longed for the comfort of his home. Back when things were simple. Comfort was a distant memory now.

But then—

Then Fletcher got an idea. And his mind was suddenly a summer day.

·····•·•····

He told Beth his idea, and she looked at him for a moment, as if she want-ed to say something. Instead, she swallowed it. She then exhaled deeply, in what might have been a sigh—but Fletcher wasn't concerned with such nuances. His idea was a good one. It was something he deserved, like everything else.

She told him that his plan would take some time, but—with the help of the staff—it hardly took a week. It was a Saturday afternoon (not that days mattered) when Beth knocked on his door and told him it was done. He followed her to the elevator and up to the fifth floor. Sunshine (who used to be Shannon), Ripley (who used to be Sarah) and Xena (who used to be Krishna) greeted him as the elevator opened. Sunshine (who used to be Shannon) wore a hard hat that was too big for her head.

"Welcome," she said as Fletcher stepped off the elevator, "to your new home."

His idea had been a good one indeed.

The fifth floor had been previously empty, except for the conference room that had been turned into Fletcher's Arcade. Now the entire floor was his. The arcade was to the left, but the girls took him right, around the corner to what used to be a physicians' lounge. It had been converted into a living room of wondrous proportions. Against the far wall was a giant TV—the biggest he'd ever seen—hanging before the room like a shrine. In front of it was a couch that wrapped all the way around the room, surrounding a coffee table made of what looked like pure stone. He stood in the doorway, mouth agape.

Xena (who used to be Krishna) shoved him from behind. "Well," she said, "you gonna just look at it or what?"

He stepped forward, in awe of his own castle.

"I know it isn't perfect," said Sunshine (who used to be Shannon), adjusting an uneven poster of *The Dark Knight* that had been hung on the wall.

"It *is* perfect," he said. "All of it."

Xena (who used to be Krishna) pushed him again. "Try out the couch! It's insane."

Fletcher woke from his stupor and took a few running steps, launching himself onto the couch. It was a goddamn upholstered cloud.

The three nurses all followed suit, jumping on the couch after him. Beth leaned against the wall, unamused.

Next, they showed him his bedroom.

"This is where the magic happens," said Ripley (who used to be Sarah).

Fletcher flushed a deep red. He hoped she was just joking, that she was unaware of Dani. The bedroom used to be another large conference room, but now was something far more marvelous. It had floor-to-ceiling windows, and Fletcher could see the Pacific Ocean in the distance. There was a desk that he knew he'd never use, but still, he liked that it made the room look sophisticated. There was a big wardrobe, a dresser and a mirror, as well as a little table with chairs. In the middle of it all was a king bed, with a frame that also seemed to be made for royalty. It was built from heavy oak, with four ornately carved bed posts and a headboard looming against the wall like a work of art. Fletcher figured that, as far as a monarch went in this post-Delilah world, he wasn't too far off.

"We raided the shit out of a Bed Bath & Beyond," said Xena (who used to be Krishna). She grinned and patted the foot of the bed proudly. "Three whole trips in Big Nurse."

The women showed him the rest of his suite. There was an office that was converted into a gym. He acted excited, knowing he wouldn't exercise any more than he was required to. Another office had been turned into a small kitchen, with an oven, a microwave and a refrigerator. Most importantly, there was a coffee maker. Fletcher's coffee intake was at an all-time high.

There were plenty of empty rooms, too. "We ran out of ideas," admitted Sunshine (who used to be Shannon).

Fletcher told them this was better than anything he could have hoped for. And it was. Partially, he thought, because the girls helped make it. They told him that a lot of the other girls helped as well: Lobster (who used to be Michelle), Crash (who used to be Carly), Raff (who used to be Madison), Morning (who used to be Annie) and Bobina (who used to be Serena). Fletcher nearly burst with pride.

The girls finally left Fletcher alone in his new suite after he thanked them too many times. He went to his bedroom and looked out the window at the California coastline, glowing with the bonfire tinges of sunset.

He deserved to have different living quarters than everyone else, because there was nobody else like him. He thought back to nearly nine months ago when he first arrived here, a scared, trembling mess of a boy. At that moment it almost seemed impossible that he had ever been so weak, so timid. At that moment, in his new kingdom, he could almost laugh at his pathetic old self.

·····•·••··

Early one morning, after a week or so of living large in his new fifth-floor penthouse, there was a knock on Fletcher's door. The sun was barely even up, and His Highness had been getting quite used to sleeping in as much as he pleased.

"What is it?" Fletcher groaned as he opened the door.

"They're back," said Beth.

"What?" said Fletcher, wiping grit from his eye. "Who's—oh shit. You don't mean—"

"I do," she said. "Jordan, Natalie and Michelle have returned."

"They're back?"

"Yes."

"*Back* back?" He blinked rapidly, short-circuiting.

"Yes."

"How long have they been gone?" he asked.

"Just over three months," said Beth.

"Hey," said Fletcher, shifting his weight awkwardly. "Remember ... just ... don't say anything about the ... visitor we had."

"Of course," said Beth.

"I'm serious."

"I'm always serious," said Beth.

Fletcher got dressed and hurried downstairs. His heart was racing. His head was spinning. His stomach was sinking.

There in the lobby, unmistakable as soon as he turned the corner, was a bouncing head of curls and a crooked smile that Fletcher knew and loved. Jordan was in a circle with Natalie and Michelle, talking to Dr. Reid and a handful of the Palm Springs girls. She turned and saw him, and her smile doubled, dimples popping. She stopped whatever sentence she was in the middle of and squirmed away from the circle, running toward Fletcher. She wrapped him in her arms and squeezed him tight.

Everything was going to be just as he'd planned.

"God, I missed you!" she said. "Look at you! How much did you miss me?"

"I guess a little," said Fletcher. They looked at each other, both grinning. She hugged him again.

"I'm glad you're back," said Fletcher.

"I am *so glad* to be back," she said, as they returned to the group. "You have no idea."

"Hey, handsome," said Natalie, wrapping Fletcher in a hug of her own.

"Morning, Odin!" said Morning (who used to be the Annie).

"Good morning, Morning," said Fletcher, blushing.

There was a pause.

"Ho-lee shit," said Jordan. "Are you actually going by Odin now?"

"I mean, it's—" Fletcher stammered.

"Hell, yeah!" said Lobster (who used to be the other Michelle). "And I'm Lobster. Because I love lobster."

"I'm Bobina," said Bobina (who used to be Serena). "My dad called me that."

Stardust (who used to be Eva) and Ripley (who used to be Sarah) shared their names, too.

"Well, I'll be," said Jordan.

"Yeah," said Lobster (who used to be Michelle). "We decided it's like, a new era. You can be whoever you want. You want a new name?"

"She's Hypatia," offered Fletcher.

He noticed a few sets of eyeballs watching him and Jordan.

She smiled. "But you can still call me Jordan. Listen, I gotta go take my stuff to my room. Fletcher, wanna help a girl out? I gotta hear what you've been up to."

"Of course," said Fletcher.

"It's so good to see you," she said as they walked away. "You look good, Fletch." She paused, grinning. "I mean, *Odin*."

"You can call me whatever you want," said Fletcher, his face now on fire.

When they got to her room, Fletcher sat down on the couch—a stiff brown one just like he used to have, nothing like the cushiony wrap-around in his new room—while she unpacked.

Fletcher asked her about the trip. He said he wanted to hear all about it. It was true, but he also wanted to avoid talking about the happenings on the home front.

"It was ... intense," she said, flinging herself on her old bed. "And kind of fruitless. I mean, we got supplies, which is good. We got a ton of shit—medical supplies, testing equipment we've never had, food. Stuffed that little go-cart to the brim."

"And the doctors?" said Fletcher. They had gone with the hopes of expanding the team with some of the brilliant physicians who were supposed to be in Phoenix. Maybe even finding a new Dr. Gomez.

"Nonexistent," said Jordan. "The hospitals were deserted. All of Phoenix was. Place was a literal ghost town. So was Tucson. So was Albuquerque. So was Santa Fe. I don't know how many survivors there are, Fletcher. And so many of the people we did find were sick or hungry, so we helped out where we could. That's what took so long. It felt more like a FEMA project than a recruitment mission."

"Man, I'm sorry," said Fletcher.

"It was just exhausting," said Jordan. "But I'm glad we could help a few people out. And I'm glad to be back."

"Humanity is really on its last legs, huh?" mused Fletcher.

"Maybe," said Jordan. "But as long as there are still *acts* of humanity, there's still humanity. And I saw a lot of people helping people out there. Little communities making it work. It's not all bad."

"That's awesome."

"To be fair," she said, "I saw a lot of people hurt by people, too."

"That's not so awesome."

"But you're still here," she stopped and looked at him. "We're still here."

He searched her eyes and, instead of seeing her, found himself wondering what she was seeing.

"Well, anyway," she said, "what's been going down here?"

"Oh, you know," he said, hoping she never would. "Uh, we had a pizza party a while ago."

"God, you're a wild man." Jordan grinned. "Listen, I need to shower and stuff, then I need to brief Dr. Reid on the trip and get a download on what's been happening around here. Besides you all playing Little Caesars."

"Sure."

"But hey," she said, "why don't I come to your room tonight and we can catch up some more?"

"Sounds great," said Fletcher. "Wait—I, uh, live on the fifth floor now."

"What? Like, in the arcade?"

"Not exactly," said Fletcher. "You'll see." He casually closed the door, then hurried down the hall. He had work to do.

Chapter 18

THEY HAD DECIDED TO do dinner together, meaning Fletcher had a few hours to Jordanize his room. Tonight was a big night. Maybe *the* big night. He felt good about it, too. He was all balls and belief.

Tonight was the night that he, Fletcher Sinclair, would stop being a little wimp.

Fletcher quickly found Beth, who was sitting on a bench in the courtyard, hunched over, whittling a branch with a small pocket knife like Daniel Boone. When Fletcher approached, she lifted her head as if she had been expecting him. He told her that he needed a few things, and that, again, it required tight lips. She nodded, slowly folded her knife and stood up, then wiped the wood shavings from her pant legs and left without a word.

Fletcher bolted up to his room to clean. He started by making his bed, which was not a customary ritual of his. Then he proceeded to tidy, picking up the assortment of single socks and old T-shirts he'd left crumpled up on the couch and floor, the half-finished coffee mugs and the sticky dinner plates. He was rather impressed with the mess he'd made in just a week. But he cleaned as if his romantic life depended on it.

Beth arrived a couple hours later, bringing with her the requested items.

"Will there be anything else?" she asked.

"No, thank you," said Fletcher. "Just your—"

"Yes, my discretion." Per usual, Fletcher couldn't read her wood-carved face. "Always."

Beth gave nothing away, ever—a privacy that Fletcher admired, even envied. This woman knew practically everything about him now, including his biggest, dirtiest, Dani-sized secret. On the other hand, he knew nothing about her. He didn't know where she came from or if she'd had a family. He didn't know her motivations, hopes, fears, sexual preference, political affiliation, favorite movie or favorite color. Above all, he didn't know how she felt about him.

But that wasn't important now.

Fletcher set the flowers Beth had brought on a table by the door. Those he'd give to Jordan immediately. The flowers were plastic, yes, but they'd do. They were the best that the nearby ransacked Walmart could offer, and they were far more colorful and impressive than those flimsy origami petals he had once thought were a good idea.

That felt so pathetic now.

He put the champagne on the table in the corner of his bedroom, as well as the box of expensive-looking chocolates. He was no idiot. He knew girls liked flowers, chocolate and champagne. Everyone knows that.

He walked through the entire suite again, making sure it was in tip-top shape. He was pleased with himself. If this wasn't the spot for the moment he had been waiting for, the site where the first sparks could catch, he didn't know what was.

The scene was set. The actor was in his place. The script was etched into his brain.

Then, there was a knock on the door.

Action.

· · · • · • · · ·

Fletcher opened the door to find Jordan, looking radiant. She wasn't dressed fancy, but she wore a black blouse that Fletcher hadn't seen before. She was done up slightly more than usual, and to Fletcher this was a wonderful sign.

She walked in and took in his bachelor pad, mouth hanging open.

"Holy shit," she said. "I like what you've done with the place."

"Oh, thanks." He suddenly realized he was holding a bouquet of plastic flowers. "Hey, uh, these are for you."

"What? Oh … you didn't need to do that." She smiled her sideways smile, her eyes a little confused. Maybe *surprised*. That was better. "You're … that's very sweet, Fletch."

"I just..." Fletcher started. "I dunno ... thought you'd like them."

"I do," she said.

"Maybe it's ... I dunno," he laughed.

"I do like them, Fletcher," she said. "Thank you."

He recited his mantra in his head: *Confidence. Confidence. Confidence.*

"So, you wanna see the place?"

"Um, *yes*," she said as they walked to the right toward the living room. Fletcher showed off the couch, and they plopped down on the plush cushions.

"So, your own suite," said Jordan. "Look at you go. Where's the golf course?"

"We *do* have a bowling alley," admitted Fletcher.

"No!" Jordan cocked her head to the side.

"Eighth floor," said Fletcher.

"What else?"

"Actually," he said, "laser tag."

"Get out of here."

"Ninth floor," he said, and then caught himself. "But it's all for every-one. It was a group effort. We're just trying to make this place a little more fun, you know?"

"A little more fun," Jordan repeated. She looked around the room—his room. "For ... everyone." There was a funny juxtaposition with the expensive quality of the furniture—the couch, the tables, the big-ass TV on the wall—and the sterile hospital canvas.

A San Diego June-gloom sunset bled through the windows, washing everything inside, including Jordan and Fletcher, with its dull nectarine glow.

"Hey, explain this to me." Jordan sat the plastic flowers on the cushion next to her. "Why on Earth is there a big green monster head on display in the cafeteria?"

She grinned, but Fletcher winced. The paper bag mask of Delilah the dragon. "It was just this little play some of the girls did. Just for fun—stupid stuff."

"What?" Jordan laughed, but looked at him curiously. "The girls put on a play? All of them?"

"Oh, no," said Fletcher, searching for a way to change the subject. "Just a group of them. They just, I don't know, decided to do one. You know, like in school or when you were a kid. Just for fun."

"Just for fun," repeated Jordan. There was something weird about her voice, something that Fletcher didn't like.

"I mean," said Fletcher, forcing a laugh that didn't help, "there's zero entertainment around here, you know? So, yeah, they decided to go all theater class. It wasn't a big deal."

"Zero entertainment?" she said. "You mean besides the theater and the arcade and the bowling alley?"

"Well," said Fletcher.

"And the laser tag…"

"Well, yeah," he said. "But it was their play, though! Not mine."

"Their play, got it," she said. "But, I'm curious: was their play *for* you? Were you the only audience?"

"Well, no," Fletcher offered. "Beth and Megan and Dr. Reid and…"

"What was the play about?" she asked.

"I mean, it was just stupid stuff, just funny … just dumb stuff," said Fletcher.

"Oh, come on," she said.

"Well, it was about a knight who defeated a monster named Delilah," laughed Fletcher.

Jordan looked at him and raised her eyebrows. "What was that knight's name?"

Fletcher looked down. "Fletcher," he said. "Okay, that sounds weird, but it wasn't like that. They were just being funny. It was … like … like satire, you know? Comedy. It was all fun. They did it for fun. The Fletcher-knight thing was their idea. Ask them! They had fun."

"Okay, okay. All fun, I get it," she said. "Sheesh."

"Ask Ripley about it," said Fletcher. "She directed it and was super into it."

Jordan looked at him oddly.

"Oh, I mean, Sarah," said Fletcher.

"Gotcha."

"Listen," said Fletcher. "I feel like this sounds weird, but it wasn't. Really, you should have seen it. It was a blast. More fun than any movie night we had in old Sinclair Cinema. For real, everyone was so into it. Talked about it for weeks. Maybe they'll do another and—"

"Did you just call the theater *Sinclair Cinema*?" Her tone was different now, far away. "Fletcher, did you really name it after yourself?"

"Ah, shit—come on," said Fletcher. "I didn't mean to say that. That's not even the real name. It doesn't even have a name!" Fletcher felt like he was under interrogation and, frankly, was a little frustrated by it. She hadn't been here. She didn't get it.

"I don't know, Fletch," Jordan said, forcing a sad laugh. "I leave for a couple months and—do I even know you anymore?"

"Hey, it's all good," he said. "It's me. Spend some time and you'll see everything is good here. Better than ever, actually."

Jordan didn't say anything. She was looking out the window. The sun was now all but set, the last dark light fizzling out.

"Hey," said Fletcher. Nothing was lost. Tonight was still his night. It had to be. "Let me show you the rest of the space. Come on."

Jordan looked at him uncertainly but got up and followed, still silent.

He led her into the bedroom, where the champagne was sitting on the table like a trophy.

When they entered the room, Jordan looked at the bed, the desk, the dresser and the giant windows. When she saw the table with the champagne and chocolate box she did a double take, then looked at Fletcher. Her eyes smoldered in a way that Fletcher chose to interpret as enamored exhilaration.

Emboldened by his decision to cross into the realm of no return, he pushed on, blind assurance leading the way. He deserved anything and everything. He was the last man on Earth.

"How about this view, huh?" he said.

"It's lovely."

"Would you like some champagne?" He picked up the bottle and started peeling at the foil hood with his fingernails.

"No." Her mouth was a harsh horizontal line.

"I got you some chocolates, too," he said. Now it was his voice that sounded different. A little deeper, maybe.

"How thoughtful."

"Jordan, listen," he said. "I know you're confused, but this is all okay. It's good, actually."

"What is?"

"All of this." Fletcher was drunk with the fiery buzz of a dream that was finally in sight. The sweet adrenaline surged through his veins.

"All of this," echoed Jordan. There was a pause. "Kind of seems like *all of this* is you taking advantage of your situation."

"Hey," said Fletcher, "what's so wrong with getting what you can in this world? Getting what you're worth?"

Jordan's eyes narrowed. Fletcher took this to mean that his assertiveness was inciting even more passion.

Onward.

Only onward.

"But Jordan, see—I don't want all this to myself," he said. "I want to share it. With you."

He remembered what Dani had said—about being a team in this new world. He wanted that, only with Jordan.

"We can share this suite," he continued. "We can share this new world and make it what we want. Anything we can dream up, it can be ours." He looked out the window at the silvery orb hanging in the sky and felt a surge of poetic romance. "See that moon?" He gestured out the giant windows. "We can share the moon, too. We can have it all. We can share it all."

"What does that even *mean?*" Jordan had been mannequin-still, and this sudden burst startled Fletcher. "What—does—that—mean? You might think you run shit around here, but Fletcher—oh, Fletcher, you poor, poor thing—you don't. You don't *own* anything. It's *us* who are trying to save humanity. You're just a part of it. Or you were."

"What?" Fletcher croaked, pieces of his outer shell falling away like stones in an ancient wall, letting in the cold, dark, ugly truth. "Jordan, come on."

This will all be over soon.

"You're talking like you're king of the world," she said. "But you're not. You're just a guy who was spared for some mysterious reason."

"You know what?" said Fletcher, holding onto who he had become and what he deserved, forcing those stones back into place with sheer will, or sheer desperation. "If there ever *was* a king of the world, it's me. Who else? Whatever I say happens because the world *needs* me. How is that a bad thing?"

"Seriously?"

"And I could have anyone, too. *Anyone*. But I'm choosing *you*, Jordan. I want us to take on this world together! You'd be the queen, so to speak."

It felt good to say it. All of it. He made his stand, took his shot. He had offered her the world. Who could say no to that? What girl didn't want to be a queen?

Jordan looked silently out the window. She shook her head. Still facing the dark ocean, she finally spoke. "You wanna know something? I had actually *fallen* for Fletcher. Can you believe that? I was ready to come back here and let him know that." She turned to him and her eyes were dark, deep, sorrowful wells that chilled his guts. "But everything changed while I was gone, didn't it? Fletcher isn't here anymore. And I'm sorry, but I have no interest in the guy that took his place. *Odin*, is it?"

She turned and walked toward the exit.

"Jordan, wait." The pieces of his shell now piled up around him. "This all got twisted up. Let's start over. It's not—you know I'm a good guy, Jordan. You know me. Let me explain everything. It's still me."

Jordan didn't turn around, cutting through the moonlit suite like a dagger. "You are what you repeatedly do," she said sadly, shutting the door behind her.

············

Fletcher didn't sleep much that night. He lay awake thinking. He couldn't make sense of it. The thing was, no women had liked old Fletcher, old pre-Delilah Fletcher. That's why Jordan's words didn't compute. No, girls had always wanted men with confidence, men who took what they wanted, men who had power—who had awesome suites with big living rooms and nice views. He had seen it his whole life. Then, out of nowhere, Jordan throws him this bullshit curveball about falling for the old Fletcher. Maybe she had been mistaken, or confused, or caught up in the emotion of the moment. Nobody had fallen for that guy—not in high school and not in this strange hospital. Not Jordan. Not anybody.

Oh, but women catered to the whims of the new and improved model. Women (the Danis, probably the Chesas, definitely the Imaginary Jessicas) offered themselves up to the upgraded version. The confident one. The last man standing. Motherfucking Odin.

So why was Jordan being so weird? He was sure he could fix things. He could do whatever he wanted now. This was his world. He told himself this over and over, like a desperate prayer, as he stared at the ceiling above his big, fancy bed.

But he soon learned there would be no fixing this. When he finally got vertical, he found an envelope under his door. Inside was a note from Jordan.

Fletcher,

I'm leaving. Again. I stayed up all night talking it over with Natalie, and this is what's best. This place has lost its direction ... and I think you have, too.

You should know that you were always special. At least to me. That's why I can't watch whatever is happening to you.

So I'm going. I'm going to find people who still want to help. They're out there. I know it. And I'll find them. Somebody somewhere can cure this thing.

I'll come back, though. Someday. Hopefully with answers. Maybe with new doctors. But I'll come back. I just hope you do, too. If you know what I mean.

Well, off I go. I'm going to keep trying to save this lovely world of ours. But only you can save yourself, old friend.

I hope you do.

Jordan

There was another letter in the envelope. This one was from Natalie.

Fletcher,

Pull yourself together, dude. You're not a dick. No matter how hard you try, you're not a dick. But I'm going with Jordan, because the world needs us or some shit. She's very convincing.

So, I'll see you when I see you.

xoxo

Natalie

Fletcher read each letter twice. He then threw his empty water glass against the wall, which broke into a few smaller pieces instead of shattering into oblivion like he had hoped. It was not nearly as satisfying as how guys in movies made it look. He shrugged and slumped down on the couch. He looked out the window, all melodrama, all messed up.

How had Jordan just left? Just like that? And Natalie, too? What great friends they were.

This will all be over soon.

Whatever, he thought. He could have anything and everything—except Jordan, apparently. And Natalie. But who needed them when he had everything else? He remembered what he told her last night: "If there ever was a king of the world, it's me."

So that's what he would be, he thought. Long live King Odin.

Chapter 19

FLETCHER TOLD BETH THAT things were changing: any women who came looking for him were now to be brought to his suite. Fletcher reminded her, unnecessarily and without prompting, that he could always leave and go … *socialize* … on his own. Of course, for the sake of preserving Fletcher's happiness and thus, maintaining his participation and thus, continuing the mission to save humankind, Beth obliged.

Beth immediately came up with a system. If any woman showed up, Beth would meet with them, just as she had been. Triage. If they were indeed seeking Fletcher (and not medical attention), she would assess the risk they posed. She'd strip-search them, which, while it wouldn't exactly be the best foreplay, would at least guarantee that nobody was sneaking in a weapon to hold Fletcher hostage or who knows what. Beth would then tell the visitor that they couldn't stay. Fletcher liked this part, as it made him feel like he was off the hook, that expectations were set.

Beth made Fletcher agree to two types of protection: the kind that came in little foil packages and the kind that shot people. Beth showed him how to fire the handgun one afternoon in the courtyard, but he insisted he already knew how condoms worked. Which he did—in theory. He kept both in his nightstand. If there was ever trouble, he just had to yell. Beth or Megan would stand guard outside his room whenever he had company. He didn't love the idea, but this was non-negotiable.

Fletcher assumed Dr. Reid knew about the arrangement, too. In fact, some of those security protocols were likely of her design. And she must have been okay with it—if she wasn't, she'd try to put a stop to it. But Fletcher didn't really care. She was of no importance to him. Besides, it's not like she was running a tight ship. It's not like she knew what she was doing. And he was prepared to threaten departure the moment she uttered a dissatisfied word to him. He held all the cards.

It only took a week or so for a woman to come knocking.

She was a middle-aged woman with big breasts and blonde hair, a former suburban soccer mom, a divorcee, a real estate agent. She comforted the visibly nervous young man. She was gentle, taking the lead while Fletcher followed, helping him see that it wasn't so scary after all. Then, despite her best offers and reasons and arguments, despite her best articulations of how helpful she could be around the hospital, she was escorted out.

Five days after that, another visitor: a sharp-nosed former violinist with a whiny voice. Fletcher found that, this time, his anxiety was nearly nonexistent. Afterward, this one begged to stay, pleading, promising to do whatever was asked. Fletcher could still hear her cries after the door closed behind her.

Then—

Over the next month or so, Fletcher's revolving door spun faster and faster. The more women who laid eyes (and hands) on this fabled man, the more seemed to hear about him, until women were making pilgrimage to the hospital every few days.

Beth's system was a good one, and it made secrecy within the hospital fairly easy. After someone alerted Beth of a visitor, Beth met with them in private, and the visitor was never seen by Fletcher's hospitalmates again. (Beth used the forgotten service elevator to take them to the fifth floor.) Fletcher's neighbors likely assumed Beth had turned them away. Not that it really mattered if they found out, but he preferred his friends not knowing his personal business.

So, life for Fletcher became a cavalcade of coitus, an endless tide of navels and nipples and lips and legs. He briefly wished he could regale Simon with all these encounters. For some reason, though, he was having a hard time remembering old Simon, and trying to do so made him feel funny, so he shrugged it off. He was too busy getting busy to think backward.

Far too busy—with girl after girl. And oh, the girls!

There was the one who asked his permission to call him Brad, which Fletcher strangely agreed to; the one who tried to snip off a piece of his hair as a keepsake or, as Fletcher angrily told her, like the original Delilah; the girl who tried to stick a finger where fingers aren't supposed to be stuck; the sweet one who cuddled with Fletcher after and made him feel like a real person; the one who slapped Fletcher in the face right in the middle of it all; the ones who told him he was amazing; the ones who were honest; the girls who reminded him of Jordan; the girls who made him forget her.

The women came in every flavor, but it always ended the same way: with Beth escorting them out. Even with the expectation set at the beginning—that a visitor couldn't stay—every single woman asked Fletcher to make an exception. Every single woman told him she could make him happy, that the two of them could be so great together, that he couldn't send her back out into the world, that world that was certain death, could he?

But he could. And he did. He had to.

He did like some of their company though, so he'd occasionally let one of his guests hang out for a few hours and play a board game or lay and talk. But it never satisfied. Their conversations were never as filling as the ones he used to have with a certain dimple-cheeked nurse.

But that was an unfair comparison.

The only way he could get his mind off of Jordan was by drowning himself in a whirlpool of strangers' long hair and tangled limbs. So the women kept walking through his door. Walking out his door. Walking through his door. Walking out his door.

Fletcher wasn't an idiot. He still knew his visitors were likely motivated by one thing: They thought they could raise their status in this new world and could secure protection by cozying up to the only man around.

Supply and demand.

Truth be told, Fletcher didn't much care about motives. He wasn't looking for true love. He was looking for something else, and he was getting it, alright. Making up for lost time, alright.

And he couldn't believe what he had been missing.

There was no doubt about it now: Fletcher was the undeniable king of the world, a king who happily accepted the offerings brought by his most enthusiastic subjects.

Once an incontrovertible nobody, this scrawny, messy-haired young man was the somebody of all somebodies—and it felt fantastic. And did he mention that he had the biggest unit on Planet Earth? That had become his new favorite joke, and he told it to himself and his guests whenever the opportunity arose. But it was only a half-joke, really.

In *The Odyssey of Zordallus*, if you ever outsmarted a Troll King, you'd get your pick of the Troll Maidens (which was better than it sounded). You'd also get a +10 boost in morale. This was kind of like that. Fletcher felt as if he had outsmarted a whole city of Troll Kings.

Troll Maidens, Fletcher realized, provided a great distraction for a warrior such as he to momentarily forget about any princess who had gotten away.

············

Fletcher was lying on his big-ass couch, staring at his big-ass TV. The TV was off. Beth's now-very-familiar knock rat-tat-tatted on the door behind Fletcher. He shouted for her to enter without turning around.

"Dinner is ready down there," she said.

"Oh," said Fletcher. "Hey, maybe bring it up tonight?"

"Sure."

"Just tired is all," said Fletcher.

"Sure," said Beth. "Hey, Sinclair ... you're using your protection, yes?"

He rolled his eyes. "Of course."

"Well, then." Beth turned to leave.

"Wait, hey," said Fletcher.

"Uh-huh."

"You don't think I'm an asshole, do you?" said Fletcher. "Because, see, I'm being honest with them and I treat them all very, you know..."

Beth just looked at him and sighed. A leathery old bag deflating. She began walking away.

"Let me guess," grumbled Fletcher. "*You don't care.*"

Beth ignored him and took a few steps toward the door, but stopped.

"That is such bullshit." She turned back to face Fletcher. Her diesel-motor voice now carried a tone Fletcher had never heard. "You honestly think I'd do what I do if I didn't *care?*"

"I guess not," said Fletcher.

"I work my ass off for this place," she said. "I care more about what goes on inside these walls than you've cared about anything in your life."

"Well..."

"And that means, for some reason, I even care about your ungrateful ass." The canyons of her hard face twitched into something that was the beginnings of a sad smile if you looked closely enough.

"I'm sorry, I didn't know you felt so—" stammered Fletcher.

"Oh, don't get all sentimental, Sinclair," said Beth. "Be an asshole or don't. Do whatever you want." Then, almost under her breath: "You might just need to figure out what that is."

"Huh?"

"Agh, this is too much talk for me," she grunted. "Someone will bring up your dinner. Good chat." And with that, she left.

·······

Eventually, Fletcher stopped caring so much what other people in the hospital thought of him and his actions. Now that Jordan was gone—long gone, out of his life, by her own choice, and soon to be out of his mind, he was sure—it didn't seem to matter. Besides, Beth, Megan and likely Dr. Reid already knew what was happening on the fifth floor. If more people found out about the women, so what? What could they do to him? He was beyond reproach.

Being so beyond reproach, Fletcher decided to cast a line in the local pond. He remembered Sunshine (who used to be Shannon) being especially flirty with him once or twice. He'd never thought much of it, on account of Jordan. But now there was no Jordan. So, he asked Megan to bring up Sunshine (who used to be Shannon).

She walked in wearing yoga pants and a tight yellow tank, and Fletcher couldn't wait to see what was underneath. Her hair was up in a ponytail that bounced as he walked her through the suite, which she had helped redesign for him not long ago.

"This couch is epic," she said, slapping a playful beat on the leather backing. She went up to the window and looked out at the red sun dipping into the endless Pacific. "This *view* is epic."

She looked at Fletcher. "So, what did you want to see me for?"

He smiled what he imagined to be his sexy smile. He maintained eye contact. He put his hands on her hips. Her face twisted in what he took to be excitement. He leaned in and kissed her, forcefully. The way a man who knows what he wants would.

"Oh!" She turned her head and stepped back. "Oh!"

"What?"

"I'm sorry," said Sunshine (who used to be Shannon). She gave a sad little half-smile and looked at him the way you look at a sick puppy. She was so sweet, even as she was—what, turning him down?

"Wait, so..." Fletcher scratched his head.

"I'm sorry," she said again. "I'm not—I don't really want—I just want to be friends, you know? I don't want to, you know, complicate things."

"It won't," said Fletcher. "No complicating."

"I just want to be friends," she said again.

Fletcher grunted.

"Seriously!" she said. "You're so great and all, but—yeah."

Fletcher grunted again.

"Hey," she said. "Let's just forget it? It's totally not a big deal, right?"

"Uh ... totally." Fletcher rubbed the heel of his palm against his forehead.

"Plus, it's not like you're *lonely*." She laughed.

Was that a reference to his visitors?

"And hey," she said, "we'll still be friends."

Fletcher just sighed. He walked her to the door, said goodnight, and shut it behind her.

Whatever. What did he care? Besides, maybe it was better to leave the local pond alone. There was still plenty to catch in the great sea outside.

He crawled into bed without brushing his teeth. Instead of sleeping he looked at the ceiling in the dark, something he was doing more and more of.

·········

Fletcher eventually lost track of how many women he'd been with. Then, he seemed to lose track of everything else. He'd forget his guests' names. He'd forget how many cups of coffee he'd had, or what meal he was eating. He could no longer remember what day of the week it was. Life had become a blurred copy of a copy of a dirty photo, a *Groundhog Day* cycle of orgasms and ennui.

When things started feeling especially mundane, Fletcher turned to liquor, like so many men he respected had done. James Bond guzzled martinis constantly. John Wayne slugged whiskey like water. Don Draper drank vodka for breakfast. And so on. He initially asked Beth to find him some scotch. That felt appropriately masculine. Then, after realizing it tasted like Pennzoil, he requested something more palatable. She got him peach schnapps and coconut rum. Now those he could handle.

And he liked the feeling.

Out of the sheer monotony of it all, he quickly developed a dependable little boozy routine. In the evenings he'd start drinking—either with one of his visitors or by himself. He'd gradually work himself into a nice drunken haze, and then sink into a sleeping oblivion. In the mornings he'd wander through a hungover fog, which faded away as he did whatever was needed of him that day. Often, though, nothing was needed of him it all. The staff hardly had any tests for him, or uses for him, and there were days when he thought they may have forgotten about him altogether. Regardless of the day's events, when evening came, he'd pick up where he'd left off on whatever bottle he'd been working on the night before. It kept him entertained, and made it easier to get excited about things when he wanted to get excited, laugh at things when he wanted to laugh, or get angry about things when he wanted to get angry.

··•·•·•·••··

"Christ's sake, Sinclair."

The tile floor was cold against Fletcher's skin and it felt lovely. It was the only part of him that felt lovely. He had no idea how long he had been lying on his own floor. The guest he'd had earlier that night, the one he'd drunk himself into a stupor with, was gone. Her name had been Kristin. Or Christine. Or something like that.

Beth was there in her place, standing over the pile that was Fletcher.

"Pull yourself together," she said.

Fletcher grunted. She bent down and flopped his arms over her shoulders. In a display of surprising strength, she picked him up and lay him down on the soft couch.

"Oh, that's better," muttered Fletcher. "That's better."

"Sleep tight," said Beth. "I put a cup of water on the table. You might want to drink some."

"You're so nice to me," he said.

"Goodnight, Sinclair."

"Beth," grunted Fletcher. "Hey, Beth. Hey."

"Yes?"

"Why?" he muttered.

"Why, what?"

"Why are you nice to me?"

"I have no idea," she said.

Fletcher paused, sleep pulling him back down. Beth turned to go. "And why do you do everything else?" asked Fletcher.

"Do what?"

"Dr. Reid says, get Fletcher what he wants, and you go, okay," he slurred. "Fletcher says, I want this, I want that, I want girls. You go, okay. But ... like ... why?"

Beth sighed.

"Because I could leave?" asked Fletcher. "Or because you care. Like you said."

Beth sighed again. "When you believe in a cause, you just try to help how you can."

"Okay."

"And I ain't no doctor," said Beth.

"Yeah, okay, okay."

"Although," she said, picking up the bottle of coconut rum from the table. "I'm starting to wonder if I'm doing more harm than good. You won't be much help if you drink yourself to death."

"I'm fine," muttered Fletcher, nearly asleep again.

"Maybe just take it easy for a bit."

"Easy, easy," repeated Fletcher. "Take it easy."

And he was out again.

Chapter 20

It was a Wednesday afternoon, but he didn't know it. He had a guest whose name was Cheryl, but he didn't know that, either. He was not taking it easy.

During sex, Cheryl had exhibited all the enthusiasm and passion of someone washing dishes. Immediately after, she began making her case to be taken in—how helpful she could be, how industrious, how obedient, etcetera, etcetera. And how cruel it would be to turn away. In this, she exhibited a fountain of enthusiasm. A well of passion.

Of course, her case was rejected. When Beth arrived to escort her out, Fletcher told her to come back and see him after.

"What were your instructions to her?" Fletcher asked Beth when she returned.

"My instructions?"

"How did you prep her for her visit?" he asked, his liquored voice a little higher than usual, a little edgier.

"I'm not sure I follow," she said. "I just—"

"Did you instruct her to be miserable?" asked Fletcher.

"Excuse me?" Beth looked at him, eyebrows raised.

"Did you say, 'Hey, so here's what I want you to do. I want you to act like being with Odin is a chore. Oh, and please, look as bored as possible while you're at it.' Is that what you tell these girls?" Fletcher felt hot and his arms tingled. He wanted to break something but didn't really know why.

"Still worried about whether I think you're an asshole or not?" Beth asked dryly.

"Just—how am I supposed to remain in good spirits if I'm surrounded with these downer girls?" said Fletcher.

"So I should encourage some more *pep*?" Her sarcasm was lost on Fletcher.

"Yes, do that," said Fletcher. "That's all for now. I'd like to be alone."

Beth pressed her lips together to prevent words from bursting out. She swallowed those words and walked away.

There was a puzzle in Fletcher's brain he couldn't figure out. He had everything he wanted, but somehow still felt empty. It was a riddle he didn't much enjoy, and the confusion angered him.

Fletcher's anger became one of those unexplainable emotional snowballs. It started with a little frustration here and there—then everything began to upset him. Each thing stuck, adding to the rolling snowball, rolling and rolling and getting bigger and bigger, until it could swallow up anything in its way. He became upset by how sweet and kind Sunshine (who used to be Shannon) was, especially given that she'd had the nerve to reject his advances. Then, after seeing Crash (who used to be Carly) and Ripley (who used to be Sarah) kiss, he learned they'd been together this whole time, which made him feel like an oblivious dickhead, which made him mad that nobody had ever told him. Also, the girls' garden had begun to yield carrots and cucumbers and herbs, and everyone was all excited, but Fletcher didn't see what was so great about raw vegetables. And God—that pissed him off, too. And the snowball rolled on and on. Things that normally didn't bother him suddenly became unbearable. Raff (who used to be Madison) had a nasally laugh that now made Fletcher want to jam pencils into his ears. Lobster (who used to be Michelle) smiled too much, and it drove Fletcher crazy. Morning (who used to be Annie) talked louder than anyone else, which Fletcher now found grating to the point of madness. He didn't like being annoyed at these things. He liked these girls. He became angry with himself for being angry with them. Thus, his anger snowball grew and grew.

As it grew, its shadow cast over Fletcher, and in the darkness he found a cold and lonesome depression. The shadow spread and spread, and he could see no way out of it.

The food began to taste unpalatable. The temperature in his suite was never right. His coffee was always lukewarm. The medical quest seemed pointless, too. They hardly ever thought of any more tests to run on him, and when they did they seemed to be grasping at straws. They were never going to solve anything. He was the last man on Earth, and he would always be the last man on Earth, and when he died there would be no more men on Earth. And, to Fletcher, that was now that.

The schnapps didn't even help anymore.

No, nothing could help. Fletcher was rage. He was futility. He was emptiness. He couldn't see over the giant snowball in front of him.

Fletcher had no idea what he wanted, but he wanted it with all his heart. He wanted everything and nothing, and everyone and no one, and to own the world and to hide in its dark forgotten crevices forever.

··········

The next evening Fletcher decided to watch a movie in Sinclair Cinema, thinking a change of scenery might lift his spirits. As he approached the theater, he heard the disappointing sounds of *The Bachelor*. Oh, well. He could use a little familiar company. He could use a friendly distraction.

But he wouldn't find that here. In his beloved theater sat Arlene, Amanda (AKA "Tinkerbell") and Megan.

"Oh, hi there." Fletcher put on a strained smile. He knew Arlene and Amanda were on the Fletcher Sucks team, for whatever reason. They'd both thought the play was some conceited brainchild of Fletcher. They'd both thought the idea of making up new names was asinine. They tended to whisper and giggle and scoff a lot when Fletcher was around. But Fletcher had long ago decided he wouldn't let the resident Negative Nancys rain on his parade.

Megan was still a bit of a mystery to Fletcher, her eyes revealing nothing behind those Coke-bottle glasses. He cringed at the thought of her standing guard outside his suite, knowing the visitors that came and went. But Beth had promised her discretion. And Fletcher trusted Beth with all his heart.

"What season are you on?" asked Fletcher, giving cordiality a try.

"Oh," said Arlene, "we're on the one where this pathetic dude abuses his position and sleeps with a bunch of strangers."

"What?" Fletcher choked on his own esophagus.

"Yeah," said Amanda. "A real piece of work."

Arlene and Amanda both grinned in a way that nearly cracked Fletcher's skull.

"But—how—"

"We just watched the part where he tried to hook up with one of the girls he lives with," said Arlene. She put her hands behind her head nonchalantly, and the muscles in her arms flexed. Fletcher thought how easily she could beat the shit out of him.

"Just shoves his tongue down her throat," said Amanda, playing with a strand of blonde hair. "Poor girl."

Fletcher's mouth hung open like an idiot. His cheeks flushed nearly purple. He tried to remind himself: *Who cares.* And: *Whatever.* And: *They don't matter.* Besides, hadn't he decided he wouldn't worry about his local reputation anymore?

But he hated the idea of all his hospitalmates talking about him behind his back—discussing his new pastimes, expressing their disappointment, maybe even laughing at him. This was none of their business.

Fletcher's depression and irritability were still at the surface, and that made for a volatile cocktail.

"You," he almost-snarled to Megan. She lifted her head to look at him, as if he was an interesting bird in a tree. "How could you?"

"Excuse me?" she said.

"You're a liar." Now it was a snarl. "You aren't supposed to tell anyone what happens up there. That's what Beth said. You're a lying, untrustworthy—"

"Megan didn't say anything," said Arlene. A smile tugged at her mouth.

Fletcher cocked his head to the side.

"Shannon did," she said.

"What?" said Fletcher.

"Shannon," said Arlene. "You know, the girl you threw yourself on?"

"Yep," said Megan.

"You know," said Amanda, "the beautiful, amazing girl you actually thought would, for some reason, want *you*."

"You know," said Arlene, "the girl that's way out of your league. Even if you are the *undisputed king of the galaxy*."

Arlene and Amanda laughed. Megan just watched him with a detached, contented look on her face.

Fletcher stared at the floor. He wanted to disappear, but when you mix anger and pride you get a sort of paralysis. But he'd think of something good to say. He was still ... whatever he was. First, though, a question: "How did you learn about, well, the others? The visitors?"

"Oh, please," said Amanda. "This place is desperate for excitement. You think people can come and go without us noticing?"

Fletcher supposed he may have been a little naively optimistic about the secrecy of the operation. The visitors likely told whoever met them at the door they were there for him, didn't they? Before they were brought to Beth? That would have to spark curiosity.

"And when I say people," said Amanda, "I mean all your bitches."

They laughed again.

"Big Daddy Fletcher."

"The funniest thing to me," said Arlene, "is that you truly feel that way, don't you? Like Mr. Ladies' Man. Like, just because you have zero competition, that means every woman wants you. By process of elimination or whatnot."

"Yeah, like we're all waiting for our turn," said Amanda, "to join you on a journey to the highest heights of passion and pleasure."

"Ooh, those fragile bony arms wrapped around me," said Arlene. "Running my hands through your greasy hair."

"You do have competition, by the way," said Amanda. "It's called a vibrator."

"And it lasts longer than forty-five seconds." Arlene and Amanda cackled while Megan smiled quietly.

"And, actually, it's just as fertile as you are," said Amanda.

"Has just as much of a chance of saving the human race," added Arlene.

"Maybe it should get the big fancy suite instead," offered Amanda. "At least a vibrator won't start thinking it's God's gift to the world."

"It's not—" Fletcher felt like he was shrinking and shrinking. "Hey, I don't—"

"Oh, I'm sorry," said Amanda. "Are we making you uncomfortable?"

"God, you really are pathetic," said Arlene.

Suddenly Fletcher was back in middle school. He was in the cafeteria playing *Magic: The Gathering* with his friends when a group of skaters started mooing like cows, and then tossed an open milk carton into the middle of the table, spraying milk all over them and their cards. Fletcher had to wipe it off his glasses.

"Wait," said Amanda, "so, you're fine going through woman after woman and tossing them back onto the streets, but when we bring it up you get all squirmy?"

Fletcher was back in high school. He was late to an assembly in the gym and took the first open seat in the bleachers, which, terrifyingly, was next to Erin Hendrix. He said hi to her, and she said hi back, and they made small talk, which was noteworthy enough on its own. But then something hit Fletcher in the back of the head. It was a piece of crumpled-up paper. He unfolded it to read: "Ask her out!" His skin burned. Another one hit him. This one read: "I think she likes you!" Then another: "Kiss her!!!" Finally, Fletcher turned around. A group of baseball players—Erin's friends—stood and cheered. "Kiss her! Kiss her! Kiss her!" they chanted. Erin apologized for them, but it was too late for that. He got up and left the building, to a chorus of boos from the baseball team.

"Oh, are we making you mad?" asked Amanda in her best baby voice.

But Fletcher was in his bedroom at his parents' house, staring at his phone watching the comments unspool under the photo some asshole posted of him at the beach—the photo that gave him the nickname Skeletor. The comments, the comments, all the comments.

"What, you gonna tell Beth and Dr. Reid that you want us out of here?" asked Arlene. "Have your mommies kick us out?"

"Ha, I wouldn't doubt it," said Amanda. "You big tough man, you."

Fletcher was hardly listening anymore. A horrifying realization had crept out of the shadows: You could reskin the world, he thought, swap out its parts, paint all the pieces, but it never really changed. On a long enough timeline, everything regressed back to the mean. Take any path you wanted—they all wrapped around and brought you back to the shitty place where you belonged. Things were what they were and that's what they'd always be.

This was who Fletcher would always be.

Fletcher couldn't take it anymore. He turned and walked, then ran, back down the hallway. He could hear their laughter behind him, hunting him, haunting him. He ran past the elevators to the stairs, leaping up two steps at a time to the fifth floor. He swung open the door and locked it behind him.

Fletcher flung himself onto the couch and buried his face in the soft cushions. He screamed a muffled yell into the leather. He flipped himself around, sitting up, and stared out the window. He could see his own reflection, and it was the reflection of a skinny little boy—not a hero, not a king, not even a real man. It sure as hell wasn't Odin, King of the World. It was just Fletcher: a scared, pathetic little twerp—the same one he'd always been.

Fletcher felt like a kid in a toy castle playing fantasy with his parents, finally realizing that none of it was real—watching his parents leaving again and again to go take care of real-life things like cooking dinner and answering the phone, then coming back and picking up their toy sword again. Everyone was just humoring him.

No, Fletcher was no chosen one. He was just the period at the end of humankind's last sentence—the tiny, insignificant dot that meant it was finally all over.

Fletcher put his face in his hands and cried—a messy, shaky, loud and wet thing. He cried for what felt like hours. That big snowball of anger had melted and all that remained was a giant puddle, and that puddle looked like misery.

That's what's left when anger melts. Big, sad puddles.

In his puddly state, he realized he was sick and tired of it all: the toy castle he created; getting what he wanted all the time and never enjoying it as much as he'd thought he would; his fast courtships; the slow afternoons that meant nothing; the way Beth looked at him when he asked for more, more, more; the way the girls would look at him when Beth told them it was time to go; the way people changed when he walked in the room; the bland food; the bland conversations; the bland days; the drunkenness; the hangovers; the way he'd glimpse the truth of who he was, or who he'd become, out of the corner of his eye but would never look directly at it, like believing that the monster in the closet would go away if you only ignored it.

It all sucked.

He closed his eyes. And there: Jordan.

He hadn't realized—until that second—how devastatingly lonely he was.

The loneliest man in the world, he thought, smiling sadly.

He saw the irony of it all. He almost wanted to laugh. If young Fletcher could see him now.

It was night, and the hospital was sleeping. As if under some kind of hypnosis, some compulsion, Fletcher left his suite and walked down the stairs to the fourth floor, the living quarters for the non-Fletchers. All the doors were closed. He walked silently until he stood in front of Room 4031.

He pushed open the door to his old home. It was just as he left it. He sat on the stiff brown couch for a moment before dropping to the floor on his hands and knees and reaching around under the couch.

He pulled out the origami flower he had made for Jordan all those months ago. It was limp and unfolding, wilting like an actual flower. It was covered in dust, too. He could barely read it: "To: Jordan" on one petal, and "From: Fletcher" on another.

And there: Jordan.

He remembered a conversation he had had with her in that very room.

She had been talking excitedly about what would happen when they solved Delilah. The explosion of art and music that would arise. The second Renaissance.

"Man," he had said, "you sure got some high hopes for our diseased little world."

"Our diseased little world hasn't stopped amazing me yet," she had said.

Eons later, in that same room, with Jordan wherever she was, Fletcher missed that optimism more than ever. She had been a constant positive charge of energy. Now his battery was drained.

He put the flower in a dresser drawer and slept on that stiff brown couch that night. He slept for hours and hours, a dreamless coma. In the morning, he snuck back to his suite.

He holed himself up on the fifth floor for the next day, the next week, the next however-long, all of it blending together and melting into that puddle he was now living in, that dark, damp, timeless depression. He came out only when he had to—mainly food and medical tests.

This will all be over soon.

But Fletcher knew that, in this instance, those words simply weren't true. This would not be over soon. Or ever, maybe. He had made his puddle and he'd have to lie in it, face-first, until ... he didn't know.

Fletcher tried and failed to imagine a world in which he could undo everything he'd done.

He told Beth that he wanted no more guests of any kind. That, in fact, he wanted no more of anything. He just wanted to be alone. Forever.

As always, Beth obliged.

"I'm sorry," he said as she turned to walk away, "for everything."

"I know you are," she said.

This time he could read her expression, and it broke his heart.

Fletcher reduced his life to a brooding sort of nothingness. He'd slog through the day, eat dinner in his room, then bathe in a swamp of self-loathing until he fell asleep. This is how Fletcher lived until he was finally forced to live another way. This is how he lived, for a few weeks, until he woke in the middle of the night to find the world he knew being ripped away. To find he was leaving the hospital, and would likely never see it again.

Chapter 21

Fletcher woke with immediate resentment. Something had pulled him from a deep sleep, a sweet sleep, a mercifully dreamless sleep where he wasn't Odin, where he wasn't even Fletcher. Where he was just nothing.

Tap, tap, tap.

Fletcher opened his eyes with a groan, and then shrieked.

There, standing above his bed, was a giant woman he didn't recognize. She wore pink harem pants, like Aladdin, and a pink T-shirt. She also wore a black ski mask. She also held a handgun.

"Good morning!" she said. She was enormous, the ski mask stretching tightly over her huge head.

"What the—" Fletcher scooted back against the wall, as if he could push his way through.

"No time to explain!" she said. "You'll thank us later. Now, sorry about this, but it's for your own good." The Giant grabbed Fletcher and flipped him over as easy as making a sandwich. Before he knew it, his hands were zip-tied behind his back. "It'll all make sense," she said. "Don't be scared, now."

The Giant set something on Fletcher's nightstand and led him into the hallway. He wanted to scream for help, but his tongue had turned into a piece of dried fruit. He wanted to kick and run, but his legs were useless, empty trash bags. So, down the stairs they went, without a peep, and into the lobby.

It wouldn't have mattered if he screamed or ran. He saw that now.

Every woman who lived at the hospital was in the lobby. They were huddled up together in their sweatpants and pajamas, zip-tied just like Fletcher, looking as bewildered as he felt. There were two strangers, too.

The strangers wore the same pink harem pants as the Giant.

They also had matching black ski masks.

They also had guns.

Fletcher wanted to say something to the other captives, or their captors, but no words came to him. So he was led, silent and docile, like a sheep to slaughter.

He wondered what happened to Beth's security protocol. The 24-hour shift schedule. The two women on guard at all times. The siren-equipped bullhorn.

"Look who it is!" said one of the armed women in pink, as if her best friend had just walked into the party. She was half the size of the first, with enormous blue eyes nearly bulging out of her mask.

"Well, well, well," said the third. She was almost as tall as the Giant, but built like an Olympic athlete.

"Thank you all for your cooperation," said the Giant. "And sorry to wake you like this."

"Hope we didn't ruin any good dreams," said Big Eyes, with a strange sincerity. "I hate when that happens."

"You can't take him," said Dr. Reid. "We need him. To save the *human race*, goddamn it."

"Samesies," said Big Eyes.

"Yeah, sorry," said the Giant. "But we have to."

"Wifemother says," nodded Big Eyes.

A few of the Palm Springs women cried softly, but nobody else spoke.

"Okay," said the Giant. She turned to Fletcher's captive hospitalmates. "So, here's the deal: I put a knife in this young man's room. On his nightstand. With that knife, you'll be able to cut each other's zip ties. Another inconvenience, I know, but we need it to take some time, you see? And please don't come looking for us. We really don't want to hurt anyone, as I hope we have shown."

"Totally," said Big Eyes. "We're nice."

"Okay." The Giant turned to her gang. "Let's do it."

Fletcher looked once more at the women he'd shared this home with for so long. He wished he hadn't.

What he saw were various masks that would be burned into Fletcher's memory forever. Fear. Sorrow. Pity. Worst of all: relief.

Beth's was blank at first glance, but Fletcher thought he saw some-thing hiding underneath all that emptiness, all those rigid lines. He wasn't sure, but thought—hoped—that it might have been something like forgiveness.

·········

Fletcher was led into the parking garage, where a bright yellow Chevy Bolt awaited like the least suspecting kidnapping vehicle. It looked like a literal lemon. As they walked toward it, their sweeping flashlights landed on Big Nurse.

"Whoazer," said Big Eyes.

The Olympian looked at the Giant. "I mean, should we...?"

Fletcher felt a brief pang of panic, or maybe longing, or maybe regret. Big Nurse wasn't made for these strangers. It was made for a noble cause. Like Jordan and him mowing down a horde of zombies, or at least riding off into the sunset together. Not this.

"No," said the Giant. "Let's just get out of here."

They opened the back door to the Bolt and Fletcher crawled in. The Olympian buckled him up and sat next to him. Big Eyes sat up front. The Giant sat in the driver's seat.

The Giant barely fit, the seat seeming to groan and compress under-neath her. It reminded him of a circus bear riding a tiny bicycle. Then, with a quick, warm wave of nostalgia, it reminded him of something else. That day, nearly a whole year ago, when Dr. Gomez drove him away from his family home in Rancho Bernardo. She'd hardly fit in the front seat of that Nissan Leaf, too. He wondered what she'd say to him right now. He wondered what she would have said to him these last few months. God, maybe things would have been different. Sometimes a boy just needs a mother, whether it's his or not. Whether she's actually even a mom or not.

He wondered what his real mom would say to him right now, too. What she'd think of what he'd done, who he'd become. The shame tore him apart. He missed her greatly. And then, he began to sob.

This will all be over soon.

"Oh, no," said the Olympian. "It's okay, honey."

"Oh, pickles," said Big Eyes. "We scared him. It's probably these guns. Gosh, I'm scared of guns, too." She looked the pistol in her own hand and dropped it into the center console like a dirty diaper.

As Fletcher composed himself, the Giant turned herself around. "Hey, sorry about this, but we're not supposed to let you see where we're going." She pulled out a long strip of black cotton and her beady eyes crinkled up in what may have been an apologetic smile. "And we're kind of in a hurry."

"Why?" whimpered Fletcher, his first words in a long, long time. "What can't I know?"

"Think of it as a surprise!" said Big Eyes. "Surprises are fun."

The Olympian wrapped the blindfold around Fletcher's eyes.

They rolled out of the parking garage and into the world from which Fletcher had been hidden for so long, and which was now hidden from Fletcher. He waited for the rumble of Big Nurse, of his hospitalmates coming after him.

"Can we take these itchy masks off yet?" asked Big Eyes.

"Oh," said the Giant. "Yeah, sure, I guess. Why not."

"Thank God," said the Olympian.

"What are you doing with me?" Fletcher asked, shock hardening into panic. He suddenly wanted to puke. "Where are we going? Who are you? What are you going to do to me?"

"Oh, you just relax, mister man," said Big Eyes. Her voice was like cotton candy, bouncing with giddy excitement. "We're just taking you to—"

"Hey!" shouted the Olympian. Fletcher could hear her slap the back of Big Eyes' seat.

"Ugh!" said Big Eyes. "My bad. I'm just so fudgin' excited!"

"Really sorry for the zip ties," said the Giant warmly. "And the blindfold. But really, I swear, you're not a prisoner. Far from it, actually. They're for your own good. You'll understand everything soon."

Fletcher grunted and tested the zip ties. They didn't budge.

"We'll take them off when we get to where we're going," the Giant said.

"Where are we going?" asked Fletcher again.

"To fulfill your destiny."

"My what?"

"You'll understand everything soon."

They drove a few minutes until curiosity got the better of Fletcher. "How did you break in?" he asked. "Weren't there people on watch when you showed up? Like, security?"

"Uh, well, there were two women awake in the lobby," said the Olympian. "I think they were on watch. But they weren't really ... on guard."

"They were playing War," said Big Eyes. "I love that game."

Cool, Fletcher thought. So the system had just decayed. Like everything else in the hospital. Like everything else in the world. He could picture, say, Krishna and Serena (once known as Xena and Bobina) sitting there, playing cards, and suddenly finding themselves with three guns pointed at them. That would have been that. So much for bullhorns with alarms. So much for handguns hidden in planters. So much for firearm lessons. So much for kickboxing classes.

The electric car hummed along for an hour or so, Fletcher keeping silent and the women mostly so. There were no sounds of other cars, and definitely no souped-up apocalypse-mobile coming to the rescue. Finally, they pulled off the main road, slowed, and then stopped.

They opened the door and led him out.

A bird—a seagull, maybe—cried loudly nearby, then flapped its wings and took off. Oh, how Fletcher envied that bird.

PART IV
THE ONE FATHER

Chapter 22

Fletcher went to summer camp when he was twelve. This was the age when things got especially shitty for some of the adolescent sub-species—when the natural order began to take form, when the hierarchy of cool kids and losers solidified. This was the time when to stand out from the herd was to get eaten by a lion.

For Fletcher, this was also the time when his mom decided he needed to make some friends. (His only friend was Simon, and they had yet to meet the rest of their little coterie.) Meanwhile, Fletcher's dad thought it would be good for him to learn some outdoorsy skills. Summer camp was the middle of his parents' Venn diagram.

Simon had been supposed to go, too, but he had convinced his pushover parents to let him skip, leaving Fletcher in the trenches by himself.

So, Fletcher found himself at Camp Ponderosa, living in a cabin on a lake somewhere in Central California. The camp caste system developed quickly, with the rich kids, the jocks and the punky skater kids rising to the top—always taking their shirts off, playing loud games of basketball, laughing too much and talking to girls. Meanwhile, the outcasts began to understand their place in the pecking order, hanging out by the tetherball court or playing board games on the picnic tables in the corner of the camp's main gathering area.

Fletcher had quickly found himself in the picnic table group, which was fine. He knew where he belonged well before many of the kids. He didn't much like summer camp, but it had been tolerable until Wednesday.

Wednesday was a lake day. Fletcher liked lake days, except that he had to reveal his skeletal physique. But the water was nice. On this particular day, Fletcher's counselor took him and his cabinmates out on a rowboat with some water balloons, prepared to lay siege to a rowboat full of female campers.

Fletcher had been crushingly nervous for such a mandatory interaction with the opposite sex—in bathing suits, nonetheless, which was a big deal even at twelve. So nervous, in fact, that he hadn't realized he had to pee beforehand. It had been a fight-or-flight situation, and all attention to his bladder had been suppressed. He realized it soon enough, though, once they were out on the water. With every row of the oar, their boat got one stride closer to the girls and one stride farther away from the restroom on the shore. He could feel his bladder slowly expand. He began clenching his muscles, focusing his brain on not peeing. Soon it became unbearable and the world grew fuzzy around him. But he told himself that peeing would not be an option, that he simply could not. He would not. He absolutely would not.

But his urethral sphincter didn't care.

And so he peed. Right there, in the boat, surrounded by cool kids: Fletcher peed his bathing suit.

The cool kids howled like jackals as they looked at the skinny kid in the bright blue trunks with the big dark crotch. They asked how he could possibly pee his pants when he was surrounded by a giant toilet. They laughed and laughed. Careful not to touch the pee, the boys grabbed Fletcher's limbs and threw him in the water, yelling at the girls that Fletcher was their secret weapon, better than any water balloon. Fletcher was their pee bomb.

Fletcher wanted to sink and be forgotten.

But he floated. He surfaced. To make matters worse, Fletcher couldn't climb back in the boys' rowboat. The girls' boat, however, had a small ladder on the back. Although he'd have rather drowned, he was instructed to swim to the girls' boat and climb in, his suit sopping wet and recently pissed in.

He might as well have been tarred and feathered, or been a leper, or been given a big scarlet "P" for pants-pisser. He sniveled and sobbed in the boat as the girls reminded him how gross he was. He sniveled and sobbed on the phone when he begged his mom to pick him up. She told him that he had to stay.

"This will all be over soon, honey," she had said.

·········

A decade later, Fletcher once again found himself in a boat wishing he were anywhere else.

When the blindfold was finally removed, this is what he saw: a bright blue sky, straight above him, with a big white triangle in the middle. He was on his back on the deck of a sailboat, bobbing up and down.

The return of sight brought a return of reality. His heart clenched and his whole body began to sweat, as if the faucets leading to all his pores had been cranked open at once. Panic swelled and he felt as if his veins were going to explode.

This will all be over soon.

He sat up with a spasm. "Where am I?" he whimpered. He looked around. All he saw was the candy blue of the sky stacked on top of the steel blue of the ocean, in every direction.

The three women looked at him, their masks removed, their faces jolly and good-natured.

The Giant was in her forties, giant in every way, with a chubby face and dirty blonde hair. She looked like a 300-pound toddler, pink marbled skin and all.

Big Eyes had frizzy brown hair, and she seemed to be peeling open those enormous blue eyes as wide as she could, as if everything around her was blowing her mind. She looked to be in her young thirties.

The Olympian was right in the middle of the first two, size-wise and age-wise. She had the caramel skin of someone from Brazil, or some other beautiful place in the Southern Hemisphere. Fletcher decided beach volleyball was her likely Olympic sport.

The three women smiled down at Fletcher, as if he was their precious little baby and not their prisoner.

"Welcome to the party!" said Big Eyes. She had one hand on the wooden tiller, steering the boat.

"Don't worry, we'll take those zip ties off very soon," said the Giant, grinning sweetly, looking as though she had marshmallows in her cheeks.

The Brazilian Olympian nodded. "Just kick back and relax. We'll be there before you know it."

Fletcher tried to laugh, but it sounded more like a choked cough. *Relax?* No, there would be no relaxing, but he remained silent, staring at his sneakers. The three women kept stealing glances at him and exchanging excited whispers.

"Hey, don't miss the pretty view, silly," said Big Eyes.

Fletcher looked up, and off to the port side he saw an island. Rock cliffs climbed out of the water, while treacherous pirate caves disappeared and reappeared with each swelling wave. As they moved slowly across the sea, the jagged stone faces eventually turned into a stretch of soft beach. The hills behind were green and brown and looked uninhabited. It may as well have been Isla Nublar. As they turned the corner and revealed more of the coast, he finally saw a building on the end of a point. It was a strange, foreign-looking edifice—a giant, circular, white structure with a red roof. It looked almost identical to Jabba the Hutt's palace. Fletcher felt like he recognized it from somewhere, but he couldn't place it. As they continued to cruise, Big Eyes pulling on a line to tighten the mainsail, Fletcher saw that the point he was looking at—with Jabba's palace—was the far side of a hidden bay. As the bay came into view, so did a small town on its shore. He watched the distant city, helpless, knowing that a scream would never reach land and that it was unlikely anyone was there to hear it anyway.

They sailed past the odd island town, following the coast north until the buildings disappeared behind them. A while later, the Giant said a couple of sailing terms that Fletcher didn't understand. Apparently, they were jibing. The mainsail was suddenly released with a flutter as Big Eyes pulled the tiller toward herself. The boat turned to face the island and the wind filled the now-open sail again, propelling them toward land.

Fletcher couldn't imagine what their target was. All he saw was rock and wilderness. As their small sailboat approached land, however, he finally saw a little wooden dock. On that dock were three more women, dressed in the same pink getups as his jovial captors. The girls on the dock shouted with glee as the boat pulled up.

"It's him!" one squeaked. "It's really him!"

"I can't believe you found him!" said another.

The girls helped Fletcher off the boat and onto the landing. He looked around, bewildered.

"Everything is going to be fine," said the Olympian, sensing Fletcher's panic. "You're not in any danger."

"In fact," said the Giant, overhearing, "you're right where you need to be."

"Okay," said Fletcher, not okay.

"Here, let's untie you," she said. "You're home, now."

The Olympian unfolded a pocketknife and freed Fletcher's wrists. He rubbed them gingerly.

"Now," said the Giant. "Please don't try to run away. We're friends. More than friends, in fact."

The pink brigade led Fletcher away from the dock and along the beach for a minute, finally turning to hike up a trail that disappeared into the hill. The girls who had met him at the dock kept saying things like "She said you'd come!" and "You took your time, didn't you?" and "I can't believe you're finally here!" Fletcher couldn't believe he was there, either—wherever he was. They continued up the trail, the forest thick and enveloping, until the girls leading the troupe stopped. A flat clearing revealed itself, out of nowhere, as if they'd stumbled upon the home of some enchanted woodland witch.

They had arrived.

Chapter 23

"Welcome home," said the Olympian.

Fletcher looked around at what that meant.

The clearing was about half the size of his old high school cafeteria—mostly dirt, with patches of stringy-looking grass, and almost perfectly flat. This open space was perched on an epic cliff, surrounded on three sides by dense forest and a beautiful view of the ocean on the fourth. Organized in staggered circles around the clearing were a dozen or so big, rectangular canvas tents, the heavy-duty kind in which you could imagine a Civil War general poring over his maps. In the middle of the tent circle was an open area with a massive bonfire pit as the centerpiece. The place looked as though it might have once been some sort of upscale campground.

It also looked like a cult commune.

As if summoned by an invisible bell, they emerged: one by one, from the mouths of various tents, women materialized left and right. Each woman wore the same pink harem pants and pink T-shirts as Fletcher's sailing crew. There were young women, all in pink. There were old women, all in pink. There were skinny women, fat women, women of all races, heights and hairstyles—all in pink. They birthed from their tent flaps and floated toward Fletcher like pink moths drawn to a porch light, joyous and unnerving smiles stretched across their faces.

The Giant stopped the crowd before it could swallow Fletcher whole. She stepped in front of him and put her plump hand up, like a bodyguard addressing the paparazzi. "I know we're all excited," she said, "but the One Father has had a long day—and you'll all meet him tonight at the Hearth. Come on now, let us through."

A few women groaned in earnest disappointment as the pink sea parted for the Giant and Fletcher. The large woman led the skinny boy to one of the tents in the inside of the circle.

"This guy is yours," she said, opening the flap door and stepping inside.

It was not quite his fifth-floor hospital suite. In fact, it was not much of anything. The only furnishings were a small cot and a wooden crate next to it, acting as a bedside table.

The Giant looked at Fletcher, her small, friendly eyes squinting through her swollen face. "I'm sorry, buddy," she said. "I know it's been a big day. But it will all make sense soon."

"Who are you people?" Fletcher asked.

"Whoa, wait—did I not introduce myself?" She put her hands on her hips in disappointment. "My bad. I'm Shelly."

"I'm Fletcher," he said, shrugging.

Just then, Big Eyes and the Olympian came in.

"This," said Shelly, gesturing toward the Olympian, "is Isabella."

Isabella smiled and handed him a silver mixing bowl. Fletcher examined it.

"Your chamber pot," said Isabella.

Fletcher quickly set it down next to the crate.

"And that," said Shelly, nodding toward Big Eyes, "is Margot."

Margot was holding something behind her back and smiling with giddy enthusiasm.

"Ohhhh, we've been waiting to give you these!" said Margot, her voice bubbly and bouncing. "And, well ... here you are." She presented the hidden object to Fletcher with the flourish of a court jester's bow. The gift was a pair of blue harem pants and a blue T-shirt.

"Your new outfit," explained Shelly. She looked at Margot—who was now holding the clothes out like an offering, head lowered—and sighed.

"Okay," said Fletcher, furrowing his brow.

"I'm sure you're beat," said Shelly. "We're gonna let you rest. Don't worry, we'll explain everything soon."

Fletcher needed 'soon' to come quickly.

"Oh," said Shelly, "and she's gonna come by in a bit. Maybe put your regalia on?"

"Who's gonna come by?" said Fletcher. "What's a regalia?"

"You're holding it," said Shelly.

"Holding what?"

"Your regalia," said Shelly.

Fletcher looked at the blue pile in his arms as the girls turned to leave. "But who's coming by?" he asked.

"The Wifemother," said Shelly, turning with a chipmunk smile before shutting the canvas flap behind her.

··········

Back in his tent, Fletcher assessed his situation. He was on an island—that much he knew. Well, he supposed he couldn't even be sure about that. All he *really* knew was he got here by boat. Then, there were his new neighbors. What did he know about them? Well, they all wore pink and lived together in this little commune. That was weird. He had to admit, though: the ones he'd met didn't seem too threatening—at least, not for people who had somehow kidnapped him and tied him up. He examined his new room: canvas floor, canvas walls, canvas roof. The small military-looking cot creaked when he sat on it, and he could feel the individual springs stabbing his backside. His blue uniform sat folded up and neatly stacked on the white sheets. The wooden crate next to his bed had the words "Peter's Produce" stamped onto the side. Then there was the silver mixing bowl, which, apparently, was where he was to do his business.

And that was it. Canvas tent, creaky bed, blue costume, wooden crate, piss bowl.

Fletcher could discern very little about his current situation, but the most troubling and confusing part was trying to figure out his role. He saw an image of being tied to a stick and held over the giant bonfire like a suckling pig, to the delight of a crowd of hungry women wearing pink.

He didn't want to be dinner, so he decided to see if escape would be easy.

Fletcher slowly lifted the flap door to his tent and poked his head out. There, six inches in front of his face, were two legs in pink pants. He looked up and saw that they belonged to a person. And that person was looking down at him.

"Hello there," said Isabella.

Fletcher didn't say anything.

"You're supposed to be resting," she said.

"Just wanted to take a look," muttered Fletcher, slinking back into the tent.

So, his tent was guarded. Whether to prevent him from leaving or others from coming in, he didn't know. He sat and waited for whatever would happen next. He thought about the days at the hospital when things had been good, before he had gone and screwed everything up. He thought about sitting with Jordan, talking about Descartes, or pizza toppings or the ending of *Lost.* He wondered what she was doing now, and desperately hoped she was safe.

Then he thought about the last few months and flushed with shame. The kind of embarrassment that hits when you're all alone is a unique and rare and deep kind.

It can be hard to know you're a monster until you step out of your cave. Now that Fletcher was outside the hospital walls, he could see clear as day the scales and fangs and horns that had grown over those last few months.

Yes, woe was Fletcher. Poor, poor Fletcher, with all his self-inflicted sorrow and remorse.

Eventually poor, poor Fletcher's self-reflection was interrupted by nature. He glanced at the silver pot, then walked back to the door and whispered through the canvas flap. "Hey ... I have to use the restroom."

"What do you think the chamber pot is for?" Isabella replied cheerfully.

Fletcher sighed.

Peeing in a metal pot was not easy. There was a lot of spray-back, so the aim needed to be just right. Fletcher was on his knees, to make the pee distance shorter, and was mid-stream when the flap opened.

"Criminy!" shouted Margot, theatrically burying her eyes in the crook of her elbow and turning away from the scene. She was holding a large plastic tray that almost went flying. Fletcher hurried to zip up his jeans, turning bright red.

"I'm so sorry," said Margot. "Oh, cheese and rice, I'm so sorry."

"It's okay." Fletcher exhaled. "You didn't mean to."

"That's the thing," said Margot. "I do stupid things all the time, but I never mean to. Just how I am, I guess."

"I do stupid things, too," said Fletcher. It was difficult to remember that he was the victim in this relationship. That Margot was his captor.

"Are you the Wifemother?" asked Fletcher.

Margot burst out laughing—a dorky, nasally, snorty laugh. "Oh, gosh, that's good," she said. "Yeah, that's rich right there. Ha!"

"Okay."

"Here," said Margot, still glowing from Fletcher's good joke. "Take a seat."

Fletcher sat on the bed as Margot moved the wooden produce crate toward him with her foot. She set the plastic tray on top, in front of Fletcher. The tray held a plate with quite an odd array of foods. In the middle of the plate were three raw oysters, surrounded by a few cloves of garlic, a pile of broccoli that Fletcher could tell was from a can and a handful of walnuts. Next to the plate on the tray was a single pill capsule and a can of apple-banana juice.

"Thank you," Fletcher managed to say.

"No problemo," said Margot, taking a seat next to him. Fletcher continued studying the chef's special. "We've been stocking up on all this stuff in hopes that we found you."

"Well," said Fletcher, "you found me."

"We sure did!" said Margot. "I'm just glad we didn't waste too much food on the *imposter*. So, don't worry—there's plenty for you."

"The imposter?" asked Fletcher.

"Oh, crackers," she said. "Forget I said anything."

"What imposter?"

"Maybe ask the Wifemother about it?" said Margot, wincing. "That's above my paygrade."

"What happened to this imposter guy?" asked Fletcher, his eyes narrowing.

"Hey, am I sitting too close?" asked Margot. "People tell me I sit too close sometimes."

"You're fine," said Fletcher. "But the—"

"Oh, good," she said. "I wonder how close *is* too close? I worry about that, you know? I'm what—eighteen inches away? If I scoot an inch closer, is that still okay?"

She shifted her butt an inch closer.

"I dunno," said Fletcher. "It's still fine, but—"

"So then, what about another?" She shifted again. "You see the problem, right? Where's the line? It would be nice just to know where—"

"Hey, hold up," said Fletcher. "Can you tell me something? Where am I? What am I doing here?"

"Hey now," she said. "I'm keeping my big ol' mouth shut. I talk too much. Everyone says that. Plus, the Wifemother will explain everything. Better than I can, too, that's for sure."

"Who is this Wifemother?" asked Fletcher.

"Don't you worry, mister," she said. "You'll understand everything real soon."

"You guys keep saying that," said Fletcher. "Give me something. How did I get here? Why did you guys kidnap me?"

"Kidnap?" snorted Margot. "We didn't kidnap you! We *rescued* you. We brought you home to fulfill the whole destiny thing."

"Excuse me?" said Fletcher.

"You think we kidnapped you?" she said. "Boy, that'd be mean. No, we just *retrieved* you." She shook her head. "Psh. Kidnap."

"Margot," said Fletcher, "you held my friends at gunpoint."

"Oh, I know!" she said. "That was scary for me, too. But you gotta do what you gotta do, right?"

Fletcher sighed.

"What kind of people do you think we are?" she asked.

"I have absolutely no idea," said Fletcher.

"You're funny," she said. "Okay, well I'm not supposed to talk about any of this stuff. I should get going."

"Wait," said Fletcher. "Just tell me... what are you guys going to do to me?" He was picturing the Roasted Fletcher dinner party again.

"Relax, silly!" said Margot. "You're in a good place. The Wifemother is gonna come in soon. She'll explain some more stuff."

And just like that, Margot was gone, leaving Fletcher with his tray-full of random foods and a mixing bowl with his own pee in it.

· · · · · • • • • · · · ·

As Fletcher sat alone in his tent, he became more and more anxious to meet this "Wifemother." Anyone known by only a one-word pseudonym meant business. Like Slash. Or Cher. But "Wifemother" had even more punch. Her name was made up of two words that each held a sacred power over most men.

Fletcher didn't have to wait long. When the Wifemother pushed aside the flap to the tent and entered, Fletcher was taken aback. He hadn't known what to expect, but it definitely wasn't this. The Wifemother stood before him: barely five feet tall and a million years old, a miniature skeleton under a film of thin skin.

Fletcher hadn't seen a real-live old person in a while. Old people hadn't fared well in the world Delilah created. The difficulty of procuring food, medicine and other assistance hadn't been kind to the golden agers. The Wifemother had made it, though. She looked very much alive, even in her ancient vessel.

"You're skinnier than I expected," she said. Her voice was gravelly and low, but strong.

"Why were you expecting me?" croaked Fletcher. His sounded high and brittle.

"I'm older than you expected, aren't I?" she said. He didn't say anything, but she very much was. "It's quite alright. I'm older than I expected, too."

She stood eye to eye with Fletcher, who was sitting on the cot, and examined him like an animal at an auction.

"What do you want?" whispered Fletcher.

"Just to meet you," she said. "Before you meet the family. Call me greedy."

"Who are you people?"

"Just what I said, love," she smiled with a mouth full of yellow corn-kernel teeth. "A family."

"But ... from where?" Fletcher asked. "Where am I?"

"Well, we're not from here," she said. "But we're from most everywhere else."

"What?" Fletcher couldn't keep up.

"So," she continued, "who is Fletcher Sinclair?"

"How you know my name?"

"What do you *love*, Fletcher?" she said. "What do you *fear*?"

At that moment, she was the answer to her last question.

"I wonder," she said, "if you actually know why you're here. Deep down, in your soul, I mean: I wonder if you really know."

"I don't think I do," said Fletcher. "But I'd really like to."

"You will," she said. "Tonight."

"I want to know what happened to the other guy, too," he said. "The *imposter*."

"Ah, yes. The imposter," she smiled, distant. "The false prophet. The one who wasn't. Paul was his name once. Paul was quite the disappointment, love. Which is why we're all so pleased that *you* are finally here."

"What happened to him?" He was scared of the answer.

"He died, love," she said. "He had to die, of course. He was not the true One Father."

The room began to swim.

"Can you please tell me what you're all doing here?" he begged.

"We're here to save the world," said the Wifemother. "Just like you are."

Fletcher sighed. "But who... who are you people?"

"We're the chosen few, my dear," she said. "We're the Wives of the One Father."

Chapter 24

Fletcher was left to sit alone in that strange tent on that strange island surrounded by those strange women, with nothing to do but wait and see if his barbecued flanks were on the menu. Is that what happened to Paul? That poor bastard probably once sat on the very same cot Fletcher did.

A while later, Isabella delivered his dinner. It was a complete 180 from the mishmash spread of lunch, which he hadn't touched. On the plate was a piece of fresh, grilled fish—some sort of white fish, probably caught just off the island—and a few pieces of the same canned broccoli that had come with lunch. The fish was a welcome change, and he scarfed it down in spite of the fear that filled most of his belly.

Finally, after some more sitting and some more waiting, Margot came to retrieve him.

"Knock, knock," she said. "You're not peeing, are you?"

"I'm not peeing," Fletcher answered.

Margot pushed aside the flap and stepped in.

"Oh, rat farts," she said, looking at him and sighing and slumping in disappointment. All her actions were dramatic. "You're not even wearing your regalia."

She stepped outside, giving Fletcher a chance to put on his blue costume. He did so, and God, he felt ridiculous—but he supposed fashion was the least of his worries. He rejoined Margot, who beamed at him, and followed her into the middle of the commune. It was now dark, but the giant centerpiece bonfire was roaring. It snapped and popped and Fletcher could not dispel the image of himself on a rotisserie. The fire's glow painted the canvas tents orange.

As Margot led Fletcher toward the blazing spectacle, he saw the other women. They were standing in a large circle around the bonfire, heads bowed. Their pink shirts and pants had been replaced by pink robes with big, pointy hoods, the kind of robe that a High Mage of Stone Deep would wear in *The Odyssey of Zordallus*. Of course, the video game wizards' robes weren't pink. They were a much more respectable dark gray.

As Margot and Fletcher approached the circle, the pink-robed women tried their best not to look, but heads kept popping up one by one like a nightmarish whack-a-mole, each trying to steal a glance at Fletcher. Margot led her esteemed guest to a break in the circle that had been saved for them. When there was a lull in the flames, Fletcher could see that he stood directly across from the smallest robe of the bunch—a five-foot, child-sized woman. He saw glimpses of the Wifemother's face as the fire sent light dancing sporadically around the circle.

"Welcome!" said a voice that Fletcher swore he recognized, but couldn't place. "We've been waiting a long time for you."

"The High Priestess means you," Margot whispered.

Fletcher dug deep for strength. He refused to let whatever was going to happen to him just happen.

A real man would stand up for himself.

"What am I doing here?" he demanded of the circle, his voice only slightly shaky.

"Everything will be explained," said the voice that belonged to the High Priestess. The voice was weird—dramatic, orotund, an octave too low. It sounded like someone giving their best impression of a news anchor.

"Whatever you're going to do to me," Fletcher spoke to the fire, "know that ... know that I'm a good guy and I don't mean any harm."

"Of course you are a *good guy*," said the High Priestess. "You're the One Father."

The voice came from right behind Fletcher. He turned around to face the High Priestess. She was much bigger than Fletcher and twice the size of the Wifemother. Fletcher looked up at her face—a fat, smiling face with big teeth.

"You're the High Priestess?" Fletcher asked Shelly.

"Am I not priestessy enough for you?" she replied, breaking character for a moment. A couple women chuckled.

"Sisters," Shelly continued, back in her performative High Priestess voice. "The wait is over. The One Father has come home to his wives."

Fletcher's head spun as he tried to follow Shelly, who was walking the outside of the circle, but he kept losing her in the shadows. The inside of his head spun, too. He looked at all the women, faces shrouded by their hoods. He counted twenty-two of them, including Shelly.

"Our patience has paid off," she said. "We were deceived once, but the Lord looked favorably upon our patience and our endurance. And now He has blessed us. Behold: the one true One Father!"

A soft, excited murmur floated around the fire from under the circle of pink hoods.

"Shelly," said Fletcher, almost pleading now. "Er, uh, Grand Priestess..."

"High Priestess," she corrected.

"High Priestess," he said. "Can you please tell me what I'm doing here?"

"Indeed," she said. "It's time you heard the prophecy of the One Father."

There was nodding around the bonfire. This story appeared to be a popular one.

"The prophecy states that God would wipe away all of humankind's men. To burn away the sin that has spread over all of His creation. It states that God would smite all men in His great razing ... all except for one," said Shelly, adding an air of theatrics to her monologue. "A new flood to cleanse the world and a new Noah to rebuild it. A new Genesis and a new Adam to write mankind's next chapter. Upon the twilight of humankind's extinction, this one man would show himself—the man chosen to live, and to save us all. This one man would become the sole father of the Neo-Human race. And he would be known as the One Father. His seed and his alone would help raise humanity from the ashes."

The bonfire popped and snapped in agreement.

"Do you see how special you are now?"

All hoods looked his way. Fletcher didn't say anything. He was done with being special. Besides, he happened to know that his seeds weren't fit to grow anything. He was as fertile as a dining room chair.

"Now," Shelly continued, "we women have a role to play, too. The prophecy also speaks of the women worthy of such a savior. If the One Father carries the spark, these women supply the wood to burn. We have been chosen by God and given the divine responsibility of becoming the mothers of Neo-Humanity in accordance with the prophecy. And we..." she said, pausing for dramatic effect, "shall be known as the Wives of the One Father."

Fletcher looked around at what he could now clearly see was a bona fide cult of bonkers proportions. He couldn't help but think of the Order of the Sacred Dark in *Zordallus*. It was a coven of witches who could give you crazy powers as long as you had something they needed. Otherwise they'd take one of your character's organs in a gruesome ritual. Then you'd have a limited window to find a shaman, fairy princess or wizard, otherwise you'd die. Unfortunately, Fletcher had a feeling this island was low on shamans, fairy princesses and wizards.

The Wifemother beckoned her High Priestess over and whispered in her ear. The High Priestess nodded and walked around the outside of the circle toward Fletcher.

"We welcome you, One Father," said the play-pretend High Priestess. "And we're so happy you're finally here."

Fletcher nodded. It was all he could do.

"Our benevolent Wifemother has asked that you be given a choice. A show of our partnership in this sacred duty we share. Would you like to commence with the first ritual, tonight, at this moment?" The ring of pink hoods nodded and whispered. "Or," Shelly continued, "would you like to rest tonight and commence tomorrow?"

"Rest, please," said Fletcher, without hesitation.

The Wives of the One Father let out a collective, dismayed sigh.

"Now, now," said Shelly. "The One Father needs his strength. He's had a long journey to find us. We'll start our first ritual, right here at the Hearth, tomorrow night."

With that, Fletcher was released. Margot led him back to his tent.

"Sleep tight, One Father," said Margot as Fletcher ducked through the tent entrance. She poked her head in after him. "Hey," she said. "I'm really happy you're here."

"Goodnight, Margot," said Fletcher, shaking his head at the absurdity of it all.

He immediately got into bed and pulled the covers tight, as if it was all a bad dream and the quicker he fell asleep, the quicker he'd wake from it.

He didn't sleep quickly, though. His mind was racing with cults and robes and prophecies and rituals. The Wives of the One Father thought that he was sent by God, or chosen by God. Fletcher had never really thought much about God. He wasn't against the idea, but he wasn't exactly the praying type, either. There had been a lot of talk about God and the end times when Delilah was doing her raping and pillaging of the human race, but even then Fletcher hadn't given religion much thought.

Of course, Jordan had. She had given everything much thought. Fletcher remembered a conversation he had had with Jordan once in his room at the hospital. She had a hypothetical theory—a what-if sort of thing—that all gods and religions came from the same God, and they were all real. Like, Mohammad and Jesus were both real, both sent by the same God, but to different groups of people. It was a sort of test—mankind's purpose, maybe—to figure that out. In Jordan's scenario, our job as humans was to realize that we were the same, brothers and sisters. Fletcher had told her she was crazy.

If he were to be honest, the thought of God *had* crossed Fletcher's mind, briefly, back at the hospital—back when he was perhaps getting a little too big for his britches. He'd considered that it wasn't out of the question that he had been chosen for some reason, some divine purpose. That he was special on a hand-selected-by-God level.

That line of thinking was nothing new to humanity, of course. It was fairly common, if you flipped through the pages of history, for a totally unfit person in a position of power to believe such a thing.

But his thoughts were quite different now. He'd fallen a long way in a short time since the hubris of the hospital—the days of private suites, one-night stands and his own private arcade. Now, sitting in his little tent surrounded by a cult of women on a desert island, his thoughts were very far from that of divine specialness. If there was a God, then really—why *was* he still alive? It seemed astronomically unlikely that he was being rewarded for something. So, was he being punished? Or had he been randomly selected to represent all men in a test of Biblical proportions? Or was he just a fluke—God's little oversight? Whatever he was, he had a feeling that if tomorrow were his judgment day, he'd have a lot of explaining to do.

Chapter 25

THE NEXT MORNING FLETCHER got out of bed and put on his blue outfit like a good boy. Until he figured out how to escape this disturbing new reality, he didn't want to step out of line.

Exhibit A: Paul.

Fletcher then lay on top of his bed sheets and waited for someone to come tell him what would happen next. He didn't have to wait long.

"Good morning, mister!" came a singing, nasally voice at his entrance. "May I come in? Are you decent?"

"Come in," said Fletcher.

Margot's head popped through the flap entrance—curly hair bouncing, apple-sized eyes surveying the room. When she saw that it was safe to enter, the rest of her came crawling through the flap. She was carrying another tray: breakfast.

"Good morning, Mr. One Father, sir." She sounded like a little kid imitating an adult.

"Please just call me Fletcher," he begged. "And good morning, Margot."

"Okay, *Fletcher*," she said. "You hungry?"

Margot held his breakfast tray for him, and he swiveled himself to sit on the edge of the bed, facing her. He took the tray. It was another unexplainable buffet. There was a ball of spinach, all wilted, wet and cold, and a scoop of soggy strawberries. Fletcher realized how much he had taken the hospital's commercial kitchen (especially the freezers) for granted. It was nearly all canned foods here. And really strange ones, at that.

"So..." Fletcher examined a small cup of what he was pretty sure were pumpkin seeds. "What's with the food?"

"What do you mean?" asked Margot, looking a little hurt.

"They're all just ... never mind," he said. "You guys don't have coffee, do you?" Fletcher's body ached for caffeine. He could feel it in his teeth.

"No way, silly," said Margot.

"Okay," said Fletcher. "Hey, I got another question."

"All ears," she said. "Can I sit on your box?"

"Be my guest."

Margot scooted the wooden crate to a proper sitting spot, and plopped down on top of it. Fletcher poked at the food with his fork, as if making sure it was dead.

"Where are we?" he asked, looking up from the ball of spinach he was unraveling.

"I'm *specifically* not allowed to answer that question," said Margot solemnly.

Fletcher sighed. "Okay, well where are you from?"

"Oh, I can answer that one," she said. "I'm from 4147 North Avocado Street in beautiful Irvine, California. United States! Well, wait. No, I'm not *from* there. I'm from Oregon. But that's where I was living before here. Irvine. Where are you from?"

"I'm from Rancho Bernardo," said Fletcher. "Just north of San Diego."

He hadn't thought of home in a long time. Rancho Bernardo was just a trippy suburban dream of another life.

"Oh, that's cool," said Margot. "I love San Diego."

"You go there a lot?" asked Fletcher, yawning.

"Oh, I've never been," said Margot.

Fletcher looked at her, almost saying a bunch of things but choosing none of them. Instead he just closed his eyes.

"Where are the rest of the girls from?" asked Fletcher. "Did you know each other before... uh ... before all this?"

"Oh, no," she said. "Each of us was alone when we were found and taken in. Given a home. By the Wifemother."

"I see," said Fletcher.

"But we're from all over," said Margot. "Let's see. Shelly is from Indio. That's in California. And Isabella, well she grew up in Columbia but was living in Dana Point. Which is in California."

Columbia, not Brazil. Pretty close.

"Let's see," she continued. "Shelly is from Fontana. Which is also—"

"California," finished Fletcher. "Got it."

"Yep! And a lot of the Wives, well..." Her face got dark, dramatic. "A lot of them come from LA."

"Which is in California," said Fletcher.

"It is," she said gravely. "But it's not a place you want to visit. Trust me, LA has gone to heck."

"So I hear," said Fletcher. "I have another question."

"Of course!" Margot's furrowed face lit up, as if she had been physically yanked from whatever terrible Los Angeles memory she was reliving.

"What's with the pink sweat suits? And the pink, uh ... robes?"

"Oh," she said, "you don't like them?"

"No, it's not that," he said. "It's just ... don't you think they're a little—"

"Feminine?" Margot said.

"Well, yeah," said Fletcher, looking at his own blue outfit. "A little on the nose, don't you think?"

"No," said Margot, matter-of-factly. "Us ladies, we wanted to celebrate our femininity. In the same way that a new baby girl is celebrated with pink everything."

"And I get the blue."

"Cuz you're a boy," said Margot.

"Yes, I am."

"The last one," said Margot.

"Far as I know."

"Well, that's why we wanted to wear the pink." Margot slapped her knees in a little rhythm. "To celebrate our girlness and your boyness. 'Cause that's how we're going to fulfill the prophecy."

"Oh, yeah," said Fletcher. "That."

"Can I ask *you* a question?" said Margot.

"Go for it."

"Was it scary?" she asked. "Your journey here?"

"The boat ride?"

"No, silly," said Margot. "Your journey to becoming the One Father. The last man on stinkin' Earth. You must have really thought you were going to die. Since, you know, you didn't know the prophecy at the time. You didn't know who you were yet. You probably thought it was just a matter of time 'til you died, huh?"

"Isn't it?" said Fletcher, proud of his profound answer.

"Well," said Margot, "I hope I don't for a while."

"Same," said Fletcher.

"It would be such a bummer," she said. "I think about that a lot. I'm really not prepared for it."

"Yeah."

"Like, Isabella let me borrow her backup sandals," said Margot. "Because I lost mine. But, see, now I've forgotten where I put hers, too. So, I need to find them. But if I died before I found them, she'd probably never get them back."

Fletcher grunted.

"How embarrassing!" she said. "I'd be buried and she'd be going, hey, that girl had my sandals."

"Yeah."

"That's why I always wear a nice, clean pair of skivvies, too," she said. "If I were to die and whoever is getting me ready to be buried found me in some granny panties, how humiliating would that be?"

"Pretty rough," said Fletcher.

"I'd say." Margot's eyes were somehow bigger than ever. Her hands moved like fireworks as she talked. "I want to be prepared, you know? Last impressions are big."

"I suppose so."

"Think of people's last words," she said.

"Yeah."

"So many people had very silly last words when everyone was dying from the virus," she said. "Part of the virus and all. But what a bummer, right?"

"Definitely a bummer," said Fletcher.

"That's why I always try to think about the last thing I say to people," said Margot. "So, if I die before I see them again, at least I gave them good last words."

"You think about death a lot," said Fletcher.

"Oh, fudge sundaes—I'm talking too much," she said. "I don't mean to be a downer. I'm not a downer, I just think about these things."

"It's all good," said Fletcher. This girl was weird as hell, but at least it passed the time.

"Let's get you some fresh air, huh?" said Margot. "I'll give you a tour."

Fletcher tied his tennis shoes and followed Margot. She showed him the Hearth in the daylight—the clearing in the middle of the commune, with the big bonfire, now dormant, waiting to be woken again by a horde of pink-robed worshippers. She walked him around the inner circle of tents, pointing out who lived in each. If the resident was home, Margot would have her come out and meet Fletcher.

"Welcome, One Father!" each would say. Fletcher would shake their hand and say hello.

On the far side of the commune, opposite the edge of the cliff and beyond the rings of tents, near the forest wall, was the laundry station. A few women washed pink shirts and pants in giant buckets of water, one at a time, pulling from a giant pink pile of cotton. They hung them on a line between two trees at the edge of the clearing, like in the olden days. Fletcher remembered *Little House on the Prairie.* He wondered what Pa would think of all this.

After Fletcher met the washers, he and Margot continued counter-clockwise around the edge of the bluff-top settlement. There was a little shed, which Margot said was the supply room. It looked like it had been there for five hundred years. Outside the shed was a makeshift kitchen under a makeshift roof, made from the nylon sheet of a sail stretched from the shed to two small trees. There was a portable three-burner stove, an electric griddle and even a microwave, all connected to a little generator. A few women approached with cans of spinach, broccoli and strawberries. Fletcher wished, so very badly, that they had been cans of chili. The women hurried into the shack to drop off the food before returning to meet their supposed savior.

The tour of the grounds continued to the social area, where some couches, beanbags and tables had been set up. Shelly, who moonlit as the High Priestess, was sitting on one of the beanbags. She was lounging with an overflowing nonchalance, tree-trunk legs spread wide, head back, like a drunk who had found the softest place to fall. She looked up when Fletcher and Margot approached.

"Ayyyyye," she said. "How's it hangin'?" Her daytime voice was nothing like that strange, formal one she used as High Priestess. It was as if nobody had the heart to tell her they knew Shelly and the High Priestess were the same person.

Fletcher and Margot continued wandering toward the cliff that looked out over the water. At the precipice, Fletcher was hit in the face with an overload of blue. The August sun was high, the sky was clear and the water sparkled like an endless blanket of sapphires. He could see the sailboat that brought him here bobbing in the water far below, tied to the dock. A seagull screeched somewhere in the distance.

Fletcher had a lot to think about: What was going to happen to him? Who were these people really? What was the mysterious ritual? What mistake had Paul made to go from Fletcher's position to a dead one?

He knew there was a good chance he'd end up like Paul. It could happen at any moment. Against his will, he found himself asking whether or not he was prepared. Like Margot and her stupid underpants. If he were to go now, was he wearing his best skivvies, so to speak? He thought about the things he had done at the hospital. He wished he had time to fix them. If you are what you repeatedly do, as Jordan had told him, then he needed time to transform, to make a new habit of goodness.

"Holy cannoli, right?" said Margot, bringing Fletcher back from his rumination on mortality.

"Holy cannoli," Fletcher answered.

"This view doesn't get old, I tell ya," she said.

Shelly belched from the beanbag behind them. Fletcher wasn't sure if it was in response to Margot's comment or born on its own.

The cliff-top view was the end of the tour, and Margot took Fletcher back to his tent.

··········

"Ding-ding!" After a few hours of fruitlessly contemplative solitude, Margot was once again at his entrance.

"Hi, Margot," said Fletcher.

"That's the lunch bell," she explained. "Hope you're hungry!"

"Hmm..." Fletcher said, looking at the tray of the same food he'd had for lunch the day before: oysters, garlic, broccoli and walnuts, along with a mystery pill and a can of apple-banana juice.

"Well, I won't watch you eat," said Margot. "People have told me it's rude when I watch them eat. Although I find it quite interesting to watch, don't you? Everyone has different techniques. You have your shovelers, your bite-planners, your—"

"Hey, Margot?" Fletcher interrupted. "I have to ask."

"Yes?"

"What's with this lunch?" he said.

"You don't like it." Margot, once again, deflated like a balloon.

"No, no, no," said Fletcher. "I'm not saying that. But like, a peanut butter sandwich is a more, uh, traditional lunch. I'm just wondering the thought behind this … *creative* smorgasbord?"

"Oh!" she said. "I forget you're new to all this."

"Very new," said Fletcher.

"We've had this menu planned for you for ages," she said. "So, old news to us. New news to you. Anywho, the oysters—besides from being dee-lish-us—are one of the very best sources of zinc."

She let that sink in for dramatic effect.

"Zinc," repeated Fletcher.

"Yeah, silly. Zinc." She clapped her hands together. "Zinc helps in sperm production, *obviously.*"

Fletcher closed his eyes and sighed.

"And the garlic, of course, helps the little guys swim!" she said. "So does broccoli."

"You don't say." Fletcher shook his head.

"And the walnuts, well, they help sperm *count*," she said. "And the ginseng helps testosterone. That's the pill. Oh, and the banana juice is for libido! We want you to be just as excited as we are!"

Fletcher smiled weakly.

"We couldn't find any actual bananas," she said. "So the juice will have to do."

"You guys have really thought of everything," said Fletcher.

"We sure have," beamed Margot.

While the Wives of the One Father imagined his testicles loading up with more baby-making sperm with every bite, Fletcher would have to silently choke the food down along with his secret: those testicles had shut down production long ago. The well was dry.

He wished he could tell her the truth just so he could eat normal food, but he didn't want to go the way of Paul.

"And breakfast has spinach," Margot continued, "which is high in folates. Good for sperm. And strawberries, which have vitamin C. Also good for sperm. And pumpkin seeds, of course, which have more of that yummy zinc."

"Uh-huh."

"But *dinner*," she said, "is just whatever we can get our little hands on. Think of it as your cheat meal!"

"And let me guess," said Fletcher, "that's why I don't get coffee?"

"Darn right," she said. "Horrible for those spermies."

"How do you know all this?" he asked.

"Oh, we all do," she said. "While we were waiting for the prophecy to come true—A.K.A. *you*—we all studied these things. For months and months and months. We had different classes and all sorts of stuff. We're all trained to be great Wives to you."

"That's nice," said Fletcher.

"It was super fun," she said. "Like being at Wife Camp with a bunch of your friends."

"Very, very nice," said Fletcher. Deep down, he felt bad for her. She belonged in a world full of rainbows and butterflies, not brainwashing classes and sperm-boosting buffets.

"Okie dokie," she said. "Eat up. Big ritual tonight And about stinkin' time!"

"Margot," said Fletcher, "what happens at the ritual?"

"Oh, I'm not spoiling that for you, silly," she said. "But it's going to be magical."

"Come on," he said. "A hint?"

"Nope. Eat up, buttercup." And with that, she was gone.

And then she was back.

"Ugh," she grunted. "I'd hate for that to be the last thing I said to you, in case I kick the bucket, like we talked about. Okay, how's this: have a great afternoon, One Father. I think you're a real swell guy."

Then she was really gone.

Fletcher hadn't eaten much of his lunch yesterday, but he was hungry now, and he ate most of it. He didn't take the pill, though. Everyone knows not to take a random pill from your captors.

Fletcher ate his weird lunch and then sat in fear for the rest of the day. The word "ritual" seemed to pulse in his head with every heartbeat.

He didn't like that word. He kept picturing the scene in *Indiana Jones and the Temple of Doom* when the underground priest pulled that guy's beating heart out of his chest and burned him in a lava pit as a sacrifice. As a *ritual*. That fear led Fletcher to take the sharpest oyster shell and place it under his bed, just in case he needed a weapon. It wasn't much of a prison shank, and he was outnumbered twenty-two to one, but it was something.

So he sat on his bed, a sharp oyster-shell shiv underneath him, and waited for the ritual.

Chapter 26

THE CANVAS OF FLETCHER'S tent changed from pale yellow to fiery red and finally to inky black, and all the while Fletcher sat on his cot, waiting. Anxiety ate through his insides like a brood of termites, as he tried to hold onto a silly crumb of hope that maybe the ritual wouldn't happen tonight. Maybe they'd forget. At one point, a woman he didn't know brought in dinner: another piece of freshly caught fish. He picked at it, too nervous to really eat. Eventually he heard the snaps and pops of burning wood, then saw the glow of a bonfire on the shadow-puppet wall of his tent, and Fletcher knew that they hadn't forgotten a thing.

Finally, Margot poked her head through the entrance flap and summoned him out. She wore her pink robe, meaning it was officially ritual time. Margot led him to the Hearth where, as Fletcher expected, twenty-one other pink-robed women stood in a circle surrounding the roaring bonfire.

As on the previous night, there was a break in the circle for Fletcher and his chaperone. His eyes darted around from person to person, trying to get a feel for the mood of the group while desperately avoiding any eye contact.

The mood was bubbling excitement.

Fletcher was not excited at all.

They all stood facing the fire for a few minutes. Finally, the largest woman among them stepped out of the circle. Shelly, once again the High Priestess, walked along the outside of the gathering as she had done the night before.

"Welcome, One Father," she said. "And welcome, Wives." She was using that same voice, the one that sounded like a bad actor in a play who had been given the role of High Priestess.

"We have waited for this moment," she continued. "We have waited and waited for this: our first ritual. The ritual is the culmination, purpose and reward of our efforts."

Fletcher subtly glanced around to see if there was a good escape route. In case the sacrificial alter came out, he wanted to know the best direction to run. Contrasting with the brightness of the flames, everything on the outside of the circle was utter blackness. He'd just have to pick a direction and hope for the best. Fletcher looked to the other side of the fire and saw the small shape of the Wifemother. She was looking right at him, and he swore he could see a smile that seemed to say: don't even think about it.

"Let us begin our ritual," said Shelly. Fletcher's heart clenched. "One Father, it is our honor to be your collective Wife ... to give rebirth to the human race with you ... and to raise all of Neo-Humanity as our children."

Fletcher gulped.

"Tonight, we will make love to you as one being."

Fletcher gulped again but his throat was now too dry to finish the job.

"This is how the ritual will commence," said Shelly. "We will share you, each taking you in turn until tonight's blessed Wife receives your seed."

Fletcher's heart was in his throat. He wanted to run, but he felt as if tent stakes had been driven through his feet, holding him to the ground.

Then, the chanting began. Low at first, a whisper of twenty-two voices. The words were unidentifiable, like a ghostly wind picking up and swirling around the fire. Then it grew, from that whisper to a low hum to a full voice and then to a roar. Finally, Fletcher understood what they were saying.

"You are the Father,
We are the Wife.
Give us your seed,
To bring in new life."

Fletcher's heartbeat was now a steady jackhammer on his sternum. A metronome keeping time to their chant, their increasingly manic chant.

"You are the Father,
We are the Wife.
Give us your seed,
To bring in new life."

Fletcher looked around and tried to think, tried to slow things down and really think. Reason. Logic. All that stuff. There had to be a way out.

Then it happened. In one motion, as if by some invisible command, all twenty-two women shrugged off their pink robes.

This will all be over soon.

There, in front of and on all sides of Fletcher, were twenty-two naked women. There were big women, like Shelly the High Priestess, and small women, like Margot right next to him. So very close to him. There were women of all shapes and colors, all exposed and bouncing and drooping and bulging and curving, all of them looking at Fletcher. Even the ancient Wifemother was naked across the flames, a five-foot raisin.

"You are the Father,
We are the Wife.
Give us your seed,
To bring in new life."

There, jiggling in the dancing glow of the flames, were twenty-two sets of breasts. Fletcher was not hardwired to handle forty-four boobs at once. The boobs and the flames and the chanting and the panic and Paul's remains likely buried nearby—it was all too much. Everything blurred together, spinning around him like his own personal tornado until he collapsed on the dirt, unconscious.

· · · · · · · · · · ·

When Fletcher came to, the first things he saw were Margot's big blue eyes. Her face was inches from his and she was studying him intently, her features scrunched up in concentration. Fletcher was still lying on the cool dirt where he fell.

"Holy fish sticks!" cried Margot. "You're alive. He's alive!"

"Please and thank you!" came a nearby voice that Fletcher knew belonged to Shelly. It was her real voice. "Phoebe, if you don't get back in that tent, I'll put you there myself. That's what I thought."

Fletcher moved his head slowly. The fire was still roaring, but the women who had surrounded it were all gone. Shelly appeared above Fletcher, next to Margot. Both of them were wearing their robes again, to Fletcher's relief. As he lay on the dirt, his eyes darted around with the frantic glance of someone who had woken up on a strange planet. He tried to get up.

"Easy does it, One Father," said Shelly. "Take it slow."

Margot sighed loudly. "That would have been such a big bummer if you were dead," she said.

"Good point, Margot," said Shelly.

"Do you even know what your last words would have been?" asked Margot. Shelly shot her a look and Margot nodded in solemn obedience.

After a few minutes, they brought Fletcher to a sitting position and then walked him back to his tent. They laid him down and instructed him to rest. The ritual was postponed for another night.

"This is why we need a doctor in our family," grumbled Shelly, to no one in particular, as she and Margot walked out of Fletcher's tent.

That night Fletcher dreamed feverish dreams of medieval dungeons and ruthless rituals, all performed by horrifying, naked women. When he woke, he faintly remembered a guy being turned into stew. A psychologist would have a field day with him, he thought.

His breakfast was waiting for him when he awoke. It was the same as the day before: spinach, strawberries and pumpkin seeds. He mindlessly ate the canned food, barely registering its unpalatable flavor as he considered his situation.

After a period of deep pondering, he arrived at the following conclusion: he was screwed.

There was a time when he would have loved the opportunity to be the sole meat in a meal for nearly two dozen women, but those days were long gone. Fletcher no longer wanted sex. In fact, at the moment, Fletcher pretty much hated sex. If it weren't for sex, he might be hanging out with Jordan back at the hospital and everything would be fine. This wasn't true, and he knew it—his sins were far more than just carnal—but he needed a scapegoat, and his loss of virginity had been as clear a turning point as any.

Fletcher couldn't let this ritual happen. If New Fletcher was the guy who had ruined everything at the hospital, then he was fully committed to being New New Fletcher. New New Fletcher was going to be his redemption. He had to protect this newfangled moral integrity. He had to stand up for himself. Stand up for what was right.

Virtuous fortitude was all fine and well, but there was a big problem in the way. They had killed the last guy who didn't play the role of One Father to their liking. Maybe Paul refused to be their rape victim—which, when he really thought about it, was what this was. Maybe Paul simply told them he wasn't the guy they were looking for. Either way, he ended up dead.

The point was, before tonight's ritual, Fletcher needed a plan.

At the moment, he had nothing. His tent was guarded. He was outnumbered.

He was screwed.

··•••·•••··

Fletcher sat and thought all morning with no thoughts of value arising, only a sickly dread that seemed to fill the tent like a noxious gas. Finally, Margot poked her curly-haired head through the flap of his tent. Lunchtime already. Just another sign that time was running out.

"How ya feeling?" said Margot. She put her hand on his forehead.

"Fine, thank you," he said.

"Good!" she said. "That means we'll be able to do the ritual tonight. Hey, no better last words than that! Not that these will be our last words, but you know…" She shimmied away, buzzing like a kid on Christmas.

"Can't wait," grunted Fletcher.

Back at the hospital, Fletcher had felt like a lab rat at times: running on treadmills, taking psychological exams, giving blood samples. Looking back now, those were the good ol' days. Before he had gone and ruined things—before he had started banging strangers, calling himself Odin and ordering women around for power and pleasure—things had been pretty great. Life had been enjoyable, considering it was likely the end of humanity. That's the problem with the good ol' days: you never know you're living them until you're on the other side and pissing into a chamber pot, eating canned vegetables and waiting for a cult to ritualistically defile you.

Before he knew it, it was dinnertime. Isabella brought in the tray. Tonight, the main course was duck.

It was good. Really good. Grilled over a flame, it had that beautiful crispy char on the outside, and the meat was moist and flavorful. He scarfed it down, hardly taking a breath. When he was done, he realized he had eaten it too fast. His stomach clenched. Great, he thought. Not only was his stomach swimming with anxiety, but now it had to digest the bird he had just inhaled.

Then, in the midst of this mild discomfort, an idea came. Lo and behold and about damn time, he thought of a plan. It could only work for one night, but it might at least buy him that. It could give him another day to think of something else, a more permanent solution, a way to escape his fate. The plan was this: Fletcher needed to get sick.

He'd blame it on the duck. The downside, of course, was that he wouldn't be able to eat the delicious waterfowl again for as long as he remained a guest of the Wives of the One Father, but Fletcher hoped that wouldn't be long anyway.

What Fletcher did next was gnarly, but necessary. He jammed his fingers down his throat to force himself to vomit—but he couldn't. He decided he needed to warm himself up to it. He put a forkful of broccoli in his mouth and bit into it slowly. He focused on how disgusting the irony taste of the canned vegetables was. He chewed it and thought of any repulsive thing he could come up with, like sour milk, old crusty toenails, and hot, steamy Porta Potties. He was preparing his body ready for its expulsionary duty. He let some chewed broccoli dribble out of his mouth, starting a nice little splatter pile on the dirt floor. He took another bite and focused on how full he was. Then he did thirty jumping jacks, and his face became moist, his breathing heavy. That was good. That would help sell it. But he needed vomit, and he needed it now. Fletcher closed his eyes and inserted two fingers into his mouth. He shoved them farther down his throat. His stomach moved and his throat tightened. He was nearly there.

Just then, the flap of the door opened and Isabella poked her head through, ducking down to crawl into his tent. Fletcher quickly removed his fingers before she could see.

"Okay," she said. "It's time."

Fletcher held his hand up to wait, looking down at the ground. As a last resort, in the same way a mother finds the strength to lift a car when her child is stuck under it, his mind did what it needed to do, against all odds. It went nuclear. It conjured up an image of the broccoli he just ate, and he could see it in his mind, clear as day. It was teeming with a million shimmering, yellowish maggots. They crawled in and out of the soggy green flesh. He could feel little remnants of broccoli in his mouth and imagined they, too, were squirming bugs. He could feel them crawling around on his tongue and worming their way across his teeth to the back of his throat, all swollen and wriggling and—

Fletcher vomited violently. Duck and broccoli and all. It was glorious, and Isabella had been there to see it. He milked it for all it was worth, groaning and spitting when the puking part was over. He was sweating as he looked up at Isabella with his best kill-me-now face.

This will all be over soon.

"One Father!" she screamed.

"Was that ... duck?" Fletcher croaked. Isabella nodded. Fletcher lowered his head. "I have a sensitivity..." he spit dramatically. "To duck. I thought it was chicken."

"Are you okay?" she asked.

"I'll be fine," he said, spitting. "Eventually. I feel so stupid. I should have asked."

"No, no," she said. "It's okay! I'm so sorry..."

And just like that, Fletcher's plan had worked. The Wifemother and the High Priestess came to see him after Isabella had called for them. The Wifemother squinted at him, smiling as if she could see right through him. They had no choice, however. Their man was covered in stomach bile and chewed-up dinner. There would be no ritual tonight.

Fletcher assured them he'd be ready the next day, as he spit and groaned into his pile of puke.

And the Academy Award goes to ... Fletcher Sinclair.

Chapter 27

HIS VICTORY WAS SHORT-LIVED: the next morning he was back to square one. He was again a sex slave with no idea of how to escape his fate.

He sat in his tent and picked at his sperm-boosting breakfast.

Margot came by and asked if he wanted some fresh air. He didn't. He just lay on his cot and tried to think of a plan, but he was fishing in a dried-up pond.

A few hours passed. A few hours closer to ritual hour. Margot appeared again, this time with lunch.

"Hiya, Mr. One Father," she said.

"Hello," he said. "And, again, Fletcher is good."

"Are you okay?" she asked.

"Yeah," he lied.

"Well," she said, "can I ask you a question?"

"Sure."

"You're not sure if you're really the One Father, are you?" She bit her lip.

"What makes you say that?" asked Fletcher.

"Well, if I just found out I was the Chosen One," she said, "I feel like I'd be a little more excited."

Fletcher raised his eyebrows.

"Oh, gobstoppers." Margot winced. "I'm sorry. I'm being rude, aren't I? Am I being rude? That's probably rude."

"No," said Fletcher, smiling. "You're not being rude. I ... I dunno. It's just a lot of pressure. I'm scared I'm not up to the task."

"I get that," she said. "But like my mom always said: you might not get to choose the song, but it's your choice whether you dance or not."

"That's nice," said Fletcher.

"And I like dancing," said Margot. She spun around like a broken ballerina.

"I think you'll be a fantastic One Father," she said.

"Thanks, Margot," said Fletcher. "I'm sure you're a great sisterwife or whatever."

"Thank you, *Fletcher*," she said as she walked toward the flap. "Hey, these were good last words, so let's leave it at that. You never know."

"No," he said. "I guess you never do."

......

Hours later, just after dinner, Fletcher sat on the edge of his bed, quite pleased with himself. He had come up with yet another plan to get out of the ritual.

Fletcher was going to beat this cult at its own game. He was going to weaponize the very divinity they had given him. It was a good plan. Again, it wasn't a final plan—it wasn't an escape—but it would buy him time.

He did a bunch of jumping jacks and pushups to get nice and sweaty, but this time nausea wasn't his end game. He got all worked up, then lay down on the bed.

Then he yelled. Loudly, frantically. "I've heard!" he screamed. "I've heard the Word!"

Isabella, who was guarding the entrance, rushed in. "What happened? Are you okay?"

Fletcher heaved breath after breath. He kept his eyes as wide as he could. He let a wild smile cross his face. "God spoke to me," he said, elated. "Quick, get the High Priestess. Get the Wifemother!"

Isabella rushed off, leaving the post unattended. Although not his plan, Fletcher entertained the idea of bolting right there and then. But his screams had attracted voices, and he heard footsteps gathering around his tent.

Shelly entered first, looking at Fletcher with excitement. The Wifemother slipped in next, moving with a creaking lack of urgency. Isabella came in last, not wanting to miss the action. The Wifemother appeared to have shrunk even more since Fletcher had last seen her, looking like a little, wrinkled child next to Shelly's bloated frame. She crept toward Fletcher, an unreadable look on her face. There was a hint of a smile, and Fletcher couldn't shake the feeling that she knew what he was doing before he spoke a word.

She probably did, he thought. She had probably made up this whole circus.

Fletcher focused on breathing heavily and keeping his eyes as crazed as possible. "God spoke to me," he announced again.

"You don't say." The Wifemother's gravelly voice was a thing of broken beauty. "And what did He have to say?"

"Well," said Fletcher, "he said, 'Yeah, it's true, you're the Chosen One.' So that was cool."

"That *is* ... cool," said the Wifemother, smiling wickedly.

"Uh," said Fletcher. "And he said that he was proud of all of you, and to keep up the good work."

"That's wonderful to hear," said the Wifemother. Fletcher felt that her tone was slightly patronizing. "There was something else, though, wasn't there?"

"Well, yes," said Fletcher. "He said that I need to build up my strength. That I'm not ready for my first ritual yet. He said, 'One Father, Fletcher, son, you need more semen. Gotta build it up.' Not in those words, you know, but that was like, the message."

He looked around. Shelly was awed to be so close to such an intimate divine interaction. Isabella looked impressed, too. The Wifemother's expression didn't change.

"No," she said.

"What?" said Fletcher. "What does that mean?"

"It means no," she said again, smiling.

"But God—"

"Devils speak falsities to untrained ears, love," she said. "The Lord has warned me that evil will speak to you, and that is why I am here. To be God's true mouthpiece."

"But we have to—"

"What we have to do," said the Wifemother, "is our sacred duty. The ritual happens tonight."

"Great news!" said Shelly. "We'll begin the preparations."

"Rest up, One Father," smiled the Wifemother as she turned and left.

Fletcher wanted to throw up again.

·········

The sun was setting as Fletcher sat on his cot, alone. The ritual would happen in a half hour or so. His plan had failed.

He had already decided that he would not let this happen. That much was nonnegotiable. He was not their property, he was not their messiah and he was certainly not their willing victim.

Fletcher was done being a novelty, a prisoner of circumstance. What he really wanted was to once again slip into the dark comfort of anonymity, but those days were gone. It seemed that no matter where he went, he belonged to everyone—as if by default, by being the last one left, he had given up his say in the matter. But he was done being anybody's anything. He was going to make his stand. At all costs.

Emboldened by his new state of mind, he reached under his bed and grabbed the sharp oyster shell—his sad excuse for a weapon. He crawled onto his bed and prepared to slash through the canvas of his tent. He was going to create a backdoor and make a run for it. Right now.

If he could sneak out and get even a minute head start on the manhunt that would follow, that could be enough to give him a chance.

He thought of *The Shawshank Redemption*, where Tim Robbins dug a tunnel behind the poster in his prison cell, bit by bit, every day, until he could crawl through to safety. Well, this was Fletcher's Shawshank Prison. Tim Robbins wouldn't let them break him, and neither would Fletcher. The difference was that Fletcher had a much smaller timeline in which he needed to escape. Like, a minute or two. Thankfully, canvas was a lot thinner than a rock wall.

But ... it turned out canvas was still pretty durable.

Fletcher slashed at the canvas, but nothing happened. He repositioned the oyster shell, getting a better grip on it with the wide end against the heel of his hand and the sharpest point ready to cut. This time he moved slowly, methodically, firmly. He pressed the shell hard against the canvas and dragged it down with purpose.

He heard a satisfying noise, which he figured to be the canvas ripping. It was not.

It was the shell filing down, crumbling into tiny pieces in his hand.

He looked at the failed tool, now a palmful of gray dust, knowing his captors could emerge through the tent flap at any moment. He dropped the oyster pieces onto the bed, now holding only that fortitude he had so recently found. Fortitude couldn't rip canvas, but it could give a man enough balls to refuse surrender. He frantically scanned the room. He had a big, round chamber pot full of piss. That wouldn't do much. There was his metal cot, but that was too cumbersome to manage. The mattress had metal springs inside that could be useful, but he didn't know how he'd get to them. The "Peter's Produce" wooden crate that acted as his bedside table (and Margot's stool, occasionally) seemed as worthless as the rest. And that was everything.

He picked up the wooden crate. He *could* knock Isabella over the head with it. It would cause a commotion, but it might be his only move. He thought for a second, wishing there was a nonviolent way. He ran his hand over the crate as he thought, feeling the rough grain of the wood, the metal head of a nail sticking out ever so slightly...

He stopped.

A metal nail.

Nails are sharp. Nails can cut things.

Fletcher got to work. He set the crate on the floor and put his foot on top, bracing it in place. He grabbed one of the wooden panels at the top and pried it up. At first it didn't budge, but with a second attempt he heard the high squeak of a nail moving through wood. He pulled harder and released a wooden panel, nearly falling backward.

He looked at his new tool: it was an eighteen-inch thin wooden board, with a big, beautiful nail sticking out one side.

It reminded him of one of those baseball bats covered with nails that you see in zombie movies.

Fletcher pressed the nail end against the canvas and it punctured straight through. He then held onto the wood and pulled it toward the ground, using all his body weight. The nail carved through the canvas like a lightsaber.

Once the slit was big enough, he wasted no time admiring his work. He slipped through silently and looked around, hoping he wouldn't see pink. The coast was clear—for now.

He stayed low, scampering from tent to tent, hiding in the shadows as women walked past, making their way to their tents to prepare for the ritual. He picked his path based on the darkest shadows, hopping from one to the other. He timed his moves around the footsteps and voices—pausing, leaping, pausing, leaping. It was a messed-up game of *Frogger*, and Fletcher had one life.

Once he got past the tents, he got a little cocky. He slid into the supply shed. The purple twilight shone through a window, illuminating pallets and pallets of canned strawberries, spinach and broccoli. Next to them were flats of water bottles, stacked high. He saw a small leather satchel and began stuffing cans and bottles in. He may not have been the savviest outdoorsman, but he'd seen plenty of movies. He knew you'd die of thirst before you'd starve to death, so he packed the bag accordingly.

There was a knife sitting on one flat of cans, and he threw that in as well. It was better than an oyster shell. He tossed the satchel over his shoulder, feeling like Indiana Jones, and left the shed, disappearing into the dark of the forest.

He heard their first cry only seconds later.

"The One Father is gone!"

Chapter 28

FLETCHER HAD NEVER BEEN one for the great outdoors, but at that moment he was its biggest fan. The dense forest meant a shot at freedom from the pink psycho cult, providing him the cover he needed to make his escape. His adrenaline was high, and—in addition to terror and panic—he felt a surging excitement. This was it, baby. He was doing it.

He slid under branches and through bushes in the murky dark. Low sticks assaulted his shins, while heavy hands of needles and leaves slapped at his face, but still Fletcher pushed on, quickly and silently.

They weren't far behind him.

"One Father!" The shout sounded like it came from all around.

"Fletcher!" came another yell. He sped up ... a questionable decision for someone of Fletcher's athleticism. He tripped over a fallen log and went down like the tree it once had been. His hands were unable to catch him in time, and his face landed with a crack on a rock. He scampered to his feet and felt his cheekbone, the point of impact. Warm liquid ran over his fingers, and his skin was hot. Blinding stars floated through his vision when he looked up, almost making him doubt what he saw. What he saw was Margot, standing right in front of him. Her pink outfit was periwinkle in the moonlight.

She looked at him as though his head were on fire.

"Guys!" she yelled.

"Shh!" Fletcher extended his palms toward her, signaling her to stop.

"What are you doing?" she asked. "You're hurt! What are you doing?"

"Please," said Fletcher. "Be quiet."

"Why?"

"Because," said Fletcher, "I need to go. You have to let me go."

"Boy," said Margot. "You're acting funny. Maybe you're sick again. The Wifemother will know what—"

"Wait, stop," said Fletcher. "I can't go back."

"Of course you're going back!" said Margot.

"No," said Fletcher, thinking quickly. "This is part of the … destiny. The prophecy."

Margot contorted her face, trying to follow.

"Yep," said Fletcher. "It says I have to go. Now."

"For serious?" she said.

"For serious. God spoke to me and said I gotta go … that way." Fletcher pointed into the darkness.

"I dunno," said Margot. "It's not safe. Not for someone as important as you, especially."

"You gotta trust me, Margot," he said.

"Oh, I do," she said. "Believe me, I do. But, I should ask someone else."

Time was ticking. Voices were closer. "Please," said Fletcher. "I have to go."

"Then I'm coming with," said Margot.

"Oh, no," said Fletcher. "You are most definitely not."

"Then I yell for help," said Margot. "Three … two … I can't just let you—"

"Damn it," said Fletcher. "Fine. Let's go. Keep up and don't make a noise."

"Okie dokie," she said. "This is crazy!"

Fletcher shushed her.

"Are you going to tell me the rest of the story or what?" she said. "What God said and all that? The prophecy?"

"Later," said Fletcher. "If you keep up and don't make a noise. We can't be found."

"Why can't—"

"Destiny," said Fletcher. "Let's *go*."

He darted off into the wilderness, Margot at his heels. He didn't bother to see if she was keeping up with him or not. If he lost her, well, that was a two-for-one. He just kept running, ricocheting off trees like a pinball off the bumpers, with no destination in mind except getting as far as possible from the commune. His route started going downhill, and at one point he took a bad step and bit his tongue. The blood tasted like metal.

"How long do we run?" asked Margot out of the darkness behind him.

"No talking," panted Fletcher. "And I don't know. A long time. Keep up or go back."

"Oh, I'm keeping up," said Margot. "Not even tired."

They ran like this for an hour or more, the ground slowly becoming flatter and the forest thinner, eventually transitioning to the more shrub-like sprawl of desert flora.

"I've never been this far out," said Margot. "It's pretty!"

"No talking," wheezed Fletcher.

They ran farther still, Fletcher's hospital training finally put to use.

"I wonder how many calories we've burned," said Margot.

"No talking," coughed Fletcher.

When the pale hint of sunrise teased the eastern sky, diluting the pitch black of its distant horizon with the smallest milky drops of the next day, Fletcher finally stopped to rest. They had long since lost the shouts that had been following them, and his body was starting to turn on him. Once Fletcher caught his breath, they walked on, until dawn was in full swing—all the while Margot asking questions and Fletcher ignoring them. Finally, he stopped to look around at the world they had crossed into.

It resembled the setting of an old Western, brown for as far as he could see in every direction, with greenish-tan bushes covering the earth like diseased fur. Spots of bright trees sporadically dotted the landscape. It was impossible to tell how far the ocean was on any side.

Fletcher set his sights on a clump of trees in the distance. He figured they could hide there for a moment and recharge. When they finally reached the trees, it was no longer dawn and the cruel summer sun was too hot to seriously call it *morning*. The little oasis featured five or six trees that were filled with explosions of yellow cottony flowers. Margot told him they were acacias. Fletcher didn't really care, but he was thankful for their existence. In the middle of them was a small open space, maybe ten feet across—a clearing made for two weary travelers. It was protected from sight and from sun.

There, in the shade of the strange island trees, Fletcher and Margot laid down on the soft grass and looked up at the blue sky, framed by a ring of yellow flowers. He touched the dried blood on his face and smiled, knowing a real man would have escaped just like he did.

He was about to doze off, glasses already removed and resting on his satchel, when Margot barreled into his beautiful respite.

"Soooooo…" she said, "are you gonna make me wait all day or what?"

"Huh?"

"Hit me with it!" she said. "The big holy message you got! Your secret mission. *Our* secret mission."

"I'm pretty tired," said Fletcher. "Let's talk about it later."

"Okay, sleepy pants," said Margot. "If you say so."

Then Fletcher fell asleep, and slept hard.

······•·····

When Fletcher woke, the sun was in the middle of the sky. He rubbed his naked eyes and groped for his glasses. He put them on and turned to see Margot, sitting crisscross applesauce and looking right at him. Those big blue marbles sparkled.

"Good morning, Mr. One Father!" she said.

"Well, it's afternoon, but hello," said Fletcher. "And don't call me that. Just call me Fletcher."

"Good *afternoon*, Mr. *Fletcher*," she corrected. "Okay, so let's hear it."

Fletcher groaned. "What?"

"Spill the beans!" she said. "What did God tell you?"

"Oh," said Fletcher.

"What's the planley, Stanley?" Margot lifted her arms, palms up, in a cartoon shrug. "Where are we going? Wait … am I…? Am I chosen to be your first wife? Am I gonna be the first mother of Neo-Humanity? Oh, my goodness, what an honor that would be! But am I ready for that kind of responsibility? Holy cannoli, are we going to do the ritual? Oh, geez. When? How's my hair look? To be honest, I'm really nervous."

"Easy," said Fletcher. "Calm down. No ritual. We're not doing any ritual."

"Okay," said Margot, exhaling. "So then, what's the plan?"

"The plan," said Fletcher, stalling to think. "Is that I am supposed to go on … a journey of self-discovery."

"Oh?"

"Yeah," said Fletcher. "So, feel free to turn around."

"Heck, no!" she said. "We're doing your self-discovery together."

Fletcher grunted and crawled to the base of one of the trees and peeked out. Enough time had passed that his followers could be anywhere. All Fletcher saw were miles of browns and greens, and some distant rolling hills that carved their way into blue skies. He knew they'd keep looking for him—he was the sole purpose of their organization, after all. And the farther he was from their camp, the better chance he had of remaining hidden. So, he needed to move.

"What's the point of our self-discovery walk?" asked Margot.

"Discovering myself," said Fletcher.

"What for?" she pressed.

"Maybe we're not meant to know." Fletcher reached into his leather satchel and grabbed a can of broccoli.

"Breakfast?" said Margot. "I'm starving."

Fletcher managed to open it with the knife he had grabbed, although it wasn't pretty. He stabbed and pried until he made a hole in the top, then sawed with the unserrated blade until he reached the insipid mush inside.

He and Margot passed the can back and forth, eating all twelve ounces of soggy broccoli.

Fletcher tossed the can under a tree and began walking. Margot clicked her tongue. "Littering, huh?"

Fletcher ignored her.

Dressed in what looked like matching pink and blue children's pajamas, the two walked for the rest of the day, stopping only to take the occasional sip of water from the bottles Fletcher brought.

"I wish you would have told me about our adventure beforehand," said Margot. "I would have brought some supplies, too. We could have had matching satchels."

"Yeah," panted Fletcher, wondering how she never tired. "My bad."

He walked without much of a plan—just survival. His food and water weren't going to last long, especially now that he had to share everything with Margot. He wasn't sure what he was going to do about her, either. He couldn't exactly leave her to die in the desert. So, at the moment, his plan was to just keep moving and hope to stumble across a better one.

They walked and walked until the sun started to sink over the hills to the west. They found no sign of civilization—no shelter, no water and no food. They did find another gathering of trees, though—this one a small clump of three palms with a few mid-sized bushy trees—and that's where they stopped for the night.

"This is so exciting," said Margot. "It's like camping!"

"Man," said Fletcher, "what would you give for a hot dog right now?"

Margot thought. "I'd probably give up a tooth."

"That's fair," Fletcher nodded. "I'd give up caffeine forever."

They drank a little more water and shared a can of mushy strawberries. Fletcher's legs ached and his feet throbbed. He took off his shoes, but the throbbing wouldn't stop. He could feel his heartbeat in his toes.

"Here," he said, handing the leather satchel to Margot. "It's the best pillow for miles around. Best in the land."

"Are you serious?" said Margot. "That's the nicest thing anyone's ever done."

"Don't say chivalry is dead."

Fletcher lay back, putting his hands behind his head, and smiled up at the stars. It felt good to hurt. It felt like grit. Like perseverance.

Fletcher thought about the Robinson Crusoes and Grizzly Adams of the world. The Charles Ingalls. At that moment, he felt like he was worthy of their fraternity.

Chapter 29

WHEN DAWN CAME, FLETCHER was already half-awake. He made some not-so-subtle noise until Margot stirred and opened her eyes. They drank a few precious sips of water, trying to conserve what little they had, despite the pleading of their dry throats. Breakfast was a few wet clumps of spinach. Now that food was rationed, the wilted leaves weren't half bad. Fletcher would have had seconds given the chance.

"Hey, Margot," said Fletcher, chewing on spinach. "Let's have it. Where are we?"

"In a desert, by the looks of things," she said, taking the can from him.

"We're on an island, right?" said Fletcher. "What island?"

"Oh," said Margot. "I'm not supposed to tell you that, I don't think."

"Come on," said Fletcher. "That was then. This is now. What was that city I saw when we were coming in?"

"Loose lips sink ships," she said.

"I won't tell that you told," said Fletcher.

"I mean..." said Margot. "I guess it's probably fine. You think it's fine?"

"Totally fine," Fletcher goaded.

"Okay, okay," she said. "We are on ... drum roll, please ... Catalina Island!" She gestured at their surroundings dramatically. "Oh, and that city was Avalon. It's got that big famous casino."

Jabba the Hutt's palace.

"Catalina," he repeated. "Avalon. Okay, that's where we need to go. Avalon."

"Uh ... why?" she asked.

"I need a boat," said Fletcher.

"You're trying to get *off* the island?" Margot's eyes bulged.

"Yep," said Fletcher.

"Wait," said Margot, squinting. "Wait! Did—did you trick me?"

"Yep," said Fletcher.

"Did you stinkin' lie to me about this whole thing?" she asked.

"Yep," said Fletcher.

"Wait," she said. "You didn't get a holy message at all, did you?"

"Nope," said Fletcher.

"Oh, shin splints," she said. "We have to go back!"

Fletcher laughed. "Big nope."

"Well, then," said Margot, "I'm going to go back and tell them."

"Be my guest," said Fletcher. "I'll be long gone."

"Well," said Margot, "then I gotta stay with you and make sure you don't hurt yourself."

"Whatever floats your boat," said Fletcher.

"I'm staying," said Margot. "But I'm mad at you and I'm not talking to you."

"What a shame."

Fletcher didn't know which way to go, but he knew Avalon was somewhere on the east side of the island, facing mainland California. And he knew the sun rose in the east. So, he figured they'd move in the general direction of that fireball creeping above the horizon.

As they started out, he began to think with mild pride about his toughness—specifically how his toughness was the one thing in his control, how he could out-tough his followers, and how every step was a fight for his survival—when Margot spoke. Her vow of silence had lasted just under two minutes.

"Okay, mister," she said. "Since God didn't tell you to do it, why did you run away?"

"Because," said Fletcher, "you guys are crazy."

"*You're* crazy," she said.

"Margot," said Fletcher. "I'm not the One Father."

"Maybe you just don't realize it," she said.

"I'm infertile, Margot," said Fletcher, pointing to his crotch. "No fertilization happening here."

"What?" She stopped walking.

"Shooting blanks," he said.

"Are you sure?" she asked.

"Yep," he said. "So—not your holy One Father. And I didn't want to end up like Paul, so I bounced."

"Oh," said Margot. "Poor Paul."

"Yeah," scoffed Fletcher. "Poor Paul. So you guys just killed him because, what—he told you he wasn't your guy?"

"Excuse me?" she said.

"Yeah," said Fletcher. "No, thank you. Didn't want to stick around for that."

"You think we killed him?"

"Listen," said Fletcher. "The Wifemother told me: he died 'cause he was a false prophet or whatever."

"Well, yeah," said Margot. "Or, he was a false prophet because he died."

"What?"

"He died of a little thing called the Delilah Virus, silly," she said. "Ever heard of it? He just survived longer than most, I guess."

"You didn't kill him?" Fletcher asked.

"You, my friend," said Margot, "have quite the imagination. No! We were heartbroken. We all thought he was the One Father! He even said that he was!"

Fletcher shook his head.

"Then one day he started talking about hair styles of tennis players," said Margot. "And we all got really confused. Then he ... well ... he, you know. And then he died."

"Holy shit," said Fletcher.

"Poor Paul," she said. "Not the best last words, either."

Fletcher shook his head.

"So, we can go back," said Margot. "Right?"

"No way," said Fletcher.

"But we're not killers."

"But they're still crazy," said Fletcher. "It's fucked up. The whole thing. I want no part in that."

"You don't get it," said Margot.

"No," said Fletcher, "*you* don't get it. Walk and talk. Gotta keep moving."

"Moving to where?" she asked.

They started walking again, the morning sun already scorching.

"Well," said Fletcher, "food and water first. So we don't die. Then a boat. I have to get back to mainland. I need to find my friend Jordan." He paused, almost surprised at the words about to come. "You should come with."

"And leave the Wives?" said Margot. "Yeah, right."

"They're seriously messed up," said Fletcher.

"No, they're not."

"Margot," said Fletcher. "You really don't realize you're in a cult, do you?"

"Ha!" said Margot. "It's not a cult. It's a family."

"Then what, pray tell, is a cult?"

"I dunno," said Margot. "A group of crazies who all believe something crazy because of some crazy leader?"

"Usually with weird outfits?" said Fletcher. "And a divine purpose that's only interpreted by that leader? Oh, and maybe rituals?"

"It wasn't a cult," said Margot, frowning.

"Whatever you say," said Fletcher.

"I'm not talking to you again," said Margot.

"How generous."

· · · · • · • · · · ·

They walked for what felt like years under a sun that seemed to hang five feet above their heads. The desert was winning. Fletcher's skin grew a deeper and deeper red as blisters bubbled up on his feet. His legs ached. His head swam. His stomach screamed. Fletcher listed his ailments to Margot, asking if she had similar symptoms.

She was talking again, of course, but she only responded with a smile. And then: delirium.

They marched, Fletcher's blue shirt over his head like a turban, leather satchel slung over his skinny, tomato-red torso. Margot shambled along in her black sports bra, pink shirt wrapped around her head like Fletcher's. They sang 'Yellow Submarine' as they shuffled across the arid land. They laughed and laughed, growing more maniacal with every step. But they kept stepping. They slogged through that dense, crazy sand and that dense, crazy air, yelling into the sky, all the while laughing. All the while laughing. All the while looking for shelter, water or food for the sake of their lives.

Even one of the three would do.

One came late in the day, as the sun was lowering in the sky. They arrived at a small oasis of trees—acacias, palms and shrubs—and found a clear, flat place in the middle. Fletcher used his knife and what little strength he had left to saw off some branches from the acacias and make a little lean-to against a tree. Margot gathered palms for some half-assed thatching. It wasn't pretty, but given their condition it may as well have been the Ritz-Carlton. They crawled inside and Fletcher felt the hiss of his hot skin in the cool shade. He took a sip of water and let it sit in his mouth, wanting to get the most out of the sweet elixir before sending it to his gut to keep him alive. He passed it to Margot. She passed it back. There was one sip left.

Fletcher, ever the gentleman, let Margot finish the water. They split the last can of strawberries.

And then: they were out of food and water.

And then: their clock was ticking.

This will all be over soon.

His mother's words appeared, uninvited, in Fletcher's brain. He wasn't sure how to interpret them at the moment, but those were the words he kept hearing in the light island wind as he drifted to sleep, that strange, big-eyed, curly-haired cult girl snoring six inches to his left.

·············

The next day, Fletcher woke to crispy sunburns all over his once-milky skin. Margot was no better. Their feet were gone, replaced by giant foot-sized blisters at the ends of their legs. Those legs could barely move. They were sore and weak all over, with no fuel in their bodies, no food in their bellies and no water for as far as they could see.

Fletcher didn't know how long one could live without food and water, but he knew they couldn't wait for a delivery to their lean-to.

So, they stood up. They looked east. And they walked. His socks were crusty from the dried blood, but they walked. His knees felt as if his leg bones were rubbing together at the ends, but they walked. As badly as he wanted to lie down and cry, they walked.

Fletcher was going to out-tough this damn desert. He was determined to. He was going to prove to himself that he had something in him that couldn't be broken.

Meanwhile, Margot sang 'Yellow Submarine'. A raspier, quieter version, but it seemed that she, too, wasn't planning on breaking anytime soon.

They made it half a day until they found another small patch of trees where they could take shelter. How big was this stupid island? Were they walking in circles?

Fletcher thought he could physically feel his stomach eating the poor organs around it. His throat was beef jerky. His dry lips crumbled like an old pencil eraser. They needed to find sustenance, but they were too weak to move anymore that day. If he were in *Zordallus*, his Energy Meter would be blinking ominously. That meant one hit and he was a goner.

They made another makeshift shelter and lay down in the sweet escape of the shade.

"I used to make forts back home when I was a kid," said Margot. "Nobody made better forts than me."

"We didn't do too bad here," said Fletcher. "Where was home again?"

"Bend," said Margot. "Oregon."

"Tell me about it." He felt light. Like he might float away.

"Well," said Margot, "it has about 100,000 people. And there are more sunny days in Bend than any other city in Oregon. 158 a year."

Fletcher smiled. "Okay, Wikipedia."

"Shush," said Margot. "Let's see, it smells different there, too. Like the air is brand new. Maybe 'cause there are trees everywhere. So many trees you wouldn't believe. I always said that if God reached down and felt Bend, it would feel fuzzy."

Fletcher closed his eyes as Margot moved her hand back and forth, making a *fttt-fttt* noise to imitate the fuzziness.

"Oh, boy," continued Margot. "There'd be so much shade for us."

"So much shade," sighed Fletcher.

"Oh, and it's on the river," she said. "In the summer, you can bring a tube and just float down it. For hours. It's real neat. Like, if there were snowglobes made for summer, they'd base it off this place. You know what I mean? Like, summerglobes."

"Summerglobes," smiled Fletcher, eyes still closed. "Tell me more."

"Well," said Margot, "there are birds in every tree. Every stinkin' tree. I already told you how many trees there are. My dad was a birdwatcher. Such a weird hobby, right? But he'd take me birding, as the birders call it. I didn't care all that much about the birds, but it was so naturey out there in the forest whenever I went with him—it felt like we were a million miles from roads or towns, sometimes—and sometimes we were so out there that I felt like we were on some big important adventure, you know? Some story people would tell each other for years."

"I'd like to see this place," said Fletcher.

"You have to," said Margot.

Fletcher looked over at Margot. Her eyes were closed, too.

"You know," she said, "we're kind of on an adventure like that."

"I guess so, huh?"

"Maybe someday people will tell this story," she said.

"Maybe," said Fletcher. "Maybe."

Chapter 30

"I'm so hungry I could eat a hippo," said Margot.

They had slept all afternoon, and it was now dusk. The time of day was disorienting. Everything was disorienting. They lay in silence, caught between the impossibility of movement and the necessity of it.

Fletcher finally forced himself to wiggle out of their lean-to and into the clearing, where he sat up. The sky was a purple blanket and growing darker. The blanket had a few holes, allowing the earliest stars to show. Fletcher stared out across the dreamland terrain and saw something move. A few somethings. He froze.

They weren't people, though. They were too big for people—bigger than Shelly, even. They were ... bison? Three giant, hairy, hulking bison, lumbering along through the twilight. Fletcher blinked rapidly, trying to clear the hallucination. Maybe this was what losing your mind felt like.

"No hippos," said Fletcher. "But look."

Margot turned over and the two of them watched the animals in awe.

"Bison burgers," whispered Margot. Like either of them could hunt. Or make a fire.

Eventually the bison wandered away, leaving the humans to their growing list of woes. Fletcher scooted to the base of a tree and absent-mindedly rolled over a log. The ground underneath it moved before his eyes. This time he was sure he was seeing things. But no. Not yet, at least. The movement came from a handful of squirming, twitching little bugs, shining in the twilight. A rust-colored centipede scurried past a waddling beetle, toward another centipede. There were two snails, too, in pretty caramel shells of perfect spirals, their antennae quivering independently.

"No hippos," said Fletcher again. "And no bison burgers." He stared at the bugs, wishing he hadn't thought what he was thinking. "But... we got bugs."

Margot crawled over on her hands and knees and inspected the insects. She looked up at Fletcher, eyes like moons. Little crazy moons. "Hakuna matata?" she said.

"Are we actually considering this?" asked Fletcher. They did need energy. Food was energy.

Margot closed her eyes and pressed her lips together in silent rumination. She stood still for a few seconds before popping her eyes open, snatching a centipede between her forefinger and thumb, tilting her head back and dropping the long insect down her throat.

She squished her eyes shut again and froze. Then, her tense body softened and she opened her eyes. She stuck out her tongue proudly. "Slimy, yet satisfying," she said.

Grinning, she grabbed the other centipede and placed it in Fletcher's hand.

He looked at the bug walking figure-eights in his palm. *Man up*, he told himself. *Like her.*

He swore the insect looked up at him.

This will all be over soon.

He tossed the creature into his mouth and bit down as fast as he could—to get it over with for both of them. He felt the brush-like legs on his tongue and gagged, but he forced himself to swallow the centipede, hardly even chewing it. Keeled over, eyes watering, Fletcher smiled. There was food in his belly.

"Slimy, yet satisfying," he coughed. "Slimy, yet satisfying."

He looked at the moist earth below him and saw a fat little bug that he didn't recognize, and he tossed that into his mouth, too. It popped like a blueberry, but tasted like dirt. Fletcher remembered how he'd imagined eating maggots to induce vomiting only a few days earlier. Now here he was, eating bugs to survive.

They ate a couple more, laughing and coughing and gagging and choking through their bug breakfast. Finally, Margot rubbed her belly.

"I'm stuffed," she said, giggling. "Compliments to the chef."

Fletcher looked at her, suddenly serious. "We got this," he said. "We're gonna survive, Margot."

"Of course we are, silly," she said.

Fletcher watched her whistle as she put on her bloody sock.

"Of course we are," he said.

So they stood up, against all odds. And, against all odds, they started walking.

·········

"So who is this Jordan lady?" asked Margot, as they plodded through the sand. They were walking in pure moonlight, and the terrain looked like another planet—blue and endless.

"She's a girl," said Fletcher, "from the hospital."

"Holy moly," said Margot. "What a love story."

"What do you want me to say?"

"Well," said Margot, "tell me about her! She's your ice cream."

"Come again?"

"Your ice cream," said Margot. "When I was a kid and my mom made me go run errands with her, she always said that if I kept moving and didn't complain, I'd get ice cream afterward."

Fletcher looked at her.

Margot shrugged, as if just learning that this wasn't a universal rule. "Well, your ice cream is what keeps you going. What keeps you walking on those ouchy feet. It's a *metaphor*."

"Okay." Fletcher smiled. "Sure, I guess she's my ice cream."

He told Margot about Jordan. About their late-night talks. About the way she made him feel. He told her how he messed it all up, too. In fact, he told her the whole story—everything. What did he have to lose? He had his doubts they'd ever see another human anyway.

He told her everything, and yet her feet never stuttered. She just smiled and nodded. "Sheesh," she said. "You weren't exactly a choir boy, were you?"

She was a fabulous confidant.

"So," said Fletcher once his catharsis was over, "what's your ice cream?"

"Well," said Margot, "David died. He was my ice cream. Before all this."

They walked in silence for a long time. Dr. Gomez had once reminded Fletcher how everyone still alive had lost so much. And that nobody should have to be alone.

"But now," said Margot, out of nowhere, "well, I'm looking for a new ice cream. And I think it's getting you to Jordan so you can save the world."

"I don't think I'm saving anything," grunted Fletcher.

"But you're alive," said Margot.

"Weird, right?" Fletcher kept his eyes ahead, trying to manifest the coast or a pond or a river or a vending machine with his mind.

"Okay, then, mister," said Margot, "explain to me why you lived."

"Honestly," said Fletcher, "I have zero idea."

"I think," said Margot, "you're put here to save humanity. So there."

"I think," said Fletcher, "I just happened to be immune. A big, random, oopsie-daisy."

"I think," said Margot, "that you're scared to believe in anything bigger than little old you."

"I think," said Fletcher, "that you do it too easily."

"Sorry I believe in *something*," said Margot.

"Like cults," said Fletcher.

"I'm not talking to you again," said Margot.

"Fine by me."

And so they walked in silence across that dark planet until the ethereal spread of dawn started glowing on the horizon in front of them.

•••••••••••

As Fletcher walked, with a surprisingly silent Margot beside him, he felt a subtle sense of peace. Even though he knew that this hellscape would likely be his final resting place. It was a sense of ownership—that he owned his own life, and that if he died, it would be while trying to live, which was a very respectable thing to be doing. In fact, he felt like a respectable version of Fletcher for the first time in a long time.

That's not to say he wasn't also miserable. People can be two things. His leather throat rasped shallow breaths, and his brittle legs struggled with every uneven step. They walked for hours, across dirt and sand and around hills and rocks, through the dawn and into morning. It was all surreal. An endless test that meant everything. A blip of an instant that meant nothing. He wasn't even dead certain he was still alive.

It went like that for a while—two silent, reflective travelers stepping through morning—until they saw their first sign of hope. A dirt road. Evidence of humanity; civilization; life.

Their broken bodies walked faster, following the path. They walked the road until they saw a sign. It was the most glorious little metal sign they had ever seen.

It read: "Lake McGee."

Their reality had been pretty simple: find water or die. So, a lake was a good thing. They walked past the sign, turned the corner and there, right in front of them, was an abandoned ranch. Fletcher looked over at Margot. She was smiling ear to ear, her big eyes searching their newfound paradise. They crossed the property, the scene frozen in time: a rusty and forgotten tractor, one wheel lying on its side; a field of dust, enclosed by a broken-down pasture fence; multiple buildings and barns; some dilapidated sheds. They stumbled by what appeared to be the main house, which was covered in the same brown dust as everything else.

As Fletcher and Margot passed the once-white farmhouse, Lake McGee came into view. It was a real, live lake, its water shimmering and its shore no more than a hundred yards away. They shuffled their zombie legs as fast as they could toward the beautiful water, Fletcher praying it was not a mirage. They reached the lake's edge and, without slowing their gait one bit, splashed into the cool water. When Fletcher was up to his knees, he flung himself in face-first. It was diving into heaven itself. He lifted his head out of the water, laughing like a lunatic. Margot was laughing, too. She splashed him, giggling and cackling. He splashed back, whooping loudly, his voice carrying across the water. Fletcher took a look around, but was interrupted by Margot jumping on his back, shoving his head down under surface. He wished he could just live under that wonderful water. They floated on their backs in their soaked pink and blue uniforms, all the while laughing.

"Fudge sundaes," said Margot. "This is the life."

"Fudge sundaes is right," said Fletcher. "This might be the best feeling ever."

Eventually, though, they left the water. There was more to explore. They walked out, newly baptized. They were sopping, recharged, overjoyed and filled with a new hope that they might actually make it off this rock.

· · · · ● · ● · · · ·

The wooden porch of the ranch house creaked beneath Fletcher's feet. He tried the front door and it opened without a fight.

"Hello!" shouted Margot. "Anybody home?"

They walked into the kitchen, which featured a huge island and endless cupboards. Fletcher opened a few: canned goods, dried goods... food they could eat. There was also coffee—sweet, sweet coffee.

"Fletcher..." said Margot. She had opened a big pantry door. Fletcher walked over and nearly erupted into a happy cry. There, on the bottom shelf, were three beautiful jugs, a gallon each, of clear, wet water—unopened, waiting for someone like them. They each snatched one and drank. Fletcher could feel the life-saving liquid run through his body, down his esophagus, settling in his stomach for a moment, and then traveling through his legs and arms, all the way to his toes and fingers. He set the jug down and lay on the tile floor. He let out a satisfied sigh.

Fletcher forced himself to his feet and walked into the dining room. There were four bowls, white with little blue swirls, sitting on the table with spoons still scattered around. A cereal box was on its side. It looked as if the family had up and vanished mid-breakfast.

Fletcher crept into the living room. It was a boring room, centered around a small couch with a strange Southwestern print facing a tiny, cubic TV that looked twenty years old. Everything looked twenty years old. There was a framed cross-stitch with the words: "Home is where the cat is."

And it was. The cat was in the hallway, and Fletcher jumped back with a small shriek when he saw it.

"Mr. Tough Guy," said Margot, bending down to pet the gray and white feline. The cat allowed it for a moment before disappearing in the other direction.

They continued to the stairs. On the second floor they found another hallway. There was a bathroom, followed by a kids' room that looked as if playtime had simply been paused and could resume at any moment. It looked to belong to two boys, judging by the bunk beds and toys and décor. In the middle of the floor was a plastic baseball bat, some Teenage Mutant Ninja Turtles pajamas and an action figure of a strange squid-human hybrid, which Fletcher immediately recognized as Admiral Ackbar.

At the end of the hall were double doors leading to the primary bedroom. Fletcher opened the doors and gasped inward, his heart shooting into his throat with the second shock in just a few minutes. In the middle of the carpeted floor lay a human corpse, almost entirely decomposed. Underneath the skeleton, on the white rug, was a faded brown stain. Delilah had been here.

Fletcher thought of the abandoned breakfast table. The family fleeing in a hurry. Leaving this here. Leaving him here.

Fletcher had lived through the Delilah Virus and its carnage, so he had seen his share of death. For some reason, though, even though he didn't know this man, a somber feeling overcame him. Maybe he was just out of practice.

Careful to avoid the skeleton's empty eyes, Fletcher tiptoed across the room and opened the closet. He found some Wrangler jeans that were close to his size, a belt to help them stay up on his skinny waist, a few old plain T-shirts and some underwear. There was a woman's dresser, too, and Margot found a ridiculous sundress with sunflowers all over it. They changed in separate rooms and met back downstairs. They looked like new people without their regalia—and felt like it, too.

The electricity, water and gas didn't work, but they were more than thankful to have shelter. After a quick search around the side of the house, Fletcher discovered a big barbecue grill connected to a propane tank. Even though they had those few gallons of fresh water, they boiled a giant pot of lake water. Fletcher was no mountain man, but he knew there was something about boiling water that made it drinkable. He figured they should save the reserves while they had a big-ass lake in their front yard.

That night, they feasted. Like Catalina royalty. From a thin cardboard box and a small glass jar they conjured up a spaghetti dinner that was the single greatest indulgence of their lives. They drank water like it was fine wine. They couldn't have asked for anything more, not in all the world.

Even the cat, which Margot had named Bartholomew, feasted on a big bowl of kibble from the cupboard.

After dinner Fletcher and Margot sat on Adirondack chairs out on the porch, watching the sunset paint the lake orange. They sat in silence, in a trance, Bartholomew lying by Margot's feet.

"You know," said Margot. Breaking quietness was her specialty. "I've decided something."

"Do tell," said Fletcher.

"I've decided," she said, "that we can believe different things. You and me."

"Oh," said Fletcher. "Thank you."

"You can believe what you believe," she said. "And I can believe what I believe."

"You've got yourself a deal."

"But here's what I believe," said Margot.

"And here we go."

"I believe," she said, "that something brought us together. Some sort of destiny or something."

Fletcher grunted.

"I believe," said Margot, "that *you* were made to survive, to be the last man left. For a reason. And that I'm here for a reason, too."

"And what's that?" he asked.

"Maybe to protect you," said Margot. "Or for my cooking skills. Or because I know karate."

"You know karate?" asked Fletcher.

"No," said Margot. "I'm just saying."

They sat in silence for a moment.

"But maybe," said Margot, "maybe you just needed a friend. Maybe that's why I'm here."

Fletcher's throat tightened. A lump like a golf ball grew behind his tongue. He thought of his old friends, long dead. He thought of his new friends, and how he'd hurt them. He thought of Jordan. He thought of the loneliness that he'd so rightfully earned.

His eyes got all misty and he rubbed the wetness away. "Maybe you're right," he croaked. He laughed, a little embarrassed.

"For Frank's sake," said Margot. "Pull yourself together, you big baby." She got up and hugged him, and Fletcher never wanted it to end.

That night they slept in the kids' room. Margot begged for the top bunk, so Fletcher took the bottom, feeling right at home wrapped in

Spider-Man sheets. Bartholomew lay curled up on the floor. The three of them slept for twelve hours.

Chapter 31

FLETCHER AND MARGOT STAYED at the ranch for a couple days, regaining strength. It was a beautiful little vacation, a getaway in the middle of Armageddon. They played house. They played cards. They slept a lot and they ate even more—canned chili, canned soup, more pasta. Fletcher got his coffee fix. They even had a pet cat, for God's sake. It was a wonderful couple of days, but—like any vacation—Fletcher knew it had to come to an end.

Eventually.

Maybe tomorrow. Or the day after.

The only thing that weighed on Fletcher's mind during their ranch house respite was the lonely corpse in the room at the end of the upstairs hall.

Maybe it was the fact that the home and food that Fletcher was enjoying so very much really belonged to this man, now a pile of bones, and it just wasn't fair or explainable. Maybe it was all the people he loved—and all the ones he'd never met—who were robbed of a proper burial. Maybe it was the heat getting to his head. Maybe it was a combination of things.

Fletcher couldn't see clearly enough to put a finger on why he felt such a connection to the dead stranger. Emotional intelligence was never his strong suit. But he felt what he felt, and on the third day at the ranch, when his strength was back enough, he did what he needed to do. While Margot slept that morning, Fletcher found a shovel in a shed near the house and went to work in the soft soil of what was once a garden.

"Whatcha digging for, Farmer Joe?" asked Margot from the porch when she finally awoke.

"I'm not really sure," said Fletcher honestly.

"Well," she said, "I'll help. Maybe we'll find it faster."

They spent the whole morning digging a big hole—not the recommended six feet, but better than nothing. Bartholomew watched them curiously from a safe distance.

"Wait here," said Fletcher. He went upstairs to the primary bedroom, pulled the sheets off the bed, and wrapped up the bones like a macabre burrito. They were brittle. A few thin ones, maybe ribs, cracked. He clenched his teeth as he dutifully continued his task, ignoring the stain on the floor as best he could. He lifted the rolled-up corpse and carried it like a child across his chest.

"Oh," whispered Margot when he appeared. "I see."

Fletcher laid the rancher to rest in the shallow grave and they shoveled the dirt back in.

"You have to say some words, I think," said Margot.

They stared at the fresh grave. For a moment, it was no longer the rancher in that hole. It was his brother. Adam, whom he'd left to rot on his bed alone. Adam, whose tomb he'd sealed with a layer of duct tape.

Hell, it could be both of them. The rancher and the brother. His parents, too. And anyone else. Everyone else.

"Thank you for everything," said Fletcher. "I'm sorry I'm here and you're not. Trust me, I don't get it, either."

He wasn't a natural at sentimental eulogies, but it was as nice a service as Fletcher could give. Then he sat in the dust and cried.

Margot sat beside him and put an arm around his shoulders.

"For the record," she said, as Bartholomew leaned against Fletcher's shins, "I'm glad you're here."

·········

"I wish we could," said Margot. "But we can't."

It was later that afternoon, and they were sitting around the kitchen table playing Go Fish.

"Wish we could what?" said Fletcher.

"Stay here," said Margot. "Forever."

"I know," said Fletcher.

"Mister," she said, "we gotta go get your girl."

Fletcher smiled at her. She was right. Plus, as long as they stayed on the island, the pink brigade would be after him. They'd eventually find him. Hell, they'd found him at a hospital in La Jolla. Maybe they weren't killers, but he wasn't going back to that commune. He didn't want Margot to, either.

They needed to get to Avalon. If they could get to Avalon, they could get a boat. If they could get a boat, they'd have a shot at getting back to the mainland. He didn't exactly know how to operate a watercraft, but how hard could it be? It would be just like crossing the Last Sea in *The Odyssey of Zordallus.* And just like in *Zordallus,* a new adventure awaited on the other side.

Fletcher and Margot examined an old mid-90s Ford pickup in the dusty driveway. Once fire-engine red, it now barely held any of its original skin. Thankfully, the old jalopy still had some gas in her tank. So, in the last light of their last night, they packed anything they might need in the bed of the truck: a shovel, an axe, rope, blankets, a shit-ton of canned food and as much water as they could find containers for.

At dawn, they'd ride.

As Fletcher lay wrapped up in someone else's Spider-Man sheets that night, he stared at the ceiling and thought.

For some reason, Fletcher thought about the one party he had gone to in high school. It had been his junior year and his cooler cousin, Mark, had a friend who was throwing a party. Mark convinced Fletcher to go, and Fletcher had convinced Simon to join him as backup.

Crazy things happened at parties. Some kids got in fights. Some got laid. Some got sick. Some got arrested. Fletcher's "crazy" was having a conversation with Will. Will was inner-circle popular.

Fletcher and Simon had hung against the wall of the party, observing the wildlife from a distance.

"You fellas taking notes?" The voice belonged to Will.

Fletcher stammered a response.

"Probably the high point of his life," said Will, pointing to a beefy douchebag making out with some skinny girl. "All downhill for him after graduation."

Fletcher laughed. Then Will asked Fletcher and Simon what they were doing after graduation. It was all a bit uncanny, Fletcher and Simon and Will all talking as if they weren't crossing caste lines.

Fletcher and Simon had no real plans for after high school. They still had senior year to survive. But college, they supposed. Didn't know where. Will, of course, had plans. He already had an exchange program he wanted to do. He was going to spend a year in China.

Fletcher asked why.

"I dunno, man," he said. "What am I missing here? These parties?"

They watched the drunken crowd for a moment.

"I dunno..." Will continued. "I guess I think that a man's life is a story, and it's his responsibility to make it a good one."

Fletcher and Simon nodded.

"Well, that was corny," laughed Will.

Fletcher didn't think so. It had sounded impossibly cool.

"Anyways," Will continued, "what do I know?"

"I guess we'll find out," said Fletcher. Will then lifted his red Solo cup in a sort of salute, and left Fletcher and Simon to bask in post-Will glow.

Fletcher wished Will could see him now. And Simon, too.

"A man's life is a story, and it's his responsibility to make it a good one," Fletcher whispered sacredly in the dark, in some dead boys' room in a strange ranch house on Catalina Island.

"What?" asked Margot from the top bunk.

"Nothing," said Fletcher. "Goodnight, Margot."

"Goodnight," she said. "And, in case I die in my sleep, let me say: I'm excited for our adventure."

"So am I, Margot," said Fletcher. "But don't die in your sleep."

Fletcher thought that, above all else, he was making a pretty damn good story. And the next chapter started at dawn.

·········

They left the ranch house at first light, leaving the deck of cards on the table and a pile of dishes in the sink. They had made it only twenty feet when Fletcher stepped on the brakes and brought the big, grumbling Ford to a halt. He rolled down the window and looked at the gravesite he and Margot had filled, now an unassuming pile of dirt beside the driveway.

He opened his mouth to say something, but he was empty of meaningful words at the moment, so he just nodded. And with that, they were done with the ranch.

The truck shook and rattled down the dirt road, water jugs and tools and bags of canned food bouncing around like popcorn in the bed. Margot smiled at him from the passenger side of the bench seat. Bartholomew purred between them.

It wasn't hard to find the one real city on the island. Not with a road and a truck. They followed dirt roads to bigger dirt roads to a real paved road until they found a sign pointing them to their destination.

They rolled through the brown nothingness, the dry, hot dusty wasteland, the godforsaken rock that burned your skin and blistered your feet and made you eat bugs if you walked upon it long enough.

Finally, they saw civilization. At the top of a giant hill, the world opened up before them. The ocean sprawled out—endless and beautiful and a little bit scary now that they would be trying to navigate it on their own. And between them and the water was Avalon.

The small town was built into a small bay, a perfect little half circle. The buildings started on the coast and crawled up the hillside, an oasis of what was once human life tucked away between desolate brown slopes. Boats of all kinds lined the harbor, in perfect rows facing the same direction like a formation of soldiers prepared for battle.

They passed a million white stucco cottages with red-tiled roofs as they drove into town. The Ford puttered down toward the water, by colorful golf carts sitting outside bed-and-breakfasts and ex-vacation homes. Just miles east, they had starved and suffered. And all this had been sitting here the whole time.

The road led to the water, ending at a roundabout lined with palm trees. They parked the truck next to an Italian restaurant and an art gallery and got out, Margot holding the cat in her arms. They took in the eerie beauty of the abandoned vacation town …. everything still, everything paused. The moored boats were close enough to swim to—sailboats, dinghies, speedboats and more. Fletcher looked to his left and saw the Catalina Casino, that giant cylindrical building that looked like Jabba's palace, sitting on the point.

On the side of the bay opposite the edifice, they found what they were looking for. There was a small dock with a couple powerboats tied up—their escape pods. Fletcher looked across the water: Mainland. Jordan.

The first step was getting one of the boats fired up. He found one with an outboard motor that didn't require a key. He stood in the back and put his hand on the black powerhead of the Mercury motor and examined it. He looked at the choke, which he didn't know was the choke. He looked at the squishy primer bulb, which also meant nothing to him. He recognized the starter cord, though—just like he'd seen his dad use on their lawnmower. His dad had tried to pass on the lawn-mowing responsibilities to Fletcher for years, but Fletcher just hadn't been much of a sweat-and-hard-work kind of kid. It sure would have come in handy now.

Fletcher grabbed the handle of the starter cord and gave it a yank. It hardly moved. He readjusted, going slower and steadier this time. He succeeded in pulling the cord back, but the engine remained dormant. He flipped the choke switch back and forth a couple times for fun and examined the engine for a button he'd missed. He pulled the cord again. When this proved fruitless, he hopped out of the boat and into another. When that one wouldn't start, he marveled at his bad luck: two engines were busted. He hopped into the third and yanked the cord hopelessly.

"Son of a bitch," grunted Fletcher.

"Geez, Mr. Grumpy Pants," said Margot, still holding Bartholomew.

"I can't start it," sighed Fletcher, defeated.

"Oh," said Margot. "I can."

She stepped into the boat, handed the cat to Fletcher, fiddled with the choke and the primer, and pulled the cord. The engine coughed and then roared to life.

"No problem, señor," she said.

Fletcher looked at her. "Margot?" he asked. "Do you also happen to know how to drive one of these things?"

"Of course!" she said.

"Of course," said Fletcher, now remembering that Margot had been the one operating the sailboat on their journey here, a lifetime ago. "Well, you're the captain then."

"It is my honor," she said, and Fletcher could tell it was. "We'll go south a wee bit. Dana Point, like we came from, not Long Beach."

"To avoid LA," said Fletcher.

"Heck yeah," she said. "Trouble with a capital T."

Farther down the coast was fine with Fletcher. It simply meant they would land closer to San Diego. And hopefully to Jordan.

They packed their supplies in the boat, untied and took off for the coast of California. Margot operated the vessel effortlessly, singing 'A Pirate's Life for Me'. Fletcher sat on a bench in the bow, grinning as they bobbed up and down, spray hitting his face, all the while holding Bartholomew.

He looked back at the island, emerging from the sparkling sea. He thought it would have been a beautiful place to visit before the world ended.

As Catalina grew smaller and smaller, Fletcher's hope grew bigger and bigger. Hope that life could be good again. Hope that he and Margot would find Jordan. Hope that he could become someone he was proud of. Hope that it would all be alright.

··········

Fletcher tangled a rope around a cleat on the dock. A sailor he was not.

"Thank you for traveling with Margot Luxury Cruises," said Margot. "And welcome to Dana Point."

"Thanks, captain," said Fletcher, wobbling out of the boat and onto the concrete pier.

Margot handed Fletcher the cat and joined him on the dock. The long concrete runway stretched out before them, connecting them to the mainland. Fletcher looked around, smiling.

Dana Point was still. The marina was protected by a long jetty, and the water was glassy and calm. A forest of sailboat masts stretched in both directions. Before them, a tall bluff rose all brown and earthy, with the roofs of mansions barely visible at the top. The quiet jingle-jangle of metal chimed from the bobbing sailboats, and a single seagull screeched.

If seagulls could speak English, it may have told Fletcher that they were not alone. But they learned quickly enough.

As Fletcher and Margot walked toward land, they saw movement in the parking lot in front of them. A big, black Sprinter van whipped through the abandoned lot, coming to a stop where the dock met the land.

Between Fletcher and Margot and the rest of the world.

The doors slid open and two women hopped out—a small, dark-skinned woman with a baseball cap and a stocky, stump-like white woman with a thick neck and shoulder-length dirty blonde hair. They both wore all black like a SWAT team. The driver's door opened and an athletic woman with short, light-brown hair stepped out. The three women exchanged looks that were hard to read from the dock, but felt like surprise.

They didn't waste time. They were on the narrow pier, facing Fletcher and Margot, and moving toward them. The dock creaked and groaned.

"Well, I'll be damned," said the driver.

"Is that...?" stuttered the blonde stump.

"Is that a boy?" said the small one with the ballcap.

Fletcher and Margot stood still, not sure if their new dockmates were friend or foe.

"Oh, that's a fucking boy," said the driver. "You can smell him from here."

They didn't seem like friends.

"Hey, boy!" she shouted at Fletcher. "How come you're not dead?"

Fletcher didn't answer. He just stood there, like a cowboy waiting to draw. Or maybe like a deer in headlights. The three newcomers stopped directly in front of Fletcher and Margot. There was nowhere to go.

"Hello, ladies!" said Margot. "Can we help you?"

"Hello, darling," said the driver. "Yes, you can. You can give us your gross little pet and we can go our separate ways."

"Bartholomew?" said Margot. "But that's our cat!"

"Not the cat." The driver smiled.

"We don't want any trouble," said Fletcher. "We're just on our way to find—"

"You keep your disgusting mouth shut," said the driver. Her eyes opened unnaturally wide. Fletcher obliged.

The driver reached into her black jacket and pulled out a handgun. She pointed it at Fletcher and Margot.

"Hand over the boy," she said.

Margot stepped in front of Fletcher. "Oh, pish-posh," she said. "No need for that, now."

"Yes need for that now," said the driver. "Besides, that creature will bring you nothing but problems."

"Oh, not good old Fletcher," said Margot.

"They're all the same," said the woman with the gun. "*Man* was the true disease of so-called *man*kind. He doesn't deserve you, sister. Let him go and finally be free of him."

"Margot," said Fletcher. "It's okay. Let me go with them. I'll see what they want and..."

"Heck no!" said Margot. "You crazy?"

"Girl," said the driver, "you have three seconds to step aside."

"Step aside, Margot," urged Fletcher.

"Three," said the driver, sighing impatiently. "Two."

"Margot," said Fletcher. "Move."

"One."

"You can't have him!" said Margot, stepping forward. "He's my friend!"

Then there was the sound. A crack that ripped the air and shook the trees.

Then there was Margot. She collapsed on the ground, right in front of Fletcher, as if someone had simply flipped a switch.

Then everything was still.

The driver held her pistol in place. Her eyes were still wide. The other two women lowered their heads, as if unable to look. Fletcher dropped to his knees. The moored boats stopped their rustling and clanging to watch the scene.

The seagull was quiet, too.

Fletcher crawled to Margot. He faintly registered a horrible, distant groaning sound, unaware that it was coming from him. He held Margot's body, shaking, burying his face into her neck, her hair.

She was gone. There only seconds before. Now gone.

The stocky woman walked up, stepping over Margot's body, and grabbed Fletcher by the arm.

"Let's go," she said lowly. She lifted him up like a ragdoll and fastened his hands behind his back with a zip tie. When he refused to move—unable to leave Margot, unable to process the woman's commands—she shoved him toward mainland, past the ballcap girl and the driver. The driver still held the gun, smirking at Fletcher. Fletcher couldn't look at her. Or anything. He had lost vision, and all other awareness of self and place. Like Margot, he was just a body now.

At the top of the gangway, as Fletcher's feet touched mainland, he heard the ballcap girl behind him.

"Greer," she said. "It's just a cat."

And the crack again.

As Fletcher was thrown into the black Sprinter van, as a pillowcase was pulled over his head, as he heard the sliding door close him in, Margot's last words echoed in his brain. He thought that Margot would have been proud of those final words. They were worthy of her.

Her last words had been: "He's my friend."

Fletcher sat there, shaking.

PART V
WORM BOY

Chapter 32

When Fletcher was a sophomore, Harry Johnson was Rancho Bernardo royalty. Well, @BigHarryJohnsonRBHS, to be more specific. That was his Instagram handle. Nobody knew his real name (there was no "Harry Johnson" at their school) but everybody—*everybody*—followed him.

He was anonymous. He was infamous. He was funny. He was cruel. To some, he was the voice of the people, saying what nobody else had the balls to say. To others he was an asshole hiding behind a keyboard, spewing venom about his peers with no fear of consequence.

What was this can't-miss content that @BigHarryJohnsonRBHS posted? What was his message to the masses that filled both newsfeeds and high school hallways? Simple: he posted lots and lots of embarrassing photos. He turned these photos into memes that spread like herpes. Who could resist violence disguised as comedy?

Eventually, and it was only a matter of time, his crosshairs found Fletcher. Oh, and the crowd loved it. At first, it wasn't just him. @BigHarryJohnsonRBHS posted a photo of Fletcher, Simon, Jake, Stephen, Anton and Ash sitting around a cafeteria table playing *Orcs & Oracles*. You couldn't see the warlocks and magical weapons on their cards, but anybody who had walked by that table around lunch knew what was going on. The meme headline, superimposed on the image, said: "One photo. So much virginity."

Fletcher and his gang grumbled about it the next morning. A few kids chuckled at them as they walked down the hallway. But they had strength in numbers. The blow was spread out among six of them.

The next time Fletcher appeared in his school's social media tabloid, he wasn't so lucky. He had been dragged to a basketball game by Simon, whose dad had made him go. Late in the third quarter, a shot tipped off a player's fingers and into the crowd. The crowd where Fletcher was sitting. The crowd where Fletcher was sitting and not paying attention. The photo showed it all: the ball slapping and contorting Fletcher's face, his expression like getting shot in the stomach—eyes wide, mouth agape and crooked, tongue flailing. When this lovely portrait was posted, the message read: "When it's chicken burgers for lunch." To be fair, Rancho Bernardo High School did have notoriously vile chicken burgers. It was relatable content.

But Fletcher was horrified. He almost didn't show up to school the next day, and when he did, he wished he hadn't. People he didn't know giggled as he walked by. The ones he did know gave him their best impression of "the face" as he passed.

"Don't worry about it," said Simon. "It'll be someone else tomorrow."

And it was. But it wasn't long until it was Fletcher again. There was the photo of Fletcher standing by himself in the parking lot, zoning out, waiting for his ride: "When your own mom stands you up." There was the shot of Fletcher drinking an Agent Orange while wearing an Agent Orange T-shirt: "Agent Orange: the official drink of disappointing your father." Finally, there was Skeletor. Unfortunately, @BigHarryJohnsonRBHS had gotten his hands on a picture of Fletcher at the beach from the previous summer. Actually, it was Adam's fault. Fletcher's brother had posted the photo from when the family had gone to Ocean Beach for the day. The photo had been of Adam and his dad, but—if you looked just to Adam's left—there was Fletcher, toweling off. He was standing up and drying his back with the towel, holding it like a cape ... exposing all of his bony skinniness. And @BigHarryJohnsonRBHS had zoomed in and cropped the photo, slapping on a message that read: "Skeletor comin' for your girl."

"Skeletor isn't even skinny," Simon reminded him the next day. He was, of course, talking about the original Skeletor, of *Masters of the Universe* fame. "He's actually jacked."

"Doesn't really help, does it?" said Fletcher. People were already calling him by his new name.

"Don't let it get to you," said Simon. "Nobody takes it seriously."

"That's easy to say when you're not Skeletor," said Fletcher.

Fletcher never again felt safe in the halls of his high school. He knew they were jokes, and he tried to brush them off, but fear ate away at him like a worm in an apple. That fear was constant, and it was worse than the posts themselves. It was fear of not knowing who his tormentor was, or where the next photo would be captured, or when the next post would pop up and deliver another shot of social cyanide. He tiptoed, trying not to do anything stupid, or say anything stupid, or move his face in a way that might look stupid.

Eventually, @BigHarryJohnsonRBHS fizzled away. The owner probably graduated, and the once-legendary persona faded into oblivion. But while he was around, and for a good time after he was gone, @BigHarryJohnsonRBHS owned Fletcher. And Fletcher never even knew who he was.

··········

Years later, the Fletcher who was being jostled about in the back of a Sprinter van with a pillowcase over his head was a different Fletcher altogether. With a different state of mind. This Fletcher wasn't so easily controlled by something as floaty and imaginary as fear—not anymore. He'd been through too much. He'd been broken too much. He'd survived too much. After all, it turned out that he—little old Fletcher—was actually pretty good at surviving. Better than any man he'd ever known. Maybe better than any man ever. One thing was for sure: he was definitely better at surviving than whatever asshole had controlled @BigHarryJohnsonRBHS. He was as dead as anyone.

No, Fletcher wasn't afraid anymore. Shattered, but not afraid. Seething, but not afraid.

Mostly, he was consumed by a gut-wrenching horror that filled his stomach like black acid, liquifying his insides. It was the horror of reality sinking in: Margot was gone.

Sure, he'd lost a lot of people close to him. But that was different. Delilah was a virus. She was impartial. Without malice. This—this was murder. This was his friend, and she was murdered in front of him. Because of him.

They say there are five stages of grief: denial, anger, bargaining, depression and acceptance. But that was before Delilah. Or maybe it was all bullshit to begin with. As Fletcher lay crumpled in the corner of the van, bouncing along as they drove, he found himself swaying back and forth between that gut-wrenching horror and a hollow, flu-like daze—like he was just a butcher's bounty, a pile of meat and bone, with no thinking and no feeling.

One moment a sickening fire, the next an empty shell.

This will all be over soon.

"Betcha didn't expect to find us waiting for ya, did you?" said a faceless voice. It wasn't the driver—the murderer. It didn't sound like it could come from the stump girl either. Fletcher thought it must be the small one with the ballcap.

"I did not," said Fletcher. The pillowcase was damp around his mouth from his hurried breaths.

"Betcha wondering who we are and what we're doing, huh?" the voice said again.

"Not really," said Fletcher.

"Well, we're a little surprised ourselves. You sort of dropped into our lap."

"What a nice treat," said Fletcher.

"Hey," whined the voice. "Watch your tone."

"Yeah, you don't know who you're dealing with," said the voice of the stump girl. "We're everywhere. We see everything. Like your boat. We saw you guys coming from a mile away."

"Hey, is it true?" the ballcap girl asked. "Is there really a cult of wiener worshippers on that island? That why you were there?"

"I was on vacation," said Fletcher. Then something hard smacked into his nose, and blood flowed.

"Whoa!" said the ballcap girl.

"Don't let him talk to you like that," said the voice of the driver, apparently responsible for the blow.

Fletcher groaned and coughed and soaked up the blood with the pillowcase, conveniently already covering his head. He could feel the blood-soaked cotton spreading the red liquid all over his face as it shifted around.

There was some whispering, then Fletcher heard the ballcap girl say: "What's it matter? Mm-hmm. Okay. Fine, fine, I'll zip it."

They sat in silence for the rest of the drive, which wasn't long. A half hour? An hour? An eternity? All Fletcher could do was think about Margot. Poor, sweet Margot.

His friend.

Finally, the van came to an abrupt stop. The women piled out, mystery hands pushing and pulling Fletcher until he was finally standing on concrete.

A hand suddenly grabbed the top of his head and pulled off the blindfold. The sun melted everything into a bright whiteness, and Fletcher covered his eyes to adjust.

"Welcome," said a new voice—a smooth, confident voice—"to the City of Angels."

Chapter 33

Los Angeles.

The Odyssey of Fletcher had led its unlikely hero to the one place that he'd been told to avoid. The place that Jordan had warned him about. That poor Margot had warned him about. This was the place where the modern-day ghost stories were born, churning, bubbling and leaking into the real world.

Frodo was in Mordor at last.

Fletcher looked around. What he saw reminded him of finally arriving at the Great Citadel of Orun in *Zordallus*, only to find it in ruins. A skeleton of a once-great civilization.

Dilapidated buildings lined the downtown streets on all sides of Fletcher. The ground floors were now open wounds of shattered windows, exposing trashed lobbies and raided stores. Some buildings had been reduced to rubble, half-walls like splintered bones rising out of their crumbled remains. Cars had been left to die on sidewalks, some charred with long-ago arson. Streetlights were felled like urban trees and garbage burned in metal barrels, polluting the scene with its acrid stench.

The road was filled with women dressed in the same black outfits as Fletcher's captors—black cargo pants or black jeans, topped with black tanks or tees. They were the anonymous fatigues of a nameless army. Groups of women marched this way and that, while others stood silently under pergolas and in front of ruined buildings, most with unpleasant faces, unpleasant postures and unpleasant guns.

"Why did you blindfold me if I was going to see where we ended up anyways?" asked Fletcher as one woman checked the zip ties on his wrists.

"So we wouldn't have to look at you," said the driver. "And holy shit, you look disgusting."

Actually, he did. His face was covered in dried blood, as if he had just walked off a Viking battlefield.

"Yeah," said the ballcap girl. "You might be the last man on Earth, and I still wouldn't touch you with a ten-foot pole."

Fletcher shrugged.

He took a look at his captors. The small, dark-featured girl with the ballcap—the one who had done most of the talking in the van before being shushed—was named Frankie. She had a narrow, serious, scared face. The stump-like girl was Brooklyn. She had a rather frog-like face, exceptionally shiny with bulgy eyes a little too far apart. Then there was Greer. Greer was the one with light brown hair, who seemed to be constantly clenching her teeth. She was the one with abnormally wide eyes, burning eyes, unstable eyes. She was the one who had killed Margot.

A group of women were there to greet Greer, Frankie, Brooklyn and Fletcher, too. Front and center was Candice.

Candice was the obvious leader, but it wasn't her physical appearance that made her position clear. In fact, she was unremarkable-looking—average stature, dark brown ponytail, a face that could have belonged to anyone. No, it was the way everyone around her acted: their softened shoulders, their quick nods, their absolute silence while she spoke. She was the Alpha. Candice carried herself as such, moving in an assertive, deliberate manner and speaking with the kind of pure and believable confidence that Fletcher envied.

Greer pulled a huge black canvas duffle from the back of the Sprinter van and dropped it at Fletcher's feet. It landed with a thud and a clanging of metal from inside. "Carry this," she said.

The zipper was open just a few inches, and Fletcher could see an assortment of firearms inside. Was that what they'd been doing before seeing him? Collecting more weapons?

Fletcher's grandma had been quite religious. She had had many paintings of Jesus in her house, Jesus at all different stages of his life: just after being born, surrounded by farm animals and three rich guys, a big star hanging just above the manger; standing before droves of people, handing out a loaf of bread in one hand and a raw fish in the other; out on an angry ocean, walking across the water as his friends cheered him on; stepping out of a cave with a giant stone rolled to the side, all dressed in white and shooting light beams out in every direction. The one that always gave Fletcher a funny feeling, though, was the one of Jesus walking the dirty streets of Jerusalem, carrying his own cross. The fact that he knew he was going to die was bad enough. Then they went and made him carry his own execution device, which looked way too heavy for anyone to lift safely. But they made him walk through the streets with it anyway. In front of people who were probably saying all sorts of nasty shit to him. It just felt like overkill.

Fletcher thought of that painting now as he walked through LA, grunting with the awkward weight of the bag, sickened by the thought that he could be carrying the tools that would bring his own demise, or others like Margot. He sure didn't feel like Jesus, but he empathized with the guy in his grandma's painting. His captors—Greer, Frankie, Brooklyn, as well as Candice and a few more of her cronies—led him down the center of the street, a busted-up Chipotle on one side, the corpse of a sushi restaurant called Sugarfish on the other.

They led him like a doomed man to the gallows, past crowds of people who were ready for the show. Fletcher focused on keeping his feet moving and his head high, trying to ignore the hissed whispers. Through the streets they walked, by once-trendy restaurants where Angelinos used to eat overpriced Wagyu sliders and avocado toast, by bars they used to stumble in and out of on Friday and Saturday nights and by a gym where they used to try and undo all the damage.

Eventually Fletcher and his captors arrived at an old hotel—a big, red building made out of bricks, in the shape of a brick. Painted on the side was a giant sign, now very faded, reading: "Hotel Cecil – Low Daily Rates – Weekly Rates – 700 Rooms."

"Welcome home," said Brooklyn.

·········

"Who are you guys?" Fletcher was sitting on the bed in his new eleventh-floor cell-slash-hotel-room. "I still don't—"

"Well, we're not *guys*," said Candice. "Which is why we're still here."

Candice had asked to be left alone with the new detainee. She was sitting on an office chair backward, facing Fletcher, her arms folded and resting atop the chair's back. She looked at Fletcher the way you might watch a monkey in the zoo play with its own turd.

"But who are we?" Candice tilted her head to the side. "It's simple: We're the future. The universe said—as clearly as the universe can say anything, really—that the way of men was over. That it was time for a new way. A new leader. Well, we are the new way. We are the new leader."

She spoke with an air of authority, of incontrovertibility, like a teacher to her student.

"It's a scary time, Fletcher," she continued. "Of that there is no doubt. People are waiting and hoping and praying for someone to bring order to this world reborn. To bring security. To bring organization. So, that's what we're doing. We are rebuilding society itself. To be better than ever." She paused. "We are no longer the daughters of a broken yesterday. We, Fletcher, are the Daughters of Tomorrow."

"Well, that sounds fine," said Fletcher. "I won't get in your way. Maybe I can just walk away and you'll never see me again?"

Candice chuckled with all the warmth of a dark, frozen cave. "Here's your situation: You are just one little boy. You have no power."

Fletcher nodded. This was true enough.

"But whoever has you, well—they have power."

"Oh, I don't know..."

"Repopulation," said Candice. "Whoever controls repopulation controls how the world is rebuilt."

Fletcher nodded. He had a feeling that revealing his infertility wouldn't be good for his lifespan.

"But how will it be rebuilt?" asked Candice. "By women. For women. You, meanwhile, no longer have to worry about anything. You just eat and sleep and provide sperm and turn off that poor male brain of yours. Do this and you will not be harmed. Any female offspring will grow up as Daughters. Any male ones will join you in your simple, stress-free existence."

"As slaves." Fletcher rubbed the heel of his palm into his forehead. He was tired of new worlds.

"Fletcher," said Candice. "You must realize that all of humankind's problems are male. Just think about the evil done by those with Y chromosomes. You must see that man is a disease—one that life has weeded out for its own survival."

Fletcher nodded.

"The universe set it all in motion," said Candice.

It was always the universe or God or destiny or some shit.

"Life simply purged itself of its disease," Candice continued. "It was inevitable. Think of what the world was like when your kind was in control. Entire civilizations, thousands of years long, built to give men power and keep women subordinate. Men wrote it in their holy bibles and in their laws so it would live above question.

"And what did they do with their world? Violence was practically an international pastime—and domestic violence was especially popular. Look at movies, sports, music—they all celebrated violence. Violence was how disagreements were settled, between individuals and countries alike. Anger was strength. War was power.

"This was a world where corruption was expected. Where sex was currency. Where substance abuse was the norm. Where kindness was weakness. Where greed was admired. Where competition, not collaboration, reigned."

A silence hung in the air like a bad smell. Those were a lot of fancy words, and Fletcher didn't know what to say. Besides, he wasn't prepared to talk on behalf of every man in the history of the world.

On top of that, who was she to talk about violence?

The sound of the creaking dock.

The sound of the gunshot.

The sound of her body hitting the wood.

But he didn't say anything. He was tired. And heartbroken. And wanted nothing more than to be alone.

"Given the chance," said Candice, "you'd make the same kinds of choices men have been making for millennia. I believe you're simply born this way. The way a tiger is born with an innate need to kill. Or a mosquito to suck blood. I don't blame you. In many respects, I feel bad for you. I just want what's best for humanity, and that means finally keeping men—you and any others we find, or any others that are born—from making any more decisions for our world. So, play along and everything will be fine."

She got up and opened the door. Fletcher saw there had been three minions standing on the other side, waiting for Fletcher to inevitably fall prey to his primal male instincts and resort to violence. In which case they would have gotten to burst in and beat him to a pulp.

"Tomorrow starts today," said Candice. "Make yourself at home."

This will all be over soon.

Chapter 34

Fletcher settled into incarceration. An armed guard stood on the other side of his door every minute of every day, so he didn't have much of a choice. For the first week or so he never left his hotel room—a room that had to be as bad as an actual prison cell. If not as bad, at least as gross. If not as gross, at least as tasteless.

It felt about fifty years outdated, and looked to have been designed by someone's not-especially-artistic grandmother. The carpet was a grayish burgundy, with little white diamonds in an unnecessary pattern. There was a desk, a mirror and a dresser; all big, bulky, mahogany beasts. The TV was as deep as it was wide—a tube-style clunker from Fletcher's childhood that he found offensive on a fundamental level. To add insult to injury, it turned out the Daughters of Tomorrow hadn't figured out a power source—a luxury he'd grown accustomed to in La Jolla—so the TV was just for decoration anyway. The comforter on his bed seemed to have been lifted from an old folks' home, all creamy white with pastel flowers stretching from edge to edge like some sort of Easter nightmare. The bathroom was the size of a coffin, with a stained and rusted toilet sitting practically underneath the tiny pedestal sink. The tiled walls were turquoise and somehow always wet.

The one form of entertainment he was allowed was reading. The Daughters let him sift through boxes of books they'd found in the hotel's abandoned rooms. While it was a far cry from a nice, humming PS5 console, he supposed now was as good a time as any to try this whole reading thing.

In the morning, the Southern California sun blasted through his one square window, painting the opposite wall a mustard yellow. Fletcher was always up before that sun. Some mornings he thought about Jordan, and felt hope. Others he thought about Margot, and wept. Often he just sat and watched the light move across the wall as the earth slowly turned.

From that window Fletcher could also see the street below. Women in black ran to and fro, all day and all night, wearing guns strapped to their backs or fastened to their hips. He could hear them shooting glass bottles. This was how you built a non-violent future, apparently. A heavily guarded tank truck fueled up vehicles throughout the day. Fletcher watched as the Daughters of Tomorrow hopped into cars and disappeared, or moved debris off the streets and out of Fletcher's view. Little black ants carrying crumbs to their hive. Little black ants working for their queen. Candice, the queen of the ants, only visited Fletcher occasionally, and only for a brief continuation of her lecture. How great their new world would be. How much better it would be than all the male-run dynasties before it. Why her and her friends were the ones for the job. Fletcher felt like he should be transcribing her soliloquies into some triumphant manifesto.

He had plenty of other visitors, though.

Fletcher's life had become a series of deliveries and pickups. First, there was the Mason jar. His job—and his only job—was to put semen in this jar. No semen meant no food. Of course, *he* knew his deposits were futile and fruitless, but he was pretty sure he'd be toast if they ever learned of his sterility. So, he obliged. And that was a feat all on its own, given the general unsexiness of his new environment. On the bright side: at least whatever poor women received his sperm would never bear his child.

The other transaction was his food—a lot of canned and dried foods, as expected, but a hell of a lot better than the procreation platters served by the Wives of the One Father. As they didn't have working plumbing in the hotel, they also brought him two buckets of water: one to drink, and one with which to flush the toilet.

Fletcher's captors came and went throughout the day, bringing empty Mason jars; taking them away with disgust; bringing full trays of food; taking the empty trays out; bringing buckets of water; taking the old ones out.

Once upon a time, toward the end of his hospital stay, Fletcher had had a steady flow of women coming through his door with one purpose: to please him. Well, the steady flow was back, but these visitors had quite the opposite intention.

For the record, neither experience was healthy for Fletcher.

The couriers of jars and trays rotated between a few different women—Candice's inner circle. They each showed their distaste for their prisoner in varying, unique ways.

"Want to know what I think?" Greer asked one morning when she was delivering the day's sperm repository.

"Not really," said Fletcher.

"I think that you were simply a mistake in nature's viral cleansing," said Greer. "That you somehow slipped through the cracks."

"Very possible," said Fletcher.

"I would *love* to finish the job," she said. "Maybe someday."

"That would suck," said Fletcher. "For me and the human race."

"I don't give a shit about the human race," she said.

"I don't doubt it."

"What did the human race ever do for you?" she asked.

Fletcher shrugged.

"Hey," she said, "remember when I killed your little girlfriend? Fun times, huh?"

"Go to hell," said Fletcher.

Greer responded by smashing the empty plastic tray against the side of Fletcher's head, right on his ear, making his head ring like a thousand mosquitos had hatched inside.

Most interactions with Greer went something like that. She was the most enthusiastic in her cruelty toward Fletcher, and made it a point to remind him every day that her goal was to convince Candice to let her kill him, humanity be damned. By the end of the first week, Fletcher already had a collection of scars and bumps and bruises to remember her visits by.

Brooklyn—the stump-like woman with the frog face—was less direct. "You know tons of people have died here?" she asked Fletcher one day. "Yeah, Hotel Cecil is pretty famous as far as hotel deaths go. Lotta people say it's haunted."

She told Fletcher of the countless suicides that had taken place within the hotel's walls since the 1930s, along with a good murder or two. She told him the story of The Black Dahlia, last spotted at the hotel before her murder in 1947. She told him of legendary serial killers Richard Ramirez, AKA "The Night Stalker," and Jack Unterweger, both shacking up at the hotel during their sprees. She told of the 2013 water tank tale and how, after people complained about the hotel water tasting funny, a naked, decomposing body was found in the building's water supply. Brooklyn told Fletcher these stories the way a dad tells ghost stories around the fire.

"Who knows?" she said. "Maybe you'll join the list someday."

It felt more like morbid fascination than intimidation to Fletcher. He decided she was pretty harmless, relatively speaking.

There was also Caitlin, a pale girl with pale eyes and a starry sky of freckles on her face, who piqued Fletcher's attention when she mentioned a rise in lesbianism within the Daughters of Tomorrow. She said it was as if nature were evolving in real time, rendering men obsolete right before their eyes. In fact, she told him, some female hammerhead sharks were known to become pregnant without a male when populations got low. She said this process was called parthenogenesis. She said it was only a matter of time until that happened to the human race. It was meant to be an insult, to show how useless Fletcher was, how little men were actually needed. But Fletcher was more intrigued than offended, and not about the cool shark story. He was still a heterosexual human male, after all, and all heterosexual human males are awed by the mystery and wonder of the female homoerotic, for reasons unknown. Fun lesbianism aside, though, Caitlin was pretty cold to Fletcher and he knew her hate for him was real.

Then there was Nia, a bookish Black girl who kept the hair on her head buzzed short. Whenever Nia came for delivery or pickups, she always recited some encyclopedia excerpt about how shitty men were: the Vikings, glorified despite their zest for rape; the dowry system in India; honor killings in the Middle East; Darwin's claim that women were evolutionarily closer to lower animals than men. She echoed Candice's rhetoric about how superior this new society of women would be compared to those misogynistic regimes of yore. Fletcher pondered this and decided that the opposite of misogyny didn't have to be misandry. It could be, you know, equality or whatever. But he kept his mouth shut. He would just nod, as if apologizing for the sins of his gender.

Of all the deliverywomen, though, Fletcher's favorite was Frankie. Or, at least, she was the most amusing. She was like a cute little fluffy dog growling at the Great Dane passing by, not fooling anybody. Oh, she tried her best to be mean, but it just didn't fit.

"I hope you bite your tongue when you're eating," she said one day. "Hope you had a bad night's sleep," she said on another. She tossed her nontoxic insults with wide-eyed focus, as if determined to prove she could be the heartless militia badass she felt inside. It was all Fletcher could do to not laugh.

"I hope the end of your book is really unsatisfying," she told Fletcher one day. After every affront, Fletcher would feign offense and Frankie would flush and storm out. It was an entertaining relationship for Fletcher, and he was pretty light on both entertainment and relationships.

In they came, out they went. Insult here, lecture there, with a solid Greer fist to the side of the head from time to time for good measure. Such was his routine. In between visits, Fletcher sat, read, slept, thought and waited. For whatever they decided to do with him.

··········

Fletcher watched the sun move across the stains of the back wall another seven times without leaving his room.

Apart from his depressing daily self-love sessions, Fletcher's duties were simple: do nothing. In fact, don't even think. Men, he was repeatedly told, were done doing the world's thinking.

Here was Fletcher's little secret, though: he kept thinking anyway. That was one of the nice things about thinking. You could think whatever thoughts you wanted, and nobody ever had to know.

He thought a lot about Jordan. She was a sort of beacon for him, a mantra to say in the dark; a reason to keep fighting. His ice cream. She was his reminder that the world could be good. She was his reminder that he could be good. He remembered once—on his birthday, actually—she had given him a mug to hold the coffee he had come to love so dearly. The mug had once said "Best Dad on Earth", but Jordan had scratched out the word "Dad" and wrote in "Man" with a Sharpie: "Best Man on Earth." It was a dorky joke, but still: Fletcher knew that she had believed in him then—believed he was a good guy. Not after everything, but for a time. Fletcher often thought about how happy he used to be doing nothing with her—playing board games, building puzzles, folding origami.

The memories came and went. Sometimes he could barely remember what Jordan looked like. Maybe he'd made her up. Other times their past conversations bounced off the walls and he could remember every word and how she had enunciated them, and he could see her sitting on the bed next to him, crinkling her nose at something he'd said, and he knew every curl of hair and the shape of her dimples and every pore on her crookedly-smiling face.

He thought about Margot, too. She was the friend he had needed when he was at his lowest. She was joy incarnate, and joy was contagious. When he started to blame himself for what happened, she reached through the void and put an end to it. Her relentless optimism wouldn't allow such mopiness. (*"Pull yourself together, Mr. Grumpy Pants,"* he could hear her say.) So, he decided to live for her as much as anyone, to make her proud. To look for the light, no matter how dark it got.

He thought about his brother, Adam, and wondered how different things would have been if it had been him instead of Fletcher this whole time. He thought about his dad, and what he'd think of Fletcher's adventures. He thought about his mom, and tried to imagine what she'd say to get him through this—the motherly sorcery she'd used any time he'd come home after being bullied or teased. He thought about Dr. Gomez as well, whom he'd come to think of as his post-apocalyptic mom. She, too, would have words of comfort to keep him afloat.

He also thought about the Daughters of Tomorrow. Through bits of spiteful conversations and angry rants, he pieced together their schtick—at least to some extent. Their rise to power happened how any good rise to power does: when people are scared, helpless and lost; when people are looking for someone, anyone to follow; when they'll eagerly trade reason for a reason to not be afraid anymore. Their new world order was that security, and it was their biggest recruitment tool.

The Daughters of Tomorrow had access to resources, like food and clean water, and they promised protection against scavengers. They spoke of a future that they would build together, that they would control. Their ideology was simple: anyone who joined them would be taken care of. Everyone else was a threat to the cause. Caitlin told Fletcher about an independent militia that had formed in Silver Lake. The Daughters were going to pay them a visit soon.

Fletcher was pretty sure that meant mass murder.

Even peaceful groups who simply refused to recognize their authority were forced to rethink. Greer told Fletcher about one such community, and how the Daughters had executed one person after another until the larger group swore allegiance to them.

And, of course: If they ever found a man (insert: Fletcher), he and any male offspring were to be used as captive breeders to continue the human race. That, and as manual laborers.

Fletcher knew Candice merely used the evils of men as a scapegoat, something to point to as justification for their existence, their rise. It went like this: men had run a pretty shitty operation for a few millennia; which was why nature had finally said "enough" and cleared them out; which was why a new society was needed; which was why a new leader was needed; which was why the Daughters were stepping into that role; which was why it was perfectly reasonable for them to do, well ... whatever they wanted.

Still, while Fletcher sat there doing nothing, he couldn't help but see the validity of some of Candice's indictments. Men had indeed fucked things up pretty royally. For a long time. Worse, he couldn't help but admit his own guilt, especially during the end of his stay at the La Jolla hospital. He had been arrogant and cruel. He had treated women as objects for his pleasure. He had demanded things based on the sole merit of having a Y chromosome. He'd been horrible. And worse still: He'd been at least a *little* guilty before he was Odin, hadn't he? Hadn't he enjoyed the artful subtleties of a male-dominated world all his life? Maybe not overtly or consciously or offensively, but he was a product of that world, wasn't he?

Now, he wasn't going to try and take the sins of an entire society on his bony shoulders, even if he was all that was left. But he recognized that maybe a rebuild of humanity wasn't such a bad idea. Maybe Delilah *was* the universe or God or destiny hitting the reset button. Maybe they *could* do it right in Version 2. Maybe to all of that, but even so: the Daughters of Tomorrow had it all wrong. Fletcher didn't know much, but he was pretty sure the recipe for a harmonious future didn't include creating a gender of slaves.

Or killing anyone that opposed you, come to think of it.

··········

On his fifth day under the care of the Daughters of Tomorrow, Fletcher saw his second dead body at their hand.

The second dead body was one of their own. One afternoon, as he was sitting on his bed investigating the strange designs in the carpet, he heard a commotion on the street below. He went to the window and saw a crowd of people, their inaudible shouts rising to the eleventh floor. The action was centered around one woman. She was distraught, spinning, looking around, pleading. People shouted at her. Then the crowd spread and she stood alone in the street, hysterical.

Another woman stepped in front of her and lifted something up. Then there was the crack. That same crack from the dock in Dana Point.

There's no sound like a gunshot. Fletcher felt it in his ribcage as he watched the crying woman's body crumple to the concrete. More commotion. More shouting. A few women picked up the body and carried it off. A moment of stillness, then someone pressed play and the street returned to normal—women going this way and that. Business as usual.

"Why was that woman shot?" Fletcher asked Brooklyn later that evening when she delivered his dinner.

Brooklyn's buggy eyes bugged. "Saw that, huh?"

"Yep."

"Well," she said, "she tried to sneak out last night."

"You're not allowed to leave?"

"All members of the Daughters of Tomorrow pledge their commitment to the cause," said Brooklyn. "It's a vow that can't be broken."

"Wow, that's rough," said Fletcher.

Brooklyn shrugged. "It's a rough world."

··········

While the sun kept moving across the wall, and Fletcher kept sitting and thinking and reading, the abuse kept piling up. For example: Caitlin actually spat on Fletcher on one occasion. For example: Nia asked, a little too sincerely for Fletcher's liking, why he hadn't offed himself yet. For example: Greer, well ... she kept working on her right cross.

For example: one day Fletcher was sitting there, reading *The Lost World*, minding his own business, when Greer and Frankie entered the room. They stopped and studied him, Greer's eyes wide with her fiery instability, Frankie's with her shaky uncertainty.

"God, you're ugly," Greer said to Fletcher.

"Yeah," said Frankie.

Fletcher smiled.

"I figured it out," said Greer. "You look like an ugly little worm. Doesn't he?"

"Yeah," said Frankie. "Yeah."

"Doesn't he look like a gross little fucking worm?" said Greer.

"Yeah," said Frankie, confidence building. "With that big, stupid nose."

"Worms don't have noses," said Fletcher.

Frankie scrunched her face in mouselike disappointment, turning red.

"Shut the fuck up, Worm Boy," snapped Greer.

"Ha," said Frankie. "Worm Boy!"

"Don't let him talk to you like that," said Greer. "Didn't I tell you that? Hit him. Right in that big, stupid nose."

Frankie hesitated.

"Do it!" barked Greer.

Frankie tossed her fist weakly at Fletcher, socking him right under the eye. It stung, sure, but it was a pathetic punch. Frankie's eyes widened in horror, an unspoken apology. Fletcher nodded back in unspoken forgiveness, rubbing his cheek.

"No, no, no," said Greer. "More like this."

Her hand flew. The blood poured. The eyes watered.

"Okay," said Greer, clapping her hands together as Fletcher crumpled on the bed, blood running down his shirt. "See ya later, Worm Boy."

"Bye, Worm Boy," said Frankie.

And it stuck. From that moment forward, Fletcher was no longer Fletcher. The man who was once Fletcher, then Odin, then Fletcher again, was now Worm Boy.

Chapter 35

AFTER A COUPLE WEEKS of sedentary meditation-and-masturbation captivity, poor Worm Boy finally got a break in the monotony. He was blessed with the joys of physical labor. And it really did feel like a blessing. Leaving that hotel room was like coming up for air.

The Daughters of Tomorrow lived all over downtown LA, holed up in various hotels and random old apartment buildings. The budding militia also had no home base, no proper meeting space and no temporary digs for new recruits. Organization was at the heart of any good rebel faction, and this current set-up was not up to snuff. They wanted a fancy new headquarters, and that's where Fletcher came in. Manual labor for the only man left.

The Daughters of Tomorrow had chosen Crypto.com Arena, formerly Staples Center, to be the site. There was something symbolic about it, something grandiose. The former home of the Lakers, Clippers, Sparks and Kings would now be the home of LA's newest dynasty in the making. The Daughters had decided that the big, open arena would make for a perfect onboarding center for new recruits. They could make it feel like an army barracks in the movies, with rows of bunks and a commanding officer keeping the Daughters-to-be in line. Just across the street was a Ritz-Carlton and a Marriott hotel, which were simultaneously being renovated for the permanent homes of the gang's full-status members. The arena would be more than just the setting for the New Recruit Slumber Parties, though. Candice had all sorts of lofty plans.

"You're lucky," she told Fletcher, pacing back and forth in Fletcher's hotel room. Fletcher sat casually on his bed, his back against the wall. Candice stopped at the window and watched the scene on the street below for a moment. "You get to contribute to something great."

"Oh," said Fletcher. "Cool."

"That's the mentality you should take, you know," she continued. "As you're aware—as we've made painfully clear, I'm sure—you will have no more responsibilities of the intellectual variety, not in this life."

"Very clear," said Fletcher.

"But you can still have purpose," said Candice. "The work you'll be doing will help build a new world. A better world."

"Great," said Fletcher.

"It *will* be great," said Candice. "And I think you deserve to know what you'll be working to build."

"Okay."

"That arena will be the center of our new empire," said Candice. "Every empire needs a heart. Do you know much about the Incas? Impressive, what they accomplished, albeit with a polygamous patriarchal monarchy. Their dynasty grew outward in every direction from Cusco, their capital, spreading far and wide over most of South America. But Cusco was always the heart. And in the middle of Cusco was a square, a meeting place—now called Plaza de Armas. Their empire was built out from this point. It was the foundation. The beating heart of the Inca world."

"Okay," said Fletcher.

"Pardon the history lesson," said Candice, "but I need you to understand the importance of your work. You see, the arena will be our Plaza de Armas. It's where our women will train. We'll teach them organized group tactics and effective combat techniques. It has rooms where we can meet, where we can plan, discuss and present any upcoming operations.

"Most importantly, though," she said, growing more impassioned, "the arena is big enough for each and every woman to sit and listen to the stories that need to be told—the words that will ignite the spark within each woman's soul—the spark that will light this world on fire—and from that fire's ashes, the new world can rise."

It was a cool-sounding way of saying that Crypto.com Arena would be the ideal place for some good ol' fashioned hatred-fueling pump-up rallies. This is where Candice would deliver her speeches and the new-world-order neo-jingoistic propaganda she needed to reach the ears of the loyal Daughters. Fletcher pictured Candice on a stage like General Patton, in front of a legion of black-clad women, threading her rhetoric about their righteous cause and the threat of any unyielding groups of women, boiling the blood in the room, charging up her soldiers to go out on whatever mission she needed them to take on.

Fletcher didn't know how many Daughters there were, but he guessed a couple hundred. The fact that Candice wanted the arena told him all he needed to know about her ambitions.

The thing was, every building in downtown LA had been looted or destroyed in some way, sometime between Delilah claiming her first soul and the Daughters of Tomorrow claiming the city as theirs. So, even the grand arena was filled with trash and rubble, broken walls and shattered glass.

Fletcher's job was to clear it out. He was given a wheelbarrow, gloves and a guard with a machine gun. He was to load the debris into the wheelbarrow and transfer it to the back of a pickup truck, which was taken away and dumped somewhere else. Someone else's problem.

He walked in and out of the arena's doors countless times on that first day, through the hallowed concrete tunnels where legends like Kobe Bryant, Shaquille O'Neal and LeBron James once moved. He walked in their footsteps to go to work, just as they had, some of their jerseys still hanging from the rafters above the hardwood court. But it all meant nothing to Fletcher. He'd never been into sports, and held no reverence for those legends or their temple.

Fletcher did imagine the seats filled with 18,000 screaming fans, though, cheering him on as he removed piece after piece. And there were plenty of pieces. There were dozens of mattresses, piles of blankets. There were miscellaneous sweaters and sneakers and folded photos of loved ones and bags filled with old food wrappers. All that was left from people who had once found temporary refuge in this building. Long ago now. All dead now. In fact, he found a few skeletal remains in the corner of the court, which he delicately wrapped in sheets. He was told to throw them in with the rest of the trash, so he placed the bones as ceremoniously as he could into the back of the truck to be rumbled away and dumped wherever it was going. There were also piles of nondescript rubble—broken doors, busted furniture, smashed computers and camera equipment—stuff that served no purpose to the looters who had come through. Fletcher squatted, lifted, waddled, dropped and wheeled the mess away for ten hours on his first day of work. He didn't even make a dent.

As he lay in bed back at the Hotel Cecil that night, he examined the blisters on his hands. His knees ached and his legs felt like soft butter melting into his warm pancake bed. His back hurt, no doubt thanks to horrible lifting form, and his shoulders throbbed when he moved his arms the wrong way. But, as he lay on his bed and looked at the ceiling, Fletcher smiled. His broken body reminded him how alive he still was.

•••••••••••

The next day, Fletcher could hardly get out of bed. So, after realizing they were on pace to kill their laborer in his first week, the Daughters gave him another job—less taxing, but no less torturous. The Daughters of Tomorrow had a robust home décor plan for Crypto.com Arena as well as their new hotel homes across the street. Read as: new recruits would need beds for the arena barracks, while existing members needed new furniture to replace anything destroyed in the fires and raids suffered by the Ritz-Carlton and Marriott. All of this added up to a need for what might as well have been a million single beds—plus lovely little matching nightstands. Fletcher's second job was to build it. All of it.

The Daughters had raided every IKEA within a hundred miles. They had collected an immeasurable number of beds and nightstands—their flat, unmistakably IKEA boxes stacked up in a dozen or so trucks outside the arena. Fletcher was told to take the furniture from the backs of the trucks to a meeting room in the arena. The meeting room had a giant twenty-person conference table with big leather chairs and a 90s-looking purple-and-blue carpet. The room was in good shape, untouched by looters. In that room, Fletcher would put together the furniture. Once a set was built, he'd take it to a staging area where someone would deliver it to its next home.

"My version of Hell," Fletcher remembered his dad grumbling one night, three hours into constructing a particle-board dresser from the KOPPANG line, "is just building IKEA furniture for all of eternity."

Turns out Hell was just off the 10 in LA.

It was a strange Swedish torture method, indeed. Tiny Allen wrenches pressed into Fletcher's blisters and rubbed raw the area between his thumb and forefinger. Lost screws reappeared by boring themselves into his knees as he crawled around on the floor. A bed would be 90 percent completed only for Fletcher to learn that a board was upside down, and he'd have to start over. All the while, the little cartoon man in the instructions taunted him. He smirked at Fletcher, hands on his hips, while Fletcher tried to decode the numbers and arrows. A jeering question mark in a thought bubble appeared over the cartoon man's head every time Fletcher made a mistake. No matter where Fletcher went, every page he turned, there was Mr. IKEA, judging Fletcher's ineptitude.

This will all be over soon.

As Fletcher torqued on screws and slid wooden pegs into their holes, one after the other after the other, he thought about Sisyphus—the Greek dude who had been banished to the underworld and forced to roll that big rock up a hill, only to let it fall back down to the bottom, then have to roll it back up to the top again. Over and over for all of forever. Tiny screws, giant boulders: what was the difference?

Eons ago in the La Jolla hospital, Jordan had told Fletcher about some philosophical mumbo-jumbo she'd just read about Sisyphus. Something about how Sisyphus could find happiness in his futile work if he acknowledged the absurdity of it all, or some such bullshit.

Well, as Fletcher built bed after bed, nightstand after nightstand, connecting the "A" side on one board to the "A" side on another ad infinitum, he could certainly see the absurdity of his situation.

While it had yet to bring him his forepromised happiness, he did find comfort in reliving the conversation in his head. Each memory was a life preserver connecting him to Jordan across all those miles and months.

And, while it was a day of failures and frustrations and physical pain, Fletcher really didn't mind it all that much. All things considered. Just like the debris removal of the day before. Just like old Sisyphus and his rock. Fletcher had a new way of thinking about things, and it was this: he couldn't control what happened to him, but he could control his mindset. This sucked, sure, but it was a lot better than being dead. And besides: he could handle it. They couldn't break him. There was still hope—small though it was—that he could somehow get out, get back to Jordan, get on with his life.

There was still hope. And that was close enough to happiness.

Another debris day. Another IKEA day. Another tray with his break-fast. Another tray with his sperm jar. Another insult. Another lecture. Another swelling bruise under his eye. Round and round it all went. Sisyphus in blue jeans.

This will all be over soon.

Through it all, he'd often get lost in his memories. His sweet little defense mechanism. He found that, when he needed it most, he could conjure up a good memory and just float around in its bubble, leaving his body to lift and twist and yank and heave. Memories of home. Of his family. Of his old friends—Simon and the rest. Of Jordan. Of Natalie. Of Margot.

His thoughts were his fuel. Each good thought jolted him ever more forward, hitting like that first big gulp of coffee to the bloodstream. His mind was a world in which he was in charge. Sure, *they* had the guns, but even bullets couldn't harm his thoughts. Those were his and his alone.

In the darkest, shittiest shithole atop Earth's dying carcass, Fletcher decided that he could be the best Fletcher yet. If he made it out alive, at least he'd know what he was made of. He was a hell of a lot more of a man than the kid that used to atrophy in his parents' basement, dependent on TV screens, Agent Orange and a mom who would bring him Bagel Bites. And he was a hell of a lot more of a man than the joke who had called himself Odin not so long ago.

Fletcher fought back against the Daughters of Tomorrow with every-thing he had, but he did it silently, in secret. As he worked, he focused on things that made him happy, or things that he was still thankful for, or reasons to believe he was lucky after all. In his hotel room, he pumped out pushups and sit-ups, even though his body burned. He blasted through book after book even though his mind ached. He couldn't control his captivity, but he could decide whether he'd use it for good or not.

He was fighting back, all right. They just didn't know it yet.

Chapter 36

Fletcher worked like a dog in Crypto.com Arena over the next couple weeks. During that time, various Daughters would visit him. There was always a guard watching him, but sometimes a few off-duty guests would come by to make his life just a little less pleasant.

Usually, they'd just sit around and say mean things to him. Often, they'd waltz in later in the day with a bottle of vodka and sit on one of the beds he'd made, taking turns pointing out things they didn't like about him.

Like this: "Hey, Worm Boy," said Caitlin. The name was quite popular now. "Do you even shower? Your hair is so greasy. Almost makes me gag just looking at it."

(Actually, he didn't really shower, per se. He was given a bucket of water and soap every night, and washed himself in the hotel's defunct shower. Not exactly a spa treatment.)

Or this: "Worm Boy!" shouted Greer. "What's wrong with your shoulder blades? You look a goddamn gargoyle."

(To be fair, his shoulder blades actually protruded a little less than they used to. He was skinny, but there was a tiny layer of muscle covering those bones now. A little, but it was there.)

Or this: "Worm Boy," said Frankie. "Your nose looks like a giant pimple. And your pimples look like little noses."

(Again: manual labor without a proper shower—of course his acne was flaring up. What'd they expect?)

Sometimes they'd throw things at him. They made a game out of it. If anyone hit him with a rock, they got a point. Brooklyn was the most accurate. Greer threw the hardest.

Other times they were more violent. They'd kick him in the stomach while he was on all fours building a bedframe. They'd trip him while he carried a heavy piece of rubble. Greer once hit Fletcher across the head with a broken piece of particle board when he didn't answer one of her questions, which opened up a gash above his eye.

"You wanna hit me back?" Greer goaded. "I know you do. Do it, you little shit."

Fletcher simply removed his shirt, tied it around his head to stop the bleeding and went back to work.

"Eww," said Frankie. "You're really skinny."

The whole thing seemed a little ironic to Fletcher. Greer and her asshole friends constantly disproved Candice's ideology: that violence was a uniquely male trait, one that played a part in many of the problems of previous male-run societies. But violence doesn't come from having a dick. It comes from being a dick.

Behold the beautiful new world.

One day, as Fletcher's manual labor career dragged on, a few visitors brought some interesting news. He was in the conference room putting together his billionth HEMNES bed frame when Frankie, Brooklyn and Greer appeared in the doorway.

"Welcome to IKEA," he said. "Can I interest you in a nightstand?"

"Worm Boy!" said Greer. "Always bad to see you. Hey, I have a question: what if you *weren't* the last man around?"

"What do you mean?" Fletcher couldn't help but chase the bait.

"Well," she said, "you'd be about half as valuable, wouldn't you?"

Fletcher stood up and wiped the sweat from his eyes.

"We heard a story," said Brooklyn, bulging frog eyes lighting up with the joy of another scandal. "It's a story about another ... one of you."

"Another furniture builder?" Fletcher asked.

"Another man, man," said Frankie.

"You don't say," said Fletcher, pretending not to care. Oh, but he cared. His heartbeat moved to double time.

"Apparently this guy is a real piece of shit," said Greer. "Maybe even worse than you."

"Which is hard, Worm Boy," Frankie offered. "Because you're the worst."

"Imagine if we find him," said Brooklyn, "and his ... you know ... gets someone pregnant right away."

Fletcher breath hitched.

"Yeah," said Frankie, "what if you can't have kids?"

"What a wonderful point," said Greer. "I guess that would make you pretty useless to us, wouldn't it? Ipso facto, I would get the pleasure of putting a bullet in your face. And, now, ladies, remind me: no signs of pregnancies so far, right?"

"Nope." Brooklyn's eyes swelled even more.

"I'll try harder," said Fletcher. "So, what's this guy's deal?"

"His deal," said Brooklyn, "is that he hates women. One of our scouts heard about him from a woman on the road. Apparently, this guy forces women to be his slaves. He even has them fight each other like gladiators for his entertainment. Like some Roman emperor."

"Emperor Asshole," said Frankie.

"Nice," said Fletcher.

Frankie flushed and gritted her teeth.

"What do you think about that?" asked Greer. "Knowing that this ... Emperor Asshole is out there. You think your bro is gonna come save you?"

"I don't know any Emperor Asshole," said Fletcher, lowering himself back down to the furniture pieces at hand. "So, probably not."

"No, probably not," said Greer. "But we're gonna find him. Then maybe I get to kill you."

"Sounds about right," said Fletcher, tightening a screw with more attention than required.

"Well, see ya later, Worm Boy," said Greer. "Maybe we'll kill you tomorrow."

"Have fun, Worm Boy," said Brooklyn.

"Hope you lose a screw," said Frankie.

Greer looked at Frankie as they walked out, amazed at how unskilled in cruelty one could be.

Fletcher never thought he'd be so terrified to learn of another male survivor. But, God, if they found him, and he could impregnate one of the Daughters...

On top of everything, Fletcher realized he probably didn't even have the biggest dong in the world after all.

Fletcher continued to switch between sprucing up Crypto.com Arena and acting as a one-man IKEA factory. He no longer measured time by days or weeks; he measured his life in truckloads of debris and in beds assembled. After his hundredth bed—along with its matching night-stand—life remained unchanged. Then another one hundred beds went by and still there was cleaning to be done and more beds to assemble. It looked like they were planning for an army indeed. He had noticed more fresh faces on the streets, too, each in black, and most with shiny new guns.

All this meant to Fletcher was just new members of the Fletcher Anti-Fan Club.

But he kept moving. He took it all, all the abuse, and kept moving.

And he kept getting stronger.

After a brief self-examination in his hotel room mirror one night, Fletcher noticed that his shoulders were indeed rounder than the bony points that used to sit atop his arms. When he moved those arms, there were long striations that rippled under his skin, and they felt less like snappable chicken bones than they used to. There was also meat on his legs, which no longer looked like they belonged to an ostrich. Where ribs used to sit visibly under the skin, Fletcher now had something called obliques.

Self-improvement in the midst of slavery. Fletcher vowed to keep getting better at what he could control. That was: his brain and his body.

Fletcher's new-and-improved physical form couldn't protect him against a bullet to the face, though, if the Daughters of Tomorrow ever decided to give Greer that pleasure.

"Heya, Worm Boy," said Greer one day. She was drinking from a green longneck bottle. Fletcher was tossing pieces of shattered glass into a wheelbarrow in an arena office. "Ready to find out if your nuts are empty or not?"

Fletcher swallowed, but didn't look up from his work. "Excuse me?"

"We've been expanding our reach," said Greer, taking a sip of her beer. "Looking for an OB. A doctor. We're going to find one, you know.

And if an OB says you're sterile, you'll be dead before she finishes the sentence."

Thankfully for Fletcher, the Daughters of Tomorrow hadn't found any medical professionals. Fletcher remembered Jordan's fruitless recruiting mission to Arizona and New Mexico.

"Or if we find that other guy," said Greer. "Our Emperor Asshole. He's gotta be more of a man than you."

"Without question," agreed Fletcher.

"He'll probably get someone preggers with the first jar," she said. "Then it's bullet time for Worm Boy."

"And Emperor Asshole will take my place as the most popular man in the world," said Fletcher.

Greer walked up to Fletcher, lifted her beer up, and emptied it on Fletcher's head. "I don't like your attitude."

For the rest of the day Fletcher's eyes stung and he stank like an old bowling alley.

Fletcher had constant visitors now. He was the only show in town.

"I hope you get allergies," Frankie said once as Fletcher was chipping away at a pile of rubble and trash in the arena, "from some weird thing buried in that junk."

Another time: "You smell like wet dog."

Another time: "I hope you get a sliver."

Brooklyn excitedly told Fletcher the rumors circling about Emperor Asshole. She couldn't help herself with a good story of another's bad situation.

"Nearly every community we visit has heard of him," she said. Her wide mouth flapped gracelessly as she talked, like a hoagie sandwich slapping open and closed. "Oh, and it's some gruesome stuff. This guy is one bad man, man. Killed a thousand women, some say. Had his way with another thousand, if you know what I'm saying. Well, I guess it could be the same thousand, but—"

"Doesn't sound like much of a gentleman," said Fletcher.

"No, he does not," she said. "Get this. I've met a couple women who claim they've met someone who met him."

"Sounds credible," said Fletcher.

"The stories have to come from somewhere!" she said. "Or someone!"

Then there was Caitlin, who used her visits to inform Fletcher of the various ways in which women were objectively superior—things like higher pain tolerances, higher IQs and longer lifespans. Then there was Nia, who would remind Fletcher of men's historical shittiness—from Genghis Kahn to Adam Levine. All reasons why this new world would be so much better.

So much better.

Fletcher was shown off to new recruits as well. He hardly had a moment to himself.

Every once in a while, Candice herself visited her pet male. Her cold passion was more intimidating than Greer's fiery abuse. Candice was worse: instead of hating Fletcher, she almost pitied him. He had the horrible disease of maleness, and it was terminal.

She stood in his room one night while Fletcher sat on his bed, exhausted, aching, wanting only to lie down alone. "What you need to understand," she said, "is that you can't separate the *wet* from the *water*. You can't separate the *oxygen* from the *air*. And you can't separate the *malice* from the *man*."

Another night: "When a limb becomes diseased you have a choice: remove the limb or let the whole body die. The Delilah Virus simply removed the diseased limb."

All reasons why this new world would be so much better.

So much better.

This kind of living was strange to get used to, but Fletcher got used to it. All the while, though, he observed the scene around him, looking for weaknesses, looking for patterns, looking for opportunities. Because, one day, he'd make his escape.

He figured he had time—in fact, that was all he had. So, he'd play their game, and be patient. He'd wait for the perfect chance to leave it.

But the rules of the game were about to change, and not in Fletcher's favor. A countdown clock was on its way, and it rapidly ticked down, down, down.

•••••••••

When a Sprinter van rumbled into town, it usually meant new recruits. Women would pop their heads out of windows and doorways to watch, wanting to glimpse the newest toy soldier joining the collection. In a dead city, the slightest movement could grab everyone's attention.

Oh, how LA had changed.

These new recruits had eaten up Candice's promise of rainbows and butterflies (or at least food and protection). They arrived ready to grow a shiny new society from the steaming mulch of humanity. To Fletcher, each woman who stepped out of those vans just represented another bed and another nightstand.

One evening, after clearing out all the junk from the visitors' locker room at Crypto.com Arena, Fletcher was back in his room at the Hotel Cecil. He was lying on his bed reading *Slaughterhouse-Five*, his body throbbing with every heartbeat from the labor of the day. The door squeaked opened, presumably for his nightly treat of dinner and an insult.

But it was Candice who walked in, and she was not carrying any food.

"Well," she was saying to someone behind her, "I told you we had some strange medical needs. And sorry for the secrecy. But this ... this is why."

Medical needs.

In walked the women she was talking to as Fletcher lay there like a zoo animal, waiting to be gawked at. He was good at being gawked at these days. Physicians, however, were bad news for Fletcher—him being infertile and all. He looked up from his book to see who his new doctors of doom were.

Three young women walked in. One was stocky but athletic-looking, her caramel-colored hair in a ponytail. One was tiny—not much more than a hundred pounds—with white-yellow blonde hair. The third had a head of brown curls and looked at Fletcher through thick glasses as if she'd seen a ghost.

Fletcher recognized his former hospitalmates instantly.

Arlene, Amanda and Megan stood before him, conjured out of a past that Fletcher had thought was gone for good. There they were: two of the Palm Springs 15 and Beth's silent right-hand woman.

"What the..." Arlene gasped.

"I know," smiled Candice. "A man."

Of course these were the new recruits. These old hospital pals hadn't been his pals at all when they had shared a roof all those months ago. Why not join his newest Anti-Fan Club?

Fletcher remembered that night, not long before he was kidnapped by the Wives of the One Father, when Arlene and Amanda had mocked Fletcher for trying to hook up with Shannon. For thinking he was hot shit. He remembered Megan watching with mild amusement. Oh, how small he had felt. How far he fell. And now—

"Meet Worm Boy," said Greer, entering the room, her mean eyes smiling.

"I'm sorry," Candice said to the new recruits. "His real name is—"

Megan cut her off: "Fletcher."

The room went silent. The three new recruits continued looking at Fletcher in awe. Candice and Greer looked at the new recruits in confusion. Everyone looked at each other, waiting for an explanation.

"We worked at the hospital he was taken from," explained Arlene quietly, unable to look away from the boy lying on the bed in front of them.

"Long time, no see," said Fletcher. He didn't fully sit up.

"We figured your ass was dead a long time ago," said Amanda.

"Sorry to disappoint," he said.

"If I had it my way, he would be," muttered Greer.

"What a small world," said Candice. She was only talking to the new recruits. "Looks like I can skip the introductions. Here's what's going on. Your old friend, Fletcher ... well, like I've told you, man's time is over. That means Fletcher's time is over. It's our world now."

Fletcher watched his old acquaintances. The whole thing might have been entertaining if it weren't for the stakes.

"But even so," Candice continued, "he still has a use. You see, even manure can help something beautiful grow. And that's why you're here: to help grow crops from manure, so to speak. We're so happy to finally have some medical professionals like yourselves. Because we need your help. We're hoping that, from Fletcher's sperm, we can begin repopulating the world. All female offspring will be new Daughters. And if his immunity to the virus is passed on to a son, that boy will be another Fletcher: a laborer and a sperm donor. However, so far, fertilization has been ... unsuccessful. So, we need your help. Together, we'll build the world we deserve. Does that all make sense? Any questions so far?"

"Uh, yeah," said Arlene. "Well, not a question."

"What is it?" asked Candice.

Fletcher tried to shout at Arlene with his eyes. To ask her not to do it. Not to say it.

She didn't notice, or she didn't care.

This will all be over soon.

"Fletcher's sterile."

Chapter 37

THERE IT WAS. THE moment they'd all been waiting for. The dirty little secret Fletcher kept hidden in his gonads.

"Sterile?" asked Candice. "Are you sure?"

"Oh, he's infertile," said Arlene. "He fried his testicles with all this toxic energy drink shit. We did tests for months and months. He's got nothing."

Suddenly Fletcher was staring into the black hole at the end of a pistol. Greer had drawn her gun in half an instant, slid across the room with one ghostly movement and shoved the weapon in Fletcher's face.

"Then we have no use for him," she snarled.

"Hold on," said Candice. "Is that undoable?"

"A bullet in the head?" asked Amanda.

"Not undoable," croaked Fletcher.

"No," said Candice. "Sterility. Can sterility be reversed?"

"Sometimes," said Amanda. "But we never figured out—"

"He serves no purpose," barked Greer.

The room stood still, waiting for direction.

"Put your gun down, Greer," said Candice.

Greer gritted her teeth but obeyed her leader. Everyone obeyed Candice. Fletcher exhaled.

"You guys are the physicians here," said Candice to her new recruits. "So, tell me: do you think there's a chance that we can fix him to reproduce?"

"I honestly don't know," said Amanda. "We couldn't at the hospital. And we had more of us. But—"

"We don't like him either," said Arlene. "But let's not just *kill* him. We're not murderers."

"Speak for yourself," said Greer.

"We should at least think about it, right?" said Amanda. "What if we think of a new idea after you already, well ... you know."

"He's got to have some use," said Megan. "He's still the last man left."

"Actually," said Candice, "he's not."

The new recruits looked at Candice.

"We've heard stories of another man out there," she said. "A monster of a man. A man who does unspeakable things to women."

"Seriously?" asked Amanda.

"We heard rumors first, stories of stories," Candice spoke with a focused intensity. "But these stories have come from multiple sources. Women from different camps. Different communities. It has to be true. According to these stories, this man enslaved women and forced them to cook for him and clean for him. He abused them. He made them fight each other to the death for his own entertainment. We don't know where this devil is, but we're going to find him. And when we do, we will make him our prisoner. If he proves fertile, then we can do away with the redundancy. Until then, give Fletcher's infertility one more try."

This will all be over soon.

• • • • • • • • • •

Another twenty-two beds went by. Another few days of arena cleaning, too. Fletcher had slowed his pace on both jobs, not wanting to finish, as finishing meant reducing his usefulness even more.

He knew the powers that be were deliberating over his fate. He knew it was a death sentence—he just didn't know the timeline. That depended on if they found this Emperor Asshole.

It also depended on what the new medical recruits said. His dear old roommates.

"Help me get out of here," Fletcher whispered to them when they came by one afternoon. He was sweeping the hardwood floor of Crypto.com Arena with a big, janitorial broom. The rubble was gone in the main arena.

"Listen," said Arlene. "All that shit you pulled back at the hospital ... you were just looking after you, right? Well, now it's time for us to look out for us."

"You realize they're going to kill me," said Fletcher.

"You realize they could kill us, too," she said. "These people are ... you either join 'em or ... well, I want to be on the winning side."

"The living side," said Amanda.

They told a story they'd heard about the Daughters of Tomorrow murdering an entire little community—a small, peaceful commune—simply for refusing to give them supplies.

"If we help you, and they find out, they'll definitely kill us," said Megan.

"Fine," said Fletcher. "Well, can I ask that you not be in too big a hurry to sign my death warrant? As long as you say there's a chance you can fix me, there's a chance I stay alive. And maybe I'll figure out a way to get out of here."

The girls looked at each other and nodded.

"We'll buy you some time," said Arlene. "But I don't know how much we'll be able to do. I'd make your break for it ASAP."

"Fair," said Fletcher. "Thank you."

Arlene looked up at the guards with machine guns at either side of the court. "We never speak of this again."

"I get it," said Fletcher. "And I'm sorry about ... everything."

And they never spoke of it again.

Meanwhile, Fletcher tried to come up with a plan. It had been hard enough to figure out how to escape a band of unarmed cult followers who worshipped him. Now he had a full militia with big guns and a bigger hatred for him.

The three physicians came by most afternoons, and they brought no cruelty. Fletcher knew they didn't like him, but he could tell they pitied him, too. His situation was one that was deserving of pity, after all.

He learned how Arlene, Amanda and Megan had gotten from the hospital in La Jolla to their new friends in downtown Los Angeles. The three had split off from the hospital not long after Fletcher left. While some at the hospital still believed they could save the world, these three women thought it was time to save themselves. They had heard rumors of more looter activity and bigger gangs and were worried that a hospital would be an attractive target. They decided to focus on surviving the best they could in the world that was left.

Meanwhile, the Daughters of Tomorrow had been sending recruiters and scouts all over Southern California, looking for fresh blood to join their little faction—especially anyone with medical experience. They didn't say why, not wanting to spread the word that they had a living man, but they could be pretty convincing without much explanation. The three women were found in Carlsbad. Fletcher thought with a sick feeling in his stomach how close the Daughters of Tomorrow had been to La Jolla, and anyone still left in the hospital.

Arlene, Amanda and Megan had set up a little makeshift medical operation in Carlsbad, helping people with what they could in exchange for food and supplies. The Daughters of Tomorrow had caught wind of their outfit and gone to recruit. They told the three nurses they were starting a new society. They told them they needed physicians. They told them it was in their best interest to join. Arlene, Amanda and Megan knew who they were dealing with, and so here they were.

Fletcher couldn't blame them.

·····•·•····

Yes, things were bad for Fletcher, but bad could always get worse.

Fletcher now only worked on cleaning up Crypto.com Arena. They needed no more beds for the time being, and the labor in the arena was now light enough that he could manage back-to-back days without his body breaking down. All the heavy rubble was gone.

He was sweeping the main arcade at the stadium's entrance, giant posters of Laker legends looking down at him. Arlene, Amanda and Megan were sitting with Frankie and Caitlin in cushioned folding chairs—the ones that once held players and coaches down on the court. They were passing a bottle of wine back and forth.

"Fletch," said Amanda. "Where's the bathroom?"

Fletcher pointed down the corridor.

"Should just pee on the floor and make him clean it up," said Caitlin as Amanda walked off in the direction of the restroom.

Fletcher continued working while the women watched, armed guards at every exit. Suddenly, there was a shout.

"Worm Boy!" said Greer. She entered the arcade with Candice and two other women.

"Howdy," said Fletcher, looking up only briefly before focusing back on his broom.

"I have a question—for all of you," said Candice, gesturing to Fletcher and his wine-drinking audience. She had that stern kind of calm that demanded attention, like a priest or a president.

"Shoot," said Fletcher.

"We've learned the name of the other man," she said. "And it's a name you'd remember. We want to know if any of you have ever heard of him."

"Tell the truth, Worm Boy," said Greer. "Or—"

"You'll kill me," said Fletcher. "Sure, what is it?"

Candice spoke: "He calls himself Odin."

Fletcher froze.

At that moment, Amanda turned the corner, returning from the restroom. She burst out laughing. "No way!"

"What's so funny?" Candice turned to her.

This will all—

"You just said Odin, didn't you?" asked Amanda.

"Yes," said Candice, "We—"

"How'd you find out about *that* thing?"

"Hold on," said Fletcher.

"What thing?" asked Candice.

"Wait," said Fletcher.

This will all be over—

"Odin!" said Amanda, still laughing. "Fletcher is Odin, Odin is Fletcher—that thing!"

This will all be over soon.

"God, that was weird, even for you, Fletch." Amanda laughed some more, unaware of what she had just done.

"You don't say," said Candice, turning back to Fletcher.

"Emperor Asshole," said Greer, now grinning like a snake.

·· ·· · · · · · · ·

Next came a flurry. A whirlwind of shouting, pistol-waving and finger-pointing. Fletcher just stood in the middle with his broom in his hand, a passive viewer to his own trial.

Candice eventually demanded and received some sense of order, once again denying Greer the kill she wanted so badly. At least for now.

Thankfully for Fletcher, the three women from the hospital filled in some gaps in the story. They revealed that, when Fletcher was Odin, he had never enslaved or abused or hurt any women. He'd slept with some, but never by force. He'd had them do many things—including put on a play for his entertainment—but never a goddamn gladiator fight to the death. He'd been a douche on a power trip, but not a monstrous murderer.

His deeds had evolved over time in the rumor mill, in a giant game of telephone told around little fires in little communities all down the coast. It had started not long after Fletcher was kidnapped. Unbeknownst to Fletcher, while he was running around Catalina eating bugs and here in LA building furniture, stories of his shittiness were spreading far beyond the hospital walls. It started with the women he'd slept with—telling stories of the last man left. Then, after Fletcher was taken, the hospital team itself disbanded—disagreements pushing different women in different directions, looking for different things: some wanted to scour the earth for a Fletcher replacement; some wanted to find Fletcher, so they could keep studying him; some wanted to search for other medical communities and pool their knowledge; some wanted to get back to being caretakers and help those in need; and some wanted to leave it all behind and just try to take care of themselves in this increasingly dangerous reality.

As the women from the hospital spread, so did their stories. They spoke of some dickhead who called himself Odin, who had practically ordered them to perform for his entertainment, who made them play silly games with him, who had made them build him a movie theater, an arcade, a bowling alley, a laser tag arena and even his own suite. A dickhead who had slept with various women, only to throw them out before morning came. This was the villain they had lived with, but Southern California had always been fertile ground for rumors to blossom and spread, and the post-apocalyptic air made the conditions all the more perfect. People were eager to accept a new monster, something to fear that was more killable than an invisible virus. Ghost stories grow rapidly in hard times, and the story of this bogeyman evolved to the status of myth.

So, Emperor Asshole was actually real, which was crazy.

Crazier still, it was Fletcher.

To their credit, the three hospital women begged Candice not to kill Fletcher just yet. They asked for more time to try to understand his infertility and his immunity to the virus, now that there was no other man. They were convincing enough to spare him his life for the moment.

Fletcher was taken to his hotel room prison, where he sat and waited, passing the time until a more official decision was made. A week went by and still he sat and sat and sat. The hospital women took blood, hair, urine and semen samples to test with the rudimentary equipment they had with them, but they were just buying time.

It turned out they could buy a month. That was the deal the women made with Candice. They had a month to give it one last shot, and after that, well ... Candice was ready to officially declare Fletcher useless to the cause. Read as: they could remove the Fletcher-sized wart from their world. Besides, Candice and her inner circle believed they'd eventually find another man. Statistically speaking, it seemed likely.

Oh, but Candice did see one final purpose for Fletcher.

"Know that your *expiration* will be a great moment for the Daughters," Candice said in his room one night. She paced before Fletcher, who sat on his bed wishing she'd leave. "Your execution will be a public event, the grand finale of a celebration like nothing this world has seen. Your end will launch our new beginning. A symbol of the transition of power. I'm already writing the speech. I must say, I'm quite proud of it."

"Okay."

"I'm telling you because I want you to know, yet again, that you're playing a part in something much bigger. A better world, Fletcher. That alone should bring you peace, give you purpose." She smiled, cold and distant. "I hope you understand."

She said it in the way a politician might explain why taxes were being raised. As if it was all a slight but reasonable inconvenience.

As Fletcher sat with the news, he reflected on his life—something that's easier when a life is scheduled to end soon. It was a tender sort of reflection, wistful, and he didn't try to stop it. It felt good. In a bittersweet way.

The tenderness was toward all sorts of things that arose from the dusty, forgotten cupboards of his mind—parts of his life he didn't even know were still in there: the smell of his childhood house when everyone was home (his brother's sweaty practice gear piled by the door, coffee brewing, lavender cleaning spray); the thumbtack-hole constellations on his bedroom walls from the constant rearranging of his posters; the way his dad would hold his newly expanded belly after a big meal; Bones, the family cat, sitting on the back of the couch and licking Fletcher's scalp with his sandpaper tongue, and Fletcher weirdly liking the feeling; watching his parents dance in the kitchen to music Fletcher didn't know and didn't much care for; years later, the family sitting on the deck of a rental house in Cannon Beach, momentarily content with each other and everything, Fletcher not even really wishing he were playing video games, the four of them blissfully unaware that in a year three of them would be dead.

His tenderness applied to things in his post-Delilah life, too: giggling with Jordan in the loopy high that came around midnight; those pale blue plastic trays that carried their mediocre meals; Jordan's philosophical ramblings, paired with his own theatrical eye rolls; playing Chutes and Ladders; the way Beth would look at him like he was speaking Klingon; the smell of the sterile hospital equipment; Natalie telling him risqué stories of pre-Delilah life just to make him squirm; Natalie smiling triumphantly when she won; learning origami; the stiff brown couch; the feeling that hung once or twice in the air around Jordan and him, dense and damp, pushing them to act but neither doing so. And then Margot, and her refusal to see the world in the boring way that everyone else did; only seeing the good, too; the way her eyes lit up like floodlights when she got excited; their vacation at the ranch; her friendship when he needed it most.

Yes, Fletcher was full of sentimental tenderness at the moment, so he allowed himself a brief poetic revelation, too. Maybe it was all those books he had been reading. The poetic revelation was this: it was all wonderful—everything. He was suddenly overwhelmed by the beauty of the life he'd been fortunate enough to live. How silly that he had never seen it like this, so clearly and unmistakably. He welled with gratitude that he had felt all that he had: both the warmth of unconditional love and the iciness of invisibility. That he had tasted the sticky-sweet nectar of his once beloved Agent Orange as well as the earthy crunch of insects. That he had met people who understood him and people who never could. That he had messed things up to a place beyond repair, and that he had changed because of it. He remembered Jordan's personal philosophy: "Oh, my sweet, silly little friend," she had said, "to live is to feel. And to feel all of it." He wanted to grab her and shake her and let her know how right she was. Everything he'd felt was part of the whole journey, and whatever happened next would be, too. How lucky was he to even be something in the first place?

Drugged by his own nostalgic slideshow and poetic revelations, Fletcher was lowered into a deep sleep. Sleep like that only comes from transcendental thinking or long hikes, and Fletcher had never done much of either, so this was all new to him. And he enjoyed it.

It didn't last, though. He was robbed of the full experience, his slumber cut short by an uninvited and unannounced shadow, lurking in the darkness of his room.

PART VI
PLAIN OLD FLETCHER

Chapter 38

FLETCHER AWOKE WITH THAT mystical third-eye certainty that some-one was watching him. As Fletcher's actual eyes searched the darkness, he became aware of a shadow. And that shadow was creeping closer.

Fletcher deduced that the shadow was a person.

As the shadow person slid nearer, Fletcher could see that they were in the tactical black get-up that the Daughters of Tomorrow fancied so much. A hood and scarf covered the shadow person's head.

Fletcher, surprisingly calm, knew that this was likely his grand finale. It was probably Greer, sneaking in behind Candice's back to steal the kill for herself. Or maybe Candice had moved up the execution date, and this shadow person was here to summon Fletcher for his last dance. Either way, it was now likely a matter of minutes. Fletcher swallowed, took a deep breath, and decided he wouldn't go out all trembling and pitiful. He'd go out in a way he was proud of.

"What, never seen a man before?" Fletcher asked the shadow.

The shadow paused. Fletcher thought of Margot and her obsession with saying the perfect last words.

The shadow person stepped closer still, slowly morphing into visibili-ty, unwrapped the scarf and revealed sparkling eyes and a lopsided smirk.

Fletcher stared in disbelief.

Jordan. *The* Jordan.

"What, never seen a woman before?" she asked.

Fletcher would have loved a witty comeback. Or any comeback, for that matter. At the moment, however, he couldn't direct the muscles in his mouth to formulate words. He couldn't even remember any words.

All his brain could do was come up with an image of Princess Leia thawing out Han Solo from carbonite.

"I'll take that as a hello," said Jordan. "But we gotta go. Come on—let's get you out of here."

"I'm sorry," said Fletcher, finally finding his tongue. "I'm so sorry." Now was not the time, but it also had to be.

"Come on," said Jordan. "Get your shoes on."

"I'm sorry," he said again, "for everything."

"Apologies can come later," she said. "When you're also thanking me for saving your ass."

"I swear I've changed, though," he pleaded. "I promise."

Jordan finally looked at him. "You are what you repeatedly do."

"I know," said Fletcher, tying his sneakers.

"Okay, Mr. Odin," she said. "Let's go."

"Odin is way dead," he said. "It's just plain old Fletcher again, I swear."

"I hope so."

Jordan opened the door to the hallway and poked her head out. She put her finger to her lips and nodded to Fletcher that it was clear. Fletcher followed Jordan, as she stepped over something on the ground.

A body.

It was a woman's body wearing all black, an assault rifle lying by her side. It was Fletcher's guard.

"Holy shit," whispered Fletcher as Jordan picked up the rifle. "You *killed* someone?"

Jordan grabbed the rifle and disappeared into the next room down the hall, leaving the gun inside, and closed the door quietly.

"You killed her?" he asked again.

"Don't get too excited," said Jordan. "She's just taking a little snooze." Jordan reached a hand into the front pocket of her black hoodie and pulled out a couple of syringes, holding them up for Fletcher to see. "Perks of the job."

· · · • · • · · · ·

As Fletcher and Jordan crept down the hallway, they heard a crunchy, static noise. The radio attached to the hip of the crumpled body was awake, even if its owner wasn't. There was a voice asking for an hourly check-in that would not be coming.

Their cover was expiring.

Jordan led Fletcher past the stairwell, but Fletcher didn't say anything. She had a confidence that he didn't dare question. They turned the corner and opened a door, slipping into a rear service stairwell that Fletcher hadn't known existed. As they shut the door behind them, they heard the slapping of footsteps emerging from the main stairwell, which Fletcher was now very thankful they had avoided. Jordan pulled out a flashlight and led the way. The two of them hurried down the stairs, eventually leaping and taking them three or four at a time, the bouncing yellow light revealing their landing zones. Ten flights. Eleven flights. Twelve flights.

Fletcher and Jordan picked up the pace, hardly touching the concrete steps as they flew down flight after flight, hands gliding on the rails to keep from landing face-first. They passed ground level and made it to the basement.

Jordan opened the only door and stepped through.

She was greeted by a loud crack.

Through the narrow opening made by the door, all Fletcher saw was her body collapse. In a matter of milliseconds, he dove through the same door, unafraid, emboldened by the armor that comes with clear purpose. That clear purpose was to save Jordan from whatever she needed saving from.

By stumbling blindly into a basement where an unknown danger awaited.

He didn't get off to a good start. The armor that comes with clear purpose is more of a mental armor, and does not protect well against metal fire extinguishers. As Fletcher burst through the door, the red cylinder drove into his stomach like a battering ram. He flew to the concrete floor of the underground parking structure.

On his back, he now saw Greer coming at him. "The back stairs," she said. "I figured a worm would head underground."

The garage was illuminated only by two flashlights—Jordan's and Greer's—which were both now abandoned on the gray floor and pointing carelessly, casting long shadows and giving their stage a dungeony glow. Greer tossed the fire extinguisher to the ground with a loud clang and came after Fletcher. He scooted backward as fast as he could, unable to get up without letting her get closer. But he couldn't scoot fast enough. Greer was on him in an instant.

As she approached, she slapped her legs with her hands—feeling both the pistol on her right hip and the knife fastened to her left quad—deciding which tool she wanted to use. She smiled and grabbed the tactical blade, unfolding it as she neared Fletcher. It was a dramatic gesture, the kind of thing that bad guys did in the movies Fletcher used to watch, right before they said something clever to their prey.

"Here we are," she said, fulfilling her villainous duty and saying something clever to her prey. "The fall of man."

She pounced on Fletcher, driving the knife toward his chest. He was able to grab her forearm with both his hands before the knife plunged into his insides, which put them at a stalemate. The knife trembled, halfway between Greer and Fletcher, unsure whether to abort or finish the job. Greer took her left hand, which was free, and placed it on top of the butt of the knife. The additional force broke the stalemate, and the knife moved slowly and steadily toward Fletcher's sternum. A foot away. Six inches. Three inches.

Just when Greer was about to close the gap and insert the knife into his chest and wipe another man from the Earth, Fletcher rolled. With everything he had, he twisted his body with one fierce log roll. The knife smashed into the ground with a sharp clash. They grappled and wrestled and writhed, but Greer clearly had experience with this sort of thing. Fletcher did not. He flipped. He flopped. He—

He found himself on his back again, once more looking at the business end of a weapon. Greer had drawn her pistol and tried to point the barrel at Fletcher's head. Fletcher had a hand on the gun as well, and pushed away as hard as he could—but Greer had better leverage this time. She slowly twisted her shoulders to rotate her body and the gun, torquing the barrel closer and closer to Fletcher's face. Fletcher tried to roll again, but she had him between her knees. He was unable to move.

This will all be over soon.

There was no life flashing before his eyes. Maybe he had meditated on his life enough in his hotel room prison.

But it didn't matter. This wasn't his time to die. Not here. Not now.

Just as Greer's gun was reaching the perfect angle to put a bullet into Fletcher's skull, there was a crack—but not the crack of a gun. Greer's body went limp. She collapsed next to him, a groan escaping her lips and the gun bouncing loudly out of reach. Jordan stood above Fletcher with the fire extinguisher. She reached into her pocket and pulled out a syringe, knelt down and inserted it into Greer's neck.

Fletcher crawled over to the gun, picked it up, and pointed it Greer's lifeless body. His hand shook, but he couldn't think of a more justifiable killing.

He wrapped his finger around the trigger, a montage of her cruelty flashing in his brain. He felt the intoxicating possibility of it—how easy it would be. But he couldn't. He didn't even want to, he realized. He just wanted to be far away from there.

He lowered the gun and looked at Jordan.

She nodded. Blood was trickling from her forehead to her cheek, but a wry smile curled on her face.

"God, how have you survived this long without me?" she asked.

She grabbed a flashlight and gestured for Fletcher to do the same. She led him across the parking lot and around a corner. At the entrance to the garage was another body—more of Jordan's sedative-wielding hand-iwork. Fletcher imagined her as a character in *The Odyssey of Zordallus*, one who could join you on a mission, whose specialty was stealth and whose weapon of choice was the syringe.

The entrance to the garage was on the side of the building, away from Main Street, which, appropriately, was the main artery of the Daughters of Tomorrow's operation. Fletcher and Jordan turned off their flashlights and slinked out into the alley, into the night. Fletcher followed Jordan toward Main Street, illuminated now only by moon-light. Crouching, she ducked behind a garbage bin. She held her finger to her lips again and gestured for Fletcher to look. He poked his head out and saw another guard, ten yards away on the corner of their alley and Main. She nodded again, which apparently meant it was time to go.

Staying low, they crossed the alley and ducked behind a parked car. The guard was a few yards away. Fletcher could hear his own heartbeat thumping in his ears. He was almost surprised that the sound wasn't giving away their location in the vacuum silence of the night. He closed his eyes for a second and tried to get his breathing under control. He looked at the pistol in his hands and tried to remember his brief training with Beth. He hoped he wouldn't have to put it to the test.

As they slithered from the alley to Main Street, Jordan tapped Fletcher and pointed out two more guards at two other posts, both across the street. One was on the ground, a block or so down the road and the other was on a balcony just after that. Fletcher and Jordan jumped from car to garbage bin to electrical box, scurrying from cover to cover. They passed the first guard by crawling behind a parked car, and now watched the guard watching from her balcony. The guard stood with a long rifle, looking out over Main Street. She rocked back and forth, looking left, looking right, obviously bored. Jordan and Fletcher watched her through the windows of the parked car they hid behind. Jordan motioned for him to watch the street guard they had just passed and that she'd watch the balcony guard. When they were both looking away, they'd cross the street.

It sounded like suicide to Fletcher, but he wasn't in a position to argue. Jordan was the one doing the saving, after all.

Fletcher watched the street guard, who was looking their way. When she turned to look the other way down Main Street, he whispered: "Clear."

"No," whispered Jordan. Her guard was looking their way. "Wait ... Okay, we're good."

"Wait," whispered Fletcher. His guard had turned back toward them.

They played this game for a few minutes until both guards were looking away. Jordan nodded and took off across the street. Fletcher scrambled after her, staying low and keeping his feet light and silent. They crouched behind another trash bin, thankful that the Daughters of Tomorrow had not yet established a good sanitation department and instead just piled garbage in dumpsters.

When the coast was clear Jordan moved on, fifteen yards down the sidewalk and then a sharp left. They were in another alley and, now that they were off Main Street, they stood up and quickened to a silent run. Jordan led Fletcher to the end of the alley and took a right. On the backside of the building there was another entrance to another parking garage. She hurried down and stopped at the base of the ramp, Fletcher right behind her.

Jordan took her flashlight out of her pocket. She pointed it straight across the pitch-black garage and turned it on and off. She did this three times—three pulses, like the start of a Morse code message.

When she finished, the garage was black again.

Then Fletcher heard a low rumble, like a dragon awakening in the back of its parking garage cave. Two dragon eyes peered out from the darkness. The twin lights and the angry growl moved toward Fletcher and Jordan, closer, closer, closer, until it was upon them. And there was the beast: a big cube of reinforced steel, its snowplow grinning.

Big Nurse.

The war-ready ambulance rolled up to them and the driver's side window lowered.

"About time," said Natalie. "I was getting bored."

Chapter 39

FLETCHER SAT ON A bench in the back of Big Nurse, feeling big Millennium-Falcon-ready-to-flee-the-Death-Star vibes. He watched Natalie command the machine to crawl forward, remembering a time when he sat in that very spot, with Jordan in that same passenger seat—the two of them pretending to drive through a zombie apocalypse, the two of them laughing, the two of them sharing a look that seemed to say so much.

Before they left the garage, Jordan turned around, reached back and snatched the pistol from Fletcher's hands. "What if I need that?" he asked.

"You'd probably just shoot one of us."

Natalie laughed. "Look at you, Rambo."

"Isn't this thing full of guns?" Fletcher slapped a box next to him. He remembered Jordan showing him a giant assault rifle.

"Mainly food and extra gas, now," said Natalie. "Traded a lot of the fun stuff for, you know, survival shit."

"Besides, have you ever even shot a gun?" asked Jordan.

"Beth showed me once," said Fletcher.

"Oh, give the boy his toy," said Natalie.

"Fine." Jordan handed Fletcher back the handgun. "Keep the safety on."

Big Nurse crept up the garage ramp and into the alley, growling lowly.

"Why'd you come for me?" Fletcher asked quietly as they rolled out of the garage. "After all I did?"

Natalie looked at Jordan with a strange expression. Almost as if to say: this is your territory.

"You're still our best chance to save humanity," said Jordan coldly. She didn't turn her head, speaking only to the windshield.

"Plus," said Natalie, "we figured your damsel-in-distress ass needed a couple knights in shining armor like us."

"Now be quiet," ordered Jordan. "Let's find our way out of this hellhole."

Fletcher obeyed.

As Big Nurse crawled down the alley, Fletcher could hear a commotion, a low hum rising up. Shouts. Car engines. Footsteps all around.

Good morning, Daughters. Are you missing something?

It's hard to hide in a dead city. It's impossible, however, when you're on the move, in a big, shiny box on wheels, weighing somewhere between six and eight tons and making sounds like a construction site. Eventually, as Big Nurse rolled down a side road parallel to Main Street, they were noticed.

The Daughters of Tomorrow announced their finding with a rifle.

The automatic gun fired from a rooftop perch, screaming through the night air and exploding in bursts of concrete and brick all around the ambulance. Without saying anything, Natalie hit the acceleration.

It turned out, Natalie could drive.

Big Nurse leapt forward with surprising speed, charging like a rhino through the abandoned street and away from the bullets that were ripping apart the walls around them. Poofs of debris followed closely behind.

Suddenly, from a hidden side alley, two black vehicles bounced out into the dark street behind them. It was a Range Rover and one of their Sprinter vans, falling into pursuit like TIE Fighters, flanking them. Unlike the chase scenes in the movies, there was no epic music: only breath-holding anxiety, screeching like broken violins in Fletcher's ears.

"Can we outrun them?" asked Fletcher. "We'll never outrun them."

"You're not helping," said Natalie.

A third car, a black Tesla, joined the chase.

"Definitely not going to outrun them," Fletcher said under his breath.

The three pursuing cars followed Big Nurse down the side street, gaining quickly. Of course, bullets are even faster than cars. Fletcher watched the side mirror as a woman leaned halfway out of the passenger window of the Range Rover. Silhouetted by the headlights of the Sprinter behind her, Fletcher saw she was holding a rifle, trying to steady herself to get off a clear shot. She began firing, bursts of yellow fire blinding the mirror's reflection. With every bang of a round, Fletcher felt his whole body seize up. The bullets burrowed into the brick walls on both sides of the ambulance.

"How's the armor on this thing?" said Fletcher, referring to the sheets of steel Beth had welded on. "Is it really bulletproof? What about the places where there's no armor?"

"Really not helping," hissed Natalie.

And then—

A metallic crack that Fletcher felt in his guts. A bullet finally found Big Nurse, hammering into the steel plating on the back door.

"Holy shit!" he yelped.

"Calm down, princess," said Natalie from the driver's seat, cranking the steering wheel.

Bap! Bap! Bap!

More bullets pelted the steel, like giant rocks of hail on a car roof. Fletcher silently thanked Beth for covering the windows on the back doors with her armor.

Suddenly, a different sound—like an aluminum can being ripped in two. Fletcher stared in disbelief at two small circles. A hole in the back, above the steel reinforcement, where the bullet had entered, and another in the roof where it had continued on its journey.

"Holy shit!" he yelped again.

They roared through downtown, heading north. Then, straight ahead, a roadblock of debris: a metal barrel of trash; a shopping cart; a busted bookshelf; a foosball table; the hull of a burned-out car.

"How's the snowplow?" asked Fletcher. "Do you see that shit up there? Does the snowplow work?"

"I swear to God," said Natalie. She stepped on the gas, blasting through the pile of garbage like bowling pins. "You just sit back there and look pretty."

Two more bullets thumped into the back of the ambulance.

"What about the box of nails and whatnot?" He gestured to the lever. He remembered Jordan saying that it opened a box under the back bumper that was filled with nails and pots and pans.

"Actually," said Jordan, "yeah. Wait until they're close."

Natalie let off the gas and the Range Rover closed in on them. The sides of the alley seemed to close in on them, too.

"Ready," said Jordan, watching the mirror. The Range Rover was now no more than ten yards back, the Sprinter van and Tesla close behind. "Go!"

Fletcher pulled the lever and a cacophony of metallic clanging erupted behind them. In the mirror, Fletcher watched pots, pans and a small toaster bounce through the air. The Range Rover swerved, tires screeching. A cast iron pan smashed into the windshield. The car lunged to its left, crunching into a brick wall.

Jordan whooped and clapped.

"Hell, yeah!" said Fletcher.

"Not bad," said Natalie.

Finally, they saw a freeway entrance and Natalie turned onto the onramp, the Sprinter and Tesla still close behind.

One upside of post-apocalyptic LA was the lack of traffic. The freeway was a silent racetrack—but the race wasn't fair. The ambulance was never going to beat out the Tesla. And probably not the Sprinter, either. But thankfully, this was no autobahn. Abandoned vehicles lay scattered on the freeway, popping out of the darkness into their headlights, and Fletcher thought their only hope of escape was for their pursuers to crash.

Now on the 110, Natalie wasn't afraid to punch it. Fletcher didn't know how she avoided the cars in the road, weaving between junk like a slalom skier. Yeah, they had a snowplow, but scooping up one of the dead cars would slow them enough to become sitting ducks.

They rocketed by Dodger Stadium on their left, a looming black silhouette against the night sky. By the time they reached I-5, the Sprinter had taken position directly behind Big Nurse.

Jordan turned around to face Fletcher. "Hey, those smoke grenades." She pointed to a box. "Worth a shot."

Fletcher opened the box and pulled out a canister, still holding the pistol in his left hand. God, so much destruction at his fingertips.

"You can slide that little window open," said Jordan. Beth had built custom sliding doors, about the size of postcards, into the sides and back of Big Nurse in case they ever needed to safely return fire.

"Do I just pull this ring and...?"

"I think so," said Jordan.

Fletcher pulled the ring, wincing, praying it wouldn't fill the cabin with smoke. That'd sure shorten their road trip.

Nothing happened, so he slid open the window. He risked a peek out and saw the Sprinter right there. He tossed the canister and watched. It bounced and—

By the time the smoke grenade erupted, all the cars had passed it. Fletcher saw a plume of gray in the distance.

Fletcher turned and looked ahead out the windshield. "Shit!" he screamed.

A mangled pickup appeared in front of them, and Natalie pulled hard on the wheel. Big Nurse screeched into a slide, drifting sideways around the truck. Natalie smoothed out the turn once they cleared the wreckage and continued north.

Then—a crunch like a wrecking ball. Fletcher slid the back window open again and saw the Sprinter on its side next to the pickup. Two down.

But there was still the Tesla. Right behind them. A woman leaned out the passenger window with an automatic rifle. Fletcher quickly shut his and hit the floor, just as the metal sheet was peppered with bullet spray. Two new holes ripped through the spaces not covered by the steel. In the side mirror, Fletcher watched the Tesla slingshot out and speed up. Suddenly, it was right alongside Big Nurse. Right next to Jordan.

A woman in all black looked over from the driver's seat. Her eyes were blank and cold—not mean, not hateful, just as blank and cold as new snow. The woman in the passenger seat was climbing out her window, positioning herself so that her torso was above the roof of the car.

"Fletcher!" cried Jordan. "The gun!"

Without hesitation, Fletcher tossed her the pistol he'd been holding.

Without hesitation, Jordan opened her door a crack and fired, aiming at the rear tire. She missed. She fired again. Suddenly there was a screech, and Fletcher watched the Tesla spin and drift into the concrete freeway barrier with a satisfying thwack.

"Did you see that?" Jordan cried. Fletcher cheered and shook Jordan's shoulders.

Natalie glanced over, a slight smile tugged at the corner of her mouth. "Nice shot," she said.

They watched the road behind them, Fletcher peering out the secret window in the back, waiting to see another car, another fleet of cars.

But nothing.

Just like that, they had left the Daughters of Tomorrow in the past.

They drove along for a while in silence. Fletcher stared at Southern California flying by through the tiny window in the side of the ambulance as the first signs of dawn crept up from the east.

Nobody talked for a long time. And then Jordan did.

"I found your stupid origami flower," she said.

Fletcher had forgotten about that piece of folded paper. He had written Jordan's name on it, and once—a million years ago—was going to give it to her as a gift, a token of affection, a romantic thought before he slaughtered all the romance in the hospital. And probably all of San Diego County.

There was another silence.

"Oh," Fletcher finally said. He let out a tiny, soft laugh that sounded incredibly sad.

Another silence.

"She didn't think it was stupid," said Natalie. She gave a half smile in the rearview mirror.

· · • • • • • • · ·

Fletcher eventually learned the plan. The three of them were driving about as far north in the United States, or what used to be the United States, as they could: Seattle. The girls had caught wind of some people at a hospital there who were doing some good work toward saving humanity. They heard there were physicians with advanced knowledge of cell mutation and pathology, and Natalie and Jordan believed this was where they needed to be. More importantly, they felt that the medical anomaly in the backseat would be in the best hands in this community.

So, they had a long car ride.

"Listen," said Fletcher as they drove along the deserted I-5, "I want you guys to know that I've changed."

"Yeah, you said that," said Jordan.

"I know," he said. "Aristotle, and you-are-what-you-repeatedly-do, and all that." He could sense a smile, even though she didn't turn around. "But it's true."

Jordan didn't say anything, so Natalie did. "I hope so. You were a little shit there for a while."

He knew a real man would own up to what he had done.

"You have no idea," he said.

So he told them. All of it. He told them about the ridiculous demands he made at the hospital while they were gone looking for help—things they'd never even heard about. He told them about the ego he grew and how sure he was of his own importance. He told them about the women he slept with, and of the coldness he showed them. He told them all the shitty things he did, all the ways he mistreated people, all the poisoned thoughts he had that now looked so twisted and arrogant and heartless and non-Fletcher.

Jordan and Natalie couldn't hide their shock. Disgust, even. And Fletcher knew it was warranted. But still he didn't stop, spilling his secrets like a busted oil tanker pouring its toxic blood into the sea. It was cathartic. He was tired of his secrets, and how heavy they had become. He wanted a chance to be made new, and that couldn't happen with those thousand-pound secrets clanging around in his pockets. He wanted to be judged, and without any missing pieces. He wanted any assessment of the new-and-improved Fletcher to be considered alongside where he came from, the self-dug pit he had crawled out of. He didn't want to leave any skeletons in his closet for someone to discover years down the road. He wanted to wash his hands. Confess his sins. He wanted to be free.

Despite their shock and disgust, Jordan and Natalie tried to be supportive. They knew this was part of the process. Surgery wasn't often pretty to look at, but if the patient needed it…

Fletcher's story didn't end there, though. He told them about the breakdown he had at the end of his hospital stay—how far he fell, his self-imposed isolation and how it was the start of realizing what he had become. He told about the Wives of the One Father, their ritual, and his newfound commitment to keeping what little integrity he had left. He told of his escape. And of Margot. He told the story of their desert trek on Catalina and her friendship. He told about their ranch house vacation.

Their boat ride to come find Jordan. He told of finding the Daughters of Tomorrow waiting for them at the dock. And the murder of Margot. Fletcher told of the abuse he received as a prisoner of the Daughters, of his endless solitude, and of the mental middle finger he gave them every day by refusing to break.

When he finished, there was more silence. Then, finally, finally, finally...

"Holy shit, buddy," said Natalie. Then she laughed, bright and loud, and said again: "Ho-lee shit."

Jordan laughed, too. Then Fletcher laughed. It was something Fletcher hadn't done in a long, long time.

Chapter 40

FLETCHER LEARNED THAT, IN the time since he had last seen them, Jordan and Natalie had been on their own adventure.

As the three drove toward Seattle, the empty highway theirs alone, the two women told Fletcher all that had happened. He listened as he looked out the window from the back of Big Nurse. He watched the world change from the urban decay of dilapidated strip malls, abandoned cars, worn-out taco shops and faded apartment buildings to a new expanse of nothingness: rolling hills of dead earthy colors, layered behind each other like a watercolor painting, already burning in the new sunrise.

The day after Jordan and Natalie had returned from their trip, they departed again in Dr. Gomez's old Nissan Leaf. They had driven around Southern California, finding communities of people, learning what each knew about this new world and searching for any ongoing efforts to find a cure.

At one point they returned to the hospital to check in. To their horror, Fletcher wasn't there. In fact, Beth was the only one left. Well, Beth and a middle-aged woman named Sandra, who now lived with Beth in that hospital home, and who had made Jordan and Natalie mojitos.

"Beth was the happiest I'd ever seen her," said Natalie. "Pretty sure I even saw a smile."

Beth told them that Fletcher had been kidnapped, and that everyone else had gone their separate ways. She insisted that Jordan and Natalie take Big Nurse. She could always make another, she said.

So, Jordan and Natalie hit the road again. They went from community to community, trying to find useful info, trying to find a place where they could pick up the trail and keep marching toward bringing the human race back from the brink of extinction.

"Sounds dangerous," said Fletcher. "With the looters and gangs and all that."

"Hey," said Jordan, "you're the one who keeps getting kidnapped. We can look after ourselves."

"Damn right," said Natalie.

"Fair enough," smiled Fletcher.

Their journey had indeed introduced them to some unsavory individuals. There was a standoff in Bakersfield with a gang that wanted their ambulance, which ended with Natalie and Jordan sprinting for their lives to Big Nurse and whipping away in the nick of time. There was a group of women in Orange who stole nearly everything they had when they tried to trade for food. There was even a small community of crazy women in Borrego Springs that, after taking Natalie and Jordan in for a while and giving them food and shelter, refused to let them leave, forcing the two to sneak out in the night.

But they met some wonderful people, too. Those still existed, they found, and that gave them hope. There was a community in Temecula that was self-sufficient, who took care of each other, who each contributed to the whole in a different way. Some tended gardens. Some raised animals. Some helped with the solar power infrastructure. They took Jordan and Natalie in when they had nothing, put them to work, let them rest and eat and be a part of the community. There were others in Huntington Beach, a group of beach bums who had come together to create a little commune that was some sort of bohemian utopia. The concept felt like it belonged in the 1960s, but happened to work just as well in the rubble of an apocalypse. They lived simply, wanting for nothing, surfing and smoking and singing songs and finding the beauty in the world around them. Jordan and Natalie found all sorts of communities of good people who cared about and for each other, from Oceanside to Riverside, from San Diego to San Bernardino.

It turned out that, at the end of the world, there were still people who loved it. There was still hope. There had to be. If humanity was to survive, it would be partially thanks to that very, very human thing: hope.

Hope is what kept Jordan and Natalie moving all that time. Searching for answers in a world that promised none. One question that they asked everyone they met was this: "Have you heard anything about a living man?"

"So you were looking for me?" asked Fletcher. It sounded sort of pathetic.

"Purely for the mission," said Jordan. "You know, some women we talked to actually had heard rumors of you. But they were all rumors from your time at the hospital."

"Makes sense now," said Natalie. "You did become *acquainted* with quite a few outsiders, by the sound of things."

Emperor Asshole.

"So," he asked, "how'd you come to LA?"

"We met a girl who had escaped the Daughters," said Jordan.

"She was shook," said Natalie. "Paranoid they were after her."

"I'm sure they were," said Fletcher. "They shoot deserters. I saw it."

"Well, this one told us about their male prisoner," said Jordan. "We figured it was likely you. But, to be blunt, if he wasn't you—well, any man would do."

"Okay," said Fletcher. "So you knew they had me. Or at least a man. But how did you actually find me? LA isn't small."

"Uh…" said Jordan. Both she and Natalie laughed.

"We took a prisoner of our own," said Natalie.

"Stop," said Fletcher.

"A guard who'd been posted up on the outskirts," said Natalie.

"You know," said Jordan, "Natalie can be very convincing."

"I bet," laughed Fletcher.

"Poor girl peed herself," said Jordan.

"No," said Fletcher.

"True story," said Natalie. "But she also told us where you were."

"Well, I hate to break it to you," said Fletcher, "but Megan, Arlene and Amanda got to me first."

"Seriously?" asked Natalie.

"Yep. Couple weeks ago."

"My Tinkerbell?" asked Natalie. "That Amanda?"

"Yep," said Fletcher. "Weren't on much of a rescue mission, though. They're Daughters now."

"Those bitches," said Natalie.

"I don't think they had much of a choice," said Fletcher. "And they helped me, at least a little. Bought me time."

The three kept driving north, stopping at various communities to trade food and medical supplies for gas. Anytime they found other humans, Fletcher hid on the floor in the back under a blanket like an illegal stowaway. He trembled at each stop, waiting to hear a gunshot or a scream. He had assumed that humanity as a whole had descended into some primal state of tribal caveman violence, but that wasn't exactly the case. He had forgotten that humanity was made up of people, and people were always good for surprises. They continued finding help, and they continued on.

They drove past the brick buildings of Sacramento, by freeway signs pointing to San Jose and San Francisco. They drove by chain hotels and shopping centers full of Best Buys, Walmarts and Chuck E. Cheeses in Redding—souvenirs of a different time. They drove over the emerald waters of Shasta Lake and through forests of towering trees, all unchanged and unaffected by these recent human problems. They drove across the Oregon–California border and through small towns that probably weren't much louder in their prime than they were in the post-apocalyptic era.

Near Eugene there was a sign for Bend, Oregon.

Margot's Bend.

"You know there are more sunny days in Bend than any other city in Oregon?" asked Fletcher. "158 a year."

Jordan and Natalie looked at him. Fletcher smiled to himself and made a silent promise that he'd see it someday. He needed to smell the brand-new air Margot had told him about. He needed to hear the birds and see the trees and the river. Margot had described it as the perfect summerglobe, if they ever made such a thing. He'd make that trip soon.

But today, they had other plans.

They crossed the Willamette River in Eugene, then sliced through miles of Oregon farmland. They crossed the Willamette once again in Portland, where countless bridges tried to stitch up the gaping river. Next, they crossed the Columbia, signaling their arrival in Washington. The farther north they ventured, the greener the world outside the window became: farms, tree-lined towns, dense forests. They drove through Olympia, past the concrete airport north of Tacoma and finally, as they turned a corner with forest on one side and industrial sprawl on the other, they saw a gleaming city, rising out of the denim island-dotted waters, a beautiful spawn of Mother Nature and Father Progress. Fletcher saw what he knew to be the futuristic Space Needle.

Seattle.

The three passengers had talked through their entire road trip, and Fletcher had come to a bittersweet realization. He knew now that he was never going to ride off into the sunset with Jordan. He had smashed that dream too much to simply glue the pieces together. He understood this with solemn acceptance. Throughout the miles of road and hours of conversation, though, he found that forgiveness and friendship were realistic goals—with both Jordan and Natalie. He could still build something wonderful with those broken pieces, it would just look different than the original design. Forgiveness and friendship were the most he could hope for, the most he could earn, but it was okay. It was all okay. He could see a future where they looked at him and saw everything he had been and everything he was and everything he could be, and accepted him for it all. And he needed friends now, far more than the fantasy that had kept him going.

His ice cream had served its purpose.

They pulled Big Nurse in front of a giant, concrete, prison-looking hospital overlooking the sparkling downtown skyline and the waters of Puget Sound. As they got out of the car and stretched their legs, looking around at what would become their new home, Jordan walked over to Fletcher. She wrapped him in a hug. He reciprocated, tentatively, not wanting to give away how much it meant.

"I want you to know that I do think you're a good man, Fletch," she whispered to him. "You just weren't for a while is all."

She let him go, gave him her lopsided grin, then clapped her hands together.

"Let's go save the world, huh?" she said.

Fletcher and Natalie followed, laughing the laugh that comes with a jolt of new hope.

There's that word again: hope.

EPILOGUE
TWO YEARS LATER

Fletcher sat in the waiting room, chewing his fingernails. People are always nervous in waiting rooms, and on this day, Fletcher was no exception. He sat, he stood, he sat again, he stood again. He paced. He thought about the events that had led him—and, oh, the rest of humanity—to this moment.

They had cracked the code. Fletcher, Jordan, Natalie and the Seattle physicians: all of them, together, had discovered the cure to Delilah, and why Fletcher's scrawny ass had survived.

It turned out that he was not some divine Chosen One. Instead, he had simply consumed enough of his beloved, toxic Agent Orange Energy Elixir. The four cans a day Fletcher used to drink had saved his life. Each Agent Orange contained a staggering 500 milligrams of the manmade chemical compound Xploserine. Fletcher's new doctor and scientist friends discovered that his overzealous intake of Xploserine had essentially caused a cell mutation. This is what made Fletcher invincible to Delilah's attack.

And maybe he wasn't the only one.

Over the last two years at the hospital, some rumors had reached its walls. Rumors of others. Like Fletcher. They came from the mouths of rambling nomads—with all their stories, and stories of stories—so they were far from confirmed. But they were optimistic tales, nonetheless. And without global communication, stories were all they had. It stood to reason that there could and would be other male survivors in other parts of the country and the world—the most fervent fans of manmade stimulants, immune on account of their bad habits.

As they'd learned in La Jolla, Xploserine had also made Fletcher unable to have children. In some sort of poetic balance, his sperm cells were too fried from the same thing that had saved his life.

The infertile One Father.

But they found a workaround. The physicians quickly learned ways to harness the mutation that Fletcher had cooked up. They adapted it and applied it to a few frozen sperm cells.

After some trial and error, they had eventually felt confident enough to attempt the real deal. With a real woman and her real egg.

That's why Fletcher was there in that waiting room. Today was the day. Their brave volunteer was set to have the first baby the Earth had seen in years.

Minutes drag slowly in waiting rooms, until they don't. Suddenly there was a doctor telling Fletcher he could go back and see her. Then a flash of hallway, a turn of a corner, a doorway, and then—

Natalie lay in bed holding her baby. She smiled at Fletcher—the smile only a mother can make. Her baby squeaked and squirmed, trying to find the most comfortable spot for a nap in this exhausting new world. It had been a big morning already.

Jordan stood next to Natalie. With a crooked grin, she nodded toward the new mom, gesturing to Fletcher to unstick his feet from the floor.

Fletcher inched toward the bed, careful not to disrupt the perfect nativity. He looked down at Natalie and her baby. Her boy. Her real baby boy. A lump the size of an egg grew in his throat and his eyes welled.

"Meet Luke," said Natalie. "Luke, meet Uncle Fletcher."

"Hi, Luke," croaked Fletcher.

"I named him after Dr. Lucia Gomez," she said.

"I like it," said Fletcher.

"It's a lot better than Odin," she said.

"It is."

Fletcher had only one thought as he looked down at the baby boy, the youngest human being alive: *God, let him be a good man.*

Acknowledgements

So, let me start by saying that writing a post-pandemic book during a very present pandemic is kind of a trip. While the first few drafts were written just before 2020 (which is to say: this thing was not COVID-inspired), the book was far from done. As you can see by the 2023 publication date. Anyway, I want to thank everyone who read a draft in one form or another during those pandemic days. I'm sure they would have preferred a premise that was, I don't know, literally anything else.

Specifically, I want to thank Oliver, Rachel and Ryan for all their conversations about Fletcher and friends—and all their thoughts that shaped the final version of this story. Oliver warned me against making Fletcher too unredeemable during his fall from grace—and I'm very glad he did. Rachel helped me see parts of the book from different points of view, which probably saved me from looking like a big dummy. And I had no idea Ryan was such a sci-fi nerd, but his knowledge of post-apocalyptic canon was ... straight-up inspiring. And super helpful. For example: Big Nurse? She's all Ryan. He also helped lead me to restructuring the intro, which was huge. And all three of them poked their fingers into plot holes and questioned doubtful character motivations and ... long story short made the book so much better than it was before they got their hands on it. So again: I can't thank them enough.

Speaking of making this book better, I want to thank my editor, Nick Hodgson. You know that old story where a sculptor explains the secret to making a statue of an elephant? "Get the biggest stone block you can find and just chip away everything that doesn't look like an elephant." Well, looking back, I feel like I handed Nick a Fletcher-sized lump of stone. I am so grateful for (and amazed by) all the genius ways she helped me chip away everything that wasn't Fletcher—and polish everything that was.

Also, thanks to Katie (Katrina, in her fancy Hollywood circles) for the very-last-minute suggestions that were very smart. And thanks to Lynne for her help with this very Acknowledgements section! How meta is that?!

Now, words are great and all ... but covers are more fun to look at. And I think this cover is pretty dope. I want to thank Brendan, my once and always Art Director partner, for all the time and energy and thought and back and forth that was put into it. And for all the supporting pieces. And all sorts of other stuff. I'm sure it was more than he thought he signed up for, but—like with everything he does—he was all enthusiasm and rad ideas from start to finish. And I have to say: the image of him trying out various orange drink spills in his living room studio still warms my heart.

I'd also like to give a shoutout to Todd, my brother from another mother. There's a scene in the second half of this book where Fletcher recalls the one party he'd gone to in high school. At the party he meets Will, who is impossibly cool yet equally caring, and who talks to Fletcher even though Fletcher is so beneath him in the social pecking order. Well, Will is pretty much Todd. I mean, Todd even studied abroad in China, just like Will. And Will's corny quote ("A man's life is a story, and it's his responsibility to make it a good one.") sounds like something Todd would have said—maybe on one of those overly philosophical summer afternoons while the two of us pulled weeds or painted fences for various nice old ladies. Anyway, Todd would have probably talked to Fletcher at that party, too—because Todd was interested in every person he met. Todd passed away before this book was born, but I think he would have really liked it. And I'm happy he's in here.

Side note: while indeed very Todd-like, that corny quote *actually* came from an overly philosophical conversation with another friend, James—this one of the beer-fueled variety on a rooftop in San Diego. In case you were wondering.

Next, I can't put a piece of writing out into the world without thanking my mom. She's the reason I can even put this many words together in an order that makes any sense. And more importantly, she's the reason I love doing it. She taught me, from before I can even remember, the power of reading and writing. I didn't know it was unique at the time, but I later learned that not every kid grew up being encouraged to write stories on rainy days. (And, it turns out, not every kid grew up in a place with so many rainy days.) My mom also read to us kids every night. She wrote me letters—both in times of celebration and when I was being an idiot. Then, when she saw I was becoming interested in writing, she gave me journals and books on the craft and read every single word I wrote. She's always been my first editor, and I'll always appreciate her insight. But more importantly, I want to thank her for showing me this world. Among many others.

And then there's Kendall. So, so, so much of this book is her. Because of course it is. I couldn't have finished this book if it hadn't been for all those late-night convos, where she helped me through various forks in the plot road. Also, fun fact, but Margot was never supposed to be as big of a character as she ended up being. That was Kendall saying: "Erik, we need more of her. Go." And man, was she right. But Kendall's role in this goes far beyond the words. She helped protect my early morning writing time. She encouraged me to keep writing, to make it happen. And she was always there when I resurfaced from the story. Above all that, Kendall is the main reason I think my life is pretty great. She's the bright thing my little world spins around. I guess what I'm saying is that Finn and I (and baby girl on the way) are lucky to have her, and since I have my soapbox here for a second, I want to put that out into the world. So there.

Finally, thank you. For reading this. It's a wild thing, thinking that this project I've been working on for years is here in your hands. And I'm so humbled that it is. Now, if you enjoyed it and, say, want to help an indie author out, a review on Amazon or Goodreads would mean the world to me. You may be surprised to learn that this book doesn't have Stephen King's marketing budget. So your reviews really do help. Anyway, if you've made it this far, you've really read the whole thing—so once more: thank you. I hope you had half as much fun reading it as I did writing it.

Erik Dargitz
May 2023

Erik Dargitz lives in Seattle, where he works as a creative director at an ad agency. His short stories have been published in Erato Magazine, Woodcrest Magazine, Dream Pop Press, Mystery Tribune, and elsewhere. When not writing, he's probably talking to his dog, chasing his toddler, or losing to his wife at gin. This is his debut novel.

www.ingramcontent.com/pod-product-compliance
Lightning Source LLC
Chambersburg PA
CBHW030142310726
48970CB00005B/1550